THE HONOURABLE ROGUE

Tony J Forder

A DI Bliss Novel

Copyright © 2025 Tony Forder

The right of Tony Forder to be identified as the Author of the Work has been asserted by him in accordance Copyright, Designs and Patents Act 1988.

First published in 2025 by Spare Nib Books

Apart from any use permitted under UK copyright law, this publication may only be reproduced, stored, or transmitted, in any form, or by any means, with prior permission in writing of the publisher or, in the case of reprographic production, in accordance with the terms of licences issued by the Copyright Licensing Agency.

All characters in this publication are fictitious and any resemblance to real persons, living or dead, is purely coincidental.

tonyjforder.com
tony@tonyjforder.com

Also by Tony J Forder

The DI Bliss Series
Bad to the Bone
The Scent of Guilt
If Fear Wins
The Reach of Shadows
The Death of Justice
Endless Silent Scream
Slow Slicing
Bliss Uncovered (novella)
The Autumn Tree
Darker Days to Come
The Lightning Rod
What Dies Inside Us
Something More to Say

Standalones
Fifteen Coffins
Degrees of Darkness

The Mike Lynch Series
Scream Blue Murder
Cold Winter Sun

The DS Chase Series
The Huntsmen
The Predators

"Rogues are always found out in some way. Whoever is a wolf will act like a wolf, that is most certain."
— Jean de la Fontaine

"Men, who are rogues individually, are in the mass very honourable people."
— Baron de Montesquieu

"Time to remind them that trapping a Rogue doesn't make him dead, just deadlier."
— Michael A Stackpole

This book is dedicated to my mother. Although at the time of writing she is still very much going strong, we almost lost her back in 2023. But, as I always suspected, she is wilful and stubborn and determined to outlive me so that she can squander my inheritance on enjoying the rest of her life. I raise a glass and cheer her on from a considerable distance for that aim. An avid reader of my work, she is now my entire fanbase in northern California. Long may she remain cheering me on from the sidelines, and long may she remain driving her friends insane. Love you, Mum. x

ONE

An early low-lying mist had all but dissipated, gradually revealing a stark ground frost that coated everything it touched as far as the eye could see. The surrounding flat landscape resembled a watercolour whose white canvas had bled through the paint.

She approached the farm on ungritted roads, her stomach clenching every time the world lurched sideways beneath the wheels of her car. Hunching over the steering wheel as if clinging desperately to a raft in the middle of a raging ocean, she felt the demister belching warm air over her pinched features. People often said it was too cold to snow, though she knew different. It could be too *dry* to snow, but today was not one of those days. She awaited the first swirling flakes with anxious misgivings.

Skilfully, and with intense concentration, she negotiated patches of black ice severe enough to test the nerves of the most accomplished driver. She gripped the wheel like a vice, her focus so penetrating that her temples began to pound behind the bony ridges above both eyes. This part of the Fens was no place to slide off the road, not with the depth and capacity of local drainage ditches likely to swallow her tiny Fiat 500 whole.

Heaving a long sigh of relief as the flint farmhouse eased into view, she gently applied the foot brake while also using gear changes to slow her car. One tortuous slide while rounding a bend caused her to gasp out loud, but she quickly straightened the vehicle to prevent a full-blown skid.

Why did you come out here this morning? she chided herself.

Because it was the neighbourly thing to do.

You could have left it until later, waited for some kind of thaw.

By which time I'd be up to my neck at work and no way of knowing when I'd get another opportunity to pop over.

The inner conflict continued for a few seconds longer before reality won the argument; she was here now. What was there to be gained from continuing a purely internal debate?

When a brief elevation in the road corresponded with the stone boundary wall giving way to wooden fencing posts and taut wire strung between them, she spotted a blue van parked outside two ramshackle outhouses. A prickle of apprehension brushed across her flesh like an invisible cobweb, and the young woman started to question everything she had ever learned, known, or achieved prior to this point. Here was a situation she instinctively ought to know how to deal with, yet in the moment her mind froze, and her body began to follow suit.

The flint-constructed property belonged to seventy-two-year-old Sheila Musgrove. Four weeks ago, three self-proclaimed roofers had scammed her out of five thousand pounds. They took her money in exchange for half a day's work and no more than two buckets of a sand and cement concoction slathered over angled sections of the roof between slate tiles and stonework where the lead flashing was at its thinnest. The driver of the Fiat had liaised with Mrs Musgrove over the past month, mainly because they lived close to each other in the same rural community. She had decided to visit the farm that morning to update the poor woman on the status of the case, albeit there wasn't a great deal to report.

Now here was a dark blue Mercedes Sprinter. The very same make, model, and colour of vehicle used by the cowboy builders. Both the farmer and her nearest neighbour had selected it from an array of photographs shown to them by local police officers. Musgrove's statement had described it in every detail other than the registration plate, and the young woman entering the frosted drive had no doubt this was the same van standing in the same yard the yard's owner had only a month ago declared off limits to the building team forevermore.

As she brought the Fiat to a gradual halt and applied the handbrake, she felt anxious and conflicted. For all she knew, the three men might have it in them to become threatening towards her, especially if they feared being caught attempting to scam the same victim out of even more of her hard-earned savings. But at the same time, a fierce anger welled up inside her, causing both cheeks to flush with the full force of her wrath. If these were the same builders, then now was the moment to stop them in their tracks. Before exiting her car, she adjusted a piece of equipment and resolved to act with authority.

Determination having won the day, she made her way around to the farmhouse's entrance, which was to the left-hand side of the building as she approached. She took great care over every step, the frost-laden ground still unreliable beneath her tread. Within a few seconds she found herself positioned halfway between the van and the front door, and while the presence of the Sprinter bothered her, the sudden sight of Sheila Musgrove's body lying across the threshold to the house sent shivers rattling down the full length of her spine.

But she was not about to turn back.

As she drew closer, she noticed more: the farm owner wore layers of winter clothing, much of which was now drenched with blood; one foot had become unshod, and a ragged hole in the sole of her thick woollen tights exposed her bare flesh to the elements; moreover, her chest no longer seemed to rise and fall.

Reaching with studious care into her shoulder bag, the Fiat's owner pulled out two items: her phone and a small, black wallet. But as she raised the mobile to dial a number, a tall and wide man with a scarf wrapped around the lower half of his face appeared in the doorway.

Their eyes met.

Neither said a word.

Before she could react or even speak, she felt a heavy jolt to the back of her head. Stunned and forced into an ungainly stagger, she spilled both the phone and wallet from her grasp as she reflexively raised them to wrap across the point of injury. She had time enough to feel her thoughts swim before a second blow with something hard and solid sent her sprawling to the ground.

As she lay there slipping into unconsciousness, the muted colours of the day becoming increasingly indistinct, she became aware of another figure emerging from the doorway, striding purposefully across the stone path and bending to retrieve her phone and wallet. He flipped it open and immediately held up a warning hand, presumably to the man who had attacked her from behind.

'No!' he cried, sounding both far away and at the same time poised inside her head. 'She's the Filth. We can do without having those bastards chasing us down for killing one of their own.'

He took a step forward, crouched low, and stared into her flickering eyes. Somewhere amidst the undulating, almost monochromatic vision, she caught his crooked grin. 'You got lucky,' he told her. 'Remember that. You owe your life to me.' Then he casually tossed the wallet, which fell open just inches from her face. As a cold darkness descended over her, the familiar contents of the wallet became imprinted on her mind.

A badge; a crown perched upon what looked like a snowflake.

The words *Detective Constable*.

And the name, Gul Ansari.

TWO

Bliss wore his heaviest overcoat and leather gloves, but still the fierce chill of the day bit into his skin when he stepped out of the Volvo. As he carefully picked his way across the salted Thorpe Wood Police Station car park, he caught up with acting detective inspector Penny Chandler. He had followed her back from the crime scene out in the Fens on the edge of Crowland, where the vicious wind had felt like dull razors scraping across their flesh. He clapped his hands together and shuddered.

'Bit taters today, Pen,' he said, his breath fogging the short distance between them. 'I meant to ask earlier how your ancient bones were coping?'

'They're managing just fine, thanks,' Chandler replied with a haughty sniff. 'Better than those brittle old twigs of yours, I'm sure.'

Bliss laughed as they entered the building and headed straight to the canteen. There, he bought an all-day breakfast for himself, a bacon roll for Chandler, and two coffees. At their corner table, she chided him for smothering his food in HP.

'Ugh! Why do you do that?' she asked, lips curling in disgust.

'Because I know you hate the taste of brown sauce. This way, you don't pick at my grub when you're done with your own.'

'Oh, so there is method in your madness, after all.'

He tapped the side of his head. 'It's all still functioning up here, sweetheart. Don't you worry about that.'

'I'm not worried. Just surprised. Man your age…' She bit into her roll and spoke around each chew. 'Anyway, how come you were late to the scene?'

'I was down in Biggleswade when I got the shout.'

'What were you doing there?'

'Working a cold case. We split duties and I pulled a witness interview. As it happens I was sitting in a café when I got the call. It reminded me of the greasy spoon shitholes I used to frequent back in London in my teenage years. Minus the chain-smoking cook dripping sweat and scattering ash over plates of burnt but undercooked botulism swimming in dirty oil. Ah, those were the days, Pen. Cast-iron guts we had. Anyway, I left as soon as I learned about the murder and the attack on Gul.'

Chandler appeared to shudder slightly. 'We're all relieved to know she only has a concussion. It could've been so much worse.'

'Absolutely. It doesn't bear thinking about. So, what's your impression?' he asked before launching into the food on his plate.

Back at the farm they hadn't discussed the case at length. For Bliss there were three initial stages of any investigation: a big-picture assessment at the scene, followed by an overall perspective and an exchange of views either in the car on the way back or over a nice cuppa, before finally drilling down into the details with the team in a Major Inquiry Room. As the pair had travelled back separately, it was only right that stage two was taking place over breakfast.

'The usual mix of good news and bad news,' Chandler said, taking a sip of her lukewarm drink. 'Thankfully, after Gul spotted the van, she had the good sense to change her dashcam settings to store everything it recorded and parked at just the right angle for it to pick up both the van and the front of the house. In the footage we saw her approach with caution, then encounter someone at the front door, and finally the attack on her from behind. Then another bloke steps out of the house. It looks as if he decided not to continue the assault after picking up Gul's ID, which she dropped when she fell to the ground after getting whacked on the back of the head. Presumably that's when they discovered she was one of us.'

Bliss stared back. He'd speared a combination of sausage, mushroom, hash brown, and egg on his fork, which dripped runny yolk all over his plate. 'Sounds interesting. I'll have a butcher's at the footage myself later. Might be helpful. That was smart of her to make sure it didn't record over itself. You mentioned bad news?'

'Unfortunately, all three men were wrapped up so well due to the bad weather we haven't been able to get any decent still images of them.'

'Ah. So not quite as useful as I'd hoped. You got the van's plate, though, yes?'

'Yep. But it's come back false on the PNC, and I have no doubt we'll find the vehicle burned out somewhere not too far from the crime scene.'

After a moment of deliberation, Bliss asked, 'How many men did Gul see?'

'She remembers seeing one for sure, perhaps even two, but neither of them clearly. She wasn't aware of the third who attacked her from behind until she was struck. He must have been on the other side of the van when she bowled up.'

'And she was out cold for how long?'

'Unconscious for seconds only. After clobbering her, the three arseholes legged it and roared off in the van. She came to just as it left the yard, though she was obviously still groggy. The dashcam shows her struggling on the ground, before eventually managing to sit upright. They took her phone so Gul couldn't call us right away. She says she was aiming to make her way into the house and use whatever phone she could find inside, but it just so happened that a neighbour spotted her as she dragged herself back to her feet.'

'Her being sparko for only a few seconds suggests a decent outcome,' Bliss said, thinking about potential brain damage.

'Precisely. Obviously, the doctors are keeping her in for observation, but she was awake and lucid enough to describe everything she saw to Bish and remembered to tell him about the dashcam footage. She also gave a description of the man she saw in the doorway. His clothing, anyway.'

'We'll let her rest for the time being,' Bliss said as he continued to eat. 'But when she is able to speak to us again, have someone pop over to the hospital with some photos of the usual suspects for her to go through. Sad to say, there are plenty of chancers out there, but we might get lucky.'

'Agreed,' Chandler said. Her eyes narrowed. 'But they don't usually go this far. To escalate from ripping off vulnerable people to murdering them, I mean.'

'True. If it is the same crew that ripped her off, presumably they came back looking to turn their victim over again, only this time she told them where to go. But you're right, you have to wonder how it went from there to what we saw.'

The farmer had lost her life in an ugly fashion. It was obvious from the cuts, abrasions, bruising, and swollen face that she'd been struck several times; a heavy beating for anyone, let alone an elderly woman. A zig-zag imprint to her left cheek suggested she had also been stamped on at least once. But Bliss was willing to bet the fatal blow had come from a single puncture wound deep into the chest.

'What do we know about Mrs Musgrove and the rip off from last month?' he asked, pushing his plate aside and wiping his lips with a folded paper napkin.

Chandler retrieved her notebook and flipped back a few pages. She took a long swallow of coffee then said, 'According to Gul, the victim lived alone. Had done since her husband passed away almost five years ago. They had two children, both of whom have been informed and are on their way home. One lives in South Africa, the other in Switzerland, so it'll take them a while to get here.'

'She ran this farm on her own?'

'She did, though these days it didn't amount to much more than a smallholding. Chickens mainly, plus a dozen or so pigs and a few sheep. All for her own consumption. She rented out her two larger fields to neighbouring farmers.'

'Add them to the list of TIEs,' he said. With the murder and assault taking place in such a rural setting, Bliss didn't imagine there would be a multitude of early Trace, Interview, and Eliminate interviews carried out, but anyone connected to the victim by a financial contract had to be of interest to the investigation. 'Is the original scam case with CID or Fraud?'

'I'm not sure. I'll find out and have the files sent through. Why, what are you thinking?'

'A neighbour helped Mrs Musgrove identify the van these fuckers used,' Bliss said. 'We'll want to re-interview them. Also, let's see who else is mentioned in the investigation reports, and then think of a few fresh possibilities for ourselves.'

'Such as?'

He shrugged. 'I don't know. Did our victim or anybody else along that road get their food delivered? If so, who by? We could have Ocado, Tesco, or similar drivers who were in the area that day. Amazon, or Evri delivering parcels, somebody along those lines. Casual visitors, friends or family. A vet, maybe. A bunch of God-botherers for all I care. Anyone who might have been close by on the day Mrs Musgrove had that work done. I want to know who they are and what they saw.'

Chandler made some notes. Bliss smiled as she scribbled away with her pen. 'How are you finding the DI role?' he asked.

'Easy-Peasy,' she said, looking up at him. 'I can't think why you complained so much about it all those years. It's a doddle. You just get the other poor sods in the team to do all the hard graft while you put your feet up and file your nails in your office.'

'Precisely. My cuticles never looked so good as when I was DI.'

'Yeah, I've always thought you looked suspiciously too well-manicured. Seriously, though, it's going great so far. Bish gives me the occasional sideways look, but following your lead I always go to him for his opinions. To be fair, he's been a tremendous help to me.

'Glad to hear it,' Bliss said. 'He's the one you had to win over. You were already senior to the others in the team. Bish had his opportunity to grab that DI role with both hands and it was too much for him at the time. I'm sure his scars from that are still fresh. But you'll have his respect and hopefully the friendship will survive your promotion.'

They finished off their drinks, stacked their tray and dumped their litter then headed over to the unit. Along the way, Bliss hit his colleague with a few surreptitious sidelong glances. He'd always known she would excel at whatever rank she rose to, but Detective Inspector suited her down to the ground. As SIO, it was his remit to manage the investigation and every member of the team involved, but he was keen to allow Chandler room to grow and breathe. She had earned it.

As they headed along the corridor, he felt her eyes catch his own. 'Is that a Crombie overcoat?' she asked.

Bliss tugged on both velvet lapels. 'It is. Smart, eh?'

Chandler grinned. 'I was just thinking how Jimmy Bliss it is. I can imagine you swaggering around those east London streets wearing one. That and your Ben Sherman shirts with the button-down collar, two-tone tonic trousers, and a Harrington jacket, if I'm not very much mistaken.'

He juddered to a halt. 'What do you know about all that old clobber?'

'I'm into retro things. Please tell me you also wore a Trilby. Please. That would just about complete my mental image of the young Jimmy.'

Waving away her speculation, Bliss said, 'Let's just say I was well acquainted with all that gear in my Ska days.'

Chandler gave him a friendly punch on the arm and wagged a finger at him. 'I knew it. I just knew it.'

'How? Why?'

She laughed and winked. 'Because you're the most retro thing I know, Jimmy. After the dinosaurs, that is.'

THREE

Having been made aware of DC Gul Ansari's diagnosis and subsequent optimistic prognosis, the Major Crime Unit team, their uniformed colleagues, and civilian staff, shifted focus to fully immerse themselves in the murder investigation. To begin with, they discussed the details gathered from the original scam. Bliss stood at the front of the room, book-ended by DI Chandler and DCI Diane Warburton.

'We may yet get some good fortune,' he said, 'but I think we have to assume that by the time we eventually locate the Mercedes Sprinter the gang will have burned it out and so forensically it'll be useless to us. That said, once we have its VIN, we can learn more about the van's history. If they stole it, which is likely, all we can hope is that they screwed up at the time. Perhaps they'll turn up on CCTV. At the very least, if they drove it anywhere before switching the plates out, they might crop up on ANPR.'

'I'll get on that as soon as we hear any news,' DS Bishop volunteered. Bliss knew his colleague was feeling the absence of Ansari more than most, the pair having worked together closely for several years. Their bond was tight, and Bliss would not want to be in the shoes of the man who'd clubbed her unconscious if Olly Bishop got to him first.

'Good. Finding a better witness than our victim's closest neighbour is also a priority. I've already discussed a few things with Penny, and she'll advise you of the relevant actions. One more thing to add to that, Pen,' he said, turning to Chandler. 'Have a word with Intelligence. See if they have any previous incidents featuring three men scamming people in this way. I'm betting Mrs Musgrove won't be the first vulnerable person these bastards have turned over on our manor.'

Bliss faced outward once more, softening his tone. 'I know we all desperately want to find the thugs who murdered this poor woman. And, naturally, we're all still blazing over what they did to Gul. But let's keep a lid on our tempers and work this case like any other. If we think positively, we'll get a fix on who these three pricks are. Without an ID, we're going to struggle, so that's our priority.'

DC Virgil's hand shot into the air. 'Jimmy, isn't there a chance they'll dump the motor, get hold of another and simply pick up where they left off? We could swamp the area with response vehicles for a day or two.'

'They might do precisely that, Alan, but this is almost certainly the first time one of their jobs has ended in murder. If that's the case, they're just as likely to want to get their heads down somewhere. Besides, if I'm them I'd want to expand beyond any previous location, especially anywhere close to Crowland. Probably across into another county served by a different area force. In fact, now that I think about it, let's communicate with neighbouring forces. See if they have similar scams being worked, and if not, at the very least, we can get it on their radar.'

'Do we know when forensics will be in?' DCI Warburton asked. 'And how about pathology?'

Bliss cocked his head. 'Forensic evidence might be thin on the ground, but we could still get lucky. The yard was thick with ice, so I have no idea what kind of footprints they'll be able to pull for us. But because it was freezing, our scumbags wore several layers of clothing, so there could be threads or fibres. I imagine they wore gloves the whole time they were there, but we'll see. I've had no word on when they'll do the postmortem, but I'll be popping over to the hospital to see Gul, so I'll nip down and have a word with the pathologist while I'm there. We're pretty sure Mrs Musgrove died as a result of the stab wound, though.'

'Okay. Any thoughts on why she was killed?'

'Something did just occur to me,' Chandler said. 'From what we know about the original scam, the three men pulled into the yard, convinced Mrs Musgrove that a heavy snow storm was on its way and that her roof was in need of urgent repair, or she risked allowing the elements in and perhaps even losing the lot. They did the work and were gone within hours. But what we don't appear to have is an account of how our victim paid them. I've heard nothing to suggest she visited her bank. In fact, if she'd done so, they would have queried her about withdrawing so much in cash. I'm wondering if she handed over money she already had in the house. If I'm right, that's probably why they came back.'

DCI Warburton, who had been waiting patiently, clicked her fingers and nodded at Chandler. 'Penny, let's verify that, please. I want to know everything about how the scam worked, how much our victim was able to recall when making her statement. Did she tell them how much ready cash she was able to lay her hands on? Was that how these men agreed on how much they wanted to do the job? And what was the likelihood of Mrs Musgrove having more tucked away?'

Chandler glanced at Bliss, who nodded. Warburton put back her head and groaned. 'Sorry, Jimmy,' she said. 'Old habits I'm afraid. You'll need to action that yourself as SIO for the policy book.'

'Don't worry about it,' he said. 'I don't care who it comes from, just as long as it ends up on record at the end of the day. Which reminds me, I need a list of people who attended the crime scene outside of this team here. First responders, duty inspector, CSI, paramedics. Also, these men stole Gul's phone. Let's get that logged, have tech set it to auto wipe all data next time it's switched on, but leave it trackable just in case they're stupid enough to use it.'

'Did she not have her own phone on her as well as her work device?' DC Virgil asked.

Bliss shook his head. 'She doesn't carry one while on duty, and as she stopped off at the farm on her way to work, she had just the one mobile. Okay, that's it. I'll get the policy book started before I head out to the hospital, but DI Chandler is your go-to person while I'm anywhere else.'

'Will you be going back to your cold case duty later on today?' DC Gratton asked. 'I just want to know where to find you if we get something only you can run with.'

The dual cold case and SIO roles he occupied were not always easy to navigate, but Bliss thought he had managed the choppy waters well so far. He looked up at Gratton and said, 'I don't expect to be, no. I contacted Investigator Greenhill earlier as I drove back to Peterborough, so she has matters in hand on my behalf. But thanks for piping up, Phil, because I've just remembered today is your last day with us. Drinks later?'

Gratton nodded. 'Of course. The Haycock from eight onwards.'

'I wouldn't miss it, mate. Have a good last shift.'

His words were echoed by everyone in the room. Phil Gratton was moving down south to join the Met firearms team. His replacement stood mute beside him. A DC transferred over from the Major Crime Unit based in Welwyn Garden City, Vasyl Kolesnyk had promptly answered to 'Vaseline' and later just plain 'Vas'. The forty-year-old Ukrainian had come to Hertfordshire having left the National Police of Ukraine just two weeks before his thirtieth birthday. He spoke excellent English and apparently enjoyed a wicked sense of humour. Bliss had yet to work with him, but he'd heard only positive things from Chandler and Bishop in particular.

'Vas,' he said, eyeing his new colleague. 'Stick to Phil like glue today. Whatever he works on, you work on. Whatever he discovers, you make sure you're up to speed with it. Today you are his shadow. As of tomorrow, you are him. Understood?'

'Understood.' The man straightened his back and just about clicked his heels as he nodded, leaving Bliss to wonder if Kolesnyk had a military background.

'Excellent,' he said. He ran his gaze around the room. 'Look, for my money we're still just about within the wider version of the golden hour, so let's pull up trees. By the time I get back from visiting Gul, I want to see some progress. Right?'

The team responded in various ways, but each was loud, certain, and 'Yes, Boss,' far outweighed 'Yes, Jimmy.' Almost eight months without a warrant card yet they were still very much *his* team. The thought brought a smile to his face as he turned away to speak with Warburton and Chandler before he left the station.

When it was just the three of them huddled together in his old office, the room Chandler now used when she needed to hide herself away to finish off paperwork, Bliss said, 'I just wanted to make it clear to you both how I see this. While I appreciate the number of investigations we're currently handling is through the roof, for me this is our top priority. Any issues with that?'

Chandler shook her head. DCI Warburton did the same but added, 'While I agree with you, Jimmy, we do need to consider managing our workload. We have court proceedings to prepare for, most prominently those against Ritchie Morrison and Jamar Jay Tapper. I realise you, personally, are not involved in that, but the rest of us are. Even so, you may yet have to give evidence against both our big and little motherfuckers. And given we've not quite abandoned Operation Splinter, either, I'm wary of stretching our limited resources.'

Splinter referred to a case dating back to the previous autumn, which the press had dubbed the Compass Killing. One of those investigations that had picked up little or no traction; the kind they didn't want to let go of but were now reduced to clinging to more out of desperation than their ability to close.

Bliss nodded. 'I understand. We draw a line here. Regards our Mofos, all I need is an hour at most with the CPS lawyer. I have my stories straight and my policy book is in order, so I'm ready. That's a few weeks away yet, so I'm not worried. And as far as Splinter is concerned, we're banging our heads against multiple brick walls. It won't hurt to turn our attention elsewhere. I want this crew, Diane. What they did to this poor vulnerable woman, what they did to Gul… we can't allow that to go unpunished. I want every resource we have on it.'

He didn't need to say any more. Warburton gave him the go-ahead with a single nod.

FOUR

Peterborough City Hospital on the Edith Cavell Healthcare Campus first opened its doors to patients in November 2010. A state-of-the-art facility spread over five floors, the main building was grand and imposing, with a host of additional units gathered around it like newborn pups to a mother. Bliss much preferred the site to the old district hospital in the city centre, and even the Edith Cavell hospital it had physically replaced, though there was never a positive or joyful reason to visit.

Upon arrival, he found DC Ansari alone, sitting up in bed watching a news feature on the small television mounted to a wall on an adjustable bracket. She seemed genuinely pleased and touched to see him, her face crumpling with emotion.

'How's the old swede?' he asked, striding across to the bed.

Ansari reflexively brought a hand to the back of her head, which was heavily bandaged around thick wads of gauze dressing. 'Not too bad, Jimmy,' she answered brightly. 'You never know, it might even have knocked some sense into me.'

'That's the spirit, girl. Glad to see you're not letting it get you down.'

She eyed his hands. 'They for me?'

He looked down and nodded. He held out a bunch of bananas, which he knew were Ansari's favourite. In his other hand, he clutched two packets of Penguin chocolate biscuits. 'I thought you could have your five a day while the nurses are about, then later on when the lights go off you can live a little.'

Smiling gratefully, she said, 'Thank you so much. I've had plenty of flowers and grapes, but you're the first to bring me things I actually enjoy.'

'Got to look after the foot soldiers, Gul,' Bliss said. 'Besides, I need you out there on the streets, not tucked up here in bed swinging the lead.'

'Bloody cheek. And if I have my way I won't be here for long. I told them I want to go home later today, but they insist I stay overnight so they can monitor me. Can you have a word, see what you can do?'

Bliss angled his head. 'You still living on your own?'

'Since I split up with Tariq, yes.'

'Then this is the best place for you. You know it is, Gul. Sometimes the after-effects of a bad concussion occur many hours after the injury that caused it. You get into trouble later while you're out there on your own in the sticks, there's no telling which way it might go.'

Ansari folded her arms, pursing her lips. 'Okay. I suppose I can live with that. But, Jimmy, they want me to take a minimum of fourteen days off work to recover and recuperate. Possibly even longer if my follow-up appointment doesn't go well. Surely you can do something about that.'

'It's not me you'd need to talk to,' Bliss said. 'I'm not your boss anymore, remember?' He leaned in, feigning concern. 'You do remember, yes?'

She laughed it off. 'Of course I do. Look, I'm fine. Really, I am. But you'll always be the boss to me, Jimmy.'

'Thank you for that. But you'd have to talk to either Pen or Diane. Though I wouldn't bother if I were you. They'll both tell you precisely what I would: you take as much time as your doctors insist on. Fourteen days, twenty-one, even four weeks if necessary. You don't mess with a head injury, Gul. I've had a few in my time.'

'Now, why doesn't that surprise me? In fact, it could explain a lot.'

Bliss chuckled. 'You could be right. Even so, you need to take good care of yourself, especially in the first few days. The symptoms can sneak up on you when you least expect them to.'

Ansari blew out her lips. 'Not much help, are you,' she complained.

'Not in these circumstances, no. And you, young lady, have to be honest about how you're feeling. With yourself and with your quacks.'

'I suppose so.'

'No supposing about it. But you can still help us out. You up for someone coming over later to go through some faces? The usual suspects, that sort of thing. One of them might trigger a memory.'

Sitting up straighter against the plump support pillows, his colleague's face brightened. 'Of course. Happy to. Just not during visiting hours. You know how my family feels about the police.'

The Ansaris were part of a vast Muslim population living close to the city centre. Of Pakistani heritage, their relationship with their daughter was unfathomable to Bliss. While her father in particular was all for police protection and security, he nonetheless disapproved of his precious Gul being part of that protective blanket.

'Don't worry,' he said. 'I'll make sure they pop over in between visiting sessions. But listen to me, if you feel tired or just not fully yourself, you have a nurse call to cancel and you get the rest you need. You hear me?'

Nodding, Ansari sighed and said, 'Loud and clear. You know, I'm not sure what to make of this Jimmy Bliss. The one who goes by the book.'

Bliss narrowed his gaze. 'When it comes to this type of injury, I'm all for it. Doctors know best, and you don't mess with the brain. Those of you who are fortunate enough to have one. Anyway, I'm very glad to see you awake and alert. You had us all worried there for a while, Gul.'

She shrugged and gave a gentle sigh. 'I just feel a bit stupid, to tell the truth. I should have been more aware. Getting attacked from behind is a bit of a rookie move.'

'Happens to the best of us,' he told her. 'And you're firmly in that category. But if you're concerned about this reflecting on your promotion push, forget about it. You pass those exams and DS is in your own two hands. You hear me?'

'Yes, boss.'

Bliss let that one go. He said his goodbyes and headed down into the basement to find the pathologist, Matt Wheeler. He was about to carry out the postmortem on a young woman fatally injured in a head-on collision on her way home from work the previous day.

'I suppose you want to know when I'll be getting around to your victim's PM,' Wheeler said as he removed a fresh set of scrubs and protective garments from their plastic wrappings. 'And you're in luck because I've just this minute added it to my schedule. Mrs Musgrove is on my table first thing Monday morning.'

'Why not tomorrow?' Bliss asked.

'Because tonight my wife and I plus our two children are driving down to the Kent coast, where we intend to enjoy some good food, even better drink, and a weekend away free of talk about spleens, brains, and various types of injuries.'

'Ah. Of course. I forgot you pathologists were part-timers,' Bliss joked.

Wheeler frowned at him over the rim of his spectacles. 'Careful, Jimmy. Or I might make you wait even longer.'

'Fair enough. You enjoy your break. But you've had a quick gander, yeah? Would you like to offer an opinion on cause of death?'

Wheeler ran a hand through his light brown hair and smiled, blinking a couple of times as if to punctuate each thought he gathered. 'I wouldn't like to, but as a consolation prize for you, I will. If I were a betting man, I'd put a few quid on COD being tied in with the stab wound. Your victim's head has taken a real old battering, so we could be looking at significant brain trauma. In addition, the overall impact of the assault could have brought on a myocardial infarction. However, my money is on the bloody wound being the coup de grâce.'

Bliss thanked him. 'I might see you Monday, then. Not quite sure what I'll be working on, but if not me I'll send DI Chandler in my stead. She needs a few more PMs under her belt to help with her squeamishness.'

'I can certainly help with that. Monday morning at ten, then.'

Driving back to Thorpe Wood, Bliss was confident that Wheeler's best guess would prove to be accurate. The thought of one or perhaps even two men beating and stamping on a frail, elderly, and certainly defenceless woman disgusted him. He felt the heat of anger rise up from his chest, resulting in an acrid taste of bile. It was entirely plausible to think of them demanding cash, Mrs Musgrove defiant in her refusal, which led to a fierce assault. But why kill the woman? Why take out a blade and thrust it into her? That wasn't part of the threat, wasn't included in the beating they gave her. The stabbing was a cold and deliberate action, with only one intention. Was it because she had seen their faces and could describe them? That didn't feel quite right to Bliss, because for all they knew by the time they returned to her farm she could already have offered the police a full description following their original scam.

It was one to ponder. If his team had no luck with the vehicle nor discovering the identities of the three men, working out why they had elected to kill their victim might be the next approach. One that did not fill Bliss with a great deal of hope.

FIVE

Bliss took a seat in Superintendent Edwards's neatly appointed office, surprised at having been summoned there together with Beth Greenhill, his Unsolved Cases Team colleague. He'd been about to grab a drink when he received the message. Though the two had long ago ceased being enemies, an unexpected summons upstairs was always cause for concern.

'Any update on Gul's condition?' Edwards asked as he settled into a chair facing her desk. 'I understand you visited the hospital earlier.'

'She's doing as well as can be expected,' he replied. 'She's already bored and wants to go home, but they're keeping her overnight for observation. She begged me to intervene, but I told her to stay put.'

'Do we know what to expect regards recovery and recuperation?'

'A minimum of two weeks, but potentially anywhere up to a month. That all depends on the after-effects and how honestly she deals with them. I warned her not to be flexible with the truth. I've had a couple of concussions in my time, and they can catch you unawares if you're not careful.'

'How about her memory?'

Bliss nodded. 'All good at the moment. But again, a severe concussion can cause confusion, drowsiness, headaches, and yes, some forms of amnesia. Her last boyfriend moved out, so she's living alone. We'll have to keep tabs on her. I was thinking of arranging for some staggered visits from the team. That way, we can all report back on our findings and compare notes.'

'Good idea,' Edwards said. 'Count me in. But whatever Gul's status, one thing that doesn't change is our determination to find the brutes who did this to her. We want them arrested and charged with Sheila Musgrove's murder, naturally, but also for how they left our colleague. Penny tells me the presumptive notion is that the men who took the money from our victim under false pretences a few weeks ago may have come back for more.'

'Yes. Gul happened to pay her a visit on the way to work this morning to discuss the case and the next move in finding the conmen who charged her such a ludicrous amount of money for work they never carried out. The reason we believe it was these same three men today is because of the blue Mercedes van. We can't be certain it was the same vehicle because nobody noted the plate during their first visit, but for me the same make, model, and colour is one coincidence too far.'

'That sounds like a perfectly reasonable deduction. Any clue as to why they returned and why this time they attacked this poor woman?'

'Our initial hypothesis is that Mrs Musgrove paid them last time with cash she had in the house and so they returned thinking it would be easy pickings. We suspect she resisted their demands to tell them where she kept her stash, perhaps even went as far as to let them know she'd been to the police. That might explain the savage attack to her face, and it could also be the reason why one of them chose to kill her. I'm having trouble with that motive, however. Mainly because it's a major escalation, but also because stabbing her to death still doesn't lead them to the cash. To be honest, it could be an explosion of temper that went way beyond what they'd intended.'

Nodding, Edwards agreed. 'It's a tough one.'

'It is. But we'll continue to talk it through. It looks as if Gul arrived shortly after the stabbing occurred, probably while they were still ransacking Mrs Musgrove's home. Gul naturally took it upon herself to investigate and was attacked for doing her job.'

Edwards hissed a sharp inhalation. 'The utter bastards! I want these men, Jimmy. I realise none of this began as our case, but now things have changed. And I want you to work closely with Penny on finding them.'

'We're on it, believe me. Mrs Musgrove had little or no information for the initial police investigation. Three men and a van is about it. But we're going to go door-to-door in the neighbourhood as it's likely that other locals were approached about their roofs requiring urgent repair. Either that or they may have seen something they didn't realise was important at the time. I also have the team scouring for potential delivery drivers both during the day of the scam and first thing this morning. As for the Mercedes Sprinter itself, we're assuming it's been dumped by now, but we'll see.'

'Indeed. Early days. But hopefully, this part of the investigation will turn up a few of the missing pieces. I take it you've opened a policy book as SIO?'

Nodding, Bliss said, 'Yes, Ma'am.'

'And the team has their actions and instructions?'

'Of course.'

'Excellent. Then you can return to the case as soon as we've dealt with the issue I asked you here to discuss.'

Here it is, he thought. He was about to learn why he'd been summoned, and he probably wasn't going to like it. A fan of Sun Tzu's *Art of War*, Bliss often mentally referred to quotes from the book. The first to pop into his head now was 'the wise warrior avoids the battle'.

'I'm sorry, what do you mean by "return to"?' Bliss shot back, ignoring both ancient wisdom and his own sage advice. He stared hard at the Superintendent but kept his tone neutral with the quote still fresh in his thoughts. 'This is an active murder enquiry. We also have a colleague injured during the course of her duties. I'm not walking away from that for a cold case, which I presume is why you asked Beth to join us.'

Having said nothing up to this point, Greenhill squirmed in her seat alongside him.

Edwards, however, stared him down. 'If you want to get technical, Jimmy, Gul was not injured during the course of her duties. The conning of an elderly woman was not your case. DC Ansari was simply being kind enough to keep a neighbour updated. Also, I'm not asking you to walk away. I'm saying you will return to it afterwards.'

'Afterwards? I've been waiting for you to get to the point since Beth and I sat down,' Bliss said, feeling his muscles beginning to tense up. 'After what, exactly?'

'That's a fair question. And you're quite right, there is a new cold case I'm going to need you to look into.'

Bliss had to keep himself from leaping out of his chair. 'Now? Surely an unsolved case can't be more important than focussing on Gul and our murder victim.'

'I'm not suggesting it's more important, Jimmy. But I am telling you that a clock has recently been applied to this particular cold case and we feel this might be the last chance to make progress on it.'

'Okay, but why us?' Bliss asked. He touched a hand to his chest. 'Why me? You still have Beth, Ben, and Guy to work whatever it is.'

'I do realise how many investigators make up the team, Jimmy,' Edwards said, clearly not looking to retreat. 'And I wouldn't pull you off your SIO duties unless I had no other choice. And I don't, in this case.'

'How can that be?'

'Because somebody you once arrested wants to provide you with information. You, and only you.'

Bliss eased back, tension leaving his body. He was beginning to understand the superintendent's dilemma, and also to appreciate the terrible position she'd been placed in.

'Is that somebody still inside or back on the streets?' he asked, less combative this time.

'Inside. They're not getting out again, either. Not alive, at least.'

'I wish that narrowed down the list of possibilities,' Bliss said. 'Look, I'm not happy about this, Ma'am, but I accept this is out of your hands, so there's no blame attached to you. Please, go on, tell me who and where.'

'The where is Milton Keynes.'

Bliss felt his flesh instantly starting to crawl. DSI Edwards knew precisely what that would mean to him. Tension ate into his muscles once again. He met her unflinching gaze and slowly shook his head. 'Please don't ask me to do this. Please.'

'It's not a request, I'm afraid. You're part of the Unsolved Cases Team, Jimmy. And… well, he asked for you by name. Demanded it, in fact. Said the only person he's willing to share this information with is you. In person. Face-to-face.'

'But him? Of all people.'

'I'm sorry to interrupt,' Greenhill said, speaking for the first time. 'But I'm starting to feel like a spare dick at a wedding. What am I missing here? Who is this prisoner making all these demands? Why is he so special and why will he only speak to Jimmy?'

Edwards glanced at Bliss, who nodded back before lowering his head. 'His name is Nick Nevin,' she told Greenhill, her voice hushed as she revealed the answer.

'And? I've certainly never heard of him, so how big a deal can he be?'

'No, Beth, you probably would never have heard his name before. But tragically, Jimmy has. Nick Nevin was once one of us. A police officer working in the Met at the same time as Jimmy. He's also the man who murdered Hazel Bliss – Jimmy's wife.'

SIX

It was a little under sixty miles from the station in Peterborough to the prison in Milton Keynes. Beth Greenhill let twenty of them slide by in relative silence before bringing up the elephant in the room and shining a dazzling, fat spotlight all over it.

'I can't begin to imagine what's going on inside your head right now,' she said with great warmth and tenderness. 'I find it almost beyond belief that they would ask you to do this, Jimmy. And I have to say, harder still to fathom why you would agree.'

Bliss said nothing for several seconds. The Volvo's fat tyres hissed on wet tarmac as the frost and ice beneath them finally succumbed to the earlier gritting and the sheer volume of traffic helping to break it up. Eventually, keeping his eyes fixed on the road ahead, he relented.

'From everything DSI Edwards told us after she revealed which prisoner we'd have to visit, the information he has could well be genuine. If there's even the slightest possibility of that, then I really have no choice. It's my job, Beth. It's what I signed up for.'

His colleague snapped her head around to face him. 'This? Having to sit in the same room as the man who murdered your wife? No. I'm sorry, but that's bang out of order. It's inhumane.'

'Maybe so. But it's also necessary. If he's serious about telling only me and only in person, then if I refuse that's an unsolved case that may never be closed. I don't know who or what we might be looking at, but odds are that some innocent family members are out there still waiting for closure. I can't ignore that because it doesn't suit or because my emotions are involved.'

Shaking her head this time, Greenhill said, 'You're a better person than I am. In your shoes, I would have told them where to stick their cold case.'

He smiled. Shot her a sidelong glance. 'No. No, you wouldn't have.'

A moment later: 'No. You're probably right. I'd have wanted to, though.'

'Yeah,' Bliss said. 'Me, too.'

They drove on in silence for a few minutes before Greenhill spoke again. The sky ahead was a milky grey, leached of both colour and intent. 'You want to talk about it?' she asked. 'Would it help you to vent before you actually lay eyes on him again? I mean, have you even been that close to him since… since it happened?'

'Too close,' Bliss admitted, feeling his grip on the steering wheel tighten. 'Nevin was still a serving Met officer when he first stalked and then murdered Hazel. I will never speak about why she appeared on his radar, so don't ask. But she did. I subsequently learned from her best friend that he had been bothering her for a while, but she was too scared to tell me about it. Afraid of what I might do to him.

'So, oblivious to what had been going on, I came home late one night to find Hazel stabbed to death on our bedroom floor. In the initial flurry of minutes that followed, I was a husband first and foremost, a police officer a distant second. I did everything you're not supposed to do if you want to preserve the scene of crime and not implicate yourself at the same time. Naturally, I became their prime suspect, but once the PM results came through I was able to prove where I was at the time of her death. That was when I started to hear whispers, and then completely out of the blue the subject of those whispers, Nevin, called me. He said he wanted to offer his condolences, but I heard the deceit in his voice. I knew what he'd done, though I had not a scrap of evidence to back it up. I should have demanded my accusers start an investigation against him, but instead I waited for him one night and I jumped him. He ended up hospitalised.'

Bliss exhaled. A long and weary breath carrying with it pain and regret. 'After that, my life became all about accusation and counter-accusation. Eventually he became a suspect, which did lead to his arrest, but without any evidence he was allowed to go about his business rather than held on remand. Meanwhile, plenty of colleagues knew what I'd done to the man, but I'd left them nothing to work with against me. And that seemed to be that.'

Greenhill had listened intently to his story. At this point she said, 'But a few minutes ago you implied you'd seen him since, is that right?'

Bliss was nodding at the memory. 'Oh, yes. I think I came to be the itch he couldn't scratch, and the humiliation of what I did to him was a flame he could never fully extinguish. He and a few of his old cronies who were convinced of his innocence put together a plan to discredit me for being on the take back in my Met days. I decided I'd had enough of his crap and baited him into a trap. We ended up having a bit of a barney – well, as much as two out of shape, no longer young men can have. We roughed each other up a bit, though without inflicting too much damage. But during the altercation I got him to admit what he did, without him realising that a senior officer could hear every word on the other end of a phone call I'd placed moments before the scuffle.'

'So, you finally landed him for your wife's murder after all those years,' Greenhill said, turning to him. Her eyes were bright and glistening. 'You're the sole reason he's serving time.'

'I did, and I am.'

'But going back to that day, you can't have known how that fight between you would go. He could have pulled a blade on you. A gun. Anything could have happened.'

'At the time I baited the trap, I was perfectly willing to die if that's what it took to nail the bastard. In fact, I'd go so far as to say I might have even wanted it to go that way. This was only a few years ago, Beth, but I still wasn't over losing Hazel. She was my world, and that prick took her away from me. I confess, there were times when I didn't much want to carry on living.'

'What changed?' she asked, seemingly unsurprised. 'Was it finally seeing him end up in prison?'

Bliss shook his head. 'Oddly enough, no. I was reminded that I still had people in my life who cared very much if I lived or died even if I didn't. My mum was still around at that point. Then there was Pen, and Bish, and the rest of the team. I can't say I was completely out of whatever black hole I'd ended up in, but I could at least see the light and appreciate it for the first time in a long while. One of these days, I'll tell you the story about a fifteen-year-old girl called Molly. She's probably the missing piece of my particular jigsaw. I think her predicament made me realise how important it was to push through the bad times.'

'She sounds interesting.'

'Oh, she's that all right. A diamond. A rough one, admittedly, but she's had those hard edges softened and now she's an absolute credit to the strength of love and loyalty.'

Greenhill pursed her lips, looking fairly emotional herself. 'Bloody hell. That doesn't sound much like the Jimmy Bliss I've heard so much about. That's not to say the legend is bad, just not that emotive.'

'I'm a mixed bag,' Bliss admitted. The A421 continued to swish beneath them as they drew closer to the M1 motorway, the road a sea of white and red lights under a blanket of clouds that had settled overhead. 'Marmite, you could say. But I think – I hope – my heart is in the right place.'

'Oh, I'm sure it is. Nobody has implied otherwise. But tell me, the jungle drums suggest there might be more to your relationship with Penny than merely colleagues or friends. Are they wrong?'

He thought about how best to respond. He and Greenhill had grown close both as colleagues and friends. They'd enjoyed a few drinks and a couple of meals together. Neither had suggested taking the relationship further, nor had either of them quashed the idea entirely. But Bliss liked and respected his usual cold case partner enough to reward the question with an honest response.

'No, they're spot on,' he said with genuine alacrity. 'She's not just a colleague, not just a friend. She's my best friend. Hazel was and will forever be my soulmate. But Pen is the closest to that I've known since or am ever likely to know. And to anticipate your next question, no we never have, and we never will.'

Laughing now, Greenhill gave an appreciative nod. 'I get that. I think that's what I see between you. Something you can't really quantify. I'm sure that kind of closeness can at times overcome the often-dreadful nature of the job. And thanks for opening up to me, by the way. From what I gather, that's somewhat unusual.'

'It's the new me,' Bliss told her. 'A true millennium man. A quarter of a century too late, maybe, but here I am warts and all. And listen, Beth, don't get me wrong. I won't ever get over losing Hazel, but I don't want or need anyone's sympathy. I finally came to terms with it, and I'm doing just fine. I have my fish, I have my dog, I have my job, I have great colleagues – old and new – and I have the kind of friendship some people never get to experience. That's more than enough to keep me going.'

'But none of which prepares you for days like today, I expect.'

He shook his head, chin jutting forwards. 'No, you're right about that. This is going to be hard, no question. But the way I'm choosing to look at it, all those things I just mentioned are waiting for me when I'm done with him. All he has to look forward to afterwards, on the other hand, is his tiny cell. So, fuck him. Fuck Nick Nevin. Let him do his worst.'

SEVEN

An hour and seventeen minutes after leaving Thorpe Wood, Bliss and Greenhill pulled into the visitors' car park at HMP Woodhill, the category A home to approximately 500 prisoners, including Charles Salvador – better known as Charles Bronson. A further half hour passed before they were led into a cell-sized room set aside for meetings between prisoners and their legal representatives.

Nick Nevin looked up without expression as they entered. Six years had elapsed since the two men had last met, but the ex-cop sitting at the table nibbling on a small bar of milk chocolate seemed to have aged out of all proportion. Hollow-cheeked and unshaven, ashen skin pressed tight against the skull. His eyes were glassy behind black-rimmed spectacles as they flitted from Bliss to Beth Greenhill, at which point he managed a weak leer.

'Oi, Oi, Jimmy,' he said, a harsh rasp to his voice. 'If you're not slipping this one a length, step aside and I'll do what only a real man can do.'

'If I were you, Nevin, I'd keep that tongue civil,' Bliss said without inflection as he and his partner took their seats. 'Or I might just reach over there and rip it from your mouth.'

'Ooh, touchy. I'm offended and triggered. And that's hardly the way to talk to the man who's about to offer you precious information. You need to treat me with a bit of respect, old son.'

Bliss leaned closer, his shadow pressing against the table. 'Let me tell you how it is, you miserable twat. Whatever you claim to have is in reference to an unsolved case, which by definition means it's not a crime in action. So, if it doesn't get worked, then nobody is at further risk. All of which means I can choose to walk out of here anytime I like. In which case, I suggest you take it down a notch and crack on with whatever you have to tell us. Otherwise, you can fuck right off.'

Nevin pouted. 'You used to be a lot more fun. Just like your late wife, as I remember,' he finished with a cackle that resulted in a coughing fit.

If he was looking to provoke a reaction, he got one. Just not the one he was most likely expecting. Whenever his thoughts strayed to the night Nevin brutally stabbed his wife to death, the one thing Bliss recalled most vividly was the blood. The slickness of its touch, the tangy odour, vivid, harrowing colour, and the bitter taste after he'd slumped to his knees to embrace and kiss Hazel as if doing so might somehow breathe life back to her bones. He could summon up the moment on a whim, or it might creep over him unwillingly like a dark cloud swollen with electricity and malevolent spite. As it had once again upon hearing his wife's killer mention her name.

But instead of pouncing, Bliss slowly eased himself to his feet. He regarded the man on the other side of the table with contempt and said, 'I did try to warn you, Nevin. Now, I'm guessing you asked for me because you thought you'd have the upper hand. Reckoned I'd have to sit here all afternoon and take any old shit you chose to dish up. But I don't. And I'm not about to.'

'All right,' Nevin said, raising a hand in defeat. 'I'm just having a bit of fun at your expense. You can't blame a man for trying.' He then leered at Greenhill and winked.

Bliss slapped the table with the palm of his hand, the sharp sound echoing off the four walls that already felt as if they were closing in. There was only a certain amount of this he was willing to take.

'My colleague doesn't have to put up with your shit, either. I was all for coming here alone, but my boss reckoned my colleague's presence might just keep me calm. I'm not convinced, but she is here, and you will treat her with respect. I advise you to get it into your thick skull that there will be no final warning. Tell me what you got me all the way down here to tell me or we're leaving, and you can go back to your cell and play with your limp dick or whatever it is you do to pass the time around here.'

The two men glared at each other for several long moments. Finally, Nevin gestured towards the chair Bliss had risen from. 'Okay, you win. Sit your arse back down. And despite what you might think of me, you really do want to hear what I have to say. Otherwise you wouldn't have come.'

Bliss sat once more and waited. Tension slowly bled from the room. 'You know the basics, right?' Nevin said. 'I assume your boss briefed you.'

'I do. She did. You claim that an ex-cellmate told you about a conversation he had with a fellow inmate, during which this other prisoner mentioned his involvement in a murder that was never solved.'

'Bingo.'

'And you want to tell me more about this why?'

'Because this murder took place in your neck of the woods.'

Shaking his head, Bliss said, 'No, I mean what's in it for you? I'm sure you don't give a toss one way or the other what this old lag did many moons ago.'

'You're a cynical fucker, Bliss. Yeah, I know I've done some disturbing shit in my time, but let's not forget I was once a copper. And a bloody good one at that.'

'No, no, no.' Bliss wagged a finger. 'Those days are long gone. You're a convicted murderer, and I can smell the distinct odour of bullshit coming out of your gob.'

Nevin's mouth twisted, and his nostrils flared. 'Ugh. That's a repulsive image you've left me with there.'

'Whatever. There's no way you're looking to provide me with intel out of the goodness of your heart.'

'How can you be certain of that?'

'Because there *is* no goodness in your heart, Nevin. If you have one at all, it's black and dead and rotting from the inside out.'

Blowing out his cheeks, Nevin said, 'Blimey, you're painting pretty pictures today, I'll give you that. But, okay, I get where you're coming from. And you're right. I do want something.'

'Of course you do,' Bliss said, pushing himself back. 'And what would that be?'

The man removed his glasses and pinched the bridge of his nose. His sunken eyes narrowed, and his lips arched downward. 'I don't want to die in here. It's as simple as that. No strings, no more bull. And no, I'm not asking for release or even parole on compassionate grounds. Neither of those is going to happen. I just want to be moved to a decent nick where I can feel human again.'

Puzzled, Bliss said, 'What the fuck are you banging on about? What's all this guff about dying and compassionate grounds?'

Nick Nevin's eyes sprang open wide. He slipped his glasses back on. 'Oh. You don't know. I thought they would have told you. See, the thing is, Jimmy, I ain't got long above ground. I have something called Creutzfeldt-Jakob disease. The quacks here thought it might be early onset Alzheimer's, but as my symptoms got worse, I went downhill rapidly. By the time they got me to a hospital and the doctors diagnosed me, the condition was advanced to the point where we're talking months, possibly weeks. Chances are I'll deteriorate so much before a transfer is even agreed that I won't even be aware of it, let alone benefit from a move. But even if that doesn't happen I'd cope better with whatever time I have left if I thought I might get to spend even a single day in a decent prison.'

Bliss stared at him. He felt no compassion. Neither did he feel joy that the man who had slaughtered his wife was about to die. He felt nothing at all, which he thought was how it should be. A fitting indifference.

'You do know we can check all this, right?' he said. 'Including your medical records?'

'Of course. I'm unwell, not retarded. They'll confirm what I told you. Jimmy, I ain't long for this world and all I want as I come to the end is a little bit of comfort and to be treated with some decency and dignity.'

With no tolerance or forgiveness in his heart, Bliss said, 'Then maybe you should have thought about that before you stabbed my wife to death and tried to fit me up for her murder, you miserable piece of shit. You've had many more years than you allowed her.'

'Oh, sure.' Nevin scoffed and turned his head away. 'Like you wouldn't have done the same thing.'

Bliss looked at him in disbelief. 'How d'you make that out?'

'Because we're not so different,' Nevin said.

'I'm nothing like you,' Bliss insisted, repulsed by the suggestion.

His one-time nemesis waved the denial aside. 'Of course you are. More than you like to believe. You won't admit it, but the truth is, we're both lifelong rogues, Jimmy. You're just a more honourable one than I am.'

After letting the words hang there for a second or two, Bliss said with measured composure, 'You're a murderer, Nevin. Not a rogue, not a scoundrel, not whatever fantasy your sick mind has concocted since you've been inside. You. Are. A. Murderer. And I will never allow you to forget that.'

Nevin spread his hands. 'Ah, but that's just it, Jimmy. I will forget it. I'll forget you. I'll even forget me.'

About to respond, Bliss noticed a dramatic and abrupt change in the man's demeanour and a stiffening of his body. It was as if a switch had been flicked, or a light snapped off. Nevin stared without blinking, his back ramrod straight as if made rigid by a convulsion. Bliss exchanged looks with Greenhill before frowning and saying, 'Nevin? Are you still with us?'

The prisoner blinked and jerked, as if startled by the presence of two people in the room. 'What the…' he began. 'Who the hell are you? What are doing in my office?'

Bliss knew enough about dementia not to argue or act abruptly in response to a delusion. He guessed this one was a switch in time and played along. 'We're police consultants, sir. I take it you weren't informed?'

He watched as Nevin mentally questioned himself, searching for answers even while trapped inside his own hallucination. Anguish glazed his eyes, and his tongue snaked out to wet both lips.

'It's not a problem,' Bliss insisted. 'We all know what the brass are for keeping us in the loop.'

This earned a nod, Nevin centring himself. 'Too busy nursing paper cuts,' he said, rolling his eyes. About to speak again, he sagged as if punctured and blinked several times. Each one seemed to bring him back to the present in aggregated stages. 'But will you grant me my final wish?' he said continuing the original conversation as if there had been no interlude. 'That's really what this is all about.'

'That depends entirely on what you have to say,' Bliss said, keen to keep Nevin in the present. 'But I warn you now, if I don't like what I hear or we're unable to verify your story, you can rot in this place for however long you have left.'

'Oh, you'll like what I have to tell you,' Nevin said with a gleam in his eyes. 'In fact, you're going to love it.'

EIGHT

The office was buzzing when Bliss and Greenhill walked in. They had each made a phone call during the drive back, and now Superintendent Edwards waited expectantly alongside Unsolved Cases Team investigators Guy Foley and Ben Corry. They were already deep into their current on-going cold case reinvestigation, but Greenhill had informed her colleagues that what Bliss was bringing them would take priority. Bliss had also taken a call from DS Bishop to tell him the Sprinter van had been discovered, but as expected, it had been torched. That pretty much left only the VIN information to work with, but they agreed it might bear fruit. He used the rest of the journey to work through the various permutations before settling his focus on this meeting.

'If everything this source told us is kosher,' he began, perched on the edge of his desk, 'then this investigation may be far more than it seems at first glance. Bearing in mind that what we're working with is hearsay second-hand information at best, we have to treat it with a measure of scepticism. But if it does prove to be all above board, we may need to be cautious in our approach.'

'Okay, Jimmy,' Edwards said, arms folded across her chest. 'Don't spin it out. We're hooked, so just tell us.'

Bliss nodded. 'Righto. I'll start with the fundamentals. In the late summer of 2014, a twenty-two-year-old woman, Daisy Vincent, was found dead in Thorney Play Park after a night out with friends in Peterborough. It's believed she was raped before being strangled. Nobody has ever been charged with her murder. Now we're told that at the back end of last year a prisoner serving time in HMP Woodhill confessed to having some involvement in that murder.'

'What's his name?' Foley asked. 'I'll check out everything we have on him.'

'My source refused to give it up. He's the type who enjoys playing mind games when he can and telling us only half the story is his way of having fun at my expense. He said that provided we were good at our jobs it would become clear without him having to name names.'

'Then why the need for added caution?' Foley asked.

'Because the victim's father is a renowned and feared villain in that part of the world. I've personally never encountered the man or his family, which includes two sons who are involved in the same line of criminal activity. But the Vincents are well known to CID here, as well as in Lincoln and Norfolk.'

'Can you go back a step, please?' Corry said. 'How did your source acquire this information again?'

'A fellow prisoner told my source's cellmate at the time about an unsolved murder that he claimed to be closely connected to. Evidently, he was torn because he was pretty sure he knew who did it, but feared his own involvement might put him in the frame instead if it ever came to light. That and the inevitable recriminations from the victim's family if word got out. The prisoner who made this half-arsed confession was scheduled for release at the time and is presumably now free. The ex-cellmate is also now out on licence.'

'Do we at least have *his* name and details to follow up on?'

'Yes, we do. Which gives us several openings going in. We need to chase up a current location for this man, plus we also have the Vincent family to consider. I don't see any advantage in rattling their cages before we have more substantive information, so we begin with the man who shared a cell with my source. His name is Toby Wallace. Ben, you and Guy look into him. All the usual checks, please. Beth and I will speak to whoever investigated Daisy Vincent's murder. If things go our way, eventually we're going to want to tie-in what we hear with what we learn from the murder investigation team.'

Bliss had earlier decided not to name his source at this early stage. He felt it might confuse matters by adding his personal history with Nevin into the mix, creating a distraction both Corry and Foley could do without.

'Hold on a moment,' DSI Edwards said, with a puzzled look on her face. 'You say this murder occurred in Thorney ten years ago, so why wasn't it our case?'

'That's three years before I came back to the city,' Bliss said. 'Are you sure the MCU didn't handle it?'

Nodding, Edwards said, 'I was a DI at the time, waiting for a DCI role to become available here. The victim's name does sound familiar now that you've mentioned it, but we definitely didn't work that case.'

'Then the Huntingdon unit must have handled it. I know Thorney is technically within our radius, but if you were swamped at the time, then they might have picked it up.'

'They must have done, though I don't recall anything truly major that summer. To be honest, we were all still winding down from the infamous ditch murders and the resulting conviction in February that year.'

'I remember reading about that nutbag,' Bliss said. 'Murdered three blokes and dumped them in ditches. Coincidentally, two of them close to Thorney, if I remember right. Didn't she threaten to kill Rose West to prove she was the top dog in her prison?'

'That's her.' Edwards shuddered. 'She genuinely made my skin crawl. I've never felt so close to true evil. Not before or since. As for whatever else we might have been working on, I think the Bretton underpass killing was around about that time. We also worked a murder in HMP Peterborough that year.'

'I'll get onto county HQ,' Greenhill volunteered. 'See what they have for us.'

'Yes, please do.' Bliss rubbed the tiny scar on his forehead. 'And if all roads do lead to a murder suspect, we then have to work out how to approach the Vincent family. I'll want a full background on them and their enterprise, including known associates and potential enemies. I can't imagine they're enamoured with us given we failed to solve the original case, so we shouldn't expect to be welcomed with open arms. That said, if we can go to them with a name, perhaps even an arrest, then it might not be all bad.'

'Do you know what line of business they're in?' Foley asked.

'Their legit operations range from building and garden supplies to pawn shops, some export and import, which may or may not be cover for smuggling. In terms of criminality, they are strictly small fry. They do some loansharking, run a team of bouncers who work the city pubs and clubs, move hooky gear around, have been known to do some raids on jewellers and phone stores, that kind of thing. The old man, Douglas, and his two sons Edward and Thomas, have all done a bit of bird. Nowhere near as much as they deserve, by all accounts. Like I say, I've never worked a case involving any of the family, it's just what we were told earlier. Evidently, my source did his research on them before arranging my visit.'

'And why are you so sure your source isn't screwing with us, Jimmy?' Foley demanded to know.

'The truth is, I'm not. But neither am I seeing what he has to gain from doing so. He gets what he asked for in return only if I'm satisfied that this is information we can rely on. Other than briefly having us on a wild goose chase, I can't think why he would bother.'

'And this is someone you put away?' Corry asked.

'It is.'

'So, what is he getting out of this?'

Bliss told them about the diagnosis and Nevin's limited amount of time left without referring to him by name. 'I'd never heard of this condition before today,' he admitted. 'But it's all there in his prison health records, and it's not something you can fake. It's possible that he's said all he's willing to say, but just as likely that it's only the tip of the iceberg. Evidently, we got him on a good day as his deterioration is rapid. Therefore, if he does have more to offer us, we're up against the clock.'

'I have to say, you're being extremely evasive,' Guy Foley said, blunt as ever. 'You're at pains not to name him, yet Beth must know who he is. Why the secrecy?'

'Because it's personal. I don't want the background to be the story. Let's get this running and I'll fill you in as and when.'

Bliss looked away, reluctant to say more. Edwards, perhaps sensing a mounting friction between the two men, clapped her hands and rubbed them together. 'All right. I say we treat this as a legitimate reinvestigation with the proviso that we are able to corroborate what you've been told so far. We have to accept – for the time being at least – that your source is unwilling to provide you with the name of the prisoner who confessed to playing a part in this murder. And you've said yourself that he may have more to tell us. But what was your sense, Jimmy? Do you think he knows more than he's saying?'

'No,' Bliss replied with a shake of the head. 'At least, not a great deal more, though of course I can't be certain. If he wanted to sell us a pup or omit valuable intel, he surely would have taken ownership. He'd have told us he heard the story directly from the killer himself. The way he claims to have obtained the information is via a channel he can't possibly return to. My gut tells me he's given us as much as he's prepared to for the time being, and hopefully we'll be able to confirm everything he said within the next twenty-four hours.'

Bliss noticed Foley's lips twitching. He thought he knew what might be on the man's mind but pushed him for an answer anyway. 'Something more to offer, Guy?' he asked.

'Not really. I was just wondering how this fits in with the murder investigation you're already working.'

'That I don't know. Clearly, that case is going to be my priority, but I'm sure we'll work through it. This is, what, the fourth time I've had to double up as SIO while working a cold case with you? We managed on those three previous occasions, so let's be positive and not see complications where none exist.'

Of his three Unsolved Cases Team colleagues, Guy Foley was the only one who had ever come close to raising objections concerning Bliss's dual role. He'd never made a direct or formal complaint, but Bliss sensed a hint of resentment lurking behind the man's demeanour. Time was he'd have challenged Foley on the issue, but on this occasion, he dismissed it from his mind.

Meanwhile, Edwards was pretending to reel unsteadily with a hand clamped over her heart. 'My God,' she said. 'Wonders will never cease. Jimmy Bliss talking about positivity. Whatever next?'

'A plague of locusts?' Greenhill wondered aloud. 'And now that I think about it, I'm sure I spotted a pale horse earlier.'

'Yeah, yeah. And his name that sat upon him was Death, and Hell followed with him,' Bliss muttered, completing the quote from Revelations. 'I suggest neither of you give up your day job.'

The resulting laughter broke through any tensions still residing in the room. But while he kept his own gaze averted, Bliss could still feel Foley's eyes fixated on him.

NINE

Civilian working hours for the UCT were strictly regulated, with neither flexitime allowed nor overtime payments made. Bliss's colleagues were therefore signed out by 4.00pm that Friday for the entire weekend. Bliss had exactly the same contract as the others, but he wasn't about to go anywhere other than the other side of the building.

The scant information they'd had to work with following the prison visit had garnered a surprisingly decent return in a short amount of time. Tasked with tracking down Nick Nevin's ex-cellmate, Guy Foley managed to speak with Toby Wallace's supervising officer and was rewarded with an address in Nottingham together with a contact number. Although he'd been unable to get hold of Wallace before leaving for the day, he had left a voicemail message.

Meanwhile, Beth Greenhill had volunteered to visit the county HQ at Hinchingbrooke in person, as it was on her way home. She left the building shortly before three-thirty, hoping to learn everything they needed to know about the original investigation, which would enable them to start the following week on the front foot.

Bliss had been the last one to leave the office before he too closed the door behind him and went to join his MCU colleagues in the major incident room. Working an active case created an atmosphere that was almost palpable, the sense of urgency and pressure that came with it releasing adrenaline and endorphins into the room in a way that a cold case could never recreate. And yet eight months into his new career, he was enjoying both roles equally. Something he had not anticipated. His days of burning through the hours at full tilt were gone, and he had learned not only to accept but also welcome the quieter, more reflective periods spent with the team of ex-detectives.

The first thing he did upon entering the MIR was to gather everyone together to ask for an update on their progress. With one hand buried in his trouser pocket while the other clutched vending machine hot chocolate, DS Olly Bishop was the first to speak up.

'The Sprinter is, as we rightly assumed, forensically useless to us,' he complained. 'But we lucked out with the VIN. The vehicle was reported stolen after it was taken on a test drive from a commercial vehicle dealership in St Ives and never returned. The fake buyer left behind a scan of his driving licence, which also proved to be fake but does at least give us a facial image to go on. I had a word with the member of staff who handed over the keys, and evidently the bloke who drove off in the van now has a beard and wore glasses, but the salesman insists it was the same man in the licence photo. I don't know how much we can rely on his say-so, but they sent over a PDF of their scan, and we'll show it to Gul to see if she recognises him. We're still tracking down CCTV from the area.'

'It's better than a poke in the eye with a sharp stick,' Bliss said. 'To be fair, finding these men through the van they used was always a reach. Even so, keep pressing for security feeds, Bish.

Our thief had to get to the garage somehow. Either he caught a bus, or somebody drove him. It'd be nice if we could spot him arriving in another motor.'

'I'm on it, Jimmy. Obviously, we're one down with Gul being off sick, but Vas is working with uniform and civilian staff to contact all neighbouring properties. We've learned there's a Shell garage on one side, and a One Stop motorist shop on the other. There's also a row of homes opposite, so we might get lucky with doorbell cams.'

'Good. How about our crime scene neighbours?'

As was his habit, DC Virgil stood to say his piece. 'They're few and far between, boss, and no joy so far. I've also been talking to bordering area forces checking on MO. As you might imagine, there are a fair few of these cowboy builders, so we're currently trying to narrow down our possibles.'

'I've been doing something along the same lines with our own intelligence team,' Chandler offered. 'And as Alan says, there are plenty of similar reports. We'd hope to tighten up on those over the weekend or by end of play on Monday.'

Everything was pretty much as expected. Bliss was happy to find the team pushing hard for evidence through the more obvious channels as opposed to going off on flights of fancy. The most viable leads often came from simply carrying out basic checks.

'Excellent work,' he said, making sure to take in all the faces turned his way. 'How about forensics?'

Chandler was quick to fill him in. 'We hope to have Lydia Keene dropping by tomorrow morning to give us her preliminary report. There is a slight delay due to the conditions. They might have shoe prints, but capturing hard evidence from a print in frost laying on previous hard ice is not an easy task. Hopefully she'll have something for us, even if it's only for comparison purposes.'

Bliss was pleased with the progress made. 'Good. We'll have the outcome of the postmortem on Monday, but I can't see it telling us anything other than the poor woman died as a result of that single stab wound. Overall, I think we've done all we can with what we had. If we must land on a hypothesis for the policy book, my money is still on the gang returning to the farm this morning because they believed Mrs Musgrove held a quantity of cash in the house. Pen, I'd like a few bodies inside that property carrying out a thorough search. It's possible that Gul disturbed the three men before they were able to lay their hands on the stash, so make sure the search team knows every nook and cranny is a potential hiding place.'

'Of course.' Chandler nodded, then frowned at him. 'I also have one question about next week.'

'Okay.'

'Well, we have Vas to fill the vacancy left by Phil heading down to the Met. But we now have another hole, with Gul being off work for at least a fortnight. Are we soldiering on one down in the main team or do you intend bringing in somebody else?'

Bliss silently remonstrated with himself for not considering the staffing issue earlier. 'I haven't given it any thought,' he admitted. 'We've got plenty of bodies joining us on Monday to handle general enquiries, but you're quite right to raise the question about bringing someone in on a temporary basis to fill in for Gul. I'll have a word with DCI Warburton the moment I catch up with her, but I'm thinking we carry on as we are until we know how long Gul will be off. If we do bring in a replacement I'll suggest DC John Hunt as he knows how we work.'

DC Gratton raised a hand. 'Boss, I have updates on Mrs Musgrove's children. Her daughter is flying in from Switzerland tomorrow morning. The son won't be here until Sunday.'

'Flying into…?'

'The Zurich flight is due into Stansted at 10.50am. Sunday's arrival is at Heathrow at noon.'

'Okay. I'll meet both flights and bring them back here. Let them know, please, Phil.'

'You sure you want to do both pick-ups?' Bishop asked. 'I'm happy to do one.'

'No, that really ought to be me,' Chandler said, injecting herself into the conversation. 'Jimmy, if you want to collect Iris Musgrove, I'll meet Paul the following day.'

Bliss was willing to do both, but Chandler had undoubtedly embraced her new role by stepping up to take some weight off his shoulders while at the same time pushing herself ahead of DS Bishop. He liked the fact she had done so and gave a nod of approval.

'Okay, that's settled,' he said. 'Bish, find out if they've both made hotel reservations. They won't be able to stay at the farmhouse until we've finished with the scene. If they haven't already done so, book them a room each for one night at the Holiday Inn. They can make their own arrangements after that.'

Cost was immaterial when you were dealing with a victim's grieving family members. Up to a point. The budget wasn't infinite, but the son and daughter were coming back to a home now devastated by the murder of their mother. Their heads would be all over the place, and Bliss was willing to do whatever he could to ease them in and steer them both through probably the most difficult time of their lives so far.

Moments later, his phone rang, and he took the call outside in the corridor. The name Sandra Bannister popping up on the caller ID had prompted him to move to a place where their conversation couldn't be overheard. A journalist with the city's local newspaper, the *Peterborough Telegraph*, Bannister had become a good friend as well as a trusted ally. Not all police officers would understand the self-imposed constraints of their relationship, so he tended to make sure nobody else was around when they talked.

'I heard one of your people is in hospital,' she said without preamble.

'Yeah, DC Ansari. But she's okay. Thankfully. Severe concussion, a couple of weeks' recovery, but Gul will be fine.'

'That's a relief.' He heard the reporter release a deep sigh. 'For a brief moment I thought it might be you, but then I learned it was one of your team. Is this in connection to the murder at Ravens Brook Farm on the outskirts of Crowland?'

Bliss paused. The line between what was acceptable in respect of the information the two exchanged was a fine one, and he was always careful to remain on the right side of it even if he occasionally stepped close to the boundary. 'It is,' he admitted. 'But I can't discuss the case with you, Sandra. There's an element we can't have out there in the public domain while we're still chasing it down. What I can tell you is that Gul was off duty paying a neighbour a visit when she was callously attacked from behind. She took two powerful blows to the head with a piece of wood.'

'I understand. I'll be sure to highlight the dangers of police work in whatever piece I write. So, I'm guessing DC Ansari caught whoever killed Sheila Musgrove in the act, at which point they then turned on her. Sounds as if she was lucky to escape with her life.'

'Or unlucky to arrive at just the wrong time.'

'Yes, that is another way to look at it. I've not heard about a media briefing, Jimmy. Why's that?'

'My understanding is that DCI Warburton will be releasing a statement shortly but hasn't called for a live press briefing. Don't read anything into that. I can assure you there are no shenanigans going on. We're waiting on the outcome of a few things, plus Mrs Musgrove's two children are coming home from abroad, so I doubt you'll get to ask any questions until Sunday evening at the earliest.'

'That's fine. I take it you're the SIO?'

'I am, yes.'

'Operation name?'

Bliss took two sideways steps to peer through the security window in the major inquiry room door. He checked the information whiteboard for the name DCI Warburton had scribbled on there earlier. 'Monument,' he said.

'Thanks, Jimmy. Any other scraps you can feed me?'

Bliss smiled. She was a trier. He gave her that. 'Only that we believe the murder relates to a previous incident involving the victim. Make of that what you will. I have to go now, Sandra.'

'Okay. Thanks anyway. Anything you need from me?'

'I'll give that some thought,' he said. 'There's a lot going on, plus we now have Gul in hospital and Phil Gratton's leaving do later tonight. If I think of something, I'll give you a bell.'

He said goodbye and closed the call at his end. It occurred to him that the *PT* might have looked into cowboy builders and con merchants, so Bannister might be able to lay her hands on something useful that the police intelligence teams had yet to uncover. He'd give it some thought overnight, but for now had plenty on his plate.

TEN

IN TRYING TO SQUEEZE in a hospital visit ahead of Phil Gratton's leaving bash, Bliss had completely forgotten to avoid visiting hours. As he entered the room, he groaned in the back of his throat when realising his mistake. DC Ansari's father was not a fan of their profession, and especially not his daughter's role in it. When Bliss saw the man standing at the foot of the bed, his first thought was to withdraw. But it was too late to back out without making matters even more awkward, so instead he took a deep breath and took a couple of strides forward.

'Good evening, sir,' he said, offering his most gracious smile while reaching out a hand. Mr Ansari stared at it a moment too long for comfort. 'I'm Jimmy Bliss. Until earlier this year, I was Gul's DI.'

The man continued to ignore him.

'Dad!' Gul snapped, glaring at her father. 'Please. You're embarrassing me.'

Her father's head whipped around, his own eyes blazing with anger. 'You dare speak to me this way?' he shot back. 'In the presence of this man, who is the only reason we are here at all.'

Bliss withdrew his hand but said nothing. While he had never understood Mr Ansari's antipathy towards his daughter's chosen career, it wasn't his place to involve himself in a family dispute. He couldn't imagine any circumstances under which Gul herself would thank him for doing so.

'Jimmy had nothing to do with what happened,' she said emphatically as Bliss was about to say goodbye and remove himself as a source of tension in the room. 'It wasn't our case, and I wasn't even on duty at the time.'

Regarding his daughter with real venom, Mr Ansari sneered as he responded. 'Precisely. This is my point. Do you honestly expect me to believe that is not something you learned from this man? Involving yourself in other people's business without invitation.'

'It wasn't like that. I wasn't investigating. Mrs Musgrove was a neighbour, and all I did was try to reassure her that everything that could be done was being done to find the men who took advantage of her.'

Her father gesticulated with a flapping hand and turned away towards Bliss. 'This is all your fault,' he said heatedly. 'My daughter might not be able to see it, but I can. You are a terrible influence, and I hold you fully responsible for my daughter's injuries.'

'I don't believe that's true, Mr Ansari,' Bliss said cooly. 'Listen, I'm sure you are a firm believer in standing side-by-side with your community. In essence, that's all Gul was doing. Out there in the Fens where your daughter now lives, the likes of Mrs Musgrove *are* her community. She was doing the decent thing, that's all.'

He immediately saw that all he had succeeded in doing was to pour water on blazing oil.

'I don't need someone like you to tell me this about my own daughter,' the man grumbled angrily. 'But rather than being with her own community she chose to live – and work – outside of it.'

He gestured towards the bed. 'This is what becomes of making such decisions, just as she did when choosing to join the police.'

Bliss was unable to contain himself any longer. 'Sir,' he said with firm defiance. 'No matter what you think or say, your daughter is a highly respected member of the team. Gul has distinguished herself with honour. She is brave, conscientious, loyal, and inspirational. Not only is your daughter an outstanding police officer, but she is also an equally exceptional person. Someone I'm honoured to work alongside and call a friend. These are all qualities that will see her rise high in the ranks and go on to achieve many things of which her communities – both old and new – can be proud. What's more, Mr Ansari, I believe her qualities owe a great deal to her family upbringing. I have no children, but if Gul were my flesh and blood, I'd be bloody proud of her.'

Stunned, or perhaps shamed into silence, Gul's father shrank back. He lowered his gaze and took a step closer to his daughter's bedside. Bliss turned his attention to the injured DC. 'I just came in to wish you well and to reinforce everything I told you earlier. You rest, you recover, you recuperate. Doctor's orders followed. You hear me?'

'Yes, boss.' It was great to see her smile.

'Excellent. If you need a lift home, give us a shout and we'll sort you out a ride. You should also expect several visitors in the coming days.'

Bliss gave her a wink then turned to leave the room. He hoped her father would come around and see his daughter for what she was. Gul Ansari was worthy of her family's admiration and respect, and while it should not have needed his own words to make them realise that he could only hope he'd finally opened the man's eyes to all that she was and would go on to be.

*

Phil Gratton's parents had swung for a grand leaving party in the largest of two event suites at the Haycock Manor Hotel in Wansford, a 16th century coaching inn both historical and splendorous. It was a risky business putting a free bar in front of a bunch of thirsty coppers, but in laying on this farewell celebration Gratton's mother and father were showing their guests how proud they were of their son.

Their generosity caused Bliss to think about what it meant on a wider scale. In speculating about how the team would overcome the loss of their colleague, Bliss had neglected to consider the move in terms of the effect on others. Phil Gratton wasn't just switching jobs; he was uprooting his life and that of his fiancée and moving all the way down to London.

Though born and raised in the capital, Bliss now found it a much more difficult city to negotiate. Londoners lived their lives at a pace befitting the hustle and bustle of activity on its roads and pavements. During his infrequent visits these days, he felt as if he needed to run just to catch up, leaving him breathless and less able to wind down. The throng of people and the tsunami of vehicles, whether day or night, was both awe-inspiring and terrifying in equal measure. He wished Gratton well, but had severe doubts about the young man's ability to settle in an environment so completely alien to anything he had experienced for a prolonged period before.

Thinking about people taking up new positions, he caught up with DC Kolesnyk, who had brought his English wife along. She was dark-haired, lively, with a captivating smile and a quick wit. 'How are you settling in, Vas?' he asked during a quieter moment with the music slipping into less raucous tones.

'All good, thank you, boss. I am enjoying being part of the team.'

Bliss clapped him on the upper arm. 'It's just Jimmy, Vas. At work in the office, but especially out of it, it's just Jimmy.'

'Jimmy. Yes.' The officer smiled and nodded, earnest as ever. He was a man who liked to please.

'While we're on the subject of settling in, are you still looking for a place of your own?'

Kolesnyk, his wife, and their two children were currently renting accommodation in Orton Southgate, not far from where Bliss himself lived.

'Of course. But it is difficult.'

Although he had told nobody, not even Penny Chandler, Bliss was waiting to hear about an offer he had put in on a house backing on to the River Nene at Water Newton, slightly south of where they now stood. The property came with its own mooring for his boat and offered him the privacy and tranquillity he sought. His own house was on the market, but now he wondered if serendipity was about to work its charms.

'I might just have the ideal solution for you, Vas,' he said. 'For both of us, actually. Before you commit to anything else, come and find me.'

Kolesnyk nodded enthusiastically. 'I will do that. Thank you, boss.'

Bliss narrowed his gaze.

'Jimmy. Sorry, boss. I meant Jimmy.'

The two men laughed, before Bliss set off to find the man of the hour and to give the speech Gratton had asked him to make. Touched by the request, he'd worked hard on making it both as genuine and humorous as he could. It was never nice to bid farewell to a good officer, a colleague, and a friend, but this move was something Phil had badly wanted, and Bliss had no intention of dissuading him at this late stage. The Met had been haemorrhaging armed officers for years, more so in the wake of gangster Chris Kaba's shooting and the subsequent murder trial, so those still willing to take on the job were being eagerly welcomed. The team would miss him, but Kolesnyk had already made a positive impact, and the unit was not about to crumble at the loss of one member. Even so, it was with a heavy heart that he made his way towards the table at which the Gratton family sat, reaching inside his jacket pocket for the notes he had scribbled earlier.

ELEVEN

While Oscar Wilde believed – or at least had written – that punctuality was the thief of time, Jimmy Bliss thought otherwise. He hated being late and also loathed being made to wait. Luckily for Lydia Keene, she was both prompt and prepared when she delivered her report at spot on 8.00am the following day. Habitually, the Crime Scene Investigation manager was forthright in her manner, speaking with confidence. This morning proved to be no different.

'Let me begin with footprints,' she said. 'Given the conditions gave us a fresh layer of frost over solid ice, we ruled out casting and had to rely on photography only. We took flash images from all four directions for maximum detail. Then we cut around the impressions, blew away the debris and took shots literally from ground level to capture as many ridges as possible. While the result is not as good as having a cast, we did manage to obtain some imperfections to match with suspect footwear, if you find any.'

'That's better news than I'd anticipated,' Bliss said.

'Not every print came out as we'd have liked, but there are several distinct impressions on the flagstone path, with a couple more in the surrounding soil. We'll need the footwear from anyone who responded without first putting on protective clothing, just to rule them out.'

DCI Diane Warburton was not scheduled to be on duty but had attended the briefing anyway. She and her family had moved closer to the city the previous year, which made travelling less restrictive for her. She listened intently, nodded and said, 'Of course, Lydia. I'll get that arranged as soon as we're done here. Anything for us other than footprints?'

Keene shrugged. 'The usual array of unknowns. Inside the house, we found only one set of fingerprints in key areas, matching those taken from our victim. That corresponds with her living alone for a number of years, although having no visitors at all during that time is perhaps a little surprising. The front door gave up a few different results, so we'll have them run through the system. But you have to imagine they'll be from delivery people and Royal Mail. I took a look at the footage from DC Ansari's dashcam and the three men we see are all wearing gloves. We did pull fibres from Mrs Musgrove's clothing, the colouring a good match for the hoodie one of the men was wearing. I suspect it'll be a generic material, but you can expect my complete report on Monday.'

Potential evidentiary impressions from the footprints, but little else. As expected. Bliss thanked Keene, who opted to remain in the room to familiarise herself with other aspects of the case. He let Warburton, Chandler, and Bishop catch her up while he headed off to Stansted. The airport was less than a seventy-mile drive down the A1 and M11, and Bliss arrived in good time. Iris Musgrove, late-forties, lean, with long brown hair and an oval face, spotted the sign Bliss had made with her name on and introduced herself.

Although the murder victim's daughter was solemn and largely uncommunicative during the journey north, Bliss did manage to discern from the occasional exchange that the relationship between the two women had often been fraught and maintained irregularly from a distance.

'Our mother wanted me and my brother, Paul, to take over the running of the farm when we left school,' she explained, her tone and rigid posture suggesting a lingering emotional scar. 'When we both turned our backs on that way of life, she basically lost interest in us. It was as if we were born to provide a function, and when we failed to fulfil that purpose, we became superfluous.'

Bliss wanted to know more, but elected not to bite and push for further revelations. It sounded like an unhappy period of their lives, yet one the siblings appeared to have moved on from. Physically, if not emotionally. 'Farming is not a life for everyone,' he allowed. 'I know it wouldn't be for me.'

From DS Bishop, he had learned that Iris Musgrove had studied chemical engineering at university and now worked for a biochemical company based in Horgen, just south of Zurich. Her brother had chosen the arts and earned a living as a TV and film score composer in Durban. As someone who had always been close to his parents, and despite having witnessed the consequences of dysfunctional relationships his entire career, Bliss couldn't imagine a rift so large that it would have resulted in such apathy and neglect between a mother and her children.

After settling the grateful woman into the Holiday Inn and leaving her with a Family Liaison Officer, Bliss spent the rest of the day with his team. DCs Virgil and Kolesnyk had got nowhere with CCTV in and around the area from which the Mercedes van had been stolen, so the pair decided to drive down to St Ives, which was just east of Huntingdon. Footage obtained from the Shell petrol station gave them nothing useful, but the One Stop motor store's external camera had captured the Sprinter as it was driven away. Unfortunately, the separate entrance to the site was out of view, so they were no better off.

Upon their return, Bliss instructed Virgil to run the plate through ANPR to see which cameras picked up the van that same day. He suggested both officers check relevant footage to see if any other vehicles were caught closely following the Mercedes. If the thief had been driven to the dealership, he reasoned, whoever drove him there might well have followed him part or even all the way to its ultimate destination.

'One more thing,' he added. 'Check with the dealership to see if the van had a tracker installed. I'm sure the gang would have disabled it, but where and when would be good to know.'

An hour in, DC Kolesnyk got a hit. The Automatic Number Plate Recognition system had two records in its database for the day the van was stolen. It was last picked up in Godmanchester, after which there had been no further hits. The team agreed this was where the plates had been swapped out, probably on some industrial estate. Bliss looked over the young officer's shoulder as he watched and re-watched the accompanying footage, but no other vehicle featured on both occasions. Neither were they able to pull a decent still of the driver, who hunched over the steering wheel. The final scrap of bad news was that the van had not come with a tracker.

With Chandler personally organising the more in-depth search of the farmhouse, Bliss partnered up with DS Bishop to exchange ideas and strategies. Despite their many years of experience, neither was able to see a way forward unless one of the current actions turned up a lead. Bliss believed the most likely breakthrough would come from one of the intelligence teams spotting a similar MO. If he was right, they could get a hit within the next hour or it might take a week, depending on how many people were prioritising the search and the outcome of resulting deliberations. Neither delighted nor particularly downhearted, Bliss called it a day shortly after 4.30pm and sent everybody home.

That night, Bliss and Chandler met for dinner at Middleton's Steakhouse & Grill at Cathedral Square in the city centre. They both brought a partner with them. Bliss arrived with Molly, the young woman he considered to be a surrogate daughter. Several years ago, he had prevented the one-time county lines drug mule from taking her own life. Now she was studying forensic science in Bedfordshire and spent every other weekend with him. Already seated alongside Chandler when they walked in was her daughter, Anna, who was fast approaching the end of her own studies at Cambridge.

The four had spent time together in recent weeks and enjoyed another evening wining and dining and discussing everything but work or study courses. It was a time for relaxation, fun, a few laughs, followed by more serious explorations of the future. Anna hadn't made up her mind what she wanted to be, though she favoured academia. Molly, on the other hand, was desperate to work crime scenes. The two young women discussed the endless possibilities of such a career, erring on the side of gore and gruesomeness, but every time they came back to the core of why some people chose to do the job: the search for truth and justice, which was close to the heart of Bliss's own philosophy.

On Sunday, Bliss took his dog, Max, for an early walk as usual, but hadn't felt at all well. For the better part of two decades, he had suffered with Meniere's Disease, a chronic condition with no cure. His feelings of instability during the walk felt as if they might result in a full-blown episode of vertigo, so he took himself off to bed, Max laying sprawled across his lower legs and feet. With the room spinning and tinnitus screaming in his ears, he didn't think he'd be able to sleep, but eventually he nodded off and by the time he woke up the room was in darkness.

Bliss checked his phones and discovered two voicemail messages, both from Chandler. The first was an update on the farmhouse search. The main living rooms had offered up nothing, but one of the officers had spotted a gap behind the mirrored bathroom cabinet. A deft fingertip search located a latch, and in pulling the cabinet away from the wall on a slim hinge they discovered a wall safe. Chandler had called Iris Musgrove to ask if she knew the combination, but the victim's daughter wasn't even aware of the safe's existence. She gave her permission for the search team to drill it, and half an hour later they recovered five bundles of notes wrapped in plastic, each amounting to five-thousand pounds.

It was a hefty sum, and Bliss's first thought was to wonder how a farmer who did little business and who asked for such low rents on her fields had managed to squirrel away a significant amount of cash. The second message was simply to inform him that Chandler had collected Paul Musgrove from Heathrow and had left him and his sister in the bar at the hotel. Bliss decided to question the pair on the discovery at the farmhouse the following morning.

Max's second walk of the day went much better than the first, and Bliss knew he was through the worst of it. He also recognised how often he had teetered on the brink lately, putting the decline down to subtle changes in the barometric air pressure affecting the fluids in his ears. Refusing to accept that his condition was getting worse and the symptoms appearing more frequently, he dismissed the matter over a couple of beers and a Chinese takeaway. After dinner he listened to some music, catching up on an all-female band called The Last Dinner Party, one of Molly's recommendations. He found their biggest hit so far, *Nothing Matters*, quite catchy and somewhat anthemic, but wasn't convinced by many of their other songs. Before heading to bed, he watched two episodes of the magnificent *Slow Horses*, as ever admiring Gary Oldman's performance as the obnoxious and disgusting but brilliant Mick Heron creation, Jackson Lamb.

He made a few mental notes following the more comedic insults characters threw at each other during the show, storing them up for a rainy day to use against Chandler. Bliss smiled at the thought, imagining her doing the exact same thing to throw his way.

Before turning in, he did a little bit of research on his laptop then sent a text message to the *PT* journalist, Sandra Bannister.

You followed the Sheila Musgrove scam/fraud case. If you'd even considered writing a larger piece on it you would first have checked out relevant facts and figures. If you hit upon a close MO, I'd love to know more about it.

Bliss smiled and made a bet with himself that he would be his reporter friend's first call the following day.

TWELVE

THE INSIDE OF THE van smelled so vile even Scuzzy Pete wrinkled his nose in revulsion – and this was a man who adored breathing in the wretched stench of his own worst farts. Having to burn out the Sprinter so soon after acquiring it was a pain, but they'd had no alternative following the farmhouse debacle. The twenty-year-old Ford Transit behind whose wheel he now sat was their go-to vehicle whenever a stolen motor had to be dumped, but it was on its last legs and seemed to have absorbed every essence of stale coffee, sour breath, and foul body odours from its two decades of use.

'What is your malfunction?' Doris asked, having noticed the grimace. His name was Matty Dories, but they had all agreed that giving him a girl's name instead was much more fun. 'You've got a face like a slapped arse, and you've been as miserable as fuck all morning.'

'All morning?' Scuzzy snapped back with real feeling. 'We've only been on the go for twenty minutes.'

'That's long enough in your company, you moody fucker. What's wrong with you?'

'Oh, I don't know. What could it possibly be? Let me see… oh, right. Maybe I'm going slightly mental over Paddy the Greek there stabbing an old lady to death with my favourite screwdriver.'

In truth, Scuzzy didn't know which aspect made him feel worse: seeing the woman killed, having his favourite screwdriver destroyed afterwards, or the fact that he ever had a *favourite* screwdriver.

Paddy the Greek, so named after a character mentioned in *Only Fools and Horses*, leaned forward in his seat by the passenger door and slowly turned to look at him. 'Stop your bitching and whining, will you? Just give us all a break from it. You're like an old biddy sometimes, Scuzzy. You've been on my back for three days now and I'm fucking sick of it.'

'Well, did you really have to kill her?' Scuzzy asked, unwilling to drop it. He knew he should keep his eyes on the road, but was finding it increasingly difficult to concentrate.

'Yes. As it happens, I did. She became a problem. I became the solution. While you were shitting your pants, I might add.'

'I wondered what that stink was,' Doris said, snorting with laughter.

'It's your fucking breath, mate,' Scuzzy sniped back. 'Do us all a favour and brush those railing of yours will you, even if it's only once.'

His mate laughed again. 'Yeah, I ain't the one known as "Scuzzy" though, am I?'

'Children, children,' Paddy chimed in. 'Give it a rest, will you? I don't want this carry on when we do our first job of the day. All right? Calm the fuck down the pair of you, or are we going to have a problem?'

Scuzzy slowly shook his head and switched his gaze back to the road. 'No problem here. None at all. But how about you try not stabbing this one to death, eh?'

The memory of the violent attack caused him to shudder as if an ice cube had been dropped down the back of his shirt. He tried to focus on the driving conditions, the road surface still coarse, slush piling up in the gutters, an icy drizzle spotting the windscreen. It wasn't an easy ask, because since Friday morning he had fought against the bloody and brutal images flashing inside his head and had come out on the losing side.

It was Paddy who had approached the old lady as she emerged from her front door. The plan was to convince her she needed additional urgent work to patch the roof, but she had come out all guns blazing, shrieking at them. He couldn't quite recall everything she had yelled out, but her having told the police about it was something he'd not soon forget. Unlike Paddy and Doris, he was relatively new to this game and tried to avoid confrontation for fear of where it might lead. His two friends seemed to revel in it, but even so, it came as a huge shock when Paddy started laying into her.

She was nothing but skin and bones beneath her winter woollies, and not even five feet tall. But the way she grabbed Paddy's arms suggested a hidden strength, perhaps muscle memory from her farming days. Either way, Paddy's response had been to introduce his forehead to her nose. The difference in their height meant his aim was a little off, and he'd caught more of her left eye, the power of the blow sending her reeling backwards. It seemed to suck all the air from her lungs. Eyes bulging, she slumped against the door jamb, dazed and gasping for breath as if she'd tumbled into a vacuum. She was done. They could all see that. Yet Paddy started clubbing at her with his fists, her cries becoming steadily weaker with each sickening thump that landed.

Scuzzy had looked on in fascinated horror and mounting revulsion. The pounding was unnecessarily comprehensive, the awful accompanying soundtrack of a defenceless old woman being beaten to a pulp almost worse than the ugliness of everything he witnessed through glazed eyes. When at last she fell silent, he felt his taut muscles relaxing as the rush of adrenaline ceased.

Now she was done.

Now it was over.

And so it was. Until Paddy pulled the screwdriver from his pocket and buried it deep into the woman's chest just beneath the rib cage. Scuzzy replayed that specific moment time after time after time; the crazed look on Paddy's face, the sight of the screwdriver disappearing into the woman's body, the sound like a puncture as her flesh tore apart, the blood bubbling from the wound through her clothing as he yanked it back out again, her sudden exhalation of air, followed by shallow, ragged gasps as the old woman fought to survive an unsurvivable attack. And then, with his own chest heaving and the veins in his neck like thick cords of rope, Paddy raised one leg and drove the sole of his boot into his victim's face.

In that moment, it was as if birds froze in flight, the air surrounding them blotted out the weak sunlight, and all sound died at the flick of an unseen switch. In retrospect, the flurry of violence was over in a flash, but the result of it, the slow, lingering death of the poor woman whose money they had come to steal, was now etched upon Scuzzy Pete's memory forever.

He blinked himself back inside the van. Judging by their laughter and a couple of rib-prods from Doris, Scuzzy had missed a couple of jibes at his expense. The pair often conspired against him, making him the butt of their jokes though even when combined they lacked sufficient brain power to form even a single halfwit. Which was probably why they always managed to miss the change in his demeanour; from light-hearted to a brooding darkness in an instant. His eyes clouded over, lips thinning, and he felt his teeth grind together. He was confident that he would eventually show them. Show them both precisely how much anger he had bottled up inside him. It was as inevitable as taking the next breath. And that day was coming.

But today was not that day. Today they'd do whatever work they could muster. Perhaps find another mug or two, another couple of pockets to pick. They only ever needed to work once a week to get by in relative comfort, but they were three greedy men with expensive tastes, and three or even four trips out a week were not unheard of.

No more violence, though. He couldn't take that again. Because Scuzzy Pete knew that if he started, if he allowed people to see what he was capable of, he might well not stop.

Not ever.

THIRTEEN

Switching between his twin roles had come a lot easier to Bliss than he had anticipated when looking ahead at stretching out his career by another notch. He knew it was instinctive, his many years' experience in the job culminating in a fundamental understanding of precisely where and when his input was required. Yet when he awoke early on Monday morning, he found himself inexplicably torn and unable to decide which of the two to focus on that day, wondering if there was enough of him to go around.

Or if he was needed at all.

After all, it wouldn't be the first time he had overestimated his worth. And, while it was always with reluctance, it wasn't as if he had never contemplated the moment when he might have to walk away and allow others to flourish. An end to it all was as humbling as it was inevitable.

It was a curious thing to be at odds with the passage of time flowing beneath your feet, but for him there were never enough hours in the day. In many ways, the weeks, months, and years he'd left behind like distant contrails had become indistinguishable. And just like vapour, they were impossible to grasp, to wring dry every perfect moment and capture their essence in the dry husk of life crumbling between your fingers.

Sober reflection gave Bliss pause as he showered and dressed for work after feeding and walking Max. The prospects for neither investigation were as dire as he had allowed himself to believe. Nor their current status, for that matter. The fog of sleep had simply robbed him of his natural ability to see the wood for the trees. A cautionary tale perhaps, but not a task he was unwilling to tackle.

Hopefully Ben Corry and Guy Foley would arrange their meeting with Toby Wallace, the man potentially at the centre of the reinvestigation if his memory could be relied upon. Neither investigator needed his guidance or supervision there, but Bliss was keen to learn everything that Beth Greenhill had discovered about the original investigation into Daisy Vincent's murder. He sensed something significant swirling around in the dust and debris of that case and found himself eager to immerse himself in it.

And yet the active murder case had all manner of possibilities at its core. Bliss wanted to speak at length to the victim's children. He and his team were confident that Sheila Musgrove had been murdered by three conmen who learned she had money stashed away somewhere on the property. But the amount of readily available cash bothered him. The farm was no more than a smallholding and had been for some time, turning over enough to keep a single person going but little more. That left the rent paid on fields let to two local farmers as the only additional income. The actions requesting interviews with them had not yet been allocated as other potential leads were regarded as a higher priority, but Bliss couldn't imagine two relatively small fields yielding vast sums of money, and certainly he expected the accounts to show these payments were made electronically between relevant banks.

He knew this niggle might prove to be nothing. Many people had an innate mistrust of banks, preferring to turn profits into cash for easy access and also to use as a bargaining chip for services, avoiding VAT and quite often any proper recording into company books. Even so, thirty grand – allowing for the five Mrs Musgrove had previously handed over to the scammers – was a substantial figure and had to be accounted for.

Bliss also hoped to get positive news from security camera follow-ups and neighbouring force intelligence teams searching for a reported act of fraud or theft with a similar MO. He believed that was the most likely route to making inroads into the meat of the investigation.

He mulled it all over while drinking tea and nibbling on a slice of toast, but found himself unable to fully commit. With no decision made, he called DCI Warburton. They chatted for a few minutes, Bliss walking her through his dilemma. She told him she understood, even sympathised, and eventually volunteered to step up in her role as deputy SIO while he spent time with the cold case. He thanked his old boss and left the house feeling a lot more positive without the weight of uncertainty on his shoulders.

The moment Beth Greenhill stepped inside the office, Bliss knew she had something encouraging to tell them. Her face was wreathed in smiles, and as she wriggled out of her coat, she couldn't wait to report on what she'd discovered.

'HQ is sending us the case files later today,' she said. 'But I have the gist of it, and as we thought, there's more to this than we first imagined. The original investigation supports the essential story we were given. Daisy Vincent was raped and strangled to death in 2014. Her killer was never caught, and though a number of people were questioned, not a single arrest was made. But here's the truly interesting thing: at the time of her death, Daisy was dating a slightly older man by the name of Stephen Wrigley.

Quite a few people spotted the two having a heated discussion earlier that same evening. One witness gave a statement saying they believe they saw Daisy Vincent later that night rushing from Wrigley's vehicle close to where she was murdered.'

'I take it he was arrested,' Foley said. He still wore a scarf tight against his neck, the office radiators only ever reaching tepid even when turned up all the way.

Greenhill shook her head. 'No. And this is where the whole case takes a sharp turn. The police put an arrest package together, but Wrigley was not at home when they put his door in. Neither had he been to work that day, which was the second place the team tried. They subsequently paid surprise visits to his mother and closest friends, but still no joy. The fact is, they never managed to locate him, and disturbingly the man hasn't been seen since.'

Bliss had seen it coming. He felt hairs standing erect on the back of his neck. This was something important. He sensed it deep down, knowing without actually knowing.

'The Vincents,' he said. 'Has to be. They somehow found out Wrigley was in the frame, and they got to him first.'

'You think they killed him?' Corry said, seemingly startled by the suggestion.

'It wouldn't surprise me. The father and both sons have violence in their records. I checked the PNC.'

'Okay, but violence and murder are two different things.'

'Of course. But this was one man's daughter. Sister to the other two. If they believed Stephen Wrigley was responsible for Daisy's death…'

Bliss had no need to finish. Everyone could follow the most logical pathway. 'We'll need to speak his family,' he added.

Greenhill shook her head. 'No can do, Jimmy. His father died when Stephen was a toddler. His mother was alive at the time of the investigation but has since passed away.'

'Okay. Having a word with her might have given us a clue as to whether he was still alive or not, but if we can't then we can't. Make a note of those friends you mentioned. I doubt they'll have much to say, but they might be worth a punt if we get stuck.'

'You say the girl was raped,' Foley said, looking at Greenhill. 'What did DNA tell the investigation team?'

'Nothing,' she said with regret. 'CSI discovered traces of lubricant, which they matched to a brand of condom called Notty Boy. They did, however, find hairs and fibres belonging to Stephen Wrigley on Daisy's clothing, and the pathologist observed light bruising to both upper arms consistent with the girl being held too tight. But we now know that witness evidence placed Wrigley with her earlier that evening, during which time they were heard to have a loud disagreement. The bruises were most likely made around that time, and the two being a couple would also explain the hairs and fibres.'

'What about the condom? Was that Wrigley's preferred brand?'

'Unknown. They never got to ask him, remember? Police did speak with two previous girlfriends of his who both said he left contraception to them and never wore a condom during their time together. Daisy's closest friends made statements insisting they had heard similar from her.'

'So, there's our anomaly,' Bliss said. 'If she was raped and murdered by her boyfriend following an argument, why did he even have a condom with him, let alone wear one?'

Greenhill responded in a flash. 'Here's an idea. What if the condom wasn't his. Maybe it was Daisy's. In fact, what if Wrigley somehow discovered condoms in Daisy Vincent's handbag? That would be more than enough to set him off. Perhaps make him angry enough to use one as he raped her afterwards, before strangling her while still infuriated.'

Bliss saw sense in the notion. 'That's certainly a possibility. It gives us motive, and it seems he had the opportunity if this witness who saw her getting out of his car was accurate. It places him in the area at the right time. And just because the witness saw him drive off doesn't mean he didn't circle back. Beth, what else do you have on that particular statement? Did this witness see anything more, such as the car following Daisy?'

'I haven't read it. I just got the story from one of the DCs who worked the case. The files will be with us shortly, but I'm sure the original investigators would have followed up on that.'

Nodding, Bliss said, 'All roads do seem to lead to Wrigley, with the possible exception of that condom. I can see why our lot over at HQ were interested in him. And I'm sure if I saw the possibility of the Vincent family being involved in Wrigley's disappearance, they did, too. I'll be curious to see what they did with it. As for us, we have this vital piece of fresh information. The thing is, it was already going to be a tense time approaching Douglas and Fearn Vincent with the prospect of this prisoner's confession. But if they did something to Wrigley by way of retribution for what they thought he did to Daisy, it's only going to make them edgier still.'

Foley agreed, but had been wondering about a different aspect. 'Even if the police suspected the Vincents of taking matters into their own hands, they must have had an alternative strategy for dealing with the boyfriend's disappearance.'

'Now that I do have an answer to,' Greenhill said. 'Because I asked the exact same question. What happened was, the team investigating Daisy's murder kept some focus on Wrigley as their prime suspect and followed whatever leads arose from the murder op. But a second team were assigned to follow up on the possibility that Wrigley, having murdered Daisy, subsequently fled the country, perhaps on a forged passport.'

'Presumably that led them nowhere,' Corry said.

'Precisely. Nobody has seen nor heard of Wrigley since the day after Daisy Vincent's murder.'

'In which case, I have another question,' Bliss said, somewhat dejectedly. 'We may obtain answers from scouring the case files, but what's bothering me right now is if the Vincents are responsible for taking revenge on Wrigley, how did they know? How could they have known about these statements pointing in his direction if they weren't informed?'

His colleagues looked at one another in silence. Bliss arched his eyebrows and continued. 'I'll allow for the possibility that the people who made the statements knew the Vincent family well enough to have relayed the same information to them directly. Or at the very least, told their stories to others who happened to be within the Vincents' circle of friends. But we can't ignore another alternative staring us in the face.'

'You're saying one of the investigation team gave up that information to the Vincents,' Greenhill said after a moment of hesitation.

Bliss breathed heavily through his nostrils. 'I'm suggesting it could have happened that way, yes. And if it did, what else did this officer do for the Vincent family?'

FOURTEEN

On a whim, and following a brief discussion about roles and actions, Bliss decided to accompany Guy Foley to visit Toby Wallace in Nottingham. The man's story was central to their investigation, and he wanted to hear it for himself. They got no reply to their knocks at the one-bedroom flat he rented in a house close to County Hall, but a student renting the room beneath him told them where they might find the ex-con.

From the A60 bridge traversing the River Trent, Bliss caught glimpses of the Meadow Lane stadium, home to Notts County football team, the City Ground, which Nottingham Forest had played at since the late 1800s, as well as the Trent Bridge cricket ground. He and Foley took winding stone steps down to the embankment, where they soon came upon a drink and snack kiosk. Close by, they found Wallace sitting on a low concrete wall overlooking the water. Unique for being Britain's only north-flowing river, the Trent was historically an important trading route. Today it merely looked cold and uninviting.

Toby Wallace, fast approaching sixty and long gone to seed, sipped from a tall takeaway cup. He wore a donkey jacket that looked worn enough to be on its umpteenth cycle of popularity and a black beanie hat pulled down tight over cropped white hair. His eyes wore rings of puffy darkness and coarse bristle adorned his cheeks, chin, and neck. As he drank, he idly watched the *Trent Lady* cruise ship glide by. For the sake of its passengers, Bliss hoped it had central heating, but to him it was inexplicable that anybody would want to cruise the river in deep winter.

He introduced himself and Foley to Nick Nevin's former cellmate, who gave a resigned nod. 'I recognise the names,' he said. 'My licence supervisor told me you wanted a word with me.'

'I'm guessing you'd rather not,' Foley said.

Bliss didn't always see eye to eye with his fellow investigator, but he did admire the ex-detective's direct approach to every situation.

'Put it this way,' Wallace said, his voice hoarse. 'I've had enough run-ins with you people to know there's nothing in it for me but more bother.'

'We're not police,' Bliss assured him. 'We work for them, but we don't carry warrant cards. All we're looking for from you here is your time. We have questions, that's all.'

The man took another sip from his cup, his eyes never having left the cruise ship. 'About?'

'Your stint in Woodhill.'

Wallace pursed his lips. 'I spent about eight months in there. That's maybe two-hundred and fifty days. Can you be more specific?'

Bliss smiled. Toby Wallace had lived much of his life either involved with or on the cusp of criminal activity, but despite his scruffy appearance and woebegone demeanour he was well educated and known to be both articulate and erudite. There was no point in attempting to bluff him.

'See if you remember this, Mr Wallace,' he said, shuffling inside his overcoat to hold in the warmth of his own body. 'You're sitting at a table playing cards on one of those two-hundred and fifty days when your opponent becomes inexplicably talkative. During a bit of a rant, he tells you all about a murder he was somehow involved in. The young victim was also raped, if that makes any difference to you and your willingness to talk to us. Apparently, this fellow prisoner was afraid to come forward with what he knew, in case the police latched onto him as a suspect. All of which sounds decidedly dodgy to me. Any of that ring a bell?'

Without changing his expression, Wallace said, 'You have to question a man's motives, don't you? He's possibly got away with murder, he's about to be released after serving time for a crime he did get banged up for, he knows his victim's father is willing and able to top the bloke who killed the poor kid, yet he still risks telling the whole story to a fellow inmate. An inmate who might be the kind to try buying favour with this grieving family by spilling his guts to them. Now, I ask you, Mr ex-policeman, does that make any sense to you?'

Bliss had to admit it didn't. And it had bothered him since first hearing it from Nevin.

'Me neither,' Wallace said. 'Fortunately for him, I just wanted to keep my head down, do my time, and come out without fretting about who did what to whom and whatever I might know about it. But in the meantime, I'm thinking his confession made no sense because he claims not to have committed the crimes himself. On top of that, he sounded confident about who did. I mean, I get that he was fired up about something he'd seen or heard that day, but he left me confused by the whole sorry tale.'

'I can understand that. So, you never passed on that information to the victim's family. Believe me, I understand that too. But did you ever repeat that story to anyone else?'

'Just one other living soul. My cellmate at the time. But then, you already know I did because I'm guessing that's how you come to be here talking to me.'

'So, this whole time, only a single other inmate has had exactly the same information you had.'

'That's right.' Wallace turned to face Bliss for the first time. 'You're a sharp one.'

'But it's all true,' Guy Foley said, stating rather than asking. 'Everything my colleague described to you is exactly how the conversation between you and this unnamed prisoner went down.'

'I wouldn't call it a conversation. He spoke, I listened. I didn't really want to, but it would have been rude of me to stand up and walk away. Besides, I had a decent hand.'

Bliss remembered Wallace had been playing cards when he learned of the unsolved murder. 'Okay. He makes this so-called confession while angry about something or other, but you simply volunteered that same information to your cellmate.'

'Yep.'

'Why?'

'Why not? It's a conversation starter, don't you think?'

Wallace was a slippery customer, but Bliss was growing tired of his slick responses. 'I suppose so,' he said. 'But you weren't afraid that he might do what you opted not to? And by that, I mean pass on the entire story to the Vincent family.'

'That would have been between him and his own conscience. His own choice to make. As I made mine.'

'And it didn't worry you that he might just do that? After all, you were the person this fellow con told, so he probably wouldn't have left you out of it.'

'I didn't see why he would. Nothing to be gained from it. He seemed like the type who'd want to take all the credit. One of your lot, as I recall.'

'A long time ago, Mr Wallace. And not one we hold in high regard. But as you rightly pointed out, we're here because of him. He did tell your story.'

'There you go, then.' As if somehow, that made his point.

Bliss chose to move on rather than plough the same furrow. 'There's just one important bit of information missing from what we've learned so far.'

'Oh, yeah? What's that, then?'

'We don't as yet know who told you that awful story, Mr Wallace.'

The man chuckled over the rim of his tall cup, from which no further steam billowed. 'So, my ex-cellmate didn't give up the identity, then? I can't say I blame him.'

'What was his name, Mr Wallace? This bloke who made the confession.'

The man drained his cup and tossed it into a nearby bin affixed to the wall on which he remained sitting. 'I just got done telling you how I've kept schtum all this time because I didn't want to get involved. Now you're asking me to involve myself.'

'But you already are,' Bliss pointed out. 'This fellow inmate who you played cards with implicated himself in a murder. He told you he was somehow involved and that he believed he knew who carried it out. For all you know he might even have done it himself. There are an awful lot of people who want to know who killed Daisy Vincent, Mr Wallace. And I'm one of them.'

Wallace gave a wrinkled grin. 'Yeah, but as you were at pains to point out earlier, you're not the police.'

'True. But I can have them here within minutes. You're enjoying your freedom courtesy of a licence. Your supervisor will have informed you that it's in your best interests to share any and all information with us. You have knowledge relating to an unsolved murder enquiry, Mr Wallace. I can't see a judge being too happy about you keeping the details to yourself. Now, you give me the name and I won't need to have that licence revoked.'

Wallace's shoulders heaved as he chuckled a second time, finishing with a harsh cough into the meat of a fist. 'In or out of the job, you people never change,' he grumbled. 'Always willing to use your powers against the little people. Or in this case, someone else's power.'

'It's just the name we're after,' Bliss said.

'Yeah, sure. A name, followed by a statement, followed by a grilling as to why I never told anyone in authority about it, followed by some bastard deciding that's reason enough to put me back behind bars.'

Bliss was shaking his head. 'Never going to happen. Look, I'm not going to pretend you won't have to provide us with an official account. I can obtain one from my source, but you were there, Mr Wallace. You were the man this inmate chose to tell his story to. I don't know why, but hopefully we'll get the chance to ask him. The thing is yours is the most important statement.'

'Other than his, presumably.'

'Of course. But to have the opportunity to squeeze that one out, we need his name.'

'What makes you think I even know it?' Wallace asked, the change in his disposition suggesting he'd pulled that one out of thin air.

'You served time with him. You played cards with him.'

'That doesn't necessarily mean he told me his name.'

Bliss squinted at him. 'No. It doesn't. And maybe he didn't. But I'm betting if that was the case you asked around, anyway. I know I would if a bloke had just told me that story.'

Another ship pottered by on the river, its diesel engine coughing and spluttering. Bliss started to feel the cold forcing its way between his layers of clothing. Irritation had opened a door, and by now anger wanted to walk through it. But he waited, sensing the old lag had more to say.

'The problem I have,' Wallace continued a moment later, 'is not that I know his name. It's that he knows mine. You think if you pick him up that he won't remember telling me all about it? Even if you lot keep my name out of it – which would be very unusual for such a bunch of fuck-ups – he'll put two and two together and come up with me.'

'And yet you didn't think your cellmate would do the same thing.'

'No. That's because I trust a villain more than I trust you people.'

'There's nothing to be afraid of,' Foley persisted. 'We find him, we arrest him, we charge him, and then we bang him up for his role in the murder. That's a good thing.'

'Not if you have… if you have reach. He'll have somebody find me and kill me just in case I agree to testify against him in court – which I will not do, by the way.'

Bliss could see the man was worried. He understood why. But he also saw a different problem Toby Wallace faced.

'Mr Wallace,' he said. 'You're clearly a bit rattled by all this, which is understandable. But you're not thinking clearly. Assuming the man we're talking about is walking free, do you really believe he's not thought about you since that card game? You think it's not crossed his mind that you know his darkest secret because he blabbed while his guard was down? A secret that could cost him his freedom. The fact is, for all you know he could have people looking for you as we speak. You might weigh it all up and decide you could be in a spot of bother either way, but I can assure you that cooperating with us is by far your best option. You do that, he goes away, and all bets are off. That's a win-win for you. The alternative… well, by my reckoning that leaves you fully exposed.'

He saw Wallace's brief moment of enthusiasm and hope die. First in his eyes, then in the slump of his shoulders, and finally the sag and fall of his chin. Bliss knew then the next thing out of the ex-con's mouth would be the name of the man who claimed to have been involved in the murder of Daisy Vincent.

FIFTEEN

'Can we not have that same bloody music on the drive back?' Guy Foley said as they climbed into the Volvo SUV. Bliss hadn't wanted to travel in awkward silence or indulge in small talk on their way to Nottingham, so he'd activated the sound system's USB to run through one of his playlists. He had not taken notice of which folder was up next, but had been happy enough to listen to Scott Henderson's particular brand of jazz fusion and blues. He'd long been high on the list of Bliss's favourite guitarists and he considered the style of music harmless enough to have playing in the background.

'I take it you're not a fan,' he said, pushing the 'Start' button to get the engine going.

'Not of the music nor the car.'

Bliss felt his forehead crinkling. 'What's wrong with the car?'

'It's petrol. The plate tells me it's last year's model, but you didn't even bother to go hybrid. Do you not watch the TV news or read the papers, Jimmy? The planet is dying.'

Nosing the Volvo across the bridge they'd earlier stood on and then taking the A52 towards Radcliffe, Bliss took a few beats before replying. 'Please, spare me the eco-zealotry, Guy.'

'It's not zealotry, it's called following the science.'

'Yeah, I've followed it as well and do you know what that same science tells us? That warming is cyclical. As is cooling. It's coming no matter what we do, and only our hubris says otherwise. Also, it's my life, so I get to choose.'

'And screw everyone else, right? We can all burn, drown, or go hungry.'

'Like I say, warming is going to happen eventually. Cycles, Guy. It's all about cycles. And not the type you Lycra louts ride. But if you object so much, I can always let you out and you can make your own way back to Thorpe Wood. If not, please, spare me the lecture and let's get back to work. The music we can change. Or would you prefer silence?'

'That might be a bit too uncomfortable.'

'Okay. You want Irish rebel songs? I think I've got *Whiskey in the Jar* somewhere.'

Foley turned to look at him. Bliss stared right back. Seconds later, both men broke up into waves of laughter. Wiping tears from his eyes, Foley said, 'I might have been born and raised within the shadow of the Shehy mountains – that would be the Cork and Kerry mountains to the likes of you – but I'm no rebel.'

'So, it's not all Englishmen you have a problem with, then? Just me.'

'What makes you say I have a problem with you?' Foley asked, his frown seemingly genuine.

Bliss shrugged. 'Nothing I've been able to put my finger on, though I do get the impression that you're not a fan of me pulling on my SIO hat whenever I need to.'

Foley shook his head. 'Not at all. Sure, to begin with I did wonder how that would work. The SIO gig is a greater pull, so I thought we'd probably play second fiddle. But to be fair, you've played it straight down the middle. Like now, for instance. You have a murder on your hands, plus one of your team with a concussion, but you're here. Fair play to you right enough, Jimmy. If I had doubts at the outset, they're long gone.'

'I appreciate that, Guy. Hammering my taste in music, however, is a little harder to swallow.'

'I can't be doing with all that jazzy, fusiony stuff. It grates on me. It's like musical masturbation when all I want is the real thing.'

'You might want to rephrase that,' Bliss said, chuckling.

'Ah, you know what I meant. I want real music.'

'What, like the Dubliners? The Corrs, perhaps? Anything but U2, please.'

Foley laughed again. 'I like my music with a bit of soul.'

'Ah, that'll be The Commitments, then.'

'Now you're talking. You have them on your playlist?'

'No. But I'll bear it in mind for next time. How about a sixties and seventies mix? Bound to be some decent soul tunes among them.'

'That'll be grand. Let's have some of that for the next hour. Unless you want to discuss the case, of course.'

The roads were busy and traffic slow moving on a dull day whose colour was never going to shift from the darker end of the grey palette. If Bliss had been on his own, he'd have immersed himself in some decent tunes. But Toby Wallace had given them a name, and Bliss had reacted to it with shock and more than a little apprehension.

'If everything we've been told so far is true,' he said, 'then an already problematic cold case just became a nightmare.'

During the walk back to the car, the two men had discussed the information provided by Wallace and Bliss had revealed his fears upon learning the identity of their confessor. Foley had never heard of Jack Maguire, but had reacted with concerned silence when he learned a potted history of two opposing families living in the same small village on the edge of the county.

'How far back does this turf war go between the Vincents and the Maguires?' he asked as they navigated the substantial A46 junction at Saxondale.

'It's a last Millennium thing,' Bliss replied. 'The Vincents have always been relatively small time, but renowned and feared all the same. The Maguires moved to Thorney and brought a fierce reputation with them. This was long before even my first stint up here, obviously, but the rivalry continues to this day.'

'And now we apparently have this Jack Maguire confessing to some kind of involvement in the murder of Daisy Vincent, in addition to possibly knowing who raped and killed her. If he didn't do it himself, which we can't rule out. That's a can of worms nobody wants to open.'

'I agree. The only son from one family being anywhere close to the murder of the only daughter of another is troublesome, no matter where it occurs. Not that we can avoid it kicking off if it's true.'

Foley turned to him. 'That's a couple of times now you said that, Jimmy. You have doubts?'

'Several. The biggest of which is my source. His name is Nick Nevin, by the way. Check him out on Google if you feel the need. The thing is he's ill. Dying, in fact. So, I understand why Nevin might want to spend his last few days in a better place. Then again, I find it hard to believe he'd willingly deal me a winning hand. And how coincidental is it that his cellmate happens to feed him this story involving a couple of criminal families from my neck of the woods?'

'But coincidences do happen. And Toby Wallace did just confirm it.'

Bliss nodded, having to flick the windscreen wipers on to bat away tyre spray. 'Yes. Yes, he did. But does that make it true? Or is Wallace part of a conspiracy, one that began inside Nevin's tiny little tortured soul? I know I must sound paranoid, but I can't escape the feeling that Nevin is setting me up somehow. That's much more like him, Guy. Believe me, the man is pure evil.'

They drove in silence for a good ten minutes. Then out of the blue, Foley said, 'You keep referring to your first posting to Peterborough. I won't lie, we've all heard the rumours. You can't work out of any nick for half a year and not pick up on what the jungle drums are saying. I just wondered if you'd like to confirm or deny.' He raised a hand. 'But not if it's still too painful. I don't mean to intrude.'

'Yes, you do.'

Foley grinned. 'Yes. I do.'

Bliss concentrated on the road ahead, but he was willing to play along. 'Go on then. Tell me what you think you know.'

'Fair play to you. The story goes that you and a couple of colleagues took on a bunch of bent coppers. And in doing so, you cost the lives of some and ruined the reputations of others, including a few who weren't even involved.'

'That's mostly true,' Bliss said, receding into the far reaches of his memory. 'A group of officers covered up a murder by one of their own many moons earlier. Some had moved on or retired, while others were still knocking around. Penny and I, plus a DS by the name of Bobby Dunne, worked off the books to expose them. Except that, as it turned out, Bobby was one of them. A few of the officers involved were shot and killed along the way. A couple of civilians, too. When it was all over, my DS was dead, and I was cast adrift. As for Pen, some people say the reason she didn't make DS sooner was due to that investigation. But the truth in her case is that she didn't feel up to taking that next step. It took her quite some time to start trusting her fellow officers again, and to a certain extent she was left wondering if any of them had been involved only to escape with their reputations intact.'

Foley blew out a long stream of breath. 'Bloody hell. That's crazy. How did you cope with being turfed out of your job?'

'Badly. I don't mean I turned to drink or drugs or anything like that. I like a drink, as you know, but I'm no drunk. And I've never done drugs in my life. So, basically, after a few weeks of feeling sorry for myself and thinking I might be better off out of the job altogether, I got my act together and set about rebuilding not just my career but myself. That case and everything that went with it took its toll on me. In fact, I'd go so far as to say that the events themselves affected me more than my ignominious departure from the Major Crime Unit.'

'Really? That bad, huh? I can't begin to imagine. As I understand it, you landed on your feet by moving to the National Crime Agency.'

'Close,' Bliss corrected him. 'At the time, it was still the Serious and Organised Crime Agency. But yes, I was fortunate enough to land a position there. In my time at the Met, I made some influential friends, one of whom recommended me to the SOCA boss at the time. I remained in the job as it transitioned across to the NCA.'

'Did you enjoy working OC?'

For Bliss, that was a tougher question than it first appeared. 'For a while. Probably a good ten years. About half of that I spent working out of Bedford, which was a move I requested because I couldn't settle back in London. But you have to remember I started off from a bad place. I was down on the Job, down on myself. I had to overcome those hurdles before settling in anywhere properly.'

'Which you eventually did if you lasted that long.'

'A dozen years in all. But what I had to do was keep telling myself that although things turned to shit and people died, I did the right thing. In fact, *we* did the right thing. Me and Pen. She was my rock. Still is. You don't forget it when somebody sticks by you and supports you the way she did. For a long time, I beat myself up over what happened again and again, believing I'd selfishly put her life in danger. Which was true to a certain extent. It could have ended badly for both of us. But when we spoke afterwards – which I confess wasn't anywhere near often enough – she would always dismiss my apologies and remind me that she put herself in the firing line. She drummed it into me that I did everything I could to convince her not to follow me along the path I chose to take. But even back then she was fiercely loyal, and although some of the shit stuck to her, she was able to push through to better herself.'

'You're lucky to have someone like that in your life,' Foley said, watching his own ghostly image in the passenger door window.

'Believe me, Guy, I know. I wouldn't be here now if it wasn't for her.'

'Is going up against the gangs as challenging as it sounds, Jimmy?'

'Every bit. And more. Once you get close to them, that is. The thing is, not only do you get to know them, but they also get to know you. I have to admit that in those early years I was glad to be living alone. These people don't really want to risk the wrath of the entire police force and various agencies by taking out a copper or a SOCA or NCA officer, and usually only resort to such tactics when they're cornered. But they are a vicious, remorseless, ruthless bunch of psychopaths, and I've seen things they've done to rival gang members that would curdle your blood.'

'Such as?'

Sadly, Bliss didn't have to think too hard about that one. 'Perhaps the worst I came across was the result of a feud between two gangs in south London, one from Nunhead, the other from neighbouring Peckham. One of the top men from the Nunhead gang went into hiding, so the Peckham boss ordered a hit on his family. They took out his partner and their two kids. But they did it in the most brutal way. When she was found, his partner didn't have a single fingernail or toenail remaining. She'd also been tortured with lit cigarettes and a staple gun. Then they sliced her up with dozens of slashes and puncture wounds, before decapitating her and leaving her head in the couple's bed. Lying either side of her torso which was in the kitchen, police found a five-year-old and a seven-year-old with their throats slit open.'

'Fucking hell!'

'I know. Sick bastards to a man.'

'Did you collar them?'

Bliss swallowed. 'Eventually. But not before they also took their target out when he came looking for revenge. Believe me, Guy, these people have no scruples. Like I said before, they don't really want to get too physical with us because it's not good for business, but they do enjoy other forms of intimidation.'

Foley was nodding along. 'Okay. I understand why that might get old very quickly. But what on earth drew you back here? To Thorpe Wood, I mean.'

Bliss smiled; an easy one at last. 'Working mainly organised crime burned me out to some extent. But the simple truth is, I missed working primarily murder investigations. OCG often involves many months of surveillance and planning and waiting for people to make moves. There's a lot going on, but only occasionally does it feel… immediate. My heart was not really in the work towards the end. I think because I was licking my wounds when I first went back to London and I convinced myself that the past was the past and all the bad stuff that happened was to the old me, while the new me was happy giving gangs a hard time. But when that all soured, and I finally got my head on straight, I realised Major Crime was where I'd been the happiest. When the post came up, it was a fairly urgent request, so it was felt that my knowledge of the place and some of the people might be an advantage.'

'They didn't consider the disadvantages?' Foley scoffed, hissing through his teeth. 'You must have felt like a pariah.'

'Oh, I did. For quite some time. You wouldn't believe how bad things were initially between me and Alicia Edwards. She was a DCI back then, and my direct boss. But in the dozen years I was away, the Major Crime Unit underwent a lot of changes, so there weren't too many colleagues who knew precisely what had happened. And to my genuine surprise, many of those who did were on my side. As for those who weren't, well, let's just say we had our differences, but I'm still here. Even me and Edwards found a way to make it work.'

'And no regrets about leaving your hometown behind once again?'

'Some,' Bliss admitted. 'But I think I did most of my growing up during that period. I worked hard on controlling my temper, which was admittedly short on too many occasions.'

'How did you manage that?'

'You'll probably laugh, but I really got into eastern philosophies. Zen, in particular. I studied it quite closely and tried to use its way of thinking, its approach to life, as a baseline for what I wanted to be.'

'Which was?'

'A better man. A better son. A better colleague. A better friend. A better person.'

'Doesn't sound like too much to ask,' Foley said, following up with a barked laugh.

Chuckling along, Bliss said, 'I know. It was an unrealistic goal. But even if I didn't achieve all my targets, I came close enough that it changed me. For the better. And I needed to be when that second stint at Thorpe Wood came around.'

'Must have been nice coming back to Penny Chandler.'

Bliss shot Foley a sidelong glance and noted the sly grin on his face. 'It was, but she had nothing to do with my decision. In fact, Pen was on secondment with the Met working on Operation Sapphire in their sex crimes unit. She came back to Peterborough to interview a victim and decided to stay.'

'And you're telling me there's nothing between you two?'

'Nothing but friendship, Guy. Have we engaged in a little bit of flirting? Yes. I even kissed her once when I was rat-arsed and, as it happens, about to tackle my nemesis, Nick Nevin, wondering if I'd make it out the other side. But she's my best friend, and nothing will ever come between us.'

'So, she's up for grabs, then?' Foley said. To Bliss it sounded as if he were only half joking.

'Guy, Penny is a grown woman and makes her own decisions. But just know that if you hurt her, you'll have me to deal with.'

'Aye, and I reckon you could still go a round or two, Jimmy.'

'I can. And do, recreationally. But I warn you, I fight dirty.'

Foley laughed. 'There'll be no need for that. I was just having a craic with you. I have a partner, and we're very happy together, thank you.'

'I'm sure being with you makes her a completely fulfilled woman,' Bliss said, a teasing edge to his voice.

His colleague turned his head and smiled. 'Ah, now, Jimmy, what makes you think I was talking about a woman?'

SIXTEEN

Ben Corry and Beth Greenhill beat them back to the office by ten minutes. Bliss had stopped in the city centre to pick up a couple of Five Guys cheeseburgers, which he and Foley had consumed long before they reached the station. Greenhill was typing up notes relating to their interview with the SIO assigned to the Daisy Vincent investigation, but paused to listen to Corry outlining how it had gone.

Hugh Prentiss, Detective Chief Inspector at the time of the murder, now back in uniform and permanently stationed at Hertfordshire police headquarters in Welwyn Garden City, had been forthcoming about the investigation. He made it clear that while all potential avenues were explored, the major crime team had been of one mind that Stephen Wrigley was responsible for raping and strangling to death his girlfriend, after which he'd either fled the country or had himself been the victim of foul play.

Remembering the sequence of events, Bliss asked if anyone had subsequently questioned the witness who identified Wrigley leaving the victim on the side of the road on the night of the murder to see if her story remained the same.

'They originally took her written statement two days later,' Greenhill confirmed. 'When the case ran out of steam they started from scratch and revisited every single lead. The woman's version of events had not changed. Evidently, she hadn't been able to sleep and was heading back home having taken her dog for a walk. She said she heard a car screech to a halt behind her. When she turned to see what had happened, she saw Daisy Vincent climb out of the car, slam the door, and quickly walk away. The car then took off again with its wheels spinning.'

'The witness knew Daisy Vincent by sight?'

'Evidently, most people did.'

'And the car? How did she know it was Stephen Wrigley's?'

'She recognised both. The car drew attention, it seems. He was driving a Nissan 300zx in those days, metallic bronze. Sporty number with the kind of growly engine you couldn't forget.'

'Sounds like a solid enough witness,' Bliss admitted. 'Might be worth giving her another go, just to see how well that memory has stood the test of time.'

'No can do, Jimmy,' Corry said. 'She passed away not long afterwards.'

Bliss chewed that over for a few moments. He could imagine Nevin spinning the story back to himself on a loop, wondering how he might use it to his advantage. He had to admit he'd suspected Nevin of some kind of double-dealing, but the cellmate had now confirmed his version of events. Even so, he had to wonder if his one-time enemy had thought beyond the obvious opportunities. Had he perhaps reached out to a friend still in the job to acquire background on Jack Maguire? Had he gone so far as to consider the possibility – as Bliss had – that Stephen Wrigley, Daisy Vincent's boyfriend, had been offered up as a prime suspect by a police officer close to the Vincent family?

Presented by Nevin as a gift of a cold case, the offering would carry a mighty sting if any potential police corruption got caught up in the wrapping paper and neat bow. That was much more like the actions of the ex-cop he knew and despised.

'Okay,' he said, taking a deep breath and moving away from personal reflection. 'From one end of this case, we know what we have. By his own admission, it does look as if Jack Maguire is connected to the killing, but we don't yet know how or why. And at this stage, all we have on him is the word of the fellow prisoner he told part of his story to. In addition, Maguire supposedly also knows who *did* murder Daisy, which makes him of further interest to us but in an entirely different way. We need to drill down much deeper into the original investigation to see if they moved on beyond identifying Stephen Wrigley as a prime suspect. Did they ever, at any time, have Maguire in the frame? What evidence gathered from the crime scene might help us to establish a connection between Maguire and Daisy Vincent? In fact, as a useful exercise, let's pull the entire investigation apart with an eye on Maguire's potential role. See what dots we can join.'

'Excuse me for saying so,' Beth Greenhill said tentatively, 'but isn't that a little blinkered? We wouldn't normally put up a suspect and look to find leads pointing to them. We'd find the evidence and that would lead us to our person of interest.'

'I realise that, of course,' Bliss said without malice. 'But in this case, we have an ID on that individual. One that's seeming increasingly accurate. I'm not suggesting we wander blindly down dead ends or blunder into anything. No looking to ram square pegs into round holes. Just running it down to see if and where and how Jack Maguire might fit. Or not.'

'Any suggestions as to how we proceed on that?' Foley asked.

Bliss nodded. 'With haste, but not speed. If he's our man, we can't hang about too long. The fact is he *has* been named, which is reason enough to pull him in. I'm sure his licence supervisor will advise him to talk to us. But there are a number of things I'd like to find out about Maguire before we interview him. Things we should try to know before we waste our time.'

'Name them,' Greenhill said, getting to her feet. 'I'll write them up on the board.'

'Okay. We know he's a criminal from a family involved in criminal activity, so was he even at liberty at the time of Daisy's murder? If so, where was he that night? He claims to have some involvement, which suggests he was close by. He also claims to know who did it, so perhaps he was even right there when it happened. What would his motive be? He made a casual confession to a fellow inmate whilst angry, but has he admitted it previously or since to anyone else? And if not, why do so when he did?'

Ben Corry picked him up on the list of questions. 'We can easily answer the first of those. But if he wasn't in prison, it might be a bit more difficult to find out where he was in 2014. Other than from him, of course. As for motive, I don't see how we can identify one without knowing precisely what his involvement was. I think we acknowledge he most likely confessed to Toby Wallace in a moment of frustration, but I can't see how we'd find out if he ever did so on any other occasion.'

'All valid observations,' Bliss allowed. 'So, we begin with the questions we can answer. And there are less of those. Are there any forensics to link him? Do any witnesses or CCTV indicate it could be him?'

'The logs and reports from the original case will hopefully give us an insight into the forensics and tech awareness. I reckon that's plenty to be getting on with.'

'There's also an issue of protection here, Jimmy,' Greenhill said. 'We can't know if your source got word out to Maguire prior to talking to us. From everything you've said about the man, I'm betting you wouldn't put it past him.'

'It's a possibility,' Bliss admitted. 'Personally, I think it's unlikely, but our duty of care says we have to consider it. By the way, Guy knows the name of my source. You can fill Ben in later on. But you mentioned protection, which got me thinking about Toby Wallace. I used his vulnerability against him, but his safety is a real concern to me. All the more so if we end up arresting Maguire.'

'And we shouldn't be forgetting him, either,' Corry pointed out. 'He'll need protecting from the Vincent family once his name gets out there.'

'Speaking of which, I just had a horrible thought,' Foley said. He wet his bottom lip. 'I know I can't be the only one with the idea of a bent cop still lurking in the back of my mind. Until now, I've been considering him or her as someone on Douglas Vincent's payroll. But what if they're not? What if somebody on the Maguires' side has or had them in their pocket and it was they who gave up this Wrigley lad's name before Jack Maguire's involvement could be uncovered?'

Bliss made no reply. He couldn't fault the logic, but it was a terrible thought. 'There are any number of trails we need to be following on this,' he said. 'We have to put our heads together to select actions in order of priority. But I also think we'd do well to find out if there is a bent officer working for either family, and if so, set about identifying them. And quickly. After all, this was HQs' case, and they'll be expecting regular updates. We can't afford to give them what we have so far if there's a chance that one of them might be feeding it all back to a Maguire or a Vincent.'

'And how do you intend to go about that?' Corry asked.

'I still have contacts over at Hinchingbrooke. Working as we do, people either know who the wrong'uns amongst us are, or at the very least, they suspect them of something. Rumours are always circulating, and I can find out if any of the original team have ever been mentioned.'

'It needn't necessarily be one of the HQ Major Crime team,' Greenhill reminded him. 'I mean, look at the active cases you run, Jimmy. There are always detectives roped in from other nicks, plus uniforms, civilians, not to forget those attached to the case in other ways, such as CSI, pathology, and intelligence.'

'That's a good point,' Bliss said. 'And of course you're right. But that's too broad for us to grapple with at this stage. I'll start with the Hinchingbrooke MCU, then expand if I get nowhere with them.'

'So, what do you want the rest of us to focus on?' Foley asked.

'It's open for discussion.'

'Are we approaching the Vincent family with this? At a minimum we ought to inform them that we are reinvestigating Daisy's murder.'

Bliss rubbed the small scar on his forehead. He felt heat upon his chest, and the tinnitus in both ears changed in both volume and frequency. Foley was correct, but sometimes following procedure was the wrong move. Turning your back on it was stressful, but at times necessary.

'Let's put a hold on that,' he said. 'You're absolutely right, Guy. It is what we should be doing. But I think it's too early. We need to form an overall strategy and acquire more information before we inform them of anything. The one thing we can't forget is the very real possibility that one or more of the Vincent family murdered and then disposed of Stephen Wrigley in retribution for Daisy's murder. If we eventually prove something against Jack Maguire, then all hell will let loose from the moment the Vincents are made aware. That's more than enough reason not to want to go to them half-cocked.'

'We need to tear that original investigation apart,' Beth Greenhill said. 'As you suggested, Jimmy, we can do so with the aim of pulling threads together that could tie up Maguire as a suspect. If not for the murder itself, then his supposed involvement. Nailing him for something might prompt him to tell us everything he knows. If that fails, we can go at it another way. But that's where it all began, so it's where we ought to begin, too.'

Nodding, Bliss said, 'Good. I'm going to contact a source to pull whatever they have on the story, and then later on I'll have a chat with an old friend. Before I do that, I want a list of everybody who took part in that original investigation. I need to step out of the office for a few minutes, so if one of you could print it off for me, I'd be grateful.'

'I can just send it to your phone, Jimmy,' Corry said, settling down at his laptop.

'Yeah, you do that. But print it off for me as well, please.'

'You're so analogue.'

'Tell me something I don't know.'

Out in the corridor, Bliss made two phone calls. The first was to Sandra Bannister at the *Peterborough Telegraph*. He fed her a couple of tips ahead of the evening's media briefing, asking her to reinforce how seriously the police took every attack on one of their own in addition to their determination to hunt down the wicked killer of an elderly woman. In return, he asked for anything held on file in reference to the Daisy Vincent murder. Being only a decade ago, it would have featured on the newspaper's website, but as usual he preferred to go directly to the source.

His second call failed to materialise in a conversation, as it was eventually diverted to voicemail. He left a message inviting his contact for a drink later that evening, choosing the Talbot Hotel bar in Oundle as a venue he thought would be far enough off the beaten track to afford them some privacy. He suggested eight o'clock and requested either a call or text to confirm.

For a minute or two he stood with the phone resting against his forehead. Other than the team's first cold case reinvestigation, the others had been fairly tame and relatively easy to navigate. This one had not even been on their radar, but as he thought about what they had he could imagine all manner of stark possibilities. If Jack Maguire was responsible for or even remotely connected to the death of Daisy Vincent, Bliss saw no way it would end with that one man's arrest and subsequent conviction. Douglas Vincent would not be satisfied with his imprisonment. Moreover, if a colleague had thrown the murder victim's boyfriend to the wolves, Bliss didn't want to be the one to toss that particular hand grenade into the mix.

Yet even then, he somehow knew he wouldn't be able to avoid it.

SEVENTEEN

Bliss concluded that his three cold case colleagues could pick apart the original murder investigation between them, and as he wouldn't be speaking to his HQ contact until much later in the day he decided to wander around to the other side of the building, donning his SIO hat as he went.

Everyone in the major inquiry room was hard at it, so he bided his time by reading the updates and crime log and completing elements of his policy book. Chandler eventually wandered over to inform him that the postmortem report was in. It confirmed the cause of death as heart failure due to a punctured lung. The implement used to inflict the wound was described as long and thin, possibly an ice pick or screwdriver. The pair were discussing the results when DC Virgil, clutching a folder in both hands, crossed the floor to join them.

'I've got something,' he told them. 'And I think it's good.'

Bliss nodded at the folder. 'You going to leave that here, or do you want to tell us?'

'I'll tell you if that's all right, boss.'

'Of course. Crack on, Alan.'

'Thanks. As you know, I've been communicating with other area forces, and I've got a couple of genuine possibilities. It's not so much the scams themselves because there are plenty of scrotes out there pulling these kinds of lowlife stunts. It's more the victim statements that attracted my attention. Those I have in my hand mention two things Mrs Musgrove also raised when she made hers.'

'That sounds interesting,' Chandler said. 'Go on then, spill.'

'Okay, so all three talk about their initial conversations with the builders. The story each of them were given was that these so-called roofers had finished a job early and were looking to do people a favour while earning themselves some pocket money before returning home. First off, they say they can do the job on the cheap provided they get paid in cash as soon as they're done that same day. They then make sure the homeowners can lay their hands on the money or are able to get to the bank, even offering to drive them if necessary. To shore up the deal, they guarantee they will winter-proof the roof for the time being at a much better price and will return to do a proper job at a heavy discount on the entire roof come the spring.'

'Did they provide figures at that point?' Bliss asked.

Nodding, Virgil said, 'They quote three. First, they insist that any other company would charge twelve grand just to winter-proof. Then they tell the homeowner they'd normally charge eight to do the exact same job, but because they were in a hurry and had a surplus of supplies and were looking to help out, they'd knock it down to five thousand.'

'The identical spiel in all three cases?'

'Yep.'

'The cunning bastards.' That could not be a coincidence. Certainly not one Bliss was willing to countenance. These scam artists always went in with a plan, making initial offers and then appearing to undercut themselves if the homeowner hesitated. They made it sound like the deal of the century, and imperative if the roof wasn't to deteriorate rapidly in the teeth of the winter weather. But the prices and offers made in these specific instances were too exact not to have come from the same team.

'Any improved evidence or descriptions from these other victims?' Bliss asked. 'Van plate number, maybe?'

'Sadly not. Descriptions are unspecific due to the winter clothing the men wore, which covered much of their faces. General physical presence only for all three, all matching what we saw for ourselves on Gul's dashcam footage. And not only did we not get a plate, but the gang also used different vans in both these other cases. A Ford Transit in one, and a Toyota Proace in the other. I've put out an alert to be notified about any relevant vehicle thefts shortly before the dates these other frauds took place. From what I can tell, this little crew doesn't hold on to any vehicle for longer than a week or two.'

'Good work, Alan. The thefts might give us something even if their victims can't.'

The conversation came to a sudden halt when a shrill cry came from DS Bishop. 'Got you! Got you, you bastard!'

'You finally catch one of those crabs you were complaining about, Bish?' Bliss asked as he looked up, chuckling at his colleague's raw excitement.

'Of a sort,' Bishop said, his face triumphant. 'All praise the mighty security camera. A house opposite the Mercedes dealership has two. One trained on the path leading up to the door, the other raised slightly higher. It captured the Sprinter exiting onto the road, with a perfect still of the driver's face in an unguarded moment. I just checked it against our known faces and got a hit.' He turned his laptop so that the screen faced his colleagues. 'Meet Bartek Danek.'

'What's that, a Czech name?' Chandler asked.

'Nope. Polish.'

'Great stuff,' Bliss said, unable to conceal his excitement at this fresh development. 'Okay. Bish, check out his record if he has one. Pen, you dive into his complete background history. Alan and Vas, I want his known associates.'

The team slipped into overdrive. Bishop needed all the strength in his broad shoulders to withstand the onslaught of congratulatory slaps he received. Like a grizzly fending off a pack of delinquent poodles, he beamed with pride and keen anticipation before getting back to the job in hand.

Meanwhile, Bliss mentally summarised the importance of DS Bishop's discovery. Until this point, the crew had been adept in covering their tracks; either that or they'd just ridden out a lucky streak. But capturing the image of the thief, identifying him so rapidly afterwards, was a massive break. Putting names and faces to his known associates might well be the icing on the cake, because Bliss was willing to place a significant wager on one or two of them being his accomplices in the frauds and thefts. He felt the juices flowing more easily, heightened by squirts of adrenaline. Every case had its crucial moments, and he knew this was one of them.

Bishop's PNC database search was by far the easiest, and it was no surprise when he came up with the goods first. 'Danek does have a record,' he said. 'He's got a couple of arrests for public disorder, and three… no, wait, four thefts of vehicles. One aggravated. No time served.'

'Typical,' Bliss muttered. 'Fucking miscreant. How many more offences before they bang him up? Oh, wait, we can't because there's no bloody space. Okay, so he has form for the offence we'll be charging him with. We can use his lack of prison time against him if need be by painting an ugly picture of his future behind bars.'

Chandler swivelled in her chair, eyes twinkling. 'Danek is twenty-nine. Polish national, came here with his family when he was just eight. He remained here when his parents returned home a few years ago. No employment record, but he does have an active bank account. UK driving licence. EU passport. No vehicle registered in his name. He's on and off the grid, with all the expected hallmarks of someone living off the black economy.'

'No surprises there,' Bliss said. 'My guess is this bunch promote themselves as genuine builders and roofers, only they're of the cowboy variety. Which means they do some valid work, cash in hand or using fake documentation and temporary bank accounts, but then add these scams into the mix for an easy injection of cash to top up their earnings.'

'You sound furious about that, Jimmy.'

'I am. And it's not about the black economy stuff, either. I mean, who hasn't paid a plumber or electrician with cash? I simply can't abide these arseholes who go around ripping off the old and the vulnerable. Some poor sods lose their life savings to these bastards, and if we can nail just one crew and get them off the streets it's a start. And that doesn't take into account the assault and murder charges.'

DCs Virgil and Kolesnyk came across the room, the former clutching a sheet of paper warm from the printer. 'We have good news and even better news,' Virgil said. 'We've identified six of the closest known associates. Danek himself lives on a mobile home and caravan park along White Post Road in Newborough, just north of the Dogsthorpe Star Pit nature reserve. And it just so happens that three of the KAs live at the same address.'

Bliss broke out into a wide, beaming smile. 'Well done, you two. Names?'

'Peter Holland, Matt Dories, and Patrick Walsh.'

'That has to be them, doesn't it? Mobile home and caravan park, you say. Is it a Pikey camp?'

DC Virgil shuffled in place, visibly anxious. He swallowed and lowered his chin. 'Um, I don't think we're allowed to use that term anymore, boss.'

'I can,' Bliss said defiantly. 'I'm one of them. In my blood, at least. My mother's family can be traced back to Spanish gypsies. I reckon that gives me the right to still call my people Pikeys.'

'Don't get Jimmy started,' Bishop advised DC Virgil. 'You'll bring out the caveman in him.'

'Sod that,' Bliss said with a snarl. 'I'm all for reining in the truly offensive terms, you know that, Bish. But we play around with the language so much I don't think anyone knows what not to say these days.'

'To be fair, you do know not to call them Pikeys,' Chandler argued. 'So why not just go along to get along?'

He turned square on to the acting DI. 'How long have we known each other, Pen? Over twenty years, right? Tell me when I've ever been a "go along to get along" sort of bloke.'

'But you've mellowed, haven't you? You've become a man for today and tomorrow, not a man of yesterday.'

'Have I bollocks! Take me or leave me as I am, that's me.' He turned back to DC Virgil. 'Anyway, am I right or not? Is it a Pi… traveller site?'

'Hard to say. I think it could be, but there's not a great deal of information about it, other than it's known as the White Post Site. It is residential, and it's protected. All above board, apparently.'

'Okay. Look, no offence intended but when you're pulling up on a place mob-handed to scoop up three or four blokes, there's a shit-ton of difference between doing so at a mobile home park for retirees, a mobile home park for those who can't afford more, and a mobile home park for the… travellers. There just is, and we can't afford to ignore that. The fact is we'd get three completely different kinds of response, and we have to prepare accordingly for the one we'd step into. All right?'

'Of course, boss. I understand.'

'Vas?' Bliss said, looking at their latest recruit.

'Sure.'

'Good. Then gather around, troops. That's if it's still acceptable to call you that. We need to put our heads together to come up with a plan of attack. Pen and I will shoot over to see Gul at home and show her the photos of these four men, see if any dislodge a memory or two. But even without her identifying them, we need a strategy to take down all four. I realise we're looking for a team of three, but as we don't know which of them are involved, we'll nick all four and sort it all out in the interview room.'

'Are you sure you don't want to take a breath, Jimmy?' Bishop said. 'Perhaps put surveillance on them and catch them at it.'

Bliss raised a finger. 'That's precisely why we need to discuss it at length. We have to consider all the options available to us. Do we take them on the road? On the job? Or early doors while they're tucked up in their caravans? Risk and reward versus health and safety.'

Chandler groaned. 'I bet I can guess which wins that fight.'

'Not if we don't run it past higher ranks.'

'Are you kidding? Please tell me you are.'

'No, I'm not. I'm SIO. I get to make the decisions.'

'Yes, you're SIO, Jimmy. Not God. Are you seriously not even going to run it by your deputy SIO first?'

'Diane will sit on the fence and run it up the chain of command.'

'You mean she'll do her job?'

'Yes, in part. But if it goes right to the top one of them will wet themselves when they hear about a traveller site. They'll find a way to put the kybosh on it, delay us, pull surveillance off, and end up kicking us in the balls.'

'You really think they want to make our jobs all the harder, don't you?'

Bliss shook his head. 'I thought that was one thing we could all agree on. Look, we'll leave our esteemed colleagues to weigh up the pros and cons of each option while we visit Gul. Anyone know if she likes fruit other than bananas?'

'She likes fruit pastilles,' Virgil said.

'Cheers,' Bliss said. 'You're a great help.'

He jerked his head towards the door. 'Come along acting DI Chandler. I don't want you swayed by these politically correct snowflakes in my absence. We've got a job of work to do, not a job of woke, so let's be getting on with it.'

Chandler must have caught his grin. 'You're such a bloody wind-up merchant with all that anti-woke stuff,' she said, shaking her head at him as they strolled along the corridor.

His grin widened. 'Pen, the world has started to take itself far too seriously. There are coppers coming up these days who'd consider reporting some of the banter that goes on inside that major inquiry room. Especially the shit you and I throw at each other.'

'And like a toddler that spurs you on to do it all the more.'

'And why not?' Bliss said. 'I can always blame my age. What's your excuse?'

EIGHTEEN

Detective Constable Gul Ansari's neat and comfortable two-storey cottage, garlanded with ivy and wisteria climbers, stood to the north-west of Crowland close to the River Welland. Having been born and raised in a community living cheek to jowl with family, friends, and ubiquitous neighbours, she had long expressed a desire to move somewhere more isolated. In Common Drove, Ansari had found the kind of peace and seclusion she had craved. The journey was a familiar one for Bliss and Chandler, given their friend and colleague lived less than a mile from their crime scene.

Ansari welcomed them with tea and cake, revealing she had already received unexpected visits from other members of the team since leaving hospital. 'I feel like such a fraud,' she told them as they sat in the quarry-tiled kitchen-diner. 'Here I am with my feet up watching daytime telly feeling absolutely fine, while you lot are traipsing around doing your jobs. I should be out there as well.'

Bliss wasn't having any of it. He explained to her again why rest was necessary, and that the after-effects might yet kick in. He knew Ansari wasn't happy about the situation she found herself in, but he was confident she would return to work sharper than ever. It took hardly any time at all for her to scour the photos of the four men, but it came as no surprise when she shook her head and admitted she recognised none of them. She did linger momentarily to tap on the image of Patrick Walsh, suggesting that his eyes looked right for the largest of the three men who had challenged her. Other than that, she couldn't say. Bliss noticed his colleague's use of language, perhaps deliberately shying away from employing the term 'assaulted' or 'attacked'. He wondered what that said about her current state of mind and when he and Chandler left Ansari alone, he carried away more concern than he'd brought with him.

Back at Thorpe Wood, the team struggled to find agreement over how to proceed. An informal risk assessment convinced them all that arresting the men in their homes was by far the most dangerous approach. However, that was their only common ground. DC Kolesnyk was the first to point out that the addresses they had for the four men referred to the site itself, not which specific mobile homes or caravans each of them resided in. Riding in at dawn on an early morning raid was unlikely to be greeted with wide approval by the residents, which further queered the pitch. Not knowing the precise location of their targets, together with an expected hostile reception made that option the riskiest one available to them.

'I'm in favour of taking them at work,' Virgil stated. 'We can set up on them in the early hours, wait for them to leave, follow, monitor, and assess, then take them as soon as cash changes hands.'

DS Bishop shook his head. 'While that may be better than going for them at the caravan park it's still far too risky for my liking. We do it like that and we're putting the fraud victim in harm's way. I say we get traffic involved and stop them on the road immediately once they've left the scene.'

'Surely that's an even greater risk,' Chandler chipped in. 'Granted, at the scene you also put the new victim in play, but out on the open road who knows how many innocent civilians might be driving along at the same time as we take this crew down? In a volatile situation like that, anything could go wrong.'

'We can nullify that risk,' Bliss said, siding with Bishop. 'We'll have eyeball at all times, and plenty of planning time. We can isolate the area by shutting down the roads around the scene, leaving just our own traffic vehicles inside the perimeter. Then as soon as the van hits the road, we strike.'

It felt like the more obvious move of those discussed, but the more they picked it apart the more frayed at the edges it became. Bliss analysed their options once more, only this time without regarding the element of risk. 'There is an additional benefit in waiting for them to leave the scene of their next crime,' he said. 'Arresting them in their homes means we have to rely on earlier crimes in terms of evidence. Even taking them at the scene leaves a door open to them legally, as they could always claim a misunderstanding and that they'd intended to hand some of the money back or to complete the job more fully.'

'Surely they could do that even after they've driven off,' Chandler observed.

'Yes, they could. But it won't come across nearly as well because by then they would have actually driven away from the property with the cash in their pockets. I do think it carries the least risk while affording us the greater amount of time to formulate a plan based on their location at the time.'

'Just one thing more is bothering me,' Kolesnyk said, following DC Virgil's habit by raising a hand. He didn't wait for the go-ahead to continue. 'We can't possibly know on which particular day they will commit this fraud. We have to assume that sometimes they work normally, while on other days they don't work at all, and only occasionally pull off this kind of stunt. We have no way of knowing which is which ahead of time.'

Bliss sighed heavily, cupping his chin in one hand. He'd neglected to shave that morning, which was unusual for him, and the skin felt like sandpaper. 'You're absolutely right, Vas. For all we know, they've bunkered down and won't venture out at all in the foreseeable future. And it's not as if we have any way to obtain intelligence on that. Even if they do leave the site, as you quite rightly pointed out that doesn't necessarily mean they'll try it on. It could well be that even they don't know until they drive past a house with a scruffy enough roof to even attempt it. And there must also be times when the homeowner simply refuses to fall for their game. It could be many days of constant surveillance and use of resources before they make a move. If they make a move at all.'

'So how about a compromise?' Bishop said. 'We still take them on the road, only we do it soon after they leave their camp site. At least that way we won't have dozens of irate residents resisting our efforts. Unfortunately, neither will we catch them with cash on the hip having just pulled another stroke, but we do still have those previous victims to fall back on. And Gul, of course.'

'Will that be enough?' Bliss queried.

'Maybe it has to be,' Chandler said. 'Look, none of us want to hit the site, and even if we did, they still wouldn't have carried out a new scam and have the cash on them. Waiting until they do could present us with a surveillance nightmare, not to mention a whacking great hole in our budget. We have no idea how long we might have to sit on them before they pull the same con. Plus, how will we even be sure they are when we're only seeing it from a distance? Are we likely to know the difference between a legit job and a fraudulent one without actually being there to examine it up close?'

After another long exhalation, Bliss said, 'This is why we thrash it out as a team, people. Everyone here has a voice. There are pros and cons everywhere we look, and our job is to consider every potential nook and cranny. If we take into account being risk averse, budget, duration, and expediency, then the compromise of pulling them on their way to their next job is the one we need to consider strongly. Yes, we'll have to rely on evidence gathered from previous jobs and those we can obtain from offers they've perhaps had rejected. We can nose around the close neighbours of our victims to date. But if we set up on that camp site on the morning we choose to strike, we can have the take-down teams in place and ready to go.'

He asked DC Virgil to get the mobile home park up on Google Maps. When it appeared on screen, Chandler immediately recognised the general area. 'Hold on, didn't we have a surveillance gig close to here before?' she said, squinting at the image.

'Not us,' Bliss said. 'But a surveillance team working for us, yes. If I remember rightly, it began in Bretton and took the watchers to a meeting point at the top of White Post Road. I wondered why it sounded familiar. That was where they first encountered our Range Rover woman, Danielle Halford.'

Nods all round at the memory of the Op, other than from their new team member. Bliss stared at the screen and gestured towards it. 'We could have cars parked up on Turves Drain and on Green Road should the van head north, plus a couple south of the site between the park and the A47 roundabout. We'll also have spares waiting for the nod. Whichever way they go after leaving the site we can then create a pincer movement on them.'

'It doesn't look as if it'll be easy to eyeball that site,' Chandler pointed out. 'There's a wide stretch of woodland there right opposite, book-ended by two large properties. One looks residential, the other commercial. That might be useful. We could stick a team inside a van and drive into the yard leading to the commercial property. Arrange it with the owners beforehand. The team can then use the cover of the woods.'

'Hmm, I'm not sure about that,' Virgil said. 'That Google Map image was taken with those woodland trees in full bloom by the look of it. Those same trees may now be without leaves, so how much cover will they afford?'

'Good point,' Bliss said. He licked his lips. 'Okay. This chat has been useful, but as SIO I have to make some decisions. The first of which is, I'm going with the compromise plan. We can't hang around until they pull another job. For all we know, they're lying low and won't try again for months. We can't take that risk. Second, I want two of you to take a run out there right now. Visit that commercial property, have words with the owner, obtain permission to use them as a decoy. Also, I need current photos of that wooded area, and I want your impressions of cover and whether we can put a surveillance team in there as planned. I don't care who goes, just get it done. I'll speak to surveillance and traffic myself, see how quickly we can get them on the plot.'

'Why, when do you intend to do this?' Bishop asked.

Bliss spread his hands. 'Tomorrow morning, if it's not too soon. Wednesday at the latest.'

The confidence he displayed was feigned. He didn't want to admit that his own words had spooked him. He'd suggested that the crew might be lying low, but his real fear was that by now they might be doing so at the other end of the country.

NINETEEN

The oil drum, tiny holes drilled at the bottom and standing on breeze blocks to create air flow, made an excellent brazier. The four sat on folding camping chairs, warming their hands around the burn barrel, feeding its hunger every so often with scraps of wood. Each new addition created fresh tongues of flame, looking first to envelop and then devour. Throughout the site, different music systems played different types of music at different volumes, creating a discordant backbeat alongside the screams of children playing and the cackling laughter and loud chatter of adult residents.

'The fuck's wrong with you?' Paddy the Greek said to Scuzzy Pete, crumpling the beer can he had just emptied and tossing it into the drum with a fierce clatter and a hiss of sparks. His tone suggested a challenge rather than a genuine concern.

'Nothing,' Pete replied sourly, his features lost inside the hood of his sweatshirt. 'I'm thinking is all.'

'You can do too much of that, you know.'

'Yeah, well, that's not something anyone will ever accuse you of, Paddy.'

The larger and older man, sitting to Scuzzy's left, raised his eyebrows as he drew his head back. Flickering shadows danced across his face. 'Ooh, get her. What's up with you, fuck face? You on the blob?'

Turning to face him down, Scuzzy said, 'Unlike you, I don't have the luxury of duncery. One of us has to consider what comes next, and we all know that's not going to be you.'

'What the fuck is "duncery" when it's at home?' Paddy protested.

'Precisely. Thanks for making my point for me. Listen, don't worry about it. When the shit finally hits the fan – and it will – I'll make sure you avoid the worst of the flying turds.'

'Don't you fucking worry about me, Scuzzy,' Paddy said, an edge to his voice this time. 'I can take care of myself.' He hadn't shifted at all in his seat, but somehow his form took on a more menacing presence.

Pete scoffed. 'Oh, I know that. You really proved yourself the hard man. Problem is that the next person you come up against might not be a frail old woman as fragile as a wet paper bag. And you might not have a screwdriver to hand, either.'

Yanking on a ring-pull to pop open another can of lager, Paddy took two long swallows before responding. 'Anytime you feel like trying it on, Scuzzy, you go ahead and do it instead of mouthing off. But you better make sure you put me down and out, because if you don't, I'll fecking tear you apart you little gobshite!'

'Woah, woah, woah,' Doris said, rising to his feet and walking around to their side of the roaring fire. 'Let's not fall out over this. Scuzzy, mate, what's done is done and Paddy couldn't undo it even if he wanted to. Paddy, it's just talk for now, so why not let it stay that way?'

Matt Dories had always been the best of them at peace-making. Not that he couldn't or wouldn't resort to violence when necessary, but it took a lot to push him over the edge. He preferred to ride out the disagreements, seeking conciliation wherever possible. Scuzzy nodded in mute agreement but turned his head away, staring out into the night, his gaze tracking wraiths of smoke unfurling into the overcast sky until they disappeared from view altogether.

He was aware that Paddy and Doris thought of him as the odd one out, expendable if push came to shove. Doris was a decent enough mate, but if it all kicked off, his loyalty would probably draw him over to Paddy's side. Which was fair enough. As for Bartek, he lived even further out on the edge, like a pilot fish swimming in and out of a shark's mouth to consume scraps of food caught between its razor-like teeth. He had his uses when it came to providing them with fresh transport, but wasn't anywhere close to becoming a full member of the crew. Generally, he kept his trap shut and let the other three get on with it. Which was just how Scuzzy Pete liked it.

Come the day of the rebellion, Scuzzy thought idly as he stared into the gathering gloom, he'd allow Bartek to walk away. As for Doris, his fate depended on how close he remained to Paddy. And whether he attempted to interfere.

But today was not that day.

Paddy and Doris might revel while oblivious to their predicament, but Scuzzy had more than a flimsy grasp on reality. Their ploy of defrauding the elderly or just plain stupid out of money was one thing, but extending that to murder and the assault of a police officer was quite another. One level of behaviour got you noticed, the other got you nicked. His two so-called pals considered themselves immune here in this place, impervious to harm. They were wrong. But for all Paddy's barbed remarks about him 'thinking too much' he had at least come up with a plan. The others would take some convincing, but once they knew what it was, they might just react accordingly when the time came.

And Scuzzy didn't think they'd have to wait too long.

TWENTY

WALKING MAX WAS SUPPOSED to be not only valuable exercise and enjoyment for the dog but also cathartic for Bliss as well. Wrapped up snug against the bitter chill, a dense mist creeping along beside him like a feathery shadow, this evening he was unable to shake off the investigations. Operation Monument was all set to take the next step. The surveillance team and traffic were putting a plan together based on the information Bliss had laid out for them in detail. They approved of his suggestions and were busy nailing down the various component parts to leave the fewest possible escape routes.

Detective Constables Alan Virgil and Vasyl Kolesnyk had driven out to Newborough to scout the location. The commercial site opposite the camp manufactured agricultural feed. To the front of the huge property stood a relatively new-build house, which is where they encountered the business owners, Mr and Mrs Abbott. But, as they reported back later, both officers felt unwelcome, the couple expressing open hostility against the police. DC Virgil took the decision not to mention the mobile home park, instead enquiring after stolen farming equipment and asking them to report any suspicious activity.

'I got the impression they might have sided with our suspects,' he told the team upon their return. 'I came up with an off-the-cuff lie, and their less than enthusiastic response told me I was right to pull the plug on our plans. However, when we decided to contact the homeowners on the other side of the woodland, they couldn't have been more helpful. They definitely aren't fans of the travellers, and as luck would have it their sheltered driveway is perfect for our needs. Also, lining the road between the two properties you've got boxwood evergreens, which provide great cover.'

Returning to the overhead view on GoogleMaps reminded the team of how difficult a proposition it was for a surveillance op. The site itself was split into three separate blocks, each with its own entrance. With an estimated thirty properties in total, chances were that people were going to be coming and going regularly throughout the day. That meant all police vehicles would require adequate cover to shelter behind, which was no easy task. The other obvious turd in the punchbowl was the very real possibility that the suspects might not leave the site at all – if they were even there to begin with.

This observation provoked further discussion and deliberation, with Bliss finally calling a halt and telling everyone to go home. 'Let's leave the experts to find solutions,' he said. 'Between them, traffic and surveillance will find a way to make this work. I'll speak to them again before I leave and feed in our input. I say we give ourselves a day, then regroup and assess if there's no sign. Either way, we'll have eyes on pre-dawn, and our watchers will have access to the same photo array we have up on the boards. They'll assign a Tango number to each name. If they spot our suspects inside the park, they'll inform us. The main thing is they'll be on the plot for every vehicle leaving that site. When they know, we'll know, and traffic will move in. Now, for obvious reasons, we're not going to be able to shut down the surrounding roads, so be vigilant and wary of other road users. I realise the A47 is close to the camp, but we can't risk them reaching that junction. Understood?'

He'd seen trepidation written across every face, but also the fierce determination he knew burned inside each officer. These men had not only assaulted a colleague, they were also responsible for murdering an innocent elderly woman. They had to be stopped at all costs.

Prior to leaving the office he'd called Sandra Bannister, who had not forgotten his request and promised to ping him across everything the *Telegraph* had on the original murder investigation. 'You look through it?' he asked, knowing she would have.

'Of course. Being inquisitive is in my job description.'

'And?'

'I remember it well. I hadn't been at the paper for long, and I didn't get to write it up. But I was part of the wider team who worked on it.'

'Summarise what you have for me,' he said. 'I'll read everything you mail across, but give me the gist.'

'Okay. Off the record now and also at the time internally, the boyfriend, Stephen Wrigley, did it and the Vincents caught up with him before he could get away and they murdered him for it. On the record, Wrigley did it and probably made his way out of the country in fear for his life.'

Bliss thought about that conversation as he and Max walked briskly around the fringes of the public golf course, skirting Orton Water, past the yacht club and along the path running beside the river towards the weir. The dog recognised the dock at which Bliss had his boat berthed and seemed inclined to linger, but Bliss called him on as he'd arranged to meet Beth Greenhill by Osier Lake at Orton Mere. She was waiting for him when they arrived and met with cautious approval by Max after some initial coaxing. Although initially wary of others, the animal enjoyed it when people made a fuss of him, and soon his tail was snapping sideways like a metronome dialled all the way up to eleven.

'How did things go this afternoon?' he asked, conscious that Greenhill had already taken time out of her evening to discuss the case with him and not wanting to delay her further with idle chit-chat.

'We pulled the original investigation inside out, but the name of Jack Maguire never came up. As anticipated, the team considered Daisy Vincent's boyfriend their prime suspect, and him disappearing off the face of the planet convinced them of his guilt. I have to say they never really looked elsewhere after that. If they did, it was cursory at best. I know the SIO told us otherwise, but I think he was probably covering his arse.'

'You have a thing about arses,' Bliss observed with a smile.

'As do you with testicles, or so I hear.' Her expression matched his own.

He laughed, guessing she had spoken with Chandler, and said, 'I'm admitting nothing. Anyhow, you're saying that beyond Wrigley, the SIO had no plan B?'

'No. Looking at what they had I can see why they focussed on him, but it's hard to justify them not exploring alternatives. For me, it was an investigation lacking genuine motivation.'

'Even though a young girl was raped and strangled to death.'

'It seems that way. And I have to say, that's almost certainly due to her family connection.'

Bliss thought about the implications. It was never easy telling a team their work had been less than exemplary, but everything pointed in that direction. Nobody from HQ was going to like having the Unsolved Cases Team trampling all over their work second-guessing with the benefit of hindsight, but that's precisely what was about to happen.

'Okay,' he said. 'Clearly, they had no reason to suspect Jack Maguire's involvement, but we do. With that in mind, can you see how he might be a good fit?'

Greenhill, crouching next to Max and ruffling the dog's chest and neck, looked up at Bliss and shook her head. 'Impossible to tell. We're not seeing a history between him and Daisy. But then again, if you look at her movements the night she died and where she was found, it could literally have been anyone who happened to be in the same area that night. Perhaps a complete stranger.'

'No forensic ties?'

'Nothing at all. They didn't get a great deal from the scene, and what they did get by way of fibres and hairs led back to the boyfriend.'

'Except for the condom,' Bliss was quick to point out.

'Yes. There is that. Well, the traces of lubricant from the condom.'

'That leaves us with one clear objective,' Bliss said eventually. 'We've done our due diligence by assessing the original investigation, but now we start a fresh one. We have a named suspect, and whatever we think about the source, we can't ignore that. How about our list of questions? Any further answers?'

'Yes. Maguire was not in prison when Daisy was murdered. From what we can gather, having pulled various records together he wasn't living outside the country and nor do we have any evidence to suggest he was living anywhere but at home at the time. His parents' home, that is. In Thorney. We found nothing to suggest Jack Maguire and Daisy Vincent were in the same orbit, albeit they lived at opposite ends of the village. It's unlikely they weren't aware of each other, and for all we know they may have passed like ships in the night, but there's nothing to link the two.'

'And nothing on whether Maguire spoke about his involvement with anyone else, I'm assuming.'

'Not a thing.'

Bliss had heard enough. 'We're going to have to pull him in. Voluntarily, if possible, but under caution. Get hold of his licence supervisor, obtain current contact details. Ask him to have a word with Maguire first, convince him to come in for an interview.'

'And if he won't comply?'

'We make sure we pay him a visit with a couple of uniforms in tow. If he refuses to cooperate, then they make the arrest. No way round it. If this had just happened, then I wouldn't be going near him with a barge pole before I'd gathered evidence. But we're talking ten years ago. We've no witnesses, no forensics, no CCTV, and no phone data. In short, nothing to suggest Jack Maguire was anywhere near the crime scene when Daisy was murdered.'

'Except for a confession he made willingly to one person.'

'Precisely. At this point, I see no alternative but to interview him. If only to get his statement on record, which in itself might give us more to work with because he'll have to provide an alibi.'

'Or stick to making no comment.'

'There's always that.' Bliss raised a tight fist. 'Thank you, PACE.'

Greenhill chuckled. 'Tell me, Jimmy, what kind of copper were you before PACE came along?'

'How fucking old do you think I am?' he said with an easy grin. 'I only had two years in when PACE was introduced. Time enough to learn bad habits, I suppose. And I won't insult your intelligence by insisting that we were reluctant to dish out the odd clip around the lughole when it was warranted. But we knew things were about to change and the behaviour towards suspects and villains had already started to soften. As for my older and more experienced colleagues, some of them were all for the regulatory changes, while others rued the fact that their methods were even being questioned, let alone outlawed.'

'So, no beatings with telephone books or fit-ups?'

'Me?' Bliss tapped his chest. 'No. Neither. Fit-ups I would never have approved of. Nor beatings. I can't deny I've been guilty of poor behaviour when losing my temper. But the only people I've ever really laid into, ironically enough, were a couple of coppers and one thug who came at me with a baseball bat. There was an old uniform who gave Pen a hard time, so me and him had a physical disagreement. Then there was a bent copper whose nose got in the way of my forehead one day in an interview room after our old DS, Mia Short, was killed. As for the nasty piece of work throwing a bat around, he eventually got clobbered by that very same weapon. Not by me, I hasten to add. But for all that, Beth, I'm no Gene Hunt.'

'I never imagined you were.'

He met her eyes. Nodded. 'Yes, you did.'

'Okay, maybe I did. Just a little bit. Not the full-on thuggery, but perhaps the idea of obtaining a result no matter what.'

'I admit I bend rules. Always have. But I work hard not to break them.'

'And when you do?'

A memory reached out to him. 'Then I own up and take what's coming to me. I was demoted a few years back, and that hurt. I deserved it, so no complaints. Wounded pride and all that guff, but I did something I shouldn't have done.'

'Care to elaborate on that?' Greenhill asked him.

'For you... Okay, so I tapped the phones used by a fellow cop without the authority to do so. What I caught on the recording proved he was a wrong'un – not that we could use it as evidence against him, naturally. But it did the trick. Olly Bishop was going for DI at the time, and we actually worked a few cases with him as my boss. That was an experience.'

'You miss it, don't you?' Greenhill said softly. 'Being on the Job, I mean.'

Bliss nodded and said, 'I won't deny it. I occasionally feel lost without my warrant card. I carried it for forty years, so in many ways it became an appendage. But I'm slowly coming to terms with not having it to rely on.'

Too slowly for his liking, Bliss realised. But it would come. It was just a matter of time.

TWENTY-ONE

THE ELIZABETHAN ERA TALBOT Hotel, built from honey-coloured limestone and Collyweston slate, was reported to be haunted by the ghost of Mary Queen of Scots. The connection to the story originated from the hotel's oak staircase, which came from Fotheringhay Castle, the site of her execution. Bliss did not believe in ghosts, despite having spoken to his murdered wife on many occasions. Although the old building looked tired and jaded, he liked the character and antiquated charm of the place. He had dined in the restaurant on a number of occasions, though he was more familiar with its bar.

By the time he arrived, his former colleague from Hinchingbrooke had already claimed a spot in the far corner, and like a true copper sat with his back to the wall facing the entrance. Bliss went straight to the counter and bought two pints of Tribute Cornish pale ale, sliding one across the scarred wooden table as he took a seat.

'How's it going, Carrot?' he asked. 'You get rid of those piles yet?'

The sergeant who currently worked with the dog unit rolled his eyes. His name was Bob Davis, which was the real name of comedian Jasper Carrott. He'd earned the obvious nickname early in his career. Unfortunately for him, his haemorrhoids were also legendary, though he claimed not to have suffered from them in decades.

'For fuck's sake, Jimmy,' he complained. 'That was more than twenty years ago.'

'Yeah, but do you still need the old rubber doughnut to sit on?'

'Surprisingly, no. And I haven't done since the spring of 2003, thank you very much. Not that I even knew you in those days, I'd remind you. Tell me, why the hell did I agree to meet you tonight?'

Bliss laughed. 'Because there's a free drink on offer. That's more than enough of a bribe for you, isn't it?'

Davis looked doubtful, but pulled the pint glass closer to the one he was currently nursing.

'How's the enemy, Carrot?' Bliss continued, taking a pull on his own drink.

'The gorgeous Mrs Davis is well and happy, thank you.'

'Glad to hear it. And the saucepans?'

'My kids are great, too. Is that why you asked me here tonight, Jimmy? To practice your cockney rhyming slang while grilling me on my family.'

Hiking his shoulders, Bliss said, 'I'm genuinely interested, you suspicious old bell end. Fair enough, I did invite you out to discuss work, but you're a longtime friend so I also wanted to know how you were doing.'

Davis waved it off. 'Sorry, Jimmy. I'm a bit on edge because I don't know what you want from me, and I'm guessing it's nothing good. But yeah, everything's good at home, thanks. We're doing great.'

'And the dog unit?'

'I'm enjoying it. It suits my temperament, I suppose.'

'As it happens, I clocked you on a raid my team requested back in the summer. I didn't get a chance to catch up with you because it all got a bit lairy.'

'I remember it well. That bugger with the dreads.'

'That's the one. Bit of a handful at the time. I'm glad things are working out for you, pal.

'Cheers. And you?'

'You know me, Bob. Same old, same old. Anyway, you're right to be wary about why I've asked you here tonight. Let me begin by saying that if you don't want to talk, don't want to help, don't want to get involved, I'll walk away with no hard feelings.'

Davis finished his first drink and took a sip of his second. 'That doesn't sound good right off the bat. You used my real name for starters, which is a sure sign this is something serious. What are you about to get me webbed up in, Jimmy?'

'Nothing if you choose not to,' Bliss said in earnest. 'But I am looking for your help. Tell me, can you think of any of your colleagues working out of county HQ ten or eleven years ago who you thought might be as bent as a nine-bob note? I'm especially interested in anyone still in the job?'

Cocking his head to one side, Davis said, 'Blimey. You don't ask a lot, do you?'

'It's not ratting on them if they're dodgy, Carrot. You know that as well as I do.' Bliss kept his eyes on those of his old colleague. What he saw there convinced him he'd touched a nerve.

'All the same. I mean, if they're still in the job then any doubts will have been based on rumour and speculation, because if we had proof of wrongdoing, they'd most likely be banged up. Certainly, they'd be out on their ear. Plus, you'd already know about it because I'm sure you wouldn't have asked me here tonight if you hadn't checked the records first.'

Bliss nodded. 'You're spot on. We did look and we found nothing. If they exist, I'm thinking it must be somebody who was never sloppy enough to get caught, but who was nonetheless rumoured to be working both sides of the street.'

'Any particular connection you're looking for?'

'Maybe. They might have been taking their thirty pieces from a family out in Thorney by the name of Vincent.'

'And you suspect this why?'

His old colleague was being cagey. Bliss didn't mind. He'd expected nothing less. 'They had a daughter called Daisy. She was found murdered not far from the family home. Right from the start, the boyfriend was in the frame. Our frame, not theirs. But when the MCU from Hinchingbrooke went to scoop him up he was nowhere to be found. Evidently, the Vincents displayed no great surprise when his name cropped up afterwards. Reading between the lines it looks as if one of two things happened: either he scarpered and turned out to be some kind of genius because he's managed to avoid us ever since, or the family were told he was a suspect by one of ours and got to him before we could.'

Davis nodded and blew out a long blast of air. 'I got you. And you reckon this bent cop might still be in post?'

'Let me put it this way,' Bliss said. 'My source would like nothing more than to fuck with my head. With what he's given me, I'm not seeing a downside unless I'm about to face the kind of shitshow that comes with having to work around a dodgy copper. It also makes sense if we believe the girl's boyfriend is below ground somewhere. That the Vincent family were told about him by one of us.'

'Can you give me time to mull it over?'

'I don't need to, Carrot.'

'Why's that, then?'

'Because you already have someone in mind. I saw it broadcast all over your boat the moment I mentioned it.'

'Perhaps,' Davis admitted. 'But let me run this by you first. Do you know a sergeant by the name of Reece Wilson?'

Bliss shook his head. 'No. Tell me about him.'

'He would have been here ten years ago. There was talk about him, but the rumours became too specific. Professional Standards were called in, triggering a covert investigation. I don't know the precise details, but it could have included monitoring his phone, his police and home computer use, bugging his home, car, office, and probably surveillance. They might even have considered putting an undercover officer into his team, but there were no comings or goings during that period.'

'Okay. Did this Wilson have any known links to the Vincent family?'

'Not that we ever heard, no.'

'How about the Maguires? They're from Thorney, too.'

'No. And that's why I hesitated to tell you about him, because he was suspected of taking bribes and gear from a dealer in Cambridge. It's all PSD ever got him on, but it was enough.'

Bliss weighed up this fresh information before rejecting it. 'No. Doesn't sound right to me, Bob. I'm not just looking for a bent copper, I'm looking for one with specific ties to either of those two families. And if I didn't know better, I'd say you were holding out on me, mate. You have someone else in mind besides this Reece Wilson. I know you do.'

Shaking his head, Davis said, 'I don't know, Jimmy. It's pure speculation. No proof. None at all. And believe me, I'm not the only one to have had my doubts.'

Bliss drank from his glass, then nodded. 'I understand your reluctance. You don't want to point a finger because they're still a serving copper, right?'

'Exactly.'

'Except if you're right about them they almost certainly shouldn't be.'

'True. But what if I'm wrong?'

'If you're wrong, then they'll keep their job. But if they're bent, then they deserve what's coming their way. If they're not, I'll be happy to clear their name, which will make you rest a lot easier, I'm sure. But to do that, I first need to know what that name is.'

'Rachael Skinner,' Davis said with only the briefest of pauses.

Bliss was no poker player and couldn't keep the look of surprise from his face. 'DC Skinner?'

'DS now. Still with Major Crimes.'

'What's the story there, Bob? We certainly never heard about it over at Thorpe Wood.'

'Would anyone at county HQ know about it if you suspected one of your own team?'

Bliss made no reply.

'Exactly. She's been managed to a certain degree.'

'Not well enough if she made DS,' Bliss pointed out.

'She was already a DS when the rumour started,' Davis noted. 'The truth is only two of us know about it. One of her colleagues mentioned something to me in passing when we were out on a job with her unit. Nothing overly damaging, you understand. Not that we know of.'

'But you can't be certain.'

'No. No, we can't. That's why we haven't been to Professional Standards. As you can imagine, it's a touchy subject. Neither of us wants to throw mud and see it stick, particularly if we're wrong. It's not that we suspect her of any real wrongdoing, either. But it does look as if she's been dating a villain.'

'Do you know who?'

'Dougie Vincent.'

Bliss hissed through his teeth. 'I knew that name meant something to you when I mentioned it. So, Skinner might well have been his bit on the side.'

'Might still be for all we know, Jimmy. That doesn't mean she's bent, doesn't mean she's feeding him information or taking bribes. It's still wrong, of course, we just don't know how wrong. You might think we should have ostracised her, but as I keep telling you, we had nothing firm to take her down with. You know what it's like around any nick. Once a rumour starts and tongues start wagging, it doesn't take long before it's stated as a fact. We've contained that as far as I know.'

'As far as you know,' Bliss echoed. 'But what if you're wrong? The longer it goes without you notifying PSD or at the very least running it up the chain of command the worse it looks for you when you eventually do.'

'But the truth is, this speculation about her never really amounted to much. I wouldn't have mentioned her now if you hadn't brought up the Vincent family. Somebody spotted her having drinks with Dougie. They then got to thinking about how certain things had gone Dougie Vincent's way in the past, you know, dodged a pull by not having bent gear where we were told it would be. It felt like somebody was feeding him information, and so this colleague put two and two together. That said, we don't even know if she was seeing him that far back.'

'So, how are you keeping tabs on her? Please tell me you've not mounted your own covert surveillance.'

His friend cast his gaze downward. 'Off the books. In my own time. Her team member has stepped away from it just in case she fucks up. All we have for certain is that she's been seen in Dougie Vincent's company. Nothing more than that.'

'But only by this colleague of yours?'

'Yes.'

'How often?'

'Just the once.'

'But you've not seen them together?'

'No.'

'And this colleague didn't think it might amount to more?'

'The intel she gave me didn't really pan out. Look, Jimmy, if Skinner is knocking him off, then she's playing a risky game, but it genuinely doesn't feel as if there's more to it than that. And I don't want her good name tainted over a stupid mistake.'

Bliss nodded. 'Understood. For what it's worth, if somebody made the same allegation about a member of our MCU I'd be working it off the books in my own time, too. No quarrel there, Bob. But what if she does involve herself in more and you find out too late?'

'We're keeping our eyes and ears open. Until now, nothing involving the Vincent family has come the unit's way. They're relatively small time, remember? Major Crime is unlikely to cross paths with them.'

'It wouldn't have to be MCU. She's there, she's around, she could pick up all kinds of intelligence.'

'We honestly don't think that's what's happening. Believe me, we're doing everything we can to keep a lid on it, Jimmy.'

'All right,' Bliss said eventually. 'I'll get in another round, then you and me need to talk some more.'

'About?' Davis asked, apprehensively.

'About what I'm going to say to DS Skinner when I speak to her.'

'When you what?'

Bliss understood how his friend felt, but he laid his cards on the table all the same. 'I have no choice, Bob. I have a situation involving the Vincents, and I cannot afford to have anybody jeopardise that. One set of loose lips and we could have bodies littering the streets of Thorney. So, yes, I'm going to have a word. Without naming names, I'm going to let her know that her relationship with Dougie has been noticed. I'm also going to tell her precisely what will happen to her if word of my current operation reaches his ears.'

Davis put his head in his hands. 'I knew I'd regret coming here tonight. I bloody well knew it.'

Bliss stood and clapped him on the shoulder. 'Look on the bright side, Carrot. First, you're about to get another free pint. And second, my having a word with Rachael Skinner might be the best thing to happen for all concerned.'

'How d'you make that out?'

'Because if she's just having a fling and there's bugger all else to it, she'll back off once she knows someone is on to her. That'll settle your mind, and professional standards will never know what they missed out on. But if it goes the other way, at least you can sit back and let someone else take the blame.'

'You mean you.'

'Yeah. I mean me. If it all goes tits up, then this conversation never happened and we were never here. But don't worry, I'm still going to buy you that second pint.'

TWENTY-TWO

WHENEVER HE NEEDED TO deliberate and didn't fancy a drive, Jimmy Bliss liked nothing more than to stretch out on his recliner and sip a fine drink from a crystal tumbler. Tonight's choice of tipple was a fifteen-year-old Black River Casks Jamaican rum from the Appleton Estate. It had cost him the better part of seventy quid, but a couple of fingers accompanied by some smooth sounds from Steely Dan's Gaucho album was just the ticket.

And he had a great deal to think about.

Operation Monument was coming to the boil. He hoped to have Bartek Danek and his fellow fraudsters and thieves in custody sometime the following morning, but there were as many risks as there were permutations in taking the crew down. So much could go wrong, including a no-show, which would leave both surveillance and his own team back at square one.

As for the cold case, it threw problems at the investigators with every forward step they attempted to take. Keeping apart two warring families was going to be difficult enough when you were looking to prove that a member of one family might have murdered a member of the other family, or at the very least appeared to be involved in some way. But when you introduced the possibility that the family of the murdered girl might have taken revenge on the wrong man, and added the prospect of a bent copper relaying any or all relevant information to the father of the murder victim, you had all the ingredients of a nightmare coming to life in the shadows while you were fully awake.

When *Time Out of Mind* started playing, Bliss tried to make a blank canvas of his thoughts and instead focussed only on listening. Rick Marotta's drumming could not have been more in the pocket, while Randy Brecker's trumpet and David Sanborn's alto sax were a match made in heaven. Then there was the legendary session from Dire Straits's Mark Knopfler to consider. It wasn't that the guitar work he produced was anything remarkable, but the subsequent myth had it that while he played on about half the track, the mix had him audible for barely fifteen seconds.

Not that Bliss cared either way. He caught himself humming along to the bridge and the chorus and began to settle for the first time that night. Which was when he realised what he needed most of all. Not a nighttime drive. Not his fish, nor his music, and not even Max. This time, an exquisite drink wouldn't suffice, either. Instead, he picked up his phone and called Penny Chandler.

'What you up to?' he asked.

'Not a lot. But I did think I might hear from you tonight. What do you have in mind?'

He grinned. Chandler knew him better than he knew himself. 'A quick drink.'

'It's late, Jimmy. And we both have an early start in the morning.'

'That's why I suggested having a drink. I thought a nice alcoholic buzz right before bed might make a perfect cure for my unsettled mood.'

'And what if my own mood is perfectly settled, thank you very much?'

'This is not about you. I'm the SIO, the one having to make all the decisions. You're just going to follow my orders. Therefore, it's my mood that counts.'

'You're a cheeky bugger, Jimmy Bliss.'

'If I admit to that, will you just stop whining and say yes?'

'Hmm. I assume I have to come to you.'

'You assume right. I've got a couple of pints and some fine rum inside me, so no driving. I'll take a slow walk down to the Windmill. Meet me there when you can.'

Fifteen minutes later they found an empty table and Bliss bought them both a double brandy off the top shelf. 'What's keeping that declining brain of yours working overtime?' Chandler asked, looking as if she'd been preparing to call it a night before he phoned. Her hair was loose, she wore no makeup, and seemed to have pulled on the first clothes that came to hand. Bliss imagined her taking a sniff of her sweatshirt armpits first, but decided that might be taking matters too far.

He relayed his concerns as they had come to him earlier. In her customary way, she took it all in before giving a considered response. 'I agree that tomorrow morning could go a thousand different ways. Your call as SIO, but if it were me and surveillance spot our crew, but they remain on the site as the day drags on, I'd use the availability of officers to raid them on their home ground.'

'Provided the surveillance team is able to give us precise locations.'

'Ideally, yes.'

He nodded. 'I'm inclined to agree. I was against the idea earlier, but I think it might have to go that way depending on the circumstances at any given time. That gives us a plan A and a plan B for two scenarios: the gang's appearance outside the gates and their non-appearance outside the gates. But what if only one of them leaves? Or two?'

'I think that very much depends on which one or two. Remember, at present we have nothing on the others, only Bartek Danek. For me, that makes all the difference. I'd take him even if the others weren't with him. Bird in the hand, and all that.'

'We do that, and we run the risk of scaring off the others.'

'So, we keep surveillance in place until we've reassessed or have picked them off one by one.'

Bliss smiled and raised his glass in admiration. 'I told you you'd make a bloody good DI, didn't I? Future SIO as well before long.'

'You agree with me, then?'

'I do as it happens. Of course, if that's the way it goes down in the morning, I might make a series of completely different decisions. But sitting here in the toasty warmth with a drink in my hand and no danger of fucking things up by choosing the wrong course of action, I'm inclined to think the same way, yes.'

They clinked glasses. 'To tomorrow,' Chandler said. Bliss repeated the phrase.

'If anything,' she went on, 'from what you said it sounds to me as if your cold case is going to be the real thorn in your side. Do you really think Rachael Skinner is dodgy?'

'Do you know her?' Bliss replied without answering the question.

'A little. I mainly met her at meetings, though I did assist their MCU on one case, too. She struck me as a decent copper, I have to say.'

'Which is what I'm hoping she will be. For more than one reason.'

'How are you going to approach her? It's not a subject matter you can casually introduce.'

'I know. I thought I might use the cold case as an excuse, say I want to speak to her about it for the reinvestigation. If she wonders why her, I'll say she just happens to be the first name out of the hat.'

'And then what?'

'No point in dithering. What I won't do is mention any suspicion that she might have influenced the outcome of the original case by passing on information to Dougie Vincent. That was a decade ago and these suspicions about her are more recent. I thought I'd just tell her she was observed in his company. Perhaps even suggest I was approaching her on the QT in the hope of persuading her to dump him before their relationship became common knowledge.'

'You think she'll go for that?' Chandler asked.

'Would you?' Bliss replied quickly.

'Probably. But then, if I was seeing him, it would be purely personal. For all we know, she might actually be working for the family as well as being involved with him.'

'It's a risk I have to take. Unless you can think of a different way to tackle her.'

Chandler chewed on her bottom lip. 'Would my presence make her more or less likely to talk?' she asked. 'I'd be happy to do it. I just don't know if I'd be more of a hindrance.'

Bliss considered the suggestion. 'I think you being there might make her suspicious. If I'm using the cold case as my way in, then you being with me is bound to put her on her guard. No, I think I'm going to try it one-on-one and appeal to her sensible and reasonable side if I can.'

'If she's involved with a criminal, how sensible or reasonable can she be?'

Grimacing, Bliss said, 'I suppose there's only one way to find out.'

'That's all very well, Jimmy, but what if it blows up in your face? What if she's on the take and spills her guts to Dougie Vincent after you two speak?'

Bliss knew Chandler was right. But he had to know if Skinner was in Vincent's pocket before moving in on Jack Maguire and informing the Vincent family about the reinvestigation of Daisy's murder. Or did he?

'Here's a thought,' he said. 'What if I steer clear of Jack Maguire altogether when I speak to her. I needn't even tell her we have a suspect. I'll keep the focus fixed firmly on her relationship with Dougie coming up in the course of my investigation.'

Nodding, Chandler said, 'Provided she agrees to the interview without the need for a rep or to have it on record, that could work.'

'It's just a matter of being careful. I only need to mention the reinvestigation into Daisy Vincent's murder. I tell her that her name came up and we need to extricate her before word leaks out.'

'I can see how that could work. But it does depend on DS Skinner's reaction. She will eventually come to know the name of your suspect because you'll have no option but to inform the MCU at Hinchingbrooke. The key is how she responds when you tell her what you've learned.'

'Yes,' he agreed with a ready nod. 'There's a lot riding on Skinner's compliance. And now that I think about it, even if she's willing to back off, that in itself might cause us problems.'

'In what way?' Chandler queried.

'If she and Dougie see each other on a regular basis, her suddenly stopping their assignations is bound to make him suspicious.'

'Then you get her to break it off with him first. If she's genuinely not on the take and their whole relationship boils down to an adulterous fling, she'll see that she's being offered a chance to make up for her own stupidity.'

'That makes sense,' Bliss said. 'But I hate the fact that this whole approach relies on the whims of someone whose notion of right and wrong has already proven to be skewed.'

Chandler finished her drink and smacked her lips. 'That wasn't half bad,' she said, following up with a long-drawn-out sigh. 'This bloody job doesn't get any easier, does it? How on earth are you still doing this, Jimmy? For that matter, why? I know I've probably said this to you a dozen times before, but you could have gone ten years ago, yet you didn't. And then even after they hit you with compulsory retirement you still came back.'

Once again, Bliss didn't answer her question, but instead asked, 'You think you'll walk when you've done your thirty years?'

'Absolutely.' Firm. Unequivocal.

'Liar,' he said, his gaze unswerving.

Chandler squinted at him. 'What makes you say that?'

He grinned. 'Because it takes one to know one. Just like with me, this job is in your blood, and you need it more than it needs you. Remember that when your time comes.'

'I don't know about that, Jimmy. Some days, it feels more like a curse than a calling.'

'I know that feeling. But even days like today, when I have these complex puzzles to resolve with so much at stake, still create the kind of buzz that makes me keen to get up in the morning. Nothing else can touch it, Pen. Nothing.'

Her face took on a particular shape. The one she made when he was right, and she hated to admit it. Bliss winked and pushed his own glass aside. 'You're in for the full ride, Pen. That's all there is to it. Don't worry, I'll be right alongside you for as long as I can be.'

'You'd better be,' she said, suddenly morose. 'I can't bear the thought of waking up to a day when that doesn't happen.'

Bliss smiled, then reached out to pat her hand. 'You know what? I have a feeling you'll be ready for me to jack it in at just about the same time as I am. I'll know when I've reached the end. By then, you'll know it, too.'

'You really think so?'

'No. I know so.'

Which he did. The latter part of their conversation summed up everything he loved about this woman. Incredibly strong and certain, yet at the same time vulnerable and tentative. A friend who failed to recognise her own worth, and a colleague whose drive and will had become the fuel he required to power his own desire to continue. Unencumbered by him, Chandler would undoubtedly go on to thrive. Without her in his life, he, on the other hand, might wither on the vine. Time would be the final adjudicator of that, he knew. It was only a matter of when.

When he got back home, he paid special attention to Max without consciously knowing why. Sometimes it felt like the dog came to him by rote, as if the animal remembered being instructed to do so by his previous abusive owner. Remembering, too, the dire consequences of disobedience. When Bliss squirmed back into his recliner, Max usually curled up by his feet or beneath the elevated footrest. Tonight, he climbed up, wanting to be stroked. He was heavy, but welcome. After a while – much longer than usual – Max shifted, and Bliss expected the dog to jump back down to take his usual place on the floor. Instead, he rolled over onto his back, inviting further stroking of his throat and belly. When Max looked up a couple of minutes later, Bliss felt the full weight of his stare. And when he met the dog's dark brown eyes, he read them.

I'm trusting you. This is the biggest gift I have to offer. Don't throw it back in my face. I couldn't bear for that to happen again.

Bliss cupped the dog's face, leaned forward, and planted a kiss on his head. 'Don't you worry, boy,' he whispered, choked with emotion. 'You're safe with me. I'll never let you down that way. Never.'

TWENTY-THREE

Looking back at how the events of the day had panned out, Bliss could not identify the point at which it all started to spiral out of his control. Not precisely. Perhaps there were too many holes in the dike and not enough fingers with which to plug them. Maybe the unknown unknowns had contributed without him even being aware of their impact. What he did know for sure was that very little had gone to plan. That, and he was to blame for the ensuing chaos and the death of two people.

He'd established the primary staging area by the now defunct cement works at the quarry in Dogsthorpe. Working in tandem with other units, he arranged for a variety of vehicles to position themselves in a perimeter surrounding the mobile home and caravan park but set a reasonable distance from it. A small number, including vans to take away their suspects, gathered at the secondary staging area in the Travelodge car park at the Eye Green services. It was this choice of location that Bliss later identified as the most likely cause of what occurred afterwards.

Yet it had all begun without a hitch when the surveillance team, having approached from the rear of the neighbouring property opposite the camp, moved swiftly and silently into position.

With minimal fuss they had set up cameras in five positions high among the trees, providing ideal coverage across the three separate compound areas. A drone team situated themselves a hundred yards further back, awaiting instructions. There was a little pre-dawn activity inside the compound, including two vehicles which left within minutes of each other. Back at the staging area, where the team was able to hear every conversation taking place over the operational communication channel, Bliss blew out a sigh of frustration as the surveillance commander instructed everybody to hold.

'Both vehicles one up, neither driver identified,' the message continued.

It wasn't until the brighter side of twilight pawed at the land that Bartek Danek showed his face, emerging from a caravan located to the rear of the middle compound. Wearing a heavy pullover and blue jeans, he walked down the row and entered another caravan three units along. For the purposes of the operation, the team referred to him as Tango One. Thirty minutes later, at 8.11am, Danek re-emerged. This time he headed straight for a scruffy-looking red Toyota Hilux 4x4 pickup standing close by. Of the remaining gang members, there was no sign.

'Damn!' Bliss cursed when he heard the update. In many ways, this was the worst news they could have had. If the other members of the crew had been with him, the police would have had a justifiable reason to interview them when they arrested Danek. On his own, the van thief wasn't as big a prize. Plus, that still left his fellow fraudsters to catch.

'What do you want us to do, SIO?' The question came from the operations leader on the ground.

Having run this precise scenario through his head on several occasions overnight, and one final time that morning with his team, Bliss reacted on instinct. 'Take him,' he said. 'The moment surveillance indicates which direction he's heading in, move your closest vehicles to intercept. Make the stop, make the arrest.'

Following the acknowledgement, he and his colleagues waited in anxious silence. Shortly afterwards, surveillance came across comms giving the vehicle registration and informing everybody that the truck had headed north after exiting the camp. Bliss knew that upon hearing his order to take the suspect, the drone team would have sent their Matrice 350 up into the ice-grey sky, hitting its maximum height before zeroing in on the red truck. If everything was going according to plan, police vehicles were also on the move, looking to intercept the Toyota at a designated road junction. The spot was chosen because a large hangar-like factory hid it from view of those at the camp site. Confident that Danek was in the bag, Bliss turned his attention to the other members of the gang.

'What's the feeling now that we're here and this is happening?' he asked, turning to his team who stood huddled together in the bitter cold, heavy coats, gloves, and scarves the order of the day. 'My gut tells me we let this play out, leaving surveillance in place. We get Danek on his way to Thorpe Wood as soon as he's collared. Then all vehicles regroup, and we set up as before waiting for the others to leave the camp. Take them one-by-one if necessary, as we discussed yesterday. Agreed? If not, tell me now.'

Nobody disagreed. Or if they did, they kept it to themselves. Bliss was SIO, the onus on him to make all decisions. He activated his personal Airwave. 'Everybody else hold position. Get Tango One away from the thick of it as quickly as you can, then roll back into your original starting positions. Await further information from surveillance on remaining Tangos. Drone team reset for a second flight as soon as you're sure Danek is in the bag.'

Communications chatter increased rapidly as traffic put a stop on Danek and made the arrest. They took him away in one of the vans that had been posted at Eye Green, while another officer removed the Toyota. But then, as everything began to settle back down, the operation went crazy and started to fall apart at the seams.

'We have movement,' cried the chief surveillance officer, urgency in his tone. 'Tango Four just came out of a caravan and pulled back a large tarp to reveal a stash of quad bikes. He and Tangos Two and Three are now on them and… wait one… they've scattered in different directions. Wait one.'

Time dragged to the point where it felt interminable to Bliss, but in reality lasted only a few seconds. Every muscle in his body started to cramp just as their radios crackled once again.

'Heads up. We have Tango Three heading north on White Post Road. Tango Four is moving south but across open ground. Tango Two has blasted across the road and seems to be following an access path between fields traveling west behind our observation post.'

Bliss had no time to curse his luck. 'All units, move in according to your current positions. Have the drone follow Tango Three as far as it can. Provide positional updates across open channels.'

He turned to Chandler, his breath almost catching in his chest. 'Pen, call NPAS. I want eyes in the sky from either Husbands Bosworth or North Weald. Whoever can get here the quickest.' He knew the National Police Air Service reacted swiftly and without question when summoned, though at all times their ability to deploy depended on the availability of aircraft. With fifteen bases scattered around the country, time was of the essence, and he had requested assistance from the two closest to their location.

To the rest of his team he said, 'How the fuck did they know to run?'

'Could the strike team have ballsed up and used blues and twos?' DS Bishop asked, concern written across his features.

It was always possible, but Bliss dismissed the idea. 'They're far too experienced to have made such a basic error.'

'Perhaps Danek spotted one of the cars and managed to call his mates before they put in their stop,' Virgil suggested.

Again, while he couldn't rule it out, Bliss thought it unlikely. 'They had excellent cover. He wouldn't have seen them until they pulled out to block the road. I don't see him having time to make that call.'

'Somebody, somewhere, spotted one of our vehicles,' Bishop said. 'Had to be.'

That was the moment Bliss felt a first uneasy sensation settle in his chest. All the vehicles involved were hidden away, except for one location. 'Fuck it!' he said, throwing his head back in exasperation. 'It's Eye Green. Has to be. What do we have there? A Travelodge. A petrol station. A Starbucks and a McDonalds. What are the odds that somebody either from the camp or who knows people from the camp works in one of those places? We had two vehicles exit the site prior to the Toyota truck. Either or both of them could have driven to Eye Green for all we know.'

'We had to base vehicles close by,' Chandler reminded him, rejoining the conversation after speaking to NPAS. 'What other option did we have?'

'Then we should have found a more secluded base.' He blamed himself, and as SIO he took full responsibility. 'What did NPAS say?'

'They understood. They'll inform us of the ETA as soon as something leaves the ground.'

As a group, they went back to listening to comms. Tango Four had somehow bypassed mobile units and was now hurtling across the nature reserve at the Star Pit. Tango Three was off-road and taking a north-west heading towards the village of Newborough. The drone was following, but had only ten more minutes in the air if it was going to return to its launch site. As for Tango Two, he had made it beneath the A16 bridge and was closing in on the outskirts of the Paston township. Bliss realised the operation's best chance of catching these men was if they remained on the quad bikes. If they dumped them in highly populated areas, they'd have a better chance of finding somewhere to hide out or even mingle in with the locals.

Waiting was exhausting as each of them fed off the stress and strain of the chase. As the minutes ticked by, the drone still had Tango Three in view, but the operation had been given only ninety-seconds more of its time. By now, the bike was entering the fringes of Newborough. Bliss asked the drone team to provide a final location read before turning back and then ordered additional vehicles into the area. He also had cars running up and down both the A16 and A47 to cover the most likely spots from which Tango Four might emerge from the nature reserve. For Tango Two to reach built-up cover, he'd have to cross Newborough Road, which is where Bliss had subsequently positioned two police cars. But since they were only guessing at his most likely route, another vehicle trawled the area hoping to spot the bike.

It felt as if the net was tightening. And Bliss, for all his self-doubt, started to believe things had swung back in their favour. But then came the incident that proved escaping the net was not always advantageous. It was Tango Four, Matt Dories, who failed to slow down when he hit the Welland Road roundabout. According to the patrol officers who witnessed the resulting accident, a VW Golf had barely slowed on the A47 and floored it having exited the roundabout at the same time as the quad bike appeared from a pathway leading up and out of the nature reserve. Despite a howling screech of brakes and clouds of dark smoke from the locked-up tyres, the Golf smashed into the back of the bike and sent it careering into the oncoming lane where it punched into a Mini Cooper at the point where the offside front wing panel meets the driver's door, crushing both instantly.

The quad bike virtually disintegrated upon impact.

Still anxiously grouped together outside the closed cement factory no more than a hundred yards away from the incident, Bliss and his entire team heard both impacts carried to them on the frigid breeze. By the time that Matt Dories and the driver of the Mini were pronounced dead at the scene by authorised paramedics, Bliss and his team had mobilised themselves to help with the search. Meanwhile, Tango Two and Tango Three had vanished into busy streets while a helicopter circled overhead, continuing its fruitless search for the fleeing suspects.

TWENTY-FOUR

Bartek Danek's solicitor began by informing the interviewing detectives of his client's wish to make a statement, following which he intended to offer no comment to subsequent questions. In response, DC Virgil folded his arms across his chest and said, 'Let's hear it then.'

Danek, tall, skinny, with a dark trimmed beard, and not looking in the least bit rattled, shifted forward in his chair, casually leaning both elbows on the table while he read from a sheet of paper torn from his legal representative's A4 note pad. 'In reference to why you have arrested me today, I am willing to tell you what happened. I needed a new van for my business, so I took a Mercedes for a test drive. I had just gone past the Bentley dealership at the interchange and was heading onto the A1307, but there was a lorry broken down on the single lane and one of those yellow diversion signs on the road. It led me onto a little back route, and just after it looped around to the left there was another lorry blocking the way. I had to stop behind it. As I put on the handbrake to wait, a man wearing a balaclava appeared out of nowhere and waved a shotgun at the driver's window. He shouted for me to get out, so I did. Then he climbed into the van, turned it around and drove back the way I'd come. The lorry did the same thing while I stood at the side of the lane looking on, afraid for my life. I waited a few minutes before walking back to the main road. The first lorry and the diversion sign were gone. That is it. That is all I have to say.'

Virgil raised his eyebrows. 'That's quite some story, Mr Danek. And I don't believe a single word of it,' he said, ignoring the glare he got from Percy Beeding, the solicitor. 'Either way, I need to go back a few steps with you before we can move on. Starting with the reason you just gave for taking the test drive. You claim you needed a new van for your business, yet we can find no documentation to suggest that you have any kind of business, let alone one that requires the use of a vehicle. You are not on any employment payroll, and also the HMRC has never heard of you, so we know you're not self-employed, either. How do you explain that?'

'My client has given you his agreed statement,' Beeding said.

'Yes, I'm neither blind nor deaf. But I'm still going to ask my questions. Mr Danek, please tell us why you have an urgent need of a van when we have no record of you running a business.'

'This is a new business. I just start it, yes?' Danek said, ignoring his own determination to say nothing else.

Virgil was surprised to receive a response, but didn't show it. 'I see. Doing what? What is this business of yours?'

'Removals. Carry things. Deliver things. Man with a van things.'

'And you've been doing this for how long?'

'I told you this. I just start. That is why I need a van.'

Virgil wrinkled his nose. 'Even if that were true, how exactly are you in a financial position to purchase a van of this type?'

'I get loan from a friend.'

'Must be a very good friend.'

'Yes. Very good.'

Virgil glanced across at DC Kolesnyk before continuing. 'Moving on, then, let's take a look at the next step. You took your test drive from the dealership in St Ives. How did you get there that day, Mr Danek?'

'I have a friend who drove me.'

'Ah. Would this be the same friend who is loaning you the money?'

'If you like.'

'No, it's not a matter of what I like,' DC Virgil said, shaking his head. 'You need to tell me the truth. Was this friend who was going to loan you the money the same friend who drove you to St Ives? Yes, or no?'

'Yes.'

'Okay. Now we're getting somewhere. With him being such a good friend, you'll be able to tell us his name and where he lives.'

'Perhaps. He moves around a lot. I cannot always be sure where he will be next.'

'I see. His name, then? I'm sure that moves around with him wherever he may be.'

With a shrug, Danek said, 'I know him only as Heisenberg.'

This prompted DC Virgil to roll his eyes. 'A fan of *Breaking Bad*, are we, sir?'

Unmoved, Danek was silent this time.

Virgil made a note and moved on. 'We'll come back to that later. So, this good friend of yours dropped you at the Mercedes dealership and then, what, just drove off?'

'No. He wait for me.'

'Did he?' Virgil frowned, stiffening in his seat. 'But if he waited for you, Mr Danek, why did you not contact him after you were van-jacked?'

Danek gave that some thought, the first time he had paused with his answers. 'Yes, I did do this. He come get me.'

'He collected you from the location where you were van-jacked?'

'Yes.'

'And even after you told him what had happened, neither of you thought to contact the police to report it?'

'My client has already answered that question,' Beeding interrupted. 'I suggest you move on.'

'That's for me to decide,' Virgil snapped. 'But we will come back to that as well, among other things. Now, let's talk about the dealership and what transpired there. You remember them taking your details and scanning your driving licence, Mr Danek?'

'Of course. This is procedure. What of it?'

'You've done this kind of thing before, then?'

'I… what?'

'You said it was procedure. To know that you must have done it before.'

'No. Not before. They tell me it is procedure.'

Virgil slipped a sheet of paper out of the folder he had placed in front of him on the table. 'I happen to have a copy of that driving licence. The trouble is, and something we need you to explain, this ID is fake. Fake name, fake details, fake address.'

Virgil turned the printout to show them both the scanned image. Danek's duty solicitor turned to his client and nodded. The suspect sighed and slouched back in his chair. 'That is not mine,' he said.

'Yes. I'm well aware of that,' Virgil said. 'I just told you it was fake.'

'No, I mean that is not the driving licence I gave them to copy. I do not know who that belongs to, but it is not me. I gave them mine, they scanned it, and then printed it out. I know nothing about the one you are showing me.'

His frown deepening, Virgil said, 'You're telling us that's not you in that photo?'

'No. I mean, no, it is not me.'

'It looks like you.'

'I do not think so.'

'I do. Because I believe it is you. Police officers searched you after they arrested you, but you didn't have your driving licence on you. Where is it, Mr Danek?'

'I don't know. I think I lost it.'

Virgil exhaled and ran a hand across his chin. 'Do you know what the punishment is for using a fake ID for the reasons we believe you did so, Mr Danek? It's based on a grid between culpability and harm. In terms of culpability, we reckon we have you on category A, which covers substantial financial gain or expectation of substantial financial gain, a leading role where offending is part of a group activity, plus sophisticated nature of offence or significant planning. When it comes to harm, we definitely have you on category two, which includes a document used or intended for use to assist criminal activity, used or intended for use to evade responsibility for criminal activity, and used or intended for use to falsely demonstrate a lawful right to drive in the UK. Likely custodial for that, sir, is between two-to-four years, perhaps more depending on what additional criminal activity we can tie to the theft of the van.'

Danek nodded. 'I understand. But like I said, I did not use fake ID. Whoever that licence belongs to, it is not me. The dealership must have fucked up.'

Virgil leaned forward. 'So, you're sticking to the whole "this isn't me on the licence and I was van-jacked" story?'

'It is not a story. This is what happened.'

'Okay. In a moment I'm going to walk you through the whole thing one more time, but before we do that, tell me why, after they took the van from you, you didn't even bother informing the dealership.'

At this point, the solicitor coughed to draw his client's attention. He shook his head but said nothing. Bartek Danek smiled and said, 'No comment.'

Which he repeated for the remainder of the interview.

During the first break, DCs Virgil and Kolesnyk met with the rest of the team to discuss the outcome of the interview and plan a strategy for the next. 'It's a bloody ridiculous story he's concocted,' Bliss admitted. 'But it's also going to be a ball ache to refute. When we're done, let's check to see if there are any cameras at or close to that junction he mentioned. Clearly neither the lorry nor the diversion sign exists, but let's prove that if we can. Meanwhile, I don't think we can push him on this so-called friend. He'll feed us a line if he gives us anything at all. We can keep hold of him for now, but the question before us is when, or even if, we introduce what we know. Do we tell him we have the names of Peter Holland, Matt Dories, and Patrick Walsh? And if so, do we also tell him what happened after he left the camp site, including the fate of his pal Dories?'

'Given all three did a runner and two of them remain at large,' Chandler said, 'I don't see any harm in feeding that to him in dribs and drabs. See what he has to say, monitor his reactions following each new nugget of information.'

Bliss nodded. 'Something has been bugging me. It's probably nothing, but why wasn't Danek bundled up against the cold weather this morning? If I'm remembering the sequence correctly, he came out of his caravan, entered another one, then jumped into the Toyota as soon as he emerged from it again. Why wouldn't he stop to wrap up first? It's fucking freezing out there even now. It's heavy coat weather at a minimum, not heavy jumper.'

'What are you thinking, Jimmy?' DS Bishop asked.

'I'm thinking maybe we were wrong. We've assumed that whoever phoned in a warning from one of those businesses at Eye Green did so after Danek had left the site. But what if that call came earlier? What if the others sent Danek off as a decoy, allowing them to scatter in all directions while we were occupied elsewhere?'

'That's a decent shout, boss,' Kolesnyk said. 'But how does it help us?'

'I'm not sure it does, Vas. But if it did come about that way, maybe upon reflection Danek is not entirely happy being staked out like a goat for us to pounce on. It might not be much, but we're stuck for leverage with this man and winding him up about that might expose a slight chink in his defences. Especially if his only crimes were providing them with hooky motors. Let's face it, every fraud victim has spoken about three gang members, not four. There's been no mention of a foreign accent, which I think there would have been. I'm betting Danek nicked the vehicles and was happy enough with his earnings from that, while the other three committed the frauds.'

'If you're right, that could be our only way of getting under his skin.'

'Okay,' DC Virgil said. 'Just so's I'm clear on our approach. When we restart the interview, we walk him through his previous answers. Assuming nothing changes, we tell him we know about Holland, Dories, and Walsh. If there's still no reaction, we make it clear that they fled while he was being chased down and arrested, leaving him as the scapegoat for everything. Then we let it drop that we think all he did was nick the vehicles, while his friends essentially stole money from vulnerable people. We let him stew on all that during a short tea break. Enough time for his brief to suggest we just gave him an obvious way out. If he coughs when we go back into the room, great. If not, we tell him about the manhunt and the tragic accident. Emphasise how dangerous it's all become for everyone involved, especially the only member of the gang we have in custody. Him.'

Bliss nodded as Virgil painted the scenario in all its glorious colours. 'That's the way I'd go,' he said. 'Put it all on his shoulders.'

'But won't his brief simply point out that we have no evidence against him on any other crimes?'

'I assume so. But what have we got to lose?'

'What do we have to gain, though?' Bishop asked. 'We have one suspect dead, the other two out there somewhere. We know who they are, so what more can Danek give us?'

'You just said it yourself,' Bliss said. 'We know who they are, but we currently don't know *where* they are. Danek has no phone on him, so presumably he left that behind at the camp. We can try getting a warrant to go in looking for it, but it'll be long gone by now. That means we can't use it to trace his mates' mobiles, if they even have them. Therefore, we can't get to them by usual means. But they're out there somewhere, right enough. And if Bartek Danek doesn't know precisely where they are right now, maybe he knows where they are going to be.'

TWENTY-FIVE

'Tell me about this morning's events,' Detective Chief Superintendent Marion Fletcher said. Her voice betrayed no emotion. Not even the consternation Bliss might have expected. He sat opposite the DCS in the large Thorpe Wood meeting room, DCI Warburton alongside him.

'I thought we had the area tied down,' he began. 'Not watertight, but as close as we could get. The truth is they took us by surprise. We had our plans in place, but clearly, so did they. We had prior authority to give chase if they ran and we reacted swiftly. What happened to one of the suspects and a member of the public was tragic, but other than choosing not to commit to the operation I don't know what we could have done differently to avoid it.'

Fletcher stared intently at him. 'Now the off-the-record version. And, please, be specific.'

Bliss had thought of little else since events started going pear-shaped on them, and he was clear. 'We had all our pieces in place. Our hope was that the entire crew would exit at the same time in the same vehicle, but that's not what occurred. Our Tango One target left the site on his own. I gave the word to take him.'

'I'm sure you considered all the alternatives, Jimmy,' Fletcher said. 'Was your instruction based on impulse, or had you previously decided what you would do if a suspect emerged alone?'

'I'd gone over it several times, internally at first and then later on in discussion with the team. We accounted for various circumstances altering our approach, but when the time came, I made the call. And I still think it was the right one.'

'Apprehending Tango One went about as well as could be expected. In hindsight, do you feel it went too well?'

'If you mean do I think Tango One knew we were out there waiting and deliberately headed into the trap set for him, yes I think that's possible. I suspect somebody working at the Eye Green service area noticed our vehicles and called to warn them just in case. His friends subsequently allowed Tango One to drive out as a decoy, allowing them to escape on quad bikes. That said, it's equally feasible that they sent him on some kind of fool's errand, that he was completely unaware of what he was driving into. We hope to know more at the conclusion of the second interview with him.'

Fletcher chewed that over before responding. 'Again, in hindsight, could you have located the secondary staging area in a more secluded area?'

'Possibly. Our vehicles needed to be close enough to be effective, but far enough away not to be seen. In checking out the surrounding area at all points on the compass, I felt that Eye Green was about as far out as we could go without having their effectiveness compromised by other factors.'

Offering a thin smile, Fletcher said, 'I think you're being generous, Jimmy. While you were watching your suspect being interviewed, I was debriefing both surveillance and traffic. It was made clear to me that our response teams selected Eye Green, and you went along with their recommendation.'

'That's true,' he admitted. 'But as SIO the final decision was mine. Although I can't be certain, I suspect the service area is where the operation was compromised. Whether that was a poor decision on my part or just bad luck, we may never know.'

'Knowing you, I'm sure you're kicking yourself. I suggest you stop. Nothing good can come of it now, and as far as I can tell, there's no blame attached to you. So, please continue.'

'Thank you, ma'am.' Bliss swallowed thickly, relieved by the Chief Superintendent's words of reassurance. 'The other Tangos scattered in all directions. We did our best to continue with the surveillance and to follow them, but they had the advantage not only of surprise but also in respect of the vehicles they used. Many of ours are fine off-road but are nowhere near as all-terrain as quad bikes. We lost track of one in Newborough and one in Paston. Searches are still under way. As for the third Tango, that was an unfortunate accident caused by his own negligence. I'm sure some will try to attribute the collision to the chase, but in fact he was not being directly pursued at that precise moment because we had lost sight of him and had no idea where he was.'

'Hmm. A fine line, Jimmy.'

'But a crucial one, all the same,' Bliss insisted, wanting no blame attached to the pursuit teams. 'We were not following him, so nobody forced him up onto that road at high speed into the path of another vehicle. We did happen to have a unit close by who witnessed the collisions, but he came out of the nature reserve without so much as pausing and under no immediate threat from us.'

'I do think we're clean on this one, Marion,' DCI Warburton said. Until this juncture she had listened patiently, but clearly, she felt this was the right time to interject. 'I realise a member of the public died as a result, but if there's fault to be assigned, then I suggest we look no further than our deceased Tango himself.'

'Except that the reason he fled in the first place was because of our presence.'

'With respect, what are we supposed to do? Not hunt for suspects because they might run?'

Fletcher held up a hand. 'I'm not suggesting anything of the sort. I'm on your side, Diane. Even so, we all know this is the way an unhelpful media is going to spin it.'

'I wouldn't bet on that,' Bliss said. 'Not the locals, anyway. I think we can rely on them to tell the truth without skewing it against the police.'

The DCS flashed a wry smile. 'One of these days, Jimmy,' she said, 'you really must tell me how you managed to pull off that particular magic trick.'

'Ma'am?'

'The one where at times you appear to have the *PT* singing off your song sheet.'

'It's no trick, ma'am. Just my charismatic personality and natural charm.'

'Is that so? Well, whatever it is, tread carefully. The law of averages suggests that living life on the edge the way you do will occasionally result in you stepping over it. Tell me, what plan are we now on?'

'I reckon we must be down to letter M by now,' Bliss admitted. 'But we have some distance to go before we run out of alphabet.'

'I do hope so. As for this morning's events, let's put them down to bad luck. It would be nice if you could turn that around inside the next twenty-four hours, Jimmy.'

'I'll do my best. As always.'

'And before we wrap things up, tell me, what, precisely, is your plan M?'

'Applying as much pressure as possible in the interview room to see if we can squeeze anything more out of Danek. And in addition to the teams we have out there searching for the remaining two suspects, I have also asked for as many units as possible to take up positions close to other traveller sites in the region, just in case the crew have prearranged boltholes somewhere. Oh, and on a happier note, I should also mention that CSI compared Tango Four's boots to prints discovered at the scene of Mrs Musgrove's murder and got a match.'

'That's certainly a positive break. We could do with one, that's for sure. What about the mobile home park they all fled from? Do you intend to raid it? It is, after all, where these men lived.'

Bliss ran a thumb over the tiny scar on his forehead. 'I'm taking that one under advisement. There are a few issues and stumbling blocks.'

'Which are?'

'Physical resources for one. We're already over stretched doing the things we have to do. A raid of that size and under such circumstances will require a heavy presence, and at this stage I'm not willing to pull our people off other jobs. The point is, the site remains under surveillance in case the gang is stupid enough to return, but also what are we going to find if we turn the place over? By now I'm sure their phones have been destroyed, plus any other potentially incriminating evidence such as clothing and footwear either burned or removed. Stirring up a hornet's nest for no reward doesn't feel like a good use of our time or people.'

DCI Warburton turned to him with a grin on her face and said, 'Not that I would ever dare accuse you of having sensibilities, Jimmy, heaven forbid, but are you actually taking into account the effect on the community? Is that another reason why you're holding back on raiding the camp?'

Bliss gave a wry smile and shook his head. 'Does that sound like me, boss? Believe me, if I thought we had anything to gain I'd order that site turned over just as we would any other dwelling

– at the very least the caravans those men slept in. No, I'm simply being practical at the moment. If that changes, I won't hesitate.'

'A word to the wise,' Fletcher said. 'Inform DSI Edwards before you act on that impulse. I think you're probably right to avoid it, especially as by now they must be aware of the accident and the loss of one of their own. Feelings may be running high. Just know that if you do decide to go in, provided you get the warrant you have my full support.'

'I'll try to steer clear of it,' Bliss said. 'But we both understand that might not be possible.'

He got back downstairs in time to catch the last few minutes of the second interview with Bartek Danek. This time, DC Kolesnyk was the officer asking questions.

'So, you don't know where your friends might be now? No meeting point you overheard them discussing. Another camp, maybe?'

'No comment.'

To Bliss's surprise, the young Polish officer smiled. 'Thank you,' he said. 'It is always a pleasure when a suspect makes life easier for us.'

Danek said nothing, but Bliss noticed his frown deepen.

'In many ways,' Kolesnyk continued, 'your friends also made it easier for us. I admire you, Mr Danek. Had my friends asked me to make a break for it knowing I'd be caught while they were getting away, I would not be as calm about the situation as you. Especially as they had to know you were sacrificing yourself by accepting the full weight of our charges. See, we know that you steal vans for them to order so that they can carry out their business of defrauding elderly and vulnerable people. I'm guessing that wasn't your idea, either. Did they promise you a spot on the team eventually, Mr Danek?'

'No comment.'

'Of course not. And why would you? Their plan all along was to make their get-away while you were being captured, leaving you to take the blame for everything. Because the way we see it, if you steal a vehicle knowing your friends are intent on using it to commit these crimes, then you are as guilty as they are. Perhaps you were happy to go along with that while it was only fraud. But did they even bother to tell you they'd assaulted a police officer? By the look on your face, I suspect not. So then, they definitely wouldn't have told you about the woman they murdered. See, they got greedy, went back to the same house to steal from the same woman, only this time she refused. That resulted in one of your friends losing his temper and killing her, Mr Danek. I don't know, maybe they did disclose everything to you. But either way, because you stole the van they used to commit those crimes, you are equally responsible.'

Danek looked as if he was about to protest when his solicitor's hand shot out. 'Don't take the bait,' Beeding told him. 'These people have offered no evidence to suggest that you had any prior knowledge of any actions taken by your friends. If they wish to proceed on the van theft, they have every right to do so. Equally, I will happily defend you against the slim evidence they have provided to date. Anything else is just talk on their part. They will not add any other charges against you.'

'You can obviously accept the advice you're being given, Mr Danek,' Kolesnyk said calmly. 'Or you can take note of everything I've told you. Mr Beeding has his view on the case against you, while we have ours. He can't possibly know what our decision will be on charging, and with the Crown Prosecution Service on our side he's asking you to take a massive risk. Also, the simple fact is, your friends deserted you, left you to it. If I were you, I'd be unhappy and looking for some payback.'

'Detective Constable Kolesnyk, I really must protest,' Beeding said, his voice raised. 'We both know the CPS will support no such charge, and it's wrong of you to suggest otherwise.'

'We won't know anything until they make a decision. By then, it'll be too late for your client.'

The solicitor turned to Danek. 'Listen to me. These detectives are stretching the limits of plausibility. The CPS would not agree to any such charges, but they won't need to because the police will not be charging you beyond the theft of the Mercedes van. That's *if* they have sufficient evidence to do so, which I seriously doubt.'

Bliss looked on, fascinated. He was impressed with Kolesnyk's sheer daring. The DC was close to stepping over the line, but had told no outright lies. The police still had the option of charging Danek for the robberies and the murder, and the CPS would then have to arrive at a decision. It wouldn't happen because they were nowhere near providing enough proof or even circumstantial evidence above and beyond the theft of the van. Any supposed criminal connection between stealing the van and the resulting crimes committed by the men who used it was a pure bluff. And not a subtle one, either. Now it all rested on Danek's own will and reliance upon his lawyer.

'Do you have something you wish to say to us?' Kolesnyk asked pointedly.

Danek waited a beat, then nodded. 'Yes. Yes, I do.'

The interview room was silent for a few seconds before the suspect leaned forward, smiled, and without inflection said, 'No comment.'

TWENTY-SIX

As he nudged his way out of the car park, Bliss found his passage hampered by a media van parked illegally. A tall, bearded man in a navy puffer jacket supporting a television camera on one shoulder waited alongside the vehicle's sliding side door. Beside him stood a female wearing a pink winter coat, pink boots, a pink beanie hat, clutching a long microphone in her pink gloves.

What the… is this News Reporter Barbie?

The unheralded thought prompted the memory of a deceased colleague, the vivacious and talented Detective Sergeant they had called *Cuffs & Baton Barbie*. Bliss had been about to treat the news crew to some choice language and heavy-duty sarcasm, but with his mind now on Mia Short and his mood having altered dramatically he instead powered down his window and summoned them over with his fingers. They scurried across, thinking they might be onto something juicy. Bliss was happy to disappoint them.

'I suggest you sod off while you still can,' he said. 'When you lot decide to block exits, that's when accidents occur. I've known expensive cameras broken beyond repair after being knocked to the ground, other people suffering bruises, dislocations, and fractures following unintended collisions. Even the odd boot or two run over.'

The woman's lanyard suggested she was with a cable news company, and she was undeterred. 'I recognise you,' she said. 'You're Bliss. Not even a detective anymore and yet I hear you organised the raid that left two men dead. Do you have anything to say to their grieving loved ones, Mr Bliss? Would you like to take this opportunity to apologise to them?' She stuffed the fluffy microphone towards his face.

Bliss realised this was the time to wind up the window, push his way through and out onto the road without saying another word. He also knew he was sick and tired of their bullshit.

'Not quite,' he said. 'But I definitely want to offer my condolences to Mr Kay's family. The man who caused this terrible and tragic road traffic collision was reckless in his riding and didn't care for the public's safety.'

'You're blaming one of the victims? What do you say to those who accuse the police of chasing this young man to his death?'

'I'd tell them it might be a good idea to be better informed before they opened their ignorant mouths.'

'That's your message to this city's outraged travelling community, is it, Mr Bliss? No sympathy for Mr Dories and his family, nor his people. Instead, you'd rather deny your role in this tragedy and describe them as uninformed and ignorant.'

Bliss nodded. 'Those who are, yes.'

'Are you aware that same community will be staging slow-driving protests in and around the spot at which the chase you organised ended in tragic death?'

'I wasn't, no. But it's ironic, wouldn't you say?'

The reporter cocked her head, pushed the microphone closer. 'In what way?'

'Because if that member of their community had himself been driving with even a modicum of due care and attention and at a suitable speed, Mr Kay, the driver of the Mini that Dories slammed into, wouldn't now be dead. *His* family and friends wouldn't now be grieving. I do hope these slow drivers spare a thought for him during their… protest.'

Bliss drove away this time, knowing he ought to have done so without uttering a single word, and yet not regretting doing so even for a moment.

*

The bar at the Holiday Inn hotel was long and polished so hard you could see your reflection in it. Bliss brought a tray of drinks over to a booth at which both Iris and Paul Musgrove sat waiting patiently. Over the course of the following thirty minutes, he provided as much information and detail as he was able to in respect of their mother's case. He'd spoken to their FLO ahead of the meeting, but the young family liaison officer hadn't had much to say about the siblings. This was one of those peculiar family circumstances where, despite being estranged, grief was the overwhelming emotion. Theirs was also a different kind of loss. A lot of missed opportunities, unanswered questions, emptiness where there ought to have been memories.

Not wishing to intrude further into their misery, the only question Bliss asked was whether their mother had told them about her initial run in with the builders. But neither had spoken to her since Christmas Day, so the news came as a shock to them both.

'We're working on the hypothesis that these same three men returned to scam more money from her,' Bliss revealed. 'Only this time it did not go according to plan.'

'That sounds like our mother,' Paul said, a wistful smile on his face. 'Her credo was very much along the lines of fool me once shame on you, fool me twice shame on me. It would have driven her insane knowing those men had pulled a fast one on her. It comes as no surprise to know that she most likely stood her ground the next time they tried it on.'

Amidst the mixed emotions, Bliss thought he detected a sense of pride and chose to delve further. 'Were you both aware that she kept large sums of cash on the property?' he asked.

They nodded in concert. 'You couldn't tell her what to do,' Iris insisted. 'We didn't know about the safe, and over the years I think both of us found ways to suggest better alternatives. But then, our father was much the same when it came to money. I imagine he was the one who had the safe installed.'

'Speaking of which,' Bliss said. 'The cash we did find remains in evidence for the time being. We can't know for certain that these men didn't handle any of it during their first visit, but as soon as we no longer need it, we'll make the entire amount available to the estate. On that subject, was your mother the type to leave a will?'

Paul shook his head, scoffing lightly. 'No. Not our mum. Felt the same way about lawyers as she did banks. She used both only when absolutely necessary.'

'Mine was much the same,' Bliss told them. 'Different generation, I suppose. Given there's just the two of you, I don't imagine there'll be a great deal of problem sorting things out legally. Which reminds me, we're done with the house, so it's all yours if you want to check out of this place.'

'I don't think I can sleep at the farm knowing what happened,' Iris said with a shudder. Her brother quickly agreed.

'Entirely up to you. You can collect the keys from the Thorpe Wood police station, which is just at the end of this road. If you change your minds, either of you, please inform your liaison officer. I need to know where I can find you to keep you updated. Also, please let us know what arrangements you make for your mother. I know my colleague, Gul Ansari, would like to attend.'

Paul Musgrove looked up. 'Ansari? My mother mentioned her to me. I had no idea she was a police officer. I thought she was just a neighbour.'

Bliss, who had so far revealed only minimal details about the day of the attack, decided it couldn't hurt to drip feed in a little more. 'They were part of the same small community. Gul kept your mother updated with news about the hunt for the scammers. In fact, she went to the house that very morning and was herself assaulted. We think the only reason she didn't meet the same fate was because they discovered Gul was a copper and had no desire to have us breathing down their necks for the murder of one of our own.'

The siblings appeared dismayed to learn of the additional violence and asked after Ansari's health. They seemed genuinely relieved to hear about the favourable outcome.

'It's horrible,' Iris said, hugging herself. 'I never hear of such things where I live.'

Her brother hissed air between his teeth. 'It's a daily event in my city. But out in the sticks where mum lives… lived, you just don't expect it.'

'Sadly, it's becoming more commonplace,' Bliss admitted. 'These men are cowards, their victims vulnerable and often remote.'

'You will catch them, won't you?' Iris said plaintively.

Thinking back to the events of the day, Bliss wished he had the same level of confidence as he'd had twenty-four hours previously. Still, he nodded, his gaze hardening. 'We will,' he said. 'There's nowhere they can go where we won't find them.'

*

The tiny village of Peakirk was little more than a blemish on the map, the kind of place that if you were a passenger in a vehicle passing through it and you blinked, you'd probably miss it. But what it did have was essential to Scuzzy Pete and Paddy the Greek.

Separately, some ninety minutes apart, both men approached via Glinton, making their way across a field, then onto a long public footpath that took them to the allotment gardens. Shielded by hedgerow, they skirted the area, climbed a small stone wall and eventually came upon an abandoned and dilapidated barn. Paddy's cousin owned the land, and the gang had a long-standing agreement to meet there if they ever had to flee from the police.

Under the cover of early darkness, Scuzzy was the first to arrive. Though the barn had not been used in years, its doors were padlocked to discourage casual drug users and the homeless. It took him three failed attempts before he remembered the correct four-digit combination, and he was hugely relieved to finally enter and shut the world out behind him. He fell to his knees and rubbed some warmth into his body. If he'd thought the day was bitterly cold, the night was busy decorating the landscape with yet more frost and ice.

After a few minutes, he pulled an LED torch from his jacket pocket and switched it on. Raking the powerful beam around the interior, Scuzzy was not encouraged by what he saw. Although the windows were boarded up, he spotted narrow slits through which light might leak. He realised he'd have to spend the rest of the night in darkness, but took a few minutes to acquaint himself with the layout, find a place to rest and perhaps even grab some sleep, and know that he could do so in relative safety. There were no tools or sharp implements on which he might damage himself.

In fact, he saw no objects of any kind resting on the thankfully wooden floorboards beneath him.

Swallowed up by darkness once again, he found himself starting to relax for the first time in more than fifteen hours. He had dumped the quad bike as soon as it was reasonable for him to do so, leaving it on a playing field with the key in the ignition hoping someone would come along and steal it. From then on he moved little and often, finding places to shelter for just long enough not to draw attention to himself. When refuge became hard to come by, he mingled with people going about their demanding lives, melting into the background while tramping busy pavements. As often as he could, Scuzzy popped in and out of all manner of shops to both take on some warmth and use up some precious daylight while 'browsing'.

Throughout the day he picked up on disconcerting snippets of conversation, referring to a tragic fatal accident involving two cars and a bike of some description. Pretty much all he'd heard away in the distance all day was the sound of sirens and for a while a helicopter circling the area, but he'd assumed they were all police vehicles on the hunt. Initially, he refused to even contemplate the possibility that one of his friends might be involved. But across the passage of hours, he became convinced that not only had either Doris or Paddy been part of what had happened, but also that they had perished.

Without behaving unnaturally, he managed to remain free and mobile, but caution dominated his every instinct even when darkness fell and the temperature began to plummet. The cold stayed with him inside the barn, wrapped around his body like an icy blanket. As for the caution, he felt his muscles slowly lose their rigidity and he no longer jumped at every sound; wind rushing through gaps in the wooden structure like distant screams;

a couple of dogs engaging in a bark-off of some sort; unfamiliar noises potentially carrying unseen threats.

No more than an hour and a half after he arrived, Scuzzy heard someone or something scrabbling at the barn doors. The wind's mournful howl grew louder momentarily as someone yanked a door open, then quickly closed it again.

From the inside or outside? he wondered, hairs raising on the back of his neck.

'Doris? Scuzzy? Either of you here?'

Pete put his head back and sighed. Paddy's voice. He flicked his torch on, shielding the ferocity of its glow with a cupped hand. 'Over here,' he called softly, leaving the light on until Paddy had joined him.

'Fuck me, it's bloody freezing out there,' the newcomer said, stamping his feet as hard as he dare.

'Not much better in here,' Scuzzy said.

'But no wind chill, at least.'

'Yeah, true enough. It's blowing a bit out there.'

'No sign of Doris so far, then?'

The silence that followed was broken only by a further flurry of wind outside, which seemed to provoke the dogs into a short rematch.

'I don't think he's coming,' Scuzzy eventually said.

'What d'you mean? Why wouldn't he be coming? Are you saying he's had his collar felt?'

'No. That is, I'm not sure. You didn't hear about the accident?'

'What accident?'

'A couple of cars and a bike of some sort. That's all I know, other than the people I overheard talking about saying it was a fatal.'

'What makes you think Doris was involved?'

'One of them mentioned the Star Pit. That was his escape route. I'm not saying it was him, just that I have a bad feeling.'

'Even if it was, doesn't mean he was the fatality,' Paddy reasoned.

'No. I know that. I just… like I said, a bad feeling.'

'He'll be here. He will.'

'He's not, though. That's the point.'

'For fuck's sake, Scuzzy. I only just arrived myself. Don't write him off yet. Doris is a tough nut to crack.'

And two other vehicles make for excellent nutcrackers, Scuzzy thought but didn't say.

'So, what's the plan for the morning?' he asked instead. Making a break for it on the quad bikes and separating in a starburst had been his idea. The barn and whatever followed was all down to Paddy.

'Just before dawn, we'll sneak around front to my cousin's place. We'll get some hot food and drink inside us before moving on.'

'Thank fuck for that. All I've had today is some jam doughnuts and Coke that I bought from a garage.'

'I didn't do much better than that myself. But he'll take care of us. When we're done, he'll move us to a safe location well away from here.'

Scuzzy breathed out his relief. 'Sounds good. Whereabouts?'

After a long pause, Paddy said, 'No offence, Pete, but the less you know the better. If for some reason we got separated again and the filth picked you up, what you don't know you can't tell.'

He thought about that and decided he would have reached the exact same conclusion. 'Fair enough. The main thing is we'll be off the streets while we regroup. You think they'll raid the White Post site?'

'Probably. They like giving our lot a good kicking.'

Scuzzy didn't think that was true at all, but he let it go. 'At least Bartek doesn't know where we're being taken, either. But what if Doris was involved in that accident but not badly injured? Does he know where this safe house is? Would he be able to tell them if they asked?'

If Paddy nodded, it was too dark to see the movement. 'He knows,' he said. 'But this barn was always the place where we planned to meet afterwards. If he was going to tell them anything, we'd already be nicked.'

Scuzzy Pete raised his knees to hug them. His friend's words gave little comfort. It simply meant that later when he dozed he did so with one eye open and both ears straining for the slightest sound.

TWENTY-SEVEN

Detective Sergeant Rachael Skinner was as slender as a pipe cleaner, while her skin glowed with health and vitality. Bliss had read up on her background and knew she had competed at county level as a long-distance runner, and her obvious standard of fitness showed in the way she looked and moved so effortlessly. On the phone she had come across as timid and perhaps a little nervous, but in person Bliss thought he detected an inner strength behind the degree of wariness he had anticipated.

'You wanted to discuss a cold case with me,' she said as he took a seat. He had entered the coffee shop moments after the detective, having watched her arrive before stepping out of his own vehicle. He had selected Pinnies in Godmanchester in the hope that the neutrality would loosen her tongue. DS Skinner was waiting for him with a white mug cupped in both hands. Clearly, she was eager to get down to business.

'Not quite,' Bliss said, aiming to throw her off a little. 'I am working a cold case, but that's not what I'm here to discuss with you specifically. It's just that your name has come up during our investigation.'

'Oh. In what capacity?'

'Unofficial. For now. Look, Rachael, I need to begin by telling you nobody wants this to progress any further than it already has. Whatever we talk about here today needn't go beyond these four walls. And I hope that my asking you to meet here rather than in a room at HQ or back at Thorpe Wood tells you where my interests lie.'

Her initial caution quickly turned to genuine apprehension. 'That doesn't make me feel any easier,' she said, her accent pure Yorkshire. 'It sounds very much as if I could be in some kind of trouble. Do I need my rep here?'

He kept his gaze deliberately even. 'I just told you this was unofficial, Rachael. For the time being, at least. Bringing in a rep makes it otherwise, and I don't think either of us wants that.'

'Okay. Well, then, what's this all about? You've got me worried now.'

'I'm sorry about that. I just needed you to be aware of the importance of what I'm about to reveal to you. Let me begin, though, by asking you a question. What would you say if I told you the cold case we are reinvestigating is the murder of Daisy Vincent?'

Rachael Skinner's body betrayed her. Bliss didn't need further confirmation, and opted not to wait for her to respond. 'I can see you understand where this is going,' he said more gently. 'Don't say anything for the moment, just know that if all else is above board, I will do my best to help you. If I suspect otherwise, then all bets are off. Understood?'

Her lips quivering, the DS nodded. She had the look of a frightened animal about her.

'Good. Rachael, you and I never worked a case together, but you know my reputation. I'm not here to throw you under a bus.'

'If you say so.'

'I do. Now, let me tell you what we know. A colleague of yours spotted you in the company of Dougie Vincent. This was in the White Horse pub close to Rutland Water if that helps to clarify the date. With that in mind, I'd like to share the result of subsequent discussions. The colleague who saw you noted that the pair of you were, shall we say, more than chummy? It looked to them as if you two were a couple. And quite close. Now, Rachael, I started by telling you what we've learned. You might be tempted to explain it away, but if you do and I'm not satisfied, and this conversation goes beyond yourself and my team, then I will put you under the kind of scrutiny your career cannot possibly withstand. Therefore, what I'd like you to do is start by acknowledging the relationship. If you do that, we can move on and I will have more questions for you.'

He left it there out in the open and allowed the ensuing silence to work on her clearly frazzled nerves. Eventually, she nodded. 'I admit it. I am seeing Dougie.'

Bliss welcomed her honesty. What he wanted now was further cooperation. Prior to that he had to lay all his cards on the table. 'Thank you. I'm grateful. Rachael, I realise you'll be aware of this, but I have to remind you anyway. Under the Code of Ethics and the Authorised Professional Practice document you signed, this relationship needed to be disclosed. Not doing so puts you at risk. You could face allegations that you compromised your integrity and impartiality as a police officer. Am I right in thinking you have made no such disclosure?'

'Yes. You're right. I haven't.'

'Okay. Listen, when I was growing up my old man was a sergeant at our local nick, and within our family group of friends there were as many small-time villains as there were cops. But times have changed. The only thing working in your favour right now is that I don't want to hurt you for having a fling with a known criminal.

Provided that's all there is to it. But there are certain things I need to be convinced of if we're going to keep this between us.'

Fear gripped the officer. She shivered as if exposed to the winter elements lurking outside, and she ignored her cup of hot tea, licking dry lips for all she was worth. Skinner waited for Bliss to continue slashing his way through her waking nightmare.

'First thing,' he said. 'At any point during your relationship with Dougie Vincent has he been under investigation by the police, NCA, or any other law enforcement agency?'

'No,' she said, shaking her head vigorously. 'Not to my knowledge.'

'Okay. Now, bearing in mind I already know the answer, how long has the relationship being going on?'

'About seven months, off and on. We had a break in between of around five weeks.'

Bliss had lied about knowing how long the pair had been seeing each other, but earlier he had checked the background information and knew Vincent had not been under investigation for almost two years.

'Good. That bodes well,' he said. 'It doesn't put you in the clear by any means, but by being open with me you're helping yourself. Now comes the more difficult part. Rachael, for me to overlook this entanglement, I need to be persuaded of two things: first, that you will today end things with Dougie Vincent, and second, that all you are guilty of is poor judgement and failing to disclose that relationship. Do you think you can do that?'

Nodding once more, DS Skinner said, 'I was infatuated with him more than anything. When it began, I honestly had no idea who he was. But from the moment he gave me his name, I knew what my responsibilities were. I just told myself I was doing no harm. That's no excuse, I realise. But it is the truth. Which leads me to the second part, because if you're asking me if I treated him favourably, or fed him information, or compromised myself in any other way, then the answer is no. Whether you believe me or not, that's how it was. In fact, I'm as certain as I can be that he has no idea what I do for a living. After he mentioned his name, I gave him a false one and told him I was a flight attendant working both short-haul and long-haul flights for British Airways. I thought that would be good cover in respect of my availability.'

Bliss regarded her closely. He'd spent a great deal of time in the company of liars. Each had their own tell, and he could count on the fingers of one hand the number of times he'd been fooled during a forty-year career. He didn't believe he was in the presence of a liar now.

'I'm inclined to believe you,' he admitted. 'But I will have to think about how I handle this information, Rachael.'

She cocked her head at an angle. 'You're genuinely not looking to report me?'

'I'm honestly not. I'm not here to enforce rules that haven't hurt investigations or betrayed the job in any significant way. Glass houses and wayward stones come to mind. You've been a bit silly, but I'm willing to give you the benefit of the doubt. That does still rely on you ending it with him. Today.'

She stared him down, her eyes earnest. 'I will. Of course I will. Jimmy, I don't want to lose my job. I love my work, and I don't intend to throw away my career on a fling. I understand that's what I've already put at risk, that I acted extremely foolishly, but I genuinely had no ulterior motive. Yes, I spent time with a known criminal, but that doesn't make me a bad cop.'

'No, I don't think it does,' Bliss allowed. 'But I warn you now, if I find out otherwise, you'll pay the price more fully than if you'd been honest with me from the start.'

'I have been honest with you. I swear it.' There was hope in her voice now where previously there had been none.

'Okay. Let me make it clear to you that under no circumstances are you to reveal the topic or nature of this discussion with Vincent when you break up with him or at any time afterwards. Understood?'

'Naturally. It never entered my mind to do so. I'll just tell him it's over and that I'm moving on.'

Something had been nagging at Bliss, and it suddenly popped into his head with full clarity. 'Rachael, you say you were seeing him on and off for seven months. Did you spend any of that time with him in your own home? Does Dougie Vincent know where you live?'

She shook her head and for the first time raised a ragged smile. 'No. I told him I was married, and to his credit he never pushed.'

'That's good. But can you be sure you were never followed? Criminals like Vincent tend to be careful when it comes to people entering their lives. He might have said one thing but done something else entirely.'

Skinner thought about it before shrugging. 'I suppose I can't be certain, no.'

Bliss had sensed that might be her response. 'Am I correct in saying you're not married and there are no children in the picture?'

'You are. Came close once, but it never took. Why do you ask?'

'I'm thinking about the risk factor here, Rachael. Obviously, I can't formally intervene without giving away your story, so you're going to have to be vigilant. Keep an eye on your rear-view, make sure you're not followed. Check your street for strange vehicles. If you haven't already got one, get yourself a doorbell camera fitted. And keep your head on a swivel in the days and weeks to come.' Bliss dipped his hand inside his jacket pocket and pulled out a business card. 'Call me if you have even the slightest niggle in the back of your mind. Rely on your training and instinct. If you even suspect something is not right, give me a bell. Night or day. Agreed?'

'Agreed. I'd be crazy not to. But I have to know… why? Why are you doing this?'

'You mean why am I not throwing you to the wolves?' He smiled when she nodded. 'We've all done foolish things. Things that step over the line. Only today I was cautioned against doing so myself. Fact is, I meant it when I said I have no desire to hurt you over a misdemeanour. Nobody got hurt. This time. And I get the feeling you're unlikely to do it again.'

'You're right about that, Jimmy.'

'I'm pleased to hear it. Anyhow, when you break it off with him do so over the phone. Which reminds me, I take it he has your personal mobile number?'

'He does, yes.'

'But not your work number?'

'No. I'm stupid, but not that stupid.'

'Good. Then make your call to him the last one from that number. Burn the SIM card afterwards and get yourself a new one to start afresh. It'll be a pain, I know, but better safe than sorry. If he really has no idea where you live and you kill the phone number he has for you, then you're closing the door on him permanently.'

'I'll do that. And I'll be ultra careful. But tell me, how are you going to handle this with my colleague and anybody else who might have picked up on a juicy piece of gossip? To be honest with you, this now makes sense of some sideways looks and the odd comment in recent weeks.'

'I'll kill it, Rachael. Stone dead. I'll tell them I'm completely satisfied there was no relationship, and *that* needs to be the next rumour they spread around the office.'

Skinner nodded and thanked him. After a few seconds, she took a breath and spoke almost in a whisper. 'If you don't mind my asking, do you have new evidence regarding Daisy's murder?'

There was little point in denying it. Before long, everybody in her team would have the details. 'We've already requested the original case files from your unit,' Bliss told her. 'So far, only a handful of your team are aware of our renewed interest. By tomorrow you'll be told anyway, so you might as well hear it from me first. The fact is, we have a suspect. Self-confessed. A man who claims to have been involved, while at the same time insisting he had no part in the murder.'

'But I thought it was the boyfriend. The one who later went missing.'

'And having read up on the case I can understand why. But we're taking this confession seriously.'

'He just came in and admitted everything?'

'Oh, no. Not to us. He was inside at the time. Stirred up by something he'd seen or heard, he ranted about it to an inmate he was playing cards with. That prisoner then told his cellmate all about it, who eventually gave us that information. We've spoken to them both. We're convinced the confession happened. What we don't yet know is if it was true.'

'Who is he? Is he known to us?'

Bliss paused this time. It was one thing believing Rachael Skinner's statement, but another taking her into his confidence. But once again, he knew the MCU at Hinchingbrooke would have all the details soon enough.

'It's Jack Maguire,' he said, going against his original decision to keep her in the dark.

The DS cupped both hands over her mouth, her eyes wide and staring. 'Oh, my god,' she muttered once she'd recovered from the shock. 'Are you absolutely certain?'

'We are.'

'Bloody hell. That village of theirs will become a powder keg from the moment Dougie is told.'

'Without a doubt. That's a fire we must fight before it's even begun. And on that note, Rachael, you make that call sooner rather than later. Because we hope to have Maguire in custody either later today or tomorrow, and at that time we will notify the Vincent family. I suggest you're well out of the blast zone by then.'

Nodding, her relief all too apparent, Skinner said, 'Thank you. I made a terrible mistake, and I'll be haunted by it for a long time to come. But I won't forget your kindness here today, Jimmy.'

'Just don't make me regret it,' he told her.

'I won't,' she promised. 'I owe you. More than I'll ever be able to repay.'

'Do me two things and we're even?'

'Okay…' Anxious once again, she extended the second syllable.

'First, do a great job every day. Second, don't fuck up again.'

Holding out her hand, Skinner said with a smile, 'You have yourself a deal.'

They shook on it. Bliss could only hope he was right about her and that she wouldn't call Dougie Vincent to tell him the entire story the moment she stepped outside the coffee house. He trusted his instincts and his judgement. But he wasn't infallible.

'There is just one thing you ought to know,' Skinner said as she stood to leave. 'I have no idea if this has any bearing on the case, but you're obviously worried about bent cops sniffing around this investigation. I'm assuming that reaches back to the original investigation, too. The thing is, when I joined Major Crime at Hinchingbrooke, there was a lot of talk about an officer who had recently left. People were saying how the air smelled sweeter, how they felt free to discuss operations out loud around the building, that sort of thing.'

'Do you remember this officer's name?' Bliss asked, feeling a brief hitch in his breathing.

DS Skinner nodded and told him.

TWENTY-EIGHT

Bliss offered his apologies as he drove to Thorney. He felt guilty about the amount of time he'd devoted to the active case, but he was confident that his team of ex-detectives would understand his priorities. Greenhill hadn't mentioned any unrest, which was a good sign. Back at Thorpe Wood he'd opted to visit the crime scene, and since nobody had complained he thought he'd made the right call.

'I'm with you on this case now, so let's make the most of it,' he said as they bypassed New England on the Soke Parkway. 'I'll start and then you can update me. To begin with, what I'm about to tell you never happened and we will never refer to it again. I spoke with an old mate of mine from county HQ. I asked him if there were any rumours about bent cops. He gave me a name, I checked them out and spoke to them this morning. I don't believe there was any wrongdoing on their part, so I cleared them. At the end of our chat, however, they fed me a different name. Someone who was around at the time of the original investigation but has since left the job. Driving back from that meeting, I spoke with my pal from HQ to advise him of my findings, at which point he then offered up that same name without any prompting from me. The officer in question was close to the first Daisy Vincent investigation.'

'This all sounds a bit cloak and daggery to me,' Beth Greenhill said. 'How come you're being so cagey with the details?'

'I made a promise I intend to keep.' It was as simple as that for Bliss. If he couldn't be true to his word, then he was nothing. 'Provided they stick to their side of the bargain, I won't identify the individual I spoke to. As for the second name to crop up, him we can go after. And we will. But first we have to decide on the order in which we're going to proceed.'

'Which is where we come in,' Ben Corry said from the back seat. 'And, Jimmy, don't worry about the time you need to spend on your active murder case. Truth is, we all heard what happened yesterday and can understand how you must be feeling.'

Bliss gave a grateful nod. 'It's not been easy to deal with. The lad himself made his choices, but the driver he accidentally killed had no say in it. The ripple effect from the fallout is still spreading, but I can assure you of my focus here and now. So, what news do you have for me?'

'We spoke to Jack Maguire's supervising officer, who in turn had a conversation with Maguire. He'll submit himself with his lawyer. All we have to do is say when and where.'

'Does he know why we want to speak with him?'

'We weren't specific, but I think we should assume he has an inkling.'

Bliss agreed. 'All right. Clearly, any interview with him is high on the list. At that point, I don't think we can hold off any longer on informing the Vincent family. I'm in favour of having no overlap, meaning we do both jobs at the same time. I'm open to other suggestions, though. We do also need to speak with this potential bent cop about whether they told the family the police were looking at Daisy's boyfriend. The question is, would it be beneficial to us if we knew the answer to that question prior to disclosing our new investigation to the Vincents?'

'Helpful but not essential as far as I'm concerned,' Guy Foley said. 'At this stage, we're telling them we have someone in the frame for the murder. That alone will hit them hard, especially when they find out who. If they bumped off Stephen Wrigley because they thought he'd murdered Daisy, that will add even more pressure to an already fractious situation. As for us knowing for certain, I'm not sure there's a significant advantage one way or the other.'

'I agree with Guy,' Greenhill said. 'Having that information helps if we're going to delve into the boyfriend's disappearance and look to build a case against Dougie Vincent or even one of his lads but is unimportant at this stage.'

Bliss was quiet for a few moments while he navigated the Volvo through the scene of yesterday's tragic accident, which had reduced the flow to one lane on both sides. He was at the next roundabout before spreading his hands and saying, 'Okay, but are we all agreed on doing the first two jobs at the same time?'

Corry was keen to respond. 'I think it would be good to have Jack Maguire off the streets at that point, because from everything you've told us the Vincents are not going to react well.'

'While I agree with that,' Foley said, 'I'm not convinced we even need to tell the Vincents who we're speaking to. They have a right to know we're reinvestigating, they have a right to know we have a suspect, but we don't have to tell them who.'

'But does that compromise our investigation?' Greenhill asked. 'If it does, then, no, we shouldn't give them his name. But I don't see where it does, especially if we have him in for interview with the real possibility of arresting him.'

'Surely it depends on which investigation we're talking about,' Bliss posited. 'Does it jeopardise ours? I think it might if, as we suspect, the Vincents go after Maguire.'

'But we'll have him in custody,' Foley pointed out. 'And when we're done he'll most likely be remanded back into prison.'

'You think he'll be any safer there? Not to mention the escalation of feelings between the two families and the kind of strife that will cause. But leaving Daisy's murder to one side for the moment, we're now obliged to look beyond that at Stephen Wrigley's disappearance. If I'm Dougie Vincent and I killed the lad, I might not hang around for us to come and slap cuffs on me.'

'So, you're saying we admit we're reinvestigating, that we have a suspect in for interview, but for investigative purposes we're keeping the name to ourselves.'

Nodding along, Bliss said, 'Precisely that. And if you're worried about Vincent finding out we're talking to Maguire, it just occurred to me that we should sort ourselves out an interview room elsewhere. Bedford would be my choice.'

'Jimmy,' Greenhill said. 'I honestly think you're taking it too far. I'm with you in keeping the name to ourselves while Maguire is being interviewed. But you know as well as I do that the moment we push the button on arresting him we have no option but to tell the Vincents the whole story.'

While he didn't like to hear it, Bliss knew she was right. He nodded, then eyed Corry and Foley in the rear-view mirror. 'Looks like we're going for a compromise,' he said. 'Before all that, I think while we're here we might as well make the most of it and inform the Vincents about the reinvestigation.'

Appeased but not entirely pleased, Foley grunted and sat back in his seat. Bliss was happy enough with his decision and drove on in silence. A long and straight stretch of the A47 known as The Causeway fed them into Thorney. Bliss took a right at the

Rose & Crown pub and made his way along to Thorney Abbey, where he pulled up in its car park. Wrapped up against the cold and a savage wind that blew in uninterrupted across wide, flat lands, they took a path leading through the cemetery, which led out into Thorney Play Park. A cloud of breath trailed behind them like steam from a passing train.

A fence enclosed the children's play area, with three wooden tables and bench seats for parents or park goers looking to rest or perhaps eat lunch. 'I doubt this has changed a great deal in the past decade,' Bliss said. He pointed back the way they had come. 'Daisy's body was discovered near the trees where the path we took meets the one heading north that leads back out of the park onto Wisbech Road.'

'From what I remember of the map,' Greenhill said, 'that's the way Daisy would have gone if she was walking home after getting out of her boyfriend's car where the witness spotted her.'

'That's right. Daisy would most likely have taken the same path we did.'

'Through a cemetery at night?' The way Ben Corry spoke his doubt was obvious.

'She could have cut through Church Street instead, but that would still have taken her past the cemetery.'

'But why would she not stick to the main roads is what I'm saying?'

'We don't know that she didn't,' Bliss said. 'She could have been dragged off the road into the park at any point, but there aren't that many ways through. It's more likely that she took a short-cut. After all, this park would have been familiar to her. She'd have felt at home here. I doubt it carried any threat in her mind.'

Greenhill blew out a long stream of breath. 'Once again I'm left to wonder if Daisy Vincent just got unlucky in that her path home crossed with that of her killer, or if he was stalking her and got lucky when she and her boyfriend argued, resulting in her jumping out of the car.'

'You think he might have been following her, just waiting for an opportunity?'

'Stranger things have happened.'

Thinking about the possibility, Bliss said, 'When you went through the crime logs did you happen to notice if the team ran her phone?'

'I did,' Corry replied. 'They ran hers and Wrigley's.'

'What do you remember about the data and the reports they got back?'

'Two standouts. Daisy's chimed with the witness statements. Wrigley's phone didn't move from his home all night. From the moment they discovered he'd spent some of the evening with Daisy in Peterborough, the team assumed he used a burner.'

'Any texts or calls going in or out of Daisy's phone around the time of her murder?'

'Yes. She made one call. To an untraceable number.'

'Which could have been Wrigley's phone, yes?'

'Might have been.'

Bliss nodded. 'One more thing. We keep talking around it, but I'm sure everyone here has their own opinion. From what we know and what we've been told, does anybody fancy Jack Maguire as Daisy's killer?'

All three of his colleagues raised their hands. 'With reservations,' Ben Corry said. 'If we take his so-called confession at face value, he's admitted to being involved, but has also distanced himself from being our killer. Moreover, he claims to know who the killer is.'

'And if we don't take his word for it?'

'Then perhaps he was clever enough to start laying a trail should the investigation ever find a new focus. He makes sure he blabs to somebody he knows will blab to someone else. He injects the notion that he knows something about the murder, including the identity of the killer. He wants that out there to use in his favour at some point in the future should it become necessary.'

'That's an awful lot of ifs, buts, and maybes,' Bliss said.

Frowning at him, Greenhill said, 'I don't think Ben used a single one of those words.'

Bliss grinned. 'I mentally added them, because it's all pure conjecture.'

'So, what do you think, then? Is Maguire our killer?'

'I really have no idea. I must say, I'd like to know what got him so riled up that he vented about his involvement. His slip of the tongue might have been a tall tale. One prisoner trying to impress another. He might just as easily have been telling the truth. Or, like you say, he may be responsible for the rape and the murder.'

'That's some top-class fence sitting there, Jimmy.'

He accepted the gibe from Greenhill with a shrug. 'Okay. Look, the truth is I needed to focus my mind, and I thought the best way of doing that was to visit the crime scene. You three might not have needed the jolt, but I did. I'm seeing it in my mind's eye now. We don't yet know who raped and strangled Daisy Vincent, but Stephen Wrigley is no longer around to question. Jack Maguire is therefore our prime suspect until proven otherwise, so I suggest we head to the Vincent home, get that part over and done with, then head back and start making arrangements to interview our ex-prisoner.'

Foley slapped his gloved hands together and rubbed them. 'Right. Let's get cracking.'

'Beth and I will speak to them while you and Ben wait in the car,' Bliss said. 'It doesn't require four of us to inform the Vincent family that we're taking another look at Daisy's murder. Don't worry, Guy, you'll have your chance another time when you tell them we have a suspect.'

'Oh, great,' Foley muttered. 'You light the blue touch paper and walk away while me and Ben risk tackling the unexploded firework.'

Chuckling, Bliss said, 'It's called delegation. Take a big bucket of sand with you. Besides, don't tell me that's not the part you're most interested in.'

'Ah, I'm saying nothing.'

'And I for one,' Corry interrupted, 'am grateful for your silence, my friend.'

'Just one final thing before we go, Jimmy,' Greenhill said, her voice subdued. 'We still don't know if some bent cop tipped off Dougie Vincent, but you said you were given a second name. Do you plan to share that this time or are you going to keep that one from us as well as part of your shady dealings?'

Bliss shook his head. He understood why the others might feel snubbed, but he had his reasons. 'No, I'm not,' he said. 'I was simply holding out until we'd got everything else settled. I didn't want your heads elsewhere.'

'Why would we? Do we know this officer?'

'I have no idea.' Bliss steeled himself, uncertain how his team might react. 'His name is Jeremy Benning. Police Constable Benning as was at the time of the murder.'

'Fuck!' Corry said, his shoulders slumping.

'Please tell me you're joking,' Greenhill begged him.

Looking between them, Foley said, 'What's going on? Who is this PC Benning?'

Bliss regarded him with deep foreboding. 'Jeremy Benning is David Benning's son. As in Police and Crime Commissioner, David Benning.'

TWENTY-NINE

There was no answer to Bliss's insistent ringing of the doorbell. But while the two of them stood waiting on the path they had gained an audience. He was the first to notice a woman in the garden next door pretending to pay attention to everything but them. The more he pressed the button the more she seemed keen to intervene. Eventually, she couldn't contain herself any longer.

'Can I help?' the neighbour asked, peeling off a pair of blue gardening gloves in a way that suggested she might be about to declare a duel.

'We're looking to speak with Mr or Mrs Vincent,' Bliss replied, turning to face her. 'They appear not to be at home. I don't suppose you know where we are likely to find them, do you?'

As he'd expected, the woman knew precisely where her closest neighbours were and seemed happy to point the police in their direction. Following her simple instructions, the team made their way to Thorney Rugby club which was located in the northern outskirts of the village. It boasted three full-size pitches, a substantial car park, and a modern clubhouse. Impressed with the amenities, Bliss parked facing a pitch on which a handful of players and coaches were running back line drills off the base of a ruck.

'There you go, Ben,' Bliss said, checking him out in the rear-view mirror. 'You can watch a spot of egg chasing while we're inside.' He and Corry both enjoyed the game, having played when they were younger.

'Just standing on the sidelines watching makes me feel old these days,' Corry confessed. 'They hit a lot harder than we did.'

'Don't be such a wimp. I bet you only started playing for the fights during and the beer after.'

'Is there any other reason?'

Bliss and Greenhill clambered out of the SUV and left their colleagues to it. As they walked through the clubhouse doors, Bliss immediately noticed something and nudged his partner. He pointed out a framed jersey hanging on the wall, below a banner proclaiming that the Vincent family sponsored the club. A handful of people sat at tables enjoying hot drinks and snacks, but Bliss recognised Dougie Vincent standing behind the counter. He noticed that the man had clocked the pair of them, showing an immediate interest.

Bliss flashed his credentials as they approached the bar, introducing himself and Beth Greenhill. A deep frown formed above cold, disapproving eyes. Before Vincent jumped to conclusions, Bliss said, 'Is there somewhere a little more private where we could talk? Your wife, too, if she's here.'

After a grudging nod of acceptance, they joined the petty gangster behind the counter before stepping inside a small office, where a frail-looking woman sat at a computer. She looked up and froze in place like a startled animal.

'This is my wife, Fearn. What do you want with us?' Vincent asked gruffly.

Bliss allowed no emotion to filter into his response. 'As I mentioned, sir, we're with the Unsolved Cases Team in Peterborough. As a courtesy to you and your family, we're here to talk to you about your daughter, Daisy.'

The Vincents regarded each other wide-eyed before Dougie said, 'Hold on a moment. If you have something important to tell us about Daisy, then our sons should be involved. They're out on the pitch doing a bit of training, but I can go grab them.'

Bliss held up a hand. 'I don't think that's necessary, sir. Mainly because I'm unable to provide you with any specific details at this early stage. We really only came here to let you know that we are reinvestigating your daughter's murder. It's our job to review cold cases and continue if we believe we can make progress. We've decided this one is worth pursuing.'

Gut feelings were not a leap of blind faith for Bliss. He forged them in the flames of insight, experience, and instinct. When you knew without knowing for certain, but the tightening of your stomach muscles insisted you were right. The look that passed between husband and wife in that moment was not one of hope or expectation, but of sheer dread. A long-forgotten fear disinterred, reaching from the grave of the past like a mouldering corpse taking its first gasp of breath in a decade. The glance Dougie and Fearn Vincent had just exchanged was one of apprehension. Given he had just provided them with positive news, Bliss had to wonder about that.

'You mentioned courtesy,' Dougie said eventually. 'So, please have the courtesy not to take us for idiots.'

'I don't know what you mean,' Bliss replied in his best approximation of appeasement.

'What I mean is, your lot told us ten years ago that while the case remained unsolved, it would technically stay open. But they also said that as far as they were concerned it might as well be closed because Daisy's killer was nowhere to be found. So why the sudden interest?'

'Ours is a relatively new team,' Greenhill explained. 'This is the first opportunity anyone has had to take a fresh look at this case.'

'And what difference will that make if there's no new evidence?'

'That's just the point, Mr Vincent. We won't know if there's any new evidence until we take a look.'

'I don't see how there can be,' he grumbled while his wife sat in silence looking decidedly uncomfortable. 'Nothing has changed. Not as far as we know.'

Bliss cut his partner off before she could continue. 'Neither do we at this stage. But until we get stuck in we can't know for sure. It could be that your daughter's ex-boyfriend has since turned up somewhere. We won't know until we run fresh national, Interpol and Europol searches.'

He felt the heat of Greenhill's scrutiny, but hoped she'd go along with his unscripted ruse. They, of course, were not waiting to run any new searches, because all relevant agencies had Stephen Wrigley's name flagged to report if it ever popped up.

'Okay. What happens now, then?' Vincent asked.

'We get to work. Four of us. The moment anything changes, we'll be in touch. If we reach the end of our investigation without making any conclusive progress, we'll let you know.'

'But it's still that turd Wrigley you're looking for, yes?'

'Of course. We have other angles to work, but naturally he remains our prime suspect.'

Vincent shuffled in place, not quite knowing how to respond. Bliss let him off the hook. 'Look, I realise this has come out of the blue and you must both be in shock to a certain extent. I'm not here to make any promises. But we are reviewing the original investigation, after which we'll run our own from scratch. We've had some success, but other unsolved cases remain that way for good reason. Not for want of trying, I hasten to add.'

If they were grateful, neither Dougie nor Fearn Vincent showed it. They nodded and mumbled, but appeared distinctly unimpressed with the whole thing. Bliss studied Dougie Vincent's face, wondering if DS Skinner had called to dump him yet. He couldn't quite picture the two of them together, but perhaps you had to dig deep to find any magnetism he might possess. Bliss handed over a business card, at which point the two investigators said goodbye and left the couple to it.

As they made their way out of the clubhouse, Bliss raised a hand to forestall Greenhill's pent-up ire. 'Sorry about jumping in with both size tens,' he said. 'I had a thought, said what I had to say, and didn't want you mentioning any doubts we had about the boyfriend. Thanks for playing along.'

Greenhill was fine about it. 'No problem, Jimmy. I caught on. Was it worth it?'

'I'm not sure. Dougie had a lot to say for himself at the beginning, don't you think?'

'He did. Unsurprising, though, given the circumstances.'

'I suppose. To tell the truth, I'm more interested in the question he didn't ask.'

Beth Greenhill chewed that over. After a lengthy pause, she turned to him and said, 'He kicked off by talking about fresh evidence, but didn't ask the most obvious follow-up question of them all.'

Bliss shook his head. 'No. He never thought to ask if Stephen Wrigley had shown up. Which is why I introduced the subject, just to see his reaction.'

'Hmm. Now, I wonder why he didn't mention it.'

'Me, too. Also, there was a look he and his wife shared. Did you clock that?'

'Yes, I did. Hard to mask that level of guilt and fear.'

'I think they did it,' Bliss said. 'More specifically, I think he did it and she has suspected him all along. Now all we have to do is make that knowledge work for us.'

THIRTY

THE BLIND TIGER WASN'T quite to Bliss's taste, but it was close to Sandra Bannister's place of work, so he made the effort as she was the one doing him a favour. He found a decent Pilsner for himself and wrinkled his nose in distaste at having to buy a strawberry and lime cider for his journalist friend. The simple act of placing the order left him feeling a little sick in his throat. They sat at a table beneath an image of a tiger's roaring face and sipped their drinks while exchanging initial pleasantries. Bliss had always enjoyed the reporter's company, though having to watch your every word could, on occasion, be irksome. When the conversation turned to business, she surprised him by asking if he'd considered the possibility that an insider had warned Stephen Wrigley.

For a moment, Bliss sat in stunned silence. He and his team had been so persuaded by the argument that it was Dougie Vincent who had a secret source in his pocket that none of them had thought to ask themselves this particular question. He considered the notion briefly before shaking his head, albeit a gesture lacking confidence.

'If you're suggesting somebody told Wrigley he was about to have his collar felt, at which point he had it on his toes, that's not quite how we see it,' he responded, still shaken by the idea.

'May I ask why not?'

'Not for public consumption, agreed?'

'If you say so.'

'We don't believe he could have remained off our radar for ten years. As a murder suspect, all resources would have been used to find him. Locally, nationally, and internationally. I don't doubt that he could have gone into hiding, only that I don't see how he wouldn't have surfaced somewhere by now.'

'That is, if he's still alive and kicking.'

'Precisely.'

'No, what I mean is that he could have been tipped off, found a way to skip the country, but for some reason didn't last long on the run.'

'No,' Bliss said. 'We would have heard. It's too unlikely, Sandra.'

'But not impossible. And judging by the look on your face, Jimmy, I'd say it's not a path you've ventured down.'

'True. On both counts.'

'And yet you're not at all fazed by my mentioning the notion of an insider. So, if there was one but they didn't tip off Stephen Wrigley himself, then they told who…? The Vincents? You think somebody on your side of the fence informed the Vincent family about Wrigley and they got to him first?'

'Don't tell me,' Bliss said, eyeing her keenly. 'That was your second guess.' He had always admired how shrewd she was, but on occasion it could be a pain in the backside.

Bannister nodded. 'It was. And while I understand your logic in questioning the boyfriend's ability to hide and remain hidden, I do still think it's worth your while looking into it, at the very least.'

'We may well do so. But tell me, how did you arrive at that conclusion?'

'The clues are in the documents I emailed you. Our own digging began with Daisy Vincent getting choked to death, from which point we worked backwards. We definitely have her leaving Wrigley's car, after which he drove off at speed. She didn't have far to walk, but much of her short journey was most likely through that park.'

'You were here in the city at the time,' Bliss said. 'I wasn't. Did you visit the scene at night?'

Bannister took a sip of her drink before nodding. 'Although I wasn't writing up the piece for publication, I did go there to get a sense of the place. I went with a cameraman.'

'Did you walk her likely route?'

'Yes. Straight through the graveyard path. The amber glow from the external abbey lights is a bit eerie and unnerving, but if you grew up there it's probably second nature to walk that way.'

The suggestion echoed Bliss's own thoughts. 'Okay. Sorry, I interrupted you. You were saying…?'

'Where was I? Oh, yes. So, we have Wrigley driving off, and Daisy walking in the general direction of home. But then we learn that her boyfriend is a suspect who suddenly can't be found. We never ran it in the paper, but we did ask ourselves how Wrigley knew to run.'

Despite believing in a betrayal by one of their own, Bliss was quick to inject some doubt. 'I'm not sure about your logic there, Sandra. Let's say Stephen Wrigley wakes the following morning to learn about Daisy's murder. If I'm him, I'm thinking somebody will know I was with her the previous evening. Maybe they found out that we argued, and that later on she demanded to be let out of the car or that I told her to get out. Either way, not only will the police want to have words with me, but Dougie

Vincent isn't going to be happy about it, is he? That alone might prompt me to scarper.'

Bannister allowed that Bliss could be right. But he was more interested in the first question she had thrown at him and wanted to know more. 'Tell me something. You learned that Wrigley had disappeared and went from there to one of us tipping him off. That's not a straight road, Sandra. Why did you immediately think a bent cop might be involved?'

'Because the word circulating our newsroom at the time was there might be one. Perhaps not with the MCU, but certainly working out of Hinchingbrooke.'

'Interesting. Did you ever have a name to go along with the rumour?'

'No.'

That flat denial told Bliss that whoever the newspaper's source was at county HQ, it wasn't anyone close to the original investigation. Sandra Bannister's way of thinking intrigued him, particularly with how swiftly she had jumped to the conclusion that a rogue police officer might have warned Stephen Wrigley. Now he couldn't help but wonder the same thing. Were his team wrong to have focussed on Dougie Vincent, or even Jack Maguire himself? Could Wrigley have had someone on his payroll? The thought prompted another question.

'Why the boyfriend?' he asked. 'From everything we've learned, Stephen Wrigley was not involved with the Vincents' criminal enterprise. He was no choir boy, so he dabbled here and there, but neither did he have any connections to local organised crime that we were able to uncover. Do you know otherwise?'

Bannister shook her head. 'No. It just made sense. He went missing. We didn't automatically assume that meant he was dead and that one or more of the Vincent family was responsible. We went the other way and assumed the stories we were picking up from local villagers about him going on the run were true.'

'But why? Something must have led you there?'

'As I recall it was mainly because the incident had all the trappings of him having extricated himself from a dangerous situation. As part of our story, we also investigated Wrigley's involvement. Some of his clothes were missing, in addition to toiletries and a large holdall. He'd also withdrawn two-hundred pounds from a cash machine in Peterborough; a sum of money he'd never been known to take out in one lump before.'

Nodding to himself, Bliss could see it now. If he'd had that same information, he might also have followed that path. He didn't remember any of his colleagues mentioning the packing or the cash withdrawal after they'd read the reports and crime log, but it was possible they had scanned the details relating to Wrigley because of their focus on Jack Maguire and the Vincent family.

He thanked Bannister and left the bar more confused than he had been at any stage of the reinvestigation. Walking back to the car park by the bus station, Bliss made a call to Toby Wallace, Nick Nevin's ex-cellmate now living in Nottingham. He let the man work through his irritability and frustration at being bothered yet again before asking about what had led to Jack Maguire venting that evening.

'You told us he was heated, upset, and ranting,' Bliss reminded him. 'Do you know why?'

'It was a long time ago. I had many encounters with many inmates. Am I supposed to remember them all in vivid detail?'

'Not all of them, no,' Bliss said reasonably. 'But then, I don't suppose many of those other conversations included a confession to being involved in a murder.'

'You'd be surprised,' Wallace scoffed.

'Perhaps. But I'm willing to bet this one stuck with you, Toby. I know when we spoke with you the other day you seemed to have good recall when it came to what he said. What I'm interested in now is why he said it and his demeanour at the time.'

'Okay, okay. If you promise to fuck off and leave me alone, I'll tell you.'

Smiling to himself, Bliss said, 'I can't promise, Toby. But I will try my best. That'll have to be good enough.'

The following pause lasted long enough to be a silence.

'Toby?' Bliss prompted.

'All right, all right. Yes, he was ranting that evening. He was furious. He'd been watching a true crime show. You know, the kind where a documentary crew follows a team of detectives working cases. Television stations are limited inside, but this one was on Channel Four, I think. If I remember rightly, it was called *Golden Hour*, or something along those lines. We used to joke about them being involved in a golden shower. Anyway, this one was a repeat from the very first series and in one segment they included a piece on the murder of a young woman called Daisy Vincent. Something he saw or heard during that clip drove him up the wall. He didn't say what, precisely, only that it proved him right about what really happened that night.'

Bliss thanked Wallace and made his way back to the station. He found himself alone in the office, where he decided to go through the materials sent over by the original investigation team. Among the items in the digital pack was a video file marked 'Golden Hour'. He nodded to himself, satisfied with the find. He thought it had sounded familiar when Toby Wallace mentioned it, but now he knew where he'd come across it more recently as the crew had filmed some scenes at Thorpe Wood, mainly in the custody suite.

The episode ran for forty-four minutes, of which they spent little more than seven on the Daisy Vincent murder. Bliss watched it on his laptop and was disappointed to discover that the segment was included in a larger piece about public appeals. Here, Dougie and Fearn Vincent, together with Daisy's two brothers, appeared on camera making an appeal at a police press briefing. The two lads, Eddie and Tommy, sat back with their arms folded looking enraged and fit to burst. Fearn dabbed her eyes with a balled-up tissue throughout, appearing gaunt and empty of anything resembling hope. Dougie did all the speaking, all the while turning some worry beads or something similar between his fingers. He spoke without certainty, but with an undercurrent of implied menace. The family wanted people to come forward with information about the night Daisy died and about the missing Stephen Wrigley, yet when you looked at Dougie and his sons you couldn't help but guess their reaction if you did.

Bliss watched it through twice more, struggling to work out what had provoked Jack Maguire's outrage. In the end, he decided it wasn't so much anything Vincent had said, more that he'd had the gall to make any appeal whatsoever for Stephen Wrigley to come forward. After all, why would you when you already knew he was dead? Perhaps in the fraternity of the criminal classes it was well known that Dougie Vincent had taken care of business himself upon learning that his daughter's boyfriend was the only suspect the police were looking to speak to.

Thinking about the information Sandra Bannister had passed on, Bliss could envisage a scenario in which it all fitted quite neatly. Having either learned or suspected he'd be considered guilty by the police – and worse still by the Vincent family – Wrigley had packed his bags looking to get as far away from Thorney as possible. Only to run into Dougie Vincent, perhaps together with his two boys, before he could make good his escape.

Believing something wasn't the same as proving it, however. Bliss knew he and his team would have to do better. They needed more than instinct and suspicion. He decided to run his theory by them when they returned to the office. For the time being, he'd sit and consider more the role Jack Maguire had played. And might yet continue to play.

THIRTY-ONE

THE TWO- AND THREE-STOREY sand-coloured Bedfordshire police HQ building looked depressingly uninspiring and functional from the outside. The interior was no better, though it was all a step up from the brutalist architecture of Thorpe Wood. Bliss recognized the familiar look and smell of the interview room, but although the Vincent family were none the wiser he'd still considered it a valid idea to remove a possible target from the area and was satisfied with his decision. The thirty-year-old suspect's solicitor, Naomi Ferguson, was not someone either Bliss or Greenhill had encountered before, but she came across as affable and reasonable. Maguire himself was tall, broad, strong-looking, and appeared healthy and relaxed.

'Thank you for agreeing to this interview,' Bliss said to him. 'Hopefully you can help clear a few things up for us and be out of here in no time at all.'

'No problem,' Maguire said. 'I've nothing to hide.'

The London accent surprised Bliss. He wondered if the Maguire family had moved up from the capital to Thorney. 'That's good to know. Let me dive right in, then, by asking you about Daisy Vincent.'

Maguire made a solid attempt at letting the question wash over him, but Bliss noticed the man tensing before he replied. 'What about her?'

'Oh, so you do know her, then?'

'I know of her, naturally. Look, I'm sure you lot know my family and the Vincents don't get on. You might say we're rivals. Enemies, even. So, yes, I know they had two sons, and a daughter called Daisy. Other than the fact she got murdered donkey's years ago, that's about it.'

'Since you've mentioned the murder, that is why we're here,' Beth Greenhill clarified. 'Tell me, Mr Maguire, do you happen to know where you were on the night of 14 September 2014?'

'Do you?' he scoffed, raising a quizzical eyebrow.

'Just answer the question, please.'

'That *is* my answer. Can you remember off the top of your head where you were ten years ago? Because I can't. My answer to your question is, I can't remember.'

'Let me see if I can jog your memory,' Bliss said patiently. 'That night, as they were driving home following a night out together, Daisy Vincent got into an argument with her boyfriend, Stephen Wrigley. When they reached Thorney, Daisy got out of the car and elected to walk the rest of the way home. We believe she took a shortcut past the abbey and through the park. And the reason why you should recall this very well, Mr Maguire, is that this is the same night she had the misfortune to run into somebody as she made her way home. And shortly after she did so, Miss Vincent was lying in the park strangled to death having first been raped.'

Maguire raised a hand, placed the palm against his chest. 'Are you trying to suggest that I did that to her?'

'We consider it likely, yes. We know for a fact you were there. We know for a fact you were involved. It's not too much of a stretch to imagine the rest.'

'You what?' Maguire seemed incredulous. 'You can't know anything of the sort.'

'We can,' Bliss assured him. 'We do.'

'How can you when it never happened?'

'Because you told us, Mr Maguire.'

'I did what?'

'You told us. In a roundabout fashion. We have a statement attesting to the fact that you openly revealed your involvement to a fellow prisoner while you were serving time inside HMP Woodhill. What do you have to say to that?'

The ex-con's solicitor advised him that he needn't offer any response. Maguire nodded but did so anyway. 'Let me get this straight. You're telling me somebody I did time with informed you that I confessed to raping and killing Daisy Vincent, yes? Because if that's the case, they're lying to you. I don't know why they would, only that they have to be.'

Bliss was about to reply when the man's precise wording jarred. Jack Maguire's demeanour wasn't that of an innocent man accused of such horrendous acts, but of someone paying close attention to the language used in the accusation. Based on the observation, Bliss took a chance.

'They actually said you admitted to being involved, Mr Maguire.'

'There you go, then. That's not the same thing at all, is it?'

'To be fair,' Beth Greenhill pointed out. 'We never suggested all of that. It was you who filled in the details.'

'Semantics,' Maguire snapped back. 'Let's focus on what you've been told. Or what you claim to have been told. I supposedly spoke about my involvement, but at no time did I confess to the murder. Right?'

'Correct,' Bliss confirmed. 'Nor the rape, for that matter.'

Nodding to himself, their suspect eased back into his chair. 'And did this prison snitch tell you anything else?'

Uneasy at Maguire believing he could dominate proceedings, Bliss said, 'I think we should stick to us asking the questions.'

'And I don't give a toss what you think. Did this prison snitch tell you anything else? Yes or no? Answer me or I'm done talking.'

Quickly weighing their options, Bliss decided he wanted to keep Maguire on side for the time being, and there was nothing to be gained from keeping the final part of his confession off the record. 'They did,' he admitted. 'They also added one final admission of yours. Apparently, you told them you knew who raped and murdered Daisy Vincent.'

Maguire shook his head with some vigour. 'No, no, no. That's all kinds of wrong. I don't know what your game is, but either they were telling you porkies or you're trying to pull some kind of stroke. Now, did they tell you I knew who raped and murdered Daisy, or did they tell you I knew who murdered her?'

Raising an apologetic hand, Bliss said, 'Sorry, that was entirely my fault. I misspoke. It was the murder only.'

'Not the rape?'

'No. But in the grand scheme of things, does that make any difference? After all, we know she was raped prior to being murdered.'

Maguire leaned forward, almost halfway across the narrow table. 'Well, see, now that's where you are wrong. One-hundred percent wrong.'

Bliss frowned, but shook his head. 'No, sir. We don't believe so. The post-mortem revealed recent bruising around the victim's vagina, in addition to traces of lubricant. Our forensic people even traced the lubricant to a specific brand of condom.'

'Hmm. Let me guess. Notty Boy, right?'

This time, Bliss was so surprised that he and Greenhill exchanged puzzled glances. She shrugged, unable to explain how their suspect might have acquired this information. Bliss took a beat, and in doing so decided to change his approach. The man clearly had something to tell them, so now was the right time to encourage him.

'Go on,' he said, giving Maguire a nod. 'I think there's more you want to say.'

'There might be,' Maguire said, folding his arms beneath his chest. 'But before I say another bloody word I need to know you won't try pinning this on me.'

For a second time, his solicitor advised him to say no more. For a second time, he ignored her advice. 'See, I know how you lot work,' Maguire continued. 'Bird in the hand and all that. I admit to what I know, you take that as a win and do me for the whole thing.'

'That's not how I do my job,' Bliss assured him. 'My objective here today is to get to the truth. If you played no part in the rape and murder of Daisy Vincent, then I will not be advising my warranted colleagues to arrest and charge you. But with us looking hard at you as a suspect, Mr Maguire, I do advise you to get the point before I run out of patience.'

For a moment, the room was silent. They had reached a critical and unexpected juncture, and Bliss knew it could still go either way. He'd reached similar positions before, only to have the suspect either lose their nerve or cave in to pleas from their solicitor. But eventually Maguire took a deep breath and said, 'Do you know how I was able to tell you the brand of condoms used?'

'No.' Bliss shook his head. 'I'm happy to listen to what you have to say, though.'

'Okay. I know because Notty Boy is my brand of choice. Daisy wasn't raped the night she died. And I know that as well because the bruising and the lubricant you mentioned were down to me. I fucked her that night. And I have to say it was ferocious because Daisy liked it that way. She was willing, is what I'm telling you. More than willing. In fact, she was the one who suggested it, out there in the open air. But, yes, I went along with it. Which is why I've kept schtum about it all this time. Because you lot find that out and you assume I must have gone on to strangle her as well. Well, I didn't. The truth is, when I left her, she was alive and well and as happy as I'd ever seen her.'

THIRTY-TWO

'You admit to having sexual intercourse with Daisy Vincent on the night she was murdered,' Bliss exclaimed, numbed by the admission. He couldn't tell if he felt frozen inside because he had previously assumed the man's guilt or because he strongly suspected Maguire was telling the truth.

'Consensual sex, yes,' Maguire stated plainly. 'Not rape. You got that? It's important you understand and accept the difference.'

'I need some time to consult with my client,' Naomi Ferguson said brusquely.

'Is that what you want, Mr Maguire?' Bliss asked. 'Do you feel the need to pause this interview to speak to your brief, or would you prefer to get it all off your chest right here, right now?'

'I must insist!' the solicitor almost shrieked. 'You will not ask my client any further questions and he will not offer any further admissions until such time as we have discussed these matters further on our own and off the record.'

By this time, Maguire had turned to look down his nose at her. With a sneer, he said, 'You insist fuck all on my behalf, lady. You represent me, but you don't fucking own me. I'll decide when I'm done talking. Okay?'

'Really, Jack, it's my job – my duty – to offer you the best advice possible,' Ferguson said, oblivious to his manner and admirably fronting up to the outburst. 'And I'm telling you now that continuing with this interview without us first discussing what you should or should not say is not in your best interests.'

The contemptuous stare remained in place, but this time when he spoke, Maguire lost the attitude. 'Fair enough. You have a job to do, I get that. But the way this works is, you advise and I either take that advice or I don't. What you fail to grasp is that I have an opportunity here to get something on record that's been nagging at me for ten-bloody-years. So, I'm going to get it off my chest, you understand?'

In reply, the young woman could only shrug.

Maguire nodded and turned back to the two investigators. 'Right. Let's get this sorted once and for all. Nobody knows about this because nobody *could* know about this. I'm a Maguire and Daisy was a Vincent. We ain't exactly the Montagues and Capulets, but we fancied each other rotten.' He smiled at the looks on their faces. 'Yeah, I know some Shakespeare. Big deal. The thing is, right, me and Daisy hooked up in a club early one morning. We just clicked, and I fucked her brains out in a store cupboard within an hour of meeting her for the first time. Basically, when we first got together, I was just Jack to her, and she was Daisy to me. It wasn't until later that our surnames came out. We knew that meant we couldn't go on seeing each other. So, that was that. But by then we'd swapped phone numbers, leaving the door ajar. We exchanged a few texts, followed by a few calls, and then we met up again.'

'And while this was going on between you, Daisy was still seeing Stephen Wrigley, yes?' Bliss said, his head buzzing with possibilities.

'Yeah. But she was looking to elbow him. We knew we didn't have a future together, me and her, but she wasn't happy with him, and I wasn't seeing anyone else at the time. It wasn't planned, but the night… the night she was killed she met up with Wrigley at a club in the city while she was out with her mates. He insisted on driving her home, but they continued the argument they'd begun in the club. She got pissed off enough to tell him she was seeing someone else and wanted to end it with him. He stopped the car, at which point they had a screaming match. He ended up telling her to fuck off, which is what she did.'

Bliss closed his eyes momentarily, nodding as he saw it play out inside his head. 'She called you. Told you what had happened. You went to her.'

Maguire shrugged. 'Yeah. We met in the park and couldn't keep our hands off each other. I only just about remembered to pull on the old Notty Boy. When we were done, we made arrangements to see each other again the following week. We were well aware of the risks, but we fancied each other like crazy. I offered to walk her home, but she said she wanted to keep looking up at the sky for a while. I said I'd stay with her, but she wanted to spend a few minutes on her own. We kissed goodbye. That was the last time I saw her.'

What Bliss heard in that final sentence was a deep and sincere amount of regret.

'That's an awful lot of information to digest, Mr Maguire,' Greenhill said, puffing out her cheeks. 'But I'm willing to bet there's not even a single scrap of it that you can prove.'

'That's where you're wrong, darling,' he said with a sly grin. 'See, although at the time I was using what you people might think of as a burner phone, I never got around to burning it. I'm not stupid, so I removed the battery and SIM card. But I kept them. I still have those text messages I told you about.'

'Which might just about prove you two were an item. But on the night in question, she called you. Which means there'll be a record of the call, but not of what was said. Nor what happened afterwards.'

Maguire licked his bottom lip. 'See? I knew that's what you people would do. I tell you something and you twist it around to suit your needs, not mine. Look, the fact is when I told that fucking idiot in prison what I did, I was wound up and raging. Even then, all I did was admit to being involved. I've just told you how. I always knew you'd try and spin it against me, but I had to tell somebody. I couldn't keep it to myself no longer.'

'All right, Jack,' Bliss said smoothly. 'Calm down. For argument's sake, let's say we believe you. Let's say everything you've told us is true. It explains away what we understood to have been a rape. That's all well and good, but it's not explaining what happened to Daisy afterwards. Now, the person who told us about your confession also told us something else. That you said you'd realised who murdered her. So, assume for one moment that we're interested in your story so far. To truly buy it, for you to convince us, we're going to want more. We're going to want the name of the person you say murdered Daisy Vincent.'

When Maguire nodded this time, it almost looked contemplative. As if he might be deciding how best to construct his next answer. But instead, he sucked in a deep breath and said, 'I think this is probably the right time to have a word with my brief.'

'Oh, come on!' Greenhill cried, flinging her arms in the air. 'You brought us this far. Why not give us the rest?'

'You think her boyfriend came back, don't you,' Bliss added. 'You think Stephen Wrigley killed Daisy.'

'This time, that really will be it,' Naomi Ferguson said, rising to her feet. 'I want to talk with my client in a consultation room.

Who knows what recording devices you might leave running if we stay in here?'

'Behave,' Bliss said without looking in her direction. 'You know we couldn't use it as evidence if we did that.'

'And rightly so. But you might be inclined to listen in anyway. Consultation room, please. Now. I am terminating this interview.'

Bliss knew precisely what that meant. As he and Greenhill traipsed upstairs, they discussed the implications. They agreed that Jack Maguire would offer no comment in any future interviews. Bliss was of the opinion that it had little reliance on his solicitor and everything to do with the fact that he had offered up the part of the story he wanted out there. It was something that had been weighing heavily on him for more than a decade and finally, under controlled circumstances, he had got to tell his part in Daisy Vincent's tragic story.

'Do you really believe he knows who killed her?' Greenhill asked as they reached the corridor.

'Based on what we heard today I'm not sure. If anything was going to convince me it's the fact that he brought it up during his rant in prison. Even so, I'm on the fence.'

'What made you mention Stephen Wrigley back there?'

'Just a hunch. I can see it, though, can't you? They argue, he slings her out of the motor and speeds off like a bat out of hell. But then he calms down and circles back, goes looking for her, sees her and Maguire at it, quietly seethes until it's over, and when Daisy is alone once more his temper flares one last time.'

'It's certainly feasible,' Greenhill said. 'Makes sense in a psychopathic sort of way. But what did you make of his reaction when you mentioned the boyfriend's name?'

And there was the glitch in the matrix. At the point of naming Wrigley as Daisy Vincent's killer, the world had made complete sense to Bliss. He'd considered it a moment of inspiration, the point at which he had cracked the case. And yet… Jack Maguire's facial expression and body language had not been those of a man who realised he had been bested.

'I think we have more work to do,' Bliss said after a lengthy pause. 'We have most of the story. I'm just not convinced we have it all.'

THIRTY-THREE

Leaving Beth Greenhill to update their cold case colleagues ahead of them quitting for the night, Bliss met with DCI Warburton to discuss the investigation into Sheila Musgrove's murder. Her mood was subdued as she explained that their day had been one lacking in direction and filled with frustration. Rather than set about creating new actions and running about like the proverbial headless chickens, she'd indulged in the time-honoured process of taking a step back to check and double check all the information they had to date.

'As you well know,' she said, 'this case has been fast-moving with barely enough time to catch our breaths. I used today to do just that. I thought it best to solidify what we had, what we knew, what we had done, and to create a solid foundation for us to build upon. Time to either shake things loose or shore them up. To me it made sense to establish a firm foothold before trying to come up with miracle moves that might see us marching off in the wrong direction because we'd overlooked something we already had.'

'That sounds reasonable to me,' Bliss responded with a nod. 'What did you learn from the exercise?'

'That as far as I can tell we've missed nothing. No false steps that we could see. What we boiled it down to in the end was luck. We got the good stuff prior to yesterday, after which the bad sort rained down on us like a hail of shit. As expected, the media is after our blood. You had your own run-in with them, so you'll know that the loss of life is entirely our fault as far as they're concerned. The one exception being the *Peterborough Telegraph*. Their chief crime reporter, Sandra Bannister, was at pains to point out the facts. She made it clear to everybody that Matt Dories was not being chased when he was killed because we didn't know his precise location at the time. Curiously, when a fellow journalist raised the issue of traffic officers being on the scene, Bannister was able to inform them by way of a carefully phrased question of her own that the officers were actually travelling in the opposite direction and happened to witness it – along with dozens of other vehicles.'

'Why do you say "curiously"?'

'Because it's awfully precise, wouldn't you say? Almost as if she'd been briefed.'

'I assume she did her homework. Bannister is one of the better journos out there.'

The look Warburton gave Bliss screamed scepticism, though she did not labour the point. 'However she gathered her information, it worked in our favour. Without that monkey on our backs, we're free to concentrate on what matters. As a team we spoke about how our four Tangos knew we were coming, but agreed there was little point in pursuing that aspect now. It's not a priority.'

'Agreed. I take it Danek was allowed to leave, pending further investigation?'

'He was. We couldn't hold him beyond the twenty-four. I took the decision not to go to the CPS with it, Jimmy. There was no way they'd agree to charges given what we had and taking into account his statement. Truth is, I decided we'd be better off with all resources focussed on the murder and the attack on Gul than on the theft of a vehicle.'

'I'd've done the same thing. Did you pass it on to CID?'

She shook her head. 'Not yet. I thought I'd wait to see how you felt about the decisions made in your absence. This is still your case.'

Bliss frowned. 'Diane, I'm never going to second guess you when you stand in for me. I'll back any and every decision you make. In this instance, there's not a thing I would have done differently.'

'Thank you for that,' Warburton said, offering a warm smile.

'Don't mention it. It was time to take that step back, as we'd been all guns blazing up until that point. How is the team coping?'

'Let's just say they'd appreciate a word from you before knocking off for the day.'

Ten minutes later, Bliss gathered his Major Crime crew together in the major inquiry room. In virtually every investigation, a team encountered moments during which their frustrations threatened to spill over. It was the SIO's duty to show leadership qualities throughout every case, and never more so than when it seemed about to lose momentum. Sensing the danger of this one going off the boil, he acted swiftly.

'DCI Warburton informs me that you've already taken a valuable look at the bigger picture,' he said. 'I welcome that move. It frees us up to make progress rather than dwelling on what we have or haven't achieved so far. One thing did occur to me as a result of my conversation with Diane. We found this gang by putting together a list of Bartek Danek's known associates. In that list, we discovered the names of Peter Holland, Matt Dories, and Patrick Walsh. They were the most obvious candidates given they shared an address. But there were others, and I think we need to look more closely at them.'

'You want me to pick that up, boss?' DS Bishop asked.

Bliss shook his head. 'No. Alan and Vas, I want you to tackle that one. Bish and Pen, I want you on a similar but different task. Like I said, Holland, Dories, and Walsh were Danek's known associates. And unless any of you have a better idea, I say we now build lists of *their* KAs. The events of yesterday morning tell us these gang members were prepared for a police raid. That's not unusual when you live the life these people do. But in second-guessing our moves and exploiting them, they left a lot behind. These men were settled in their homes on the camp site, presumably among friends and allies. Our accident victim had nothing on him except for some cash, which suggests his mates are in the same boat. They have to know they can't return, but if they planned their escape, then we must assume part of that plan included an eventual rendezvous point. Our next move is to either discover the location or find somebody else who knows it.'

'That all sounds good,' Chandler said. 'You're suggesting their known associates might lead us to one or the other of the outstanding Tangos.'

'I am. I suspect the meeting place is either another camp site or an isolated caravan or mobile home. And I doubt it will be too far away, but I'm guessing just enough that it puts distance between us and them. Either way, I also think there's a good chance that one of their friends, most likely someone they have in common, will act as their main point of contact. If we begin by narrowing the list of KAs to people that appear on all three lists, or two at the very least – we exclude Danek because he's obviously an outsider – then hopefully we end up with a manageable number to work with. Everyone on board with that?'

They were. Bliss detected a renewed sense of purpose. He surveyed their faces and knew what they needed to hear next. 'Okay. I suggest you all go home and get some rest. I know how knackered I am, so you lot must be running on fumes.' He dismissed their protests. 'I know you're all willing to burn yourselves out over this one, especially as one of our own got hurt by these tosspots. But I need you sharp. The investigation needs you sharp. Mrs Musgrove's family needs you sharp. If you're exhausted, that's when mistakes get made. So go home, enjoy some time with other people if you have them in your life, and come back refreshed tomorrow morning.'

In truth, Bliss wasn't sure what they would find when they began their searches. But it was a common goal, a target they could aim for when previously there wasn't one in view. It was something they could all agree upon and strive together to deliver. He saw relief in their eyes, and that was more than enough for him.

THIRTY-FOUR

Early that evening Bliss took an unexpected call from Beth Greenhill. She had stayed on in the city to meet up with an old friend over a coffee, but had later found herself at a loose end and yearning for some company. He invited her over to his place to eat provided they kept shop talk off the menu, after which he ordered a delivery of hot sandwiches from Sub-Xpress.

'You must be desperate to seek me out to spend time with,' he said when Greenhill arrived. Bliss took her coat and hung it up alongside his own in the hallway.

'I was,' she said, fussing over Max, who greeted her like an old friend. 'It was either you or the Samaritans, and they were engaged.'

'Probably because they knew you'd be calling and didn't want to listen to you whinge and whine about your day.'

Laughing, Greenhill said, 'You'd better have ordered that food, because if this is how you greet people into your home then clearly you've become a shit host.'

'Subs are on the way,' he said, leading her into the living room, still chuckling at her joke. 'But remember, no work talk. After the last couple of days, I just need to switch off.'

Greenhill moved her head from side to side, stretching her neck muscles. 'I have no problem with that, believe me. The job we're working is tough enough. At least I don't have your active case to deal with as well.'

She took a seat on the sofa. Bliss sat on his recliner, swivelling it around to face his guest. 'What can you do?' he said with a shrug. 'That's the job I signed up for. Anyhow, to what do I owe the honour of this particular visit to my humble abode?'

'Like I told you, I was close by, the evening ahead seemed to stretch out endlessly before me, and I suppose I just didn't fancy a late dinner alone at my place. You must get like that sometimes, surely.'

Bliss nodded. 'Of course. As I've often said to other people, living alone doesn't make me lonely, but I won't deny there are times when I could do with some company. The Windmill is my usual remedy. To tell the truth, I couldn't even be arsed to walk down there tonight. As it goes, you probably did me a favour. I would have sat here on my Tod, watching some boring game of football on the telly, and at some point, yesterday's failures would have sucked me in. With you here, I can focus on not focussing… if you get my drift.'

'I think I do.' Casting her gaze around the room, Greenhill said, 'I meant to say this last time I was here, but it's not exactly what I would call cosy, Jimmy. You don't have much in the way of keepsakes or photos.'

Bliss laughed, appraising the four walls for the first time in many months. 'You should have seen the place before Pen forced my hand. I had no shelves, nothing on the walls at all. That sofa was a late entry. In fact, until recently, I still had unpacked boxes stacked up in the dining room. Truth is, I only opened them up to see what I could throw if and when I move.'

'Ah, yes. The move. How's that going?'

He waggled a hand sideways and back again. 'I made an offer. I'm waiting to hear if the owners accepted it, though the agent didn't seem optimistic.'

He was about to expand further when they were both alerted to a noise coming from the front door. It wasn't the knock Bliss had been waiting for. Instead, he heard the metallic clunk of a lock disengaging. A moment later, Chandler's voice chirped, 'I hope you're decent, old man. At the very least you better have some shorts on, you...' Her words trailed off as she closed the door behind her and noticed three pairs of eyes looking back at her. Max trotted forward, tail wagging. She knelt to pet him, cringing with embarrassment.

'I'm so sorry,' she said. 'I had no idea you two were... that you two were...'

'Oh, we're not,' Greenhill said, waving aside the assumption. 'There is no "we two", Penny. I was in the city and feeling peckish, Jimmy suggested SubXpress delivered for dinner. That's all there is to it.'

'You sure you don't want to be even more emphatic about how you and I couldn't possibly be an item,' Bliss said, grinning at his cold case colleague. 'I mean, it's not such a wild suggestion, is it? Me and you. We two.'

Like an animal caught in the headlights, Beth Greenhill perched on the edge of her sofa cushion looking mutely between them both, her cheeks colouring rapidly as if they might sizzle to the touch. Chandler walked uneasily into the living room, twirling a keychain on one gloved finger as Max followed at her heels.

'I suppose you're wondering about this, right?' she said, then bit into her lip. 'Why I have a key to this house? Why I just used it without knocking?'

Greenhill raised both hands. 'I have absolutely no questions or expectations. Whatever arrangements you two have is entirely down to you, and only you.'

'There's no hidden meaning to it,' Chandler insisted. 'I do hope you realise there's nothing going on between us. I mean, this is Jimmy we're talking about, Beth.' She faked a shudder, with a hint of dry heaving.

'Well, fuck you both very much,' Bliss said. 'I won't pretend I've had women fighting over me before, but I can assure you I've never previously had two women so desperate to disassociate themselves from me, either.' He shook his head in mock displeasure and said, 'The truth is, I'm too good for you, Pen. We both know it, and I'm sure Beth would agree.'

Greenhill groaned and wrapped both hands over her head as her chin slumped to her chest. 'Please,' she whispered. 'Let this be a nightmare. Let me wake up and realise none of this ever happened.'

This elicited laughter from both Bliss and his uninvited guest. 'Let me explain,' he finally said to put Beth out of her misery. 'A while back, Pen and the others were forced to come looking for me after I failed to show up at work. The following day she and I swapped spare keys should we ever need them to gain access in similar circumstances. Pen being Pen, she takes advantage of my good nature and swans in and out whenever the notion takes her. Also, she and I both know what's really behind her letting herself in unannounced. She once got to see me in my shorts, and now finds it impossible to stop fantasising about it.'

Chandler was nodding, her eyes crinkling. 'It's true, Beth. I have a thing about dumpy old geezers with fat, hairy legs.'

They were saved from further torture by the doorbell. Bliss collected the food order and brought it into the kitchen. 'You want some, Pen?' he asked. 'We have a large mesquite and a Piri Piri.'

Declining the offer, Chandler told them she'd make herself scarce and leave them to their dinner. Greenhill wouldn't hear of it and demanded Bliss cut her sub in half to share. In the end he cut both subs into thirds and distributed them equally. He also pulled three bottles of Peroni from the fridge.

'This is a work-free zone for tonight,' he said to Chandler as he handed her a plate and a beer. When they were all settled, they got stuck into the toasted baguette sandwiches. The silence between them lasted for less than a minute.

'Is this the first time you've been here, Beth?' Chandler asked. The question seemed casual enough, though it carried enough subliminal meaning to draw a frown from Bliss.

Greenhill shook her head. 'No. Third time. In fact, I was just saying how… unlived in it looks.'

'Believe me, it's in showroom condition compared to how it used to be. I reckon Jimmy was still living out of a suitcase years after moving in.'

'Please,' he shot back. 'Do carry on talking about me as if I wasn't here.'

Chandler sneered at him. 'You were a recluse living in a sterile hermit's cave until I forced you to put a few bits and bobs around the place.'

'She bullies me,' Bliss explained.

'No, I worried about you. Everything here screamed impermanence. It was as if you couldn't wait to leave us again.'

'And that bothered you?' Greenhill asked her.

'It concerned me, yes. Not because he's any great shakes as a human being, you understand. But I'd got used to having him as my boss, and I really couldn't be doing with breaking in anyone else.'

'I can well understand that. Which reminds me, I hear you've taken a step up yourself, Penny.'

'It was about time,' Chandler said with an enthusiastic nod. 'Past time, in truth.'

'DI this year,' Bliss said. 'And when she's had enough of working at the sharp end, Chief Inspector is hers for the taking. However, we've strayed over to work, which we agreed we wouldn't talk about.'

Chandler rolled her eyes. 'Get him on the subject of fish, Beth,' she said, biting into her sandwich with a heavy crunch. 'Or if you're suffering from insomnia lately, have him bang on about music. Puts me to sleep every single time.'

'You're a philistine,' he told her. 'You wouldn't know good music if it bit you on the arse.'

'Me? You're stuck in the past, mate. You think great music began in the sixties and ended in the eighties. You think that if an album wasn't produced with the help of drugs, it isn't a proper album. That's your philosophy.'

Bliss shook his head wearily, but with a broad smile on his face. He needed this. He'd been glad when Beth had called, more thankful still when Chandler had turned up out of the blue. This was not a night for introspection followed by the inevitable doubt and second-guessing. His Op had been blown out of the water. Two men had unnecessarily lost their lives, one of them entirely innocent, though neither had deserved such an end. Those kinds of days often compelled him to question the validity of his work, or at least his impact, leaving him sleepless and miserable. Last night he'd been too tightly wound even to fret, the sense of defeat fuelling a passionate fury as opposed to rancour or sublimation.

There was time enough for all that when the investigation was over, he reckoned. The moment when he'd put himself through his own debriefing, with no holds barred and only the truth as his witness. He had a feeling he'd need to be at his best in the coming days, because the odds, while not insurmountable, were stacked against him and his colleagues.

THIRTY-FIVE

For the first time since the start of the new year, Bliss awoke to a turn in the weather. A piercing wind continued to make it bitterly cold outside when he walked Max, but the grass was no longer crisp to the touch, he saw no chunks of ice on the pond to break up, and not even a thin film of frost coated the Volvo's windscreen when he left home. He chose to take the slight increase in temperature as a portent of better things to come. Superstitious nonsense, maybe, but he welcomed any sign of optimism.

The first thing he did when he got to work was to meet with Superintendent Edwards. His name was not on her overcrowded schedule, but in the voicemail he'd left while he was out with the dog he'd asked for ten minutes of her time, claiming it was an emergency situation. Now she was asking him to explain himself, and suddenly he didn't feel quite as confident as he had when he'd entered her office.

'First of all,' he said, 'I apologise for skipping ranks. DCI Warburton could have done this on my behalf, but I wanted to cut out the middle… woman.'

'That's not a problem, Jimmy. You're here now. Please do go on.'

'Okay. There are two things. The first is something neither of us will want to touch, but which happens to be an issue I feel duty bound to report. The second is a matter of procedure.'

'Fine. Let's get the first part over with.'

Bliss related in detail his recent conversation about the current Police and Crime Commissioner's son. When he was done, Edwards nodded and revealed that the rumour had spread to the higher ranks. Although only a DCI at the time she had learned of it through Marion Fletcher.

'So, everybody knew but it got buried anyway,' Bliss said with more than a hint of resentment.

'Yes and no,' Edwards replied after a momentary pause. 'You have to realise, in those days his father was just another failed cop, and so carried no influence. Behind the scenes, the incumbent Chief Constable was briefing for a case to be put together. But before anything solid became of it, Jeremy Benning handed in his resignation. There was talk of continuing the disciplinary process even after he'd left the job, but to be perfectly honest there was little stomach for it.'

'I wish I was surprised by that. So, I should say nothing about this matter, then? I'm guessing it would be better all round if I failed to include the intel in my investigation report.'

'That's entirely up to you, Jimmy. I'm not sure what good it would do anybody if it came to light now. Quite the opposite, I suspect.'

'Do we know if he caused much damage at the time?'

'A little, but nothing we couldn't overcome. He might have been a real problem had he stayed and been good at it, but he never earned the complete trust of his colleagues. Like I say, it's up to you what you do with this intel. But you might want to consider leaving this one alone.'

'And if I find out he leaked our interest in Stephen Wrigley? A leak that might have led to Wrigley being murdered, I'd remind you.'

Releasing a long sigh, Edwards said, 'I can't tell you what to do if that proves to be the case, Jimmy. Well, I can, of course. But I won't. I know you. I know you'll want Jeremy Benning to pay if he fed that information to the Vincent family, especially if doing so got a man killed. If it were me, I dare say I'd feel the same way.'

'With respect, Alicia, you're as involved in this as I am. What is your gut telling you?'

'What it usually does. To approach with caution. In this instance, you have to balance your desire to punish an ex-copper for betraying his position against the consequences of doing so. David Benning is unlikely to take it lying down, not when his son's reputation is at stake. He'll fight you on this and given his position he'll most likely win. What will you have achieved if that's the way it turns out?'

Bliss chewed on his lip, then said, 'Once again you've turned it back on me. I asked what you would do. Will do. Other than telling me you'd act cautiously, I still don't have an answer.'

'Then you shall have it, Jimmy. I cannot report this matter unless it appears in your investigation report. If I do, people will ask why you failed to mention it. But should it make your report, should a repeat of this conversation become more formal, I will raise it up the chain of command. All I ask is that you first weigh up the pros and cons.'

'You still haven't said what you would do.'

She shook her head at his doggedness. 'If it were me and I discovered irrefutable proof that Jeremy Benning sold information to the Vincents and that information ultimately cost Stephen Wrigley his life, I'd do everything in my power to nail the bastard.'

Bliss grinned. 'I was hoping you'd say that.'

'I was hoping I wouldn't have to. But approach with caution, Jimmy.'

'I'll give it some thought.'

Edwards nodded. 'Good. Now, you said you had something procedural to discuss.'

Bliss took the hint and moved on, reserving judgement on how they had handled the issue. 'I wouldn't normally have bothered you, but this has to go through you due to budget constraints. We still have surveillance in place on the mobile home and caravan park and I'd like to keep it that way for another couple of days at least. That said, I'm also requesting additional surveillance. Well, to be strictly accurate, an extension to the remit of what's already in place.'

'Specifics, Jimmy,' Edwards said, checking her watch. 'Specifics.'

'I want to keep tabs on Bartek Danek. We know he went back to the site following his release from custody, where he has since remained. The current surveillance instructions are to watch out for our two remaining Tangos should they return to the site. But now I'd also like to add an instruction for them to follow Danek should he leave.'

'You think if they don't return, he might regroup with the others elsewhere?'

'I suspect he will, yes. Or at least, that he hopes to.'

'But I was under the distinct impression that our surveillance was blown. They knew we were there two days ago. Why wouldn't they be just as cautious now?'

Bliss had considered this argument and was ready to fend off the DSI. 'With respect, Alicia, as far as we're aware they knew only that we were close by, not our precise location. I don't believe they are aware of the cameras focussed on the site, only that we had plenty of units in the area on Tuesday morning. They likely suspected a raid based on that information, as opposed to knowing they were under constant surveillance.'

Edwards leaned forward, a pensive frown tightening her forehead. 'To be honest with you, Jimmy, I'm not convinced we require surveillance to continue at all. The suspects who escaped aren't coming back. You know that as well as I do. And for the same reasons, Danek is unlikely to be stupid enough to leave the site only to lead you right to their doorstep.'

'Normally I'd agree with that. And while I don't think they're dumb enough to return, surveillance might well spot something worthwhile all the same. As for Danek, granted, we couldn't move him on giving up his friends, but I think DC Kolesnyk ruffled his feathers just enough to put some doubt in his mind. Time occasionally works in our favour. That seed we planted might grow, might already have caused him to question his commitment to these men. He might decide to confront them. And, as I've already said, I'm not convinced they are aware of the tight surveillance. They'll be looking out for vehicles, not cameras in the trees opposite.'

'And if you're wrong?'

'It wouldn't be the first time, nor the last. But I do think it's the way to go. We have the surveillance team in place. All I'm asking for is more time and for them to stick to Danek like glue should he leave the camp.'

'The suggestion being he knows where the others are.'

Bliss nodded. 'Knows where they were going, at the very least. I don't see them splitting up the way they did without having a regroup destination in mind. Realistically, it'll be no more than some kind of way station, a place for them to run to ahead of moving on to a safe house elsewhere. Would Danek have played his part without being included in that? I think not.'

Edwards took his point, but had one of her own to make. 'Would they have included him knowing he might head straight to the prearranged rendezvous point after leaving custody, but not knowing if he'd made a deal with us prior to his release?'

'Okay. I admit that might have been a concern. Let's say you're right. I don't imagine they would have given him the location of the safe house, but I do think he would have been part of the initial conversation concerning their assembly point. That is something they might have been willing to do, knowing full well he'd be with us for at least a day. They most likely left before he was released but following him there might still give us a lead. Anything. More than we have, at any rate.'

Tapping the desktop, Edwards said, 'I can give you until the end of the week, Jimmy. Then we cut our losses.'

Bliss thought about it. He wanted longer, but what she had offered was acceptable. He had no idea if the plan would work, but if you didn't buy a ticket... 'I'll take it,' he said.

'Then tell surveillance you have my authority. However, I do hope you have other irons in the fire.'

Bliss had been expecting her to express that sentiment or something along those lines. Running an Op was like being a juggler while also spinning plates. The job required you to complete it without spilling a single item.

'I have the team combing through known associates as we speak. I don't see these men straying too far from what they know, from the familiar. We found them that way to begin with, and I think we can do so a second time.'

'Then again, they could be on an island off the coast of Scotland by now.'

Bliss shrugged. 'That's not the kind of scale we can even contemplate. We begin at home and work our way out. Just not too far, I hope.'

'Fine.' Edwards looked up expectantly. 'And our unsolved?'

Bliss brought the DCI up to speed on the team's action and results to date. She took it all in quietly before asking, 'This story from Jack Maguire. Are you buying it?'

'Leaning towards it, yes. For the most part. But if he genuinely does know who killed Daisy Vincent, he's not letting on. And I don't think he will unless we reach the point of arresting and charging him with her murder. That way, he keeps a vital card close to his chest and will only play it if he absolutely needs to.'

'Which, from what you've told me, isn't likely to happen.'

'I can't see it, no. Frankly, I don't believe he's guilty.'

'And this Wrigley fellow?'

The real fly in the ointment. A man whose full role was largely unknown, and who was not around to provide any answers to their many questions. Bliss had spent a great deal of time contemplating the man's part in that evening's events, in addition to his whereabouts or fate.

'I still believe Dougie Vincent and his two sons, or perhaps Dougie alone, murdered Wrigley,' Bliss stated flatly. 'I'm considering running a bluff with that one. Paying another visit, dropping into conversation that we've had a tip off about the whereabouts of the body, how much forensic evidence we hope to acquire, then watching and waiting to see if any of them go to check or move it.'

Edwards stared at him, guarded now. 'More surveillance, Jimmy?'

He shook his head. 'No. We'll take care of it ourselves.'

'Always assuming they buried the body rather than feeding it into a wood chipper.'

'In which case we'd be buggered.'

Edwards nodded. She interlocked her fingers on the desk. 'How about informing the Vincents of Maguire's involvement? If the girl wasn't raped as previously suspected, we have to inform the family of such a development.'

'I'm wrestling with that one,' Bliss admitted. 'As things stand, Maguire can offer no proof that the sex he had was consensual. And in terms of the PM, rape was never mentioned with any real certainty. The pathologist offered it as a possibility, which of course people leapt upon and made the most of.'

'Even so. If we so much as suspect he's telling the truth, we need to be updating the family. Knowing their daughter wasn't raped after all is likely to come as a huge relief to them. Remember, when it comes to Daisy's death, they deserve our every cooperation.'

Unable to deny Edwards' logic, he nodded and said, 'Understood. Thing is, do we also have to give them a name? After all, if the sex *was* consensual, then no crime had been committed at that point. The rape is removed as a potential charge, which leaves us with the murder only. If Maguire is telling us the truth, he was responsible for the former, not the latter. Why put him at risk and set two families at each other's throats for no good reason?'

Edwards paused long enough to suggest she agreed with him. 'I may have to take that one under advisement, Jimmy. It could depend on whether Mr Maguire remains a suspect at the time.'

'And that time may well be upon us, because as things stand, we still have an interest in him. Only, what I keep coming back to is this: we have no evidence linking him with the victim, so leaving his prison confession to one side, why even admit to having sex with Daisy that night if his version is not the truth?'

'In other words, you pretty much believe him, but not enough that you're willing to dismiss him as a suspect.'

'That's it in a nutshell, Alicia.'

'It's a tough call. I should discuss it with Marion, but I doubt that will be today.'

'Then I have a day to make further progress.'

'You do that,' Edwards said. 'Your priority being the escaped gang members. I want those killers in custody, Jimmy. Gul's attackers. Do what you have to do, but just find them again.'

'I will,' Bliss said with conviction, determined to make both men pay a heavy price.

THIRTY-SIX

Bliss reached the point where he didn't know if he was coming or going. He dashed between the MCU and UCT offices, never spending more than half an hour in either. He had to be on top of his game because both investigations were in danger of careering off the rails. Switching focus so rapidly and often, left him momentarily confused as to which case he was working on, and for the first time in as long as he could remember he felt close to helplessness. Despair, even. But then, around mid-afternoon, the first domino fell.

'Boss,' Chandler said, spinning in her office chair to face him. 'I've just heard from the surveillance team. Danek is on the move.'

'Please tell me he's using the same truck.' Bliss felt a throbbing in both temples. He had obtained permission to stick a lump on the vehicle before Danek collected it from the Thorpe Wood car park. They had hidden the tracking device so well that it couldn't have been spotted, and activating it meant they could follow him from a distance.

But Chandler was shaking her head, wrinkling her nose in disappointment. 'Nope. Sorry. It was a long shot, Jimmy. They're bound to be suspicious of it. It was worth the gamble, but they haven't fallen for it. No, he's in an old Land Rover Discovery this time. On his own as far as we can tell.'

'And we're following?'

'Yes. They have their best people on it. Usual variety of vehicles, some up ahead on the same road, others circling to join in even further on depending on which route he takes.'

'Which way's he headed?'

'He made his way to the A16 and went north. He then took the Thorney Road west and has just shot through Newborough.'

Bliss brought up a mental map of the area. 'Peakirk is next unless he diverts across country. After that, he could head to Northborough or drop down into Glinton.'

'Like I said, surveillance is moving as many watchers into position as they can.'

By now, everybody had stopped what they were doing to listen in. There appeared to be a general sense that this might be the next big move. Grabbing his coat off the back of his chair, Bliss said, 'Let's get out there. You with me. Bish, take Alan. Vas, man the fort until further notice.'

He wasted no further breath on explanations. But even before they'd reached the car park, Chandler received an update. 'It's Peakirk, Jimmy. Danek parked up and is now walking back the way he drove in. Watchers say his head is spinning like a top. He's stopping all the time, crossing the roads back and forth. Checking shop windows for reflections. Paranoid levels, evidently. Definitely suspects he's being tailed.'

'Okay. Just as long as he doesn't clock anyone to turn that suspicion into a certainty, we'll be fine. I badly want you to ask surveillance to tell their officers to exercise caution, but don't you dare. They know what they're doing. They're the best people for the job. They will be careful, and I'm just being a dick.'

'You'll get no disagreement from me there.'

They got going. It was no more than a fifteen-minute drive to Peakirk, but Bliss put his foot down as if he hoped to do it in ten. He noticed Bishop keeping close throughout the short drive. Chandler kept in touch with surveillance all the way. Taking as many main roads as possible while at the same time avoiding those known for heavy traffic, they were soon moving in on their destination. Guided by officers already on the scene, they eventually pulled up in the village hall car park, which was shielded from the main road by tall bushes and trees.

Sergeant Dave Marney greeted them with a warm handshake. 'We have Tango One surrounded,' he said to Bliss's immense relief. 'After a bit of dicking around he finally made his way to an old barn. We were unable to follow him directly as it's at the back of someone's property and we didn't want to ask permission in case the owner knew what was going on and tried to warn our suspect. But we do have all sides covered with eyeball on the barn.'

'Terrific job. Any other movement?' Bliss asked.

'You mean have we spotted the remaining Tangos?' Marney shook his head. 'No. We have Tango One entering, and that's it. But I do have some bad news for you.'

Bliss would have been more surprised if he'd not. 'Go on,' he said. 'Ruin the moment for me.'

Marney crossed both arms beneath his chest, looking regretful. 'One of my people had positioned himself in an allotment nearby and was able to get a decent view of our Tango entering the barn. Sorry, Jimmy, but he had to use a combination padlock to gain entry.'

The meaning became immediately obvious. 'Fuck it!' Bishop said with a snarl. 'If they locked it from the outside, then there's almost certainly nobody else inside.'

'That's the way we saw it,' Marney said.

'They might have had themselves locked in for security reasons,' Bliss said. 'But I tend to agree with you both. We suspected the others would be gone by now, but if they were here then they could have left something of interest behind.'

'I also don't imagine Danek will be best pleased,' DC Virgil added. 'If they've moved on to a safe house without him, he might be pissed off enough to talk to us this time.'

'And tell us what?' Chandler asked, gloomily. 'If he doesn't know where they went, then he's of no help to us.'

'Perhaps. But he might know more than he thinks.'

'Either way,' Marney interjected, 'Tango One is unlikely to hang around much longer. Are you going in?'

Bliss nodded. 'We're going in. Before we do, though, did you happen to find out who owns the property here?'

'It's in the works.'

'Okay. Never mind. We'll give them a knock. We have good enough reason to enter that barn without a warrant, but let's do this by the numbers.'

It didn't take long. Nobody was home, and when they entered the barn without obtaining the owner's permission, Danek came quietly and with minimal fuss. He answered none of Chandler's questions following his rearrest, but just as disappointment began to wash over Bliss, he took a call from DC Kolesnyk.

'Boss,' he said urgently. 'I have some interesting news. That property you hit belongs to a Thomas Walsh. He's Patrick Walsh's cousin. Not only that, but Thomas Walsh also appears on the list of known associates.'

'We'd expect him to if they're cousins and Thomas has been in trouble himself, Vas,' Bliss said.

'I understand. But it's not only Patrick Walsh's KAs I'm talking about. The cousin also cropped up on Matt Dories' list as well.'

Bliss let that sink in. Family was family, but the inclusion of Dories suggested all manner of possibilities. Whereas the fraud and theft crew appeared to have little of substance to lose and much to gain by their criminal activity, the property and land on which the barn stood implied Thomas Walsh might have more to consider when questioned. *If we reach that point*, Bliss thought, as an idea popped into his head.

'Vas,' he said, a tingle rushing across the surface of his skin. 'Look deeper into Thomas Walsh. Finances, businesses, and property. Yes, property in particular. Get back to me as quick as you can.'

He ended the call, clocking the faces of colleagues turned his way. 'What are you thinking, Jimmy?' Chandler asked.

'Only that they came here first, which must have been by arrangement because they had the combination to the padlock. That tells me they believed in Patrick's cousin and also that he was open to helping them. What's to say they haven't trusted him further?'

'You mean he might have shifted them to a safe house. Something he owns or rents.'

Nodding, Bliss said, 'That's precisely what I'm thinking, Pen. Tied to him at the very least. Something not obvious, I'm guessing. Perhaps not a house at all. But a property he owns, rents, or leases whether personally or tied to a business. It has to be considered.'

'We're not exactly stumbling over leads at the moment. It's as good as anything else we have.'

'That's me. I always strive to be only as good as anything else.'

Chandler smiled at him. 'And you always manage to live down to that. In fact, sometimes you're not even as good as anything else, so well done.'

'Remind me why we're friends again.'

'Because nobody else likes you, which makes me feel sorry for you.'

'So, I'm a pity pal?'

'At best.'

If the snorts and guffaws were anything to go by, the others were enjoying their conversation. Bliss looked around at them. 'Please, feel free to weigh in whenever you like.'

'To be fair to Pen,' Bishop said, 'she's not far wrong. We've learned to tolerate you, Jimmy, but that's as far as it goes.'

This was met with general nods of consensus.

Shaking his head in disgust, Bliss said, 'When I finally curl up my toes, you rotten lot will be sobbing and wailing, wondering how you'll manage without me in your miserable lives.'

'Of course we will, boss,' Virgil said. 'You keep telling yourself that.'

They were still laughing when DC Kolesnyk called back. 'I have a few properties listed, boss. Other than the house in Peakirk he also has a flat in Kings Lynn and a house in Cromer. Two decent possibilities there. But I also checked out the business side and I think I might have what you were looking for. There's a place called Three Holes, which is not far from Downham Market. Mr Walsh owns both a car repair and scrap merchant there at the same address. I searched on Google and sandwiched between the two sites is a relatively new-build bungalow. All three properties share the same plot of land. I think as he owns the businesses, he must also own the bungalow.'

'And I agree with you, old son,' Bliss said, barely able to conceal his excitement. 'Great job, Vas. Well done. I'll get back to you when we've come up with a plan.'

Euphoric now, Bliss passed on the information. 'I'm not saying they won't turn out to be on the coast,' he said. 'But at this time of year, I wouldn't bank on it. And while it could be the flat in

Lynn, I was thinking of somewhere less obvious. This Three Holes place seems to fit the bill. Thoughts?'

Huddling together, the team discussed their options while staring at online maps. The usual tactic would be to spend time studying the area and analysing the approach, possibly bringing the surveillance team into the conversation. But Bartek Danek wasn't going to be held in custody for long, and if Patrick Walsh's cousin got wind of the arrest, he might alert the suspects.

'I'm all for going in now,' he finally admitted. 'We're forty minutes away. If we're wrong, then we won't have wasted much time.'

'We'll need other units in place,' Chandler said. 'I don't think we want to make this an armed raid unless we absolutely have to, and there's nothing in their records to suggest either man is likely to be armed. Nor overly violent other than last week's scene.'

Bliss agreed. 'Let's have a couple of dogs and their handlers, plus backup and transport for the arrests. We time it based on their ETA on the plot, not ours. No frills. We knock, if they don't answer or they tell us to sling our hooks, we take the door down.' He turned to DS Bishop. 'You and Alan make the arrests.'

'Will do,' Bishop replied. 'But what if there are others inside the property with them?'

'We ignore them unless they get in our way,' Bliss said firmly. 'But if our two Tangos are inside, they're coming with us. One way or another.'

THIRTY-SEVEN

Just past Guyhirn, Bliss led the convoy of vehicles into a lay-by populated by a well-established roadside snack bar. There, he bought his team a hot drink and some food, happy to keep their immediate thoughts on sustenance rather than their case. It was going to take longer than he had hoped to gather all the relevant teams together and shift them over to Three Holes, so he'd elected to use some of that time wisely to get everybody refuelled. He sat munching his sausage and bacon sandwich in silence, mulling over the implications of the raid to come.

He knew nothing about the small village of Three Holes, other than the fact that it lay just over the border in Norfolk. Penny Chandler had suggested the name stemmed from the three arches featured in the Three Holes bridge, but while its origins intrigued him, his mind insisted on drawing him back to the basic strike plan that he and his colleagues had agreed upon prior to leaving Thorpe Wood.

If the location proved to be empty, if they had guessed incorrectly, he had no idea where that left them. Thomas Walsh owned other properties, but just because his barn had been used as a rendezvous point didn't necessarily mean he had helped his cousin, Patrick, and Peter Holland further. The truth was the suspects could be just about anywhere in the British Isles by now. Perhaps even further afield. Yet the intelligence gathered, combined with their own experience and common sense, told them this was the most likely location.

But even if the raid uncovered the two men skulking away in Three Holes, what solid evidence did Major Crime have against them? Very little, was the unappetising answer. Which meant that whatever they required to proceed with charges would have to be gathered while both men were in custody. If there was any evidence to be discovered.

He found himself in the same pensive mood shortly afterwards when he and his team met up with the other units in a car park belonging to a fisheries establishment located well away from passers-by in what turned out to be little more than a hamlet sitting halfway between Wisbech and Ely at the junction of Popham's Eau and the Middle Level 16 Foot River. Bliss went over the plan – such as it was – that he had devised in agreement with the rest of the team. It was as basic as it was urgent; vehicles carrying the teams would hit the address at speed, two would enter a wide gravel drive leading to the bungalow, while the others would block the entrance and fill up the road behind them. Officers would first identify themselves when knocking and then enter the premises without further warning if they received no immediate response. If someone inside the bungalow willingly opened the front door to them, then it was DS Bishop's role to insist on entering the property while proffering the warrant that DC Kolesnyk had brought with him at Bliss's insistence.

As he and Chandler killed time in the Volvo while Bishop and Virgil performed a drive-by peek at the property, Bliss mentioned his concerns at where this next phase might lead them.

'Isn't it the same risk we take on many other occasions?' she said, turning to him with her usual blunt stare when she was being serious. 'How often do we walk into an interview room holding all the cards, Jimmy? Rarely. Circumstances often dictate when we make an arrest. In this case we may not have anything more against this pair than we did two days ago, but we don't have less.'

'I know, I know,' he said on a sigh. 'I got carried away, hoping Danek might turn on Walsh and Holland, especially after they left him in the lurch. But he's solid. I don't see him breaking.'

'So, we do what we do. We take them into custody, and we work them in the room at the same time as we search for that elusive proof. We might get lucky with boot prints as we did with Matt Dories. Not proof of theft or stabbing or assault on Gul, I know, but it'd be a start. If we can place them at the farm that morning based on physical evidence from forensics, then we'll be in a position to apply more pressure.'

'I don't know what it is with me at the moment,' he said irritably. 'I feel as if all I want these days are instant results. A Big Mac and a verdict on the side, please.'

'I know precisely what's wrong with you,' Chandler said. 'You want that immediate gratification because your new role pretty much ends once we have them in a cell. You don't get to see these Ops out the way you once did. Previously you'd be in it for the duration, from the initial visit to the crime scene to seeing someone banged up. Now you point the unit in the right direction, but without crossing the finishing line with us at the end. If you were an ordinary SIO you'd be along for the full ride, but the way things stand it's Diane who gets to step up for the more tedious and, frankly, gruelling part. On top of that you have your unsolved cases to work as well, which is why it all feels so different.'

Bliss knew she was right. Was it ever in doubt? Both nail head and aim had fallen into place with almost Teutonic precision for Chandler. Her detachment perhaps allowed her to see things more clearly. Or maybe he had permitted his blindness to obscure the truth because he didn't want to accept it.

'I think I'm going to ask if I can stick with this one,' he said. 'To see it through while working the cold case. My agreement when discussing this civilian role was to act as SIO when it was expedient, to free up Diane in her DCI role, relying on my experience to lead the team. A bit like the unsolved aspect, in that we take an investigation so far and then must hand it off to others because we're no longer warranted.'

'And I take it you're not happy with that arrangement anymore?'

'Not right now, I'm not. I want these remaining two fuckers put away, and I need to be part of the team that does that. I can't snap the cuffs on, but I can make sure we get the right suspects, the right evidence, and put them together to build a case. This role was flexible, fluid, even, is how Marion Fletcher described it to me. I think now is the right time to make changes.'

Chandler nodded. 'I'm all for it, Jimmy. I'm sure Diane will be, provided it doesn't mean you neglect the cold cases. When you and I discussed it right at the beginning, you knew you'd have to assess and reassess your priorities on an almost daily basis. I think so long as you can convince everybody that things will continue in the same vein, you might be able to persuade them. But, and please don't take this the wrong way, it seems to me you have one extremely complex cold case to resolve, and that team may need you more than we do in the coming days.'

'I know what you're saying,' Bliss said. 'And you're right. It is a fine line. What isn't these days? My priorities do change on a regular basis, and I believe I can manage that and still make valid contributions to whatever I have on my plate at the time.'

'Are you worried? You think Diane, Alicia, and Marion will see things differently?'

'They might. They're accountable, remember. They won't want me burned out to the point where I start making mistakes. None of us wants that. They might decide I'd be taking on too much. Or that at the very least there's a risk of that happening, with me not getting those priorities we talked about in the right order.'

Chandler gave a rueful grin. 'All you can do is run it by them, Jimmy. Get all three of them in a room and explain it to them the way you just did to me. They'll understand. I'm not saying they'll agree, but they will understand.'

Bliss nodded. 'That might have to be enough,' he said.

'And if it's not?'

'Well, then, that's a different conversation entirely.'

And not one any of us are going to like.

THIRTY-EIGHT

Scuzzy Pete stared over the rim of his pint glass. At this angle, he was cutting Paddy the Greek's head in half. He decided it was a good look for a man he was growing increasingly irritated with. The beer helped him cope, but only to a certain degree. He would need a shit-ton more if their continued antipathy wasn't going to erupt into something far more violent than the verbal abuse they'd been exchanging for the past couple of hours.

Doris had often acted as a buffer between the two. Generally easy going by nature, he had sought to pacify and appease for the sake of the greater good, physically coming between them on more than one occasion. It was hard to think of him being gone, harder still to imagine who was going to keep the peace now.

Not that Scuzzy was overly bothered if it all kicked off. Paddy was taking too many fucking liberties, with snidey pop after snidey pop. The guy was a prick and doing his head in.

You think I'm too thick to understand what you're saying? Or is it that you consider me too cowardly to react with genuine violence as opposed to the handbags we so casually resort to most of the time?

He shook his head. What that smug-looking cretin failed to appreciate was how deep real hatred could run, and just how volatile their relationship had become. He took a couple of timely breaths, allowing it to wash over him. It was as if he had been cast adrift at sea in the eye of a storm, only to have the squall break and the roiling water all around suddenly become still and silent, lapping gently as the tide drew him slowly to shore.

Becalmed, Scuzzy turned his attention to their current predicament. The so-called 'safe house' was decent enough; he had to give Paddy credit for that. The man's cousin had come through for them, both with the overnight refuge and now this. The bungalow was warm, dry, and stocked with food and drink. Best of all, it was in a secluded spot in some forgotten Fenland hamlet where the police would never think to search.

In fact, the more he thought about it the more this place might well be the nicest he'd ever stayed in. Sure, it was primitive, the furnishing rudimentary, the style makeshift as befitted a dwelling in which nobody dwelled. But compared to the fleapit tower block flat he'd grown up in it was a virtual palace. The floor of the home he'd shared with his mother and three siblings had been littered with ageing dog shit, discarded needles, and drugs paraphernalia belonging to his drug-addled parent. Over the years, various boyfriends had come and gone, most of whom treated him worse than the dogs. He'd left home nine days after his sixteenth birthday and had never looked back. After that he spent time on the streets or sleeping on a variety of sofas, and at eighteen he'd met Paddy the Greek and Doris. Theirs was a tentative friendship at first, but while he had never quite taken to Paddy, he and Doris had formed a strong bond. Now his rock was gone and all that remained was this obnoxious piece of shit; a volatile freak who smelled bad and behaved even worse. Thought he was the big 'I am' dog's bollocks and tried to lord it over his supposed friends.

Well, not for much longer, Scuzzy thought. One more dig at his expense and he was going to lose his shit. Big time.

Over the past thirty minutes or so, things had settled down a little. Paddy had the living room sofa all to himself. He sat with his back to the arm, a cushion tucked behind him for lumbar support, feet up and long legs spread apart. The sofa stood to Scuzzy's left, facing a basic widescreen TV. From his own position sitting in one of the room's two armchairs, he could also watch the telly and only had to turn his gaze a fraction to pull Paddy into focus. Well, the top of his head at least.

Scuzzy smiled and lowered the glass, but then for reasons he was later unable to understand his idle gaze became a full-on glower. Just like that. Nought to sixty in an instant. He felt a vein in his neck pulse like a nervous tic, understanding that this was anger bubbling beneath the surface expressing itself the only way it knew how. Though infrequent, his most intense outbursts were almost always volcanic in their nature; as if he could feel the steady flow of magma rising up from the pit of his stomach aching to be released in a flood of lava.

It wanted him to vent.

It needed him to vent.

'What did you do with my favourite screwdriver?' he asked in a calm but loud voice.

Paddy dragged his attention away from the screen, looked at Scuzzy blankly for no more than a second, then turned back to the TV and some kind of quiz show featuring a whole raft of so-called celebrities known only to the terminally shallow.

To accompany his pint of beer, Scuzzy had also poured himself a bowl of salted cashew nuts, which sat on the arm of the chair. He dipped a hand into the bowl, grabbed a small portion and lobbed them at the rude fuck-pig who had just ignored him.

Paddy didn't disregard him a second time.

'What the fuck?! Did you just throw nuts at me you crazy bastard?'

'I did. And I'm not crazy. I've been tested, so I know.'

Maintaining his languid position on the sofa, Paddy said, 'Oh, no. You're not crazy at all. I mean, how could a man who has a favourite screwdriver be crazy?'

'So, you did hear me, then?'

'Yeah. What of it?'

'Answer me then, you fucking ignorant prick!'

For the longest time, it looked as if Paddy couldn't be bothered to respond, but then he slowly swung his legs around and planted his stockinged feet on the floor. He fixed Scuzzy with what he probably believed was some kind of 'death stare' but which in reality wasn't savage enough to startle a kitten.

'Well?' Scuzzy demanded.

'Are you serious?' Paddy looked at him as if he were demented. 'I mean, really, are you seriously questioning me about a fucking screwdriver?'

'I am, yes. Because it wasn't any old screwdriver. It was my favourite screwdriver. Not to mention the same screwdriver you used to kill an old woman with. That makes it even more special.'

Another lengthy pause. Their gazes interlocked, squinting like black hat and white hat cowboys looking to draw down on each other. But then Paddy's lips curled into a smile and a gleam of delight reflected off his eyes. 'I think you'll find the only prints on that screwdriver, Scuzzy, my old mucker, are yours.'

Pete caught the mocking tone. And the tense. Along with the meaning of both.

He inched forward in his seat, cheeks flushing. 'You told me you destroyed it,' he said. 'How can it still have prints on it if you destroyed it, Paddy?'

'I've told you a lot of things over the years. Don't make them true.'

'But you assured me. Assured us – me and Doris. You said you left it in the van when we torched it.'

'That was just to shut you up about your favourite-fucking-screwdriver, Scuzzy. Honestly, you sounded like a fucking madman. You still do.'

'Why did you keep it? Why did you lie?'

Paddy's grin dripped contempt from his moist lips. 'Why d'you think? It's *your* favourite screwdriver, Scuzzy. Everybody who knows you knows that. And it has your prints all over it, not mine, because I wore gloves that day. So, should the Filth catch up with us at some point in the future and you decide your loyalties lie elsewhere, I have some leverage tucked away where only I can find it.'

Scuzzy swallowed. It tasted like bile going down. His eyes burned with hatred, molten in their sockets. 'You'd do that to me?'

Hands spread wide, Paddy said, 'I'm not saying I want to, Pete. But I can't have you shooting your mouth off, can I?'

'Why would I do that?'

'Any number of reasons I should imagine. But now you know not to.'

Scuzzy thought it all through, his mind jumping from one angle to the next. Eventually, one of them stuck and held his attention. 'When you say nobody else will find it, that includes the old Bill, yeah?'

'Of course,' Paddy said with a snort of derision. 'It's safe until I don't want it to be.'

'Which means if you're not around to tell them where it is, they're not finding it.'

The look he got back this time was a serving of quizzical with a slice of anxiety on the side. 'Now, what the fuck does that mean?' Paddy asked, jumping to his feet.

Scuzzy Pete also stood, but he did so deliberately, taking his time about it. The two men stood facing each other.

Which was when they both heard the gunning engines and the screech and slide of tyres on gravel outside. Paddy turned towards the source of the noises and activity. Scuzzy continued to face him.

And Scuzzy was the first to react.

*

They came hard and fast. No lights. No sirens. The support and dog vans darting off the road and skidding into the driveway, Bliss's Volvo and DS Bishop's pool car up next with other vehicles filling in behind out on the pavement. Two teams immediately headed around to the rear of the property to prevent any escape via a back door or window, while others lined up at the sides to protect against local intrusion should anyone from the garage or breaker's yard look to get involved.

Bliss's instructions back at the staging area had been simple and clear, and the first of his colleagues to approach the bungalow front door carried them out to the letter. A double-tap knock. A single shouted sentence informing those inside the property that the police demanded they open up. A five-second wait. Then the door went in, instantly followed by the designated strike team plus two dogs and their handlers swarming into the property. No more than a minute later, a figure appeared in the doorway beckoning Bliss and Chandler.

They and the rest of the team entered to be confronted by a scene Bliss had only partially expected. Peter Holland stood in the centre of the room, struggling in the grasp of two support officers, his hands already cuffed behind his back. He said nothing as he wriggled and squirmed while two dogs growled at him, but by the time Bliss noticed blood on the man's clothing and boots, he had already spotted the source.

Patrick Walsh lay like a crumpled starfish on the floor, his face buried in the thick beige carpet. One officer knelt by his side attempting to stir the stricken man, while another colleague spoke urgently into his radio demanding a paramedic. Bliss thought they'd probably need a mortuary attendant as well, because from his position it looked very much as if Walsh was close to dying.

Blood pooled on the floor around the victim, the result of an obvious violent struggle. Protruding from one of several savage wounds in Walsh's back and sides was the plastic handle of a slim tool. If its bulky, corrugated circumference was anything to go by, several inches of it right up to the ferrule were now buried deep inside the man's flesh. The officer attempting to revive the stricken figure looked up and shook his head just as the paramedics hurried through the doorway.

Bliss turned his attention back to Holland, aware that the man had stopped resisting and now stood quietly as he panted, his gasps obvious even in all the commotion going on around him. And then, just as Bliss tried to make sense of what he was seeing, he watched in horrified fascination as the assailant's expression changed from one of resolute aggression to a look of unadulterated delight.

He's proud of himself, Bliss thought in that moment.

'Is this your work, Mr Holland?' he asked coolly.

Their suspect's smile radiated all the more. He looked demonic, reminding Bliss of a younger, scruffier Charles Manson. Holland nodded by way of an answer. Then he shot a look of pure loathing and venom at his fallen companion.

'Fuck you, Paddy!' he cried, white flecks of spittle invading the surrounding air. 'You won't fucking underestimate me again, will you?'

'How did he misjudge you?' Bliss asked, desperate to keep the man talking.

But as it turned out, Peter Holland had only one more thing to say.

'It never occurred to him that I had a second favourite screwdriver.'

THIRTY-NINE

There were times – perhaps too many – when Jimmy Bliss wondered where all the chaos, madness, horror, and carnage took root inside his head. He'd wandered those dark passages in search of answers on numerous occasions but today, as with every previous attempt that came before it, he'd found only abandoned chambers and a desolate landscape in which nothing good could possibly grow. Uninhabited and potentially uninhabitable, he knew those areas of the brain had become scarred and ugly over time. But, he reasoned, maybe it was their very barrenness that allowed him to continue unscathed. If he ever managed to unlock a door to find the malevolence within, he feared he might be unable to prevent the insanity from wrapping itself around him and drawing him into the darkness.

Bliss took a breath, which brought him back to a place less unpleasant. The murder of Patrick Walsh was far from the worst crime scene he had ever attended, yet the dead look in the killer's eyes continued their effortless attack on his senses deep into the afternoon. He'd seen neither compassion nor remorse in those dull orbs. Curiously, no evil or satiated desire, either. It was the complete lack of humanity, the hollow, uncaring indifference in them that bothered Bliss so much.

Combatting such an absence of empathy would, he knew, require the exact opposite in terms of depth of feeling. Detective Constable Gul Ansari was by far the best interviewer on the team, but as she wasn't available to him and DCs Virgil and Kolesnyk had made a good fist of their previous time in the room, Bliss went with them.

Peter 'Scuzzy' Holland had requested a duty solicitor when advised of his rights by the custody officer. He declined to inform anyone of his presence at Thorpe Wood. He also insisted he had no medical issues in need of attention. He was compliant, if somewhat subdued. At no point did his behaviour suggest he was at all concerned either for himself or by what he had done. The custody officer asked Bliss, Bishop, and Chandler if Holland's apparent lack of apprehension warranted a mental health appraisal, but between them they decided all he lacked was a conscience.

His interview began just shy of three hours after his arrest. By this time, he'd changed into a grey tracksuit, his own clothes having been removed for forensic examination. He'd had two cups of tea and a bacon sandwich. Other than responding to formal questions as he was booked in, he offered no conversation whatsoever.

As anticipated, the solicitor submitted a statement from his client in which he claimed he had defended himself against attack. In response, DC Virgil studied the man with open disdain and said, 'A number of police officers and two paramedics overheard you state that the murder weapon, a Phillips-head screwdriver, was your "second favourite". Are you now claiming the screwdriver wasn't yours?'

Holland shook his head, his sunken, beady eyes giving nothing away. 'No, that is mine. But it was Paddy the Greek who came at me with it, not the other way around.'

'By "Paddy the Greek" do you mean Patrick Walsh?'

'The arrogant prick, yes.'

'You say he came at you brandishing the tool, yet it was Mr Walsh who was murdered using the screwdriver. How do you explain that?'

A nonchalant shrug. 'We wrestled for it. He's strong, but I was fighting for my life. I wrenched it out of his hands. He told me he was going to take it back off me and then kill me with it, so all I did was defend myself.'

'How many times?'

'What?' Puzzled now, or so his querulous look suggested.

'How many times did you defend yourself with the screwdriver, Mr Holland?'

'Oh, I see what you're saying. Truth is, I don't know. Look, I feared for my life. I was scared and I panicked. I just hit him with it until he was on the floor.'

'You say you defended yourself against him, yet each of the wounds on Mr Walsh's body were either in his sides or on his back. Nothing to the front, which suggests he was facing away from you. How do you account for that?'

'I already told you, I thought he was going to kill me, so I lashed out to keep him from grabbing hold of me. His body must have twisted round at some point. Look, if he'd got his hands on that screwdriver again it'd be me lying dead.'

Virgil made a note on a spiral-bound pad he'd laid out on the table before continuing. 'You also say the two of you fought, that you wrestled for the murder weapon, and yet somehow you managed to escape completely unscathed. Not a single defensive wound on you. How do you suppose that happened?'

The solicitor spoke for the first time since identifying himself for the recording. 'I object to your use of the term "murder weapon". You've yet to establish murder, and my client has confirmed he acted purely in self-defence.'

'You're not in court now, Mr Sparrow,' Virgil said.

'Nonetheless...'

'Mr Walsh. How do you suppose that happened?' Virgil repeated as if the solicitor had not interrupted.

'I just got lucky, I suppose.'

'Extremely so, I'd say. A larger man comes at you, armed, determined to harm you, and yet you have not a single injury while he had many and died as a result. I don't believe anybody is that fortunate.'

Morgan Sparrow shook his head and said, 'No, no, no. That won't do, DC Virgil. The cause of death has yet to be established by a pathologist.'

'The screwdriver sticking out of Mr Walsh's back gave us a clue,' Virgil insisted.

'Nevertheless. Please, do stick to the facts in evidence.'

'Okay. The facts in evidence are that when we entered the property in Three Holes, Mr Walsh was lying on the floor having bled from multiple stab wounds, while your client stood over him covered in the victim's blood banging on about the weapon in Mr Walsh's back being his second favourite screwdriver. Your client claims he attacked Mr Walsh in self-defence, yet there is no evidence whatsoever to back up that claim.'

'Look, you want to know how I knew he'd follow through on his threat?' Holland said in a raised voice. 'I'll tell you. Because I had to watch him kill that old lady last week. The one on the farm outside Crowland. He stabbed her. With my favourite screwdriver.'

Virgil blinked a couple of times at that, made a mental note and then looked over at DC Kolesnyk, who followed up without missing a beat. 'So, you're admitting you were there at that farmhouse, Mr Holland,' he said. 'And that the weapon used to kill Mrs Musgrove was, in fact, yours.'

'Yes.'

'Just as the weapon used to kill Mr Walsh was also yours.'

'Yes. He was a fucking thief as well as a killer.'

'Tell me more about that, Mr Holland.'

As if the pair had rehearsed the entire interview so far, Holland stayed silent while his solicitor shook his head and said, 'My client will only offer no comment to any further questions.'

DC Virgil responded with a deep sigh. 'Having said just enough to confirm he was at the scene of two murders, and that on both occasions the weapon used was his, but that he is responsible for neither.'

'I can't comment on the incident in Crowland. That's not why we're here today. My client offered that information of his own free will and now wishes to comply with his right not to speak.'

Virgil kept his gaze fixed on Holland. 'The more you explain yourself the more you help your case,' he said. 'Why would you elect not to do that?'

'No comment,' Holland said. No smirk. No aggression. In fact, his features and his tone were expressionless. Animated when speaking, he now sat passively and quite content.

Watching on the monitor in a different room, Bliss groaned and fired off a few profanities. That was it. Peter 'Scuzzy' Holland had said everything he wanted to say and was just about smart enough to utter nothing more. Revealing who stabbed Mrs Musgrove was no slip of the tongue; he'd deliberately put it on record to distance himself from that murder. Naming Patrick Walsh as the woman's assailant might also lend credence to the allegation about the man's volatility, supporting Holland's claim of self-defence. Bliss wondered who had formed that plan coming into the interview.

Knowing he'd be working on this investigation for a while longer, Bliss called Beth Greenhill to ask how things were in the UCT office. His colleague admitted the team had made little progress in either discovering a fresh lead or when considering a new way forward. No more and no less than he'd expected.

'I think it may be time to pull a bluff,' he said. 'I'm reluctant, but if we play it right and they have buried him somewhere, then we might just trigger a response.'

'Okay. Sounds interesting. How do you propose we go about it?'

'I'm thinking we approach the Vincents with news about Jack Maguire. We tell them about him and Daisy, let them know we're satisfied he played no part in her murder and that we believe it was Wrigley who returned and reacted badly to seeing the two of them together.'

'Which might well be the truth.'

'Absolutely. It's the most likely scenario now that we have more pieces of the puzzle. And once we've firmly established that in their minds, maybe pull a Columbo on them and just as we're leaving one of us drops a hint that we have a lead on Wrigley's whereabouts.'

After a moment, Greenhill said, 'I don't see that we have much to lose. It could prove to be a cunning plan.'

'A plan so cunning you could put a tail on it and call it a weasel?'

The pair laughed. 'I had no idea you were a *Blackadder* fan, Beth,' Bliss said, having quoted a line spoken by the lead character. 'We must compare notes some time.'

'I'm game,' she replied. 'But once you get me started on comedy shows there's no shutting me up.'

'Tell me about it. I'm one of those sad bores who used to quote Monty Python all the time.'

'And I'm one of those even sadder bores who laughs at those quotes in response. Anyway, back to the case. You were saying…?'

'Yes. Where was I? Oh, right. Provided you, Guy, and Ben agree to working off schedule, we put the pair of them on the house while we hang back. I'll ask DCI Warburton to authorise putting a lump on Dougie Vincent's motor if we can find the right time and place to do it.'

'Sounds like a plan. Maybe even another cunning one.'

Bliss laughed again. Not the best of strategies, admittedly, he thought. But doing something proactive was better than sitting around pontificating. Every now and then, you had to step up to make something work for you, even if the move you made was somewhat unorthodox.

'Okay,' he said, realising the day was slipping away from them. 'Look, I'm tied up for now, but I'll try to get to you before you go home tonight. If I don't make it, we'll meet up in the morning to thrash out the details.'

While he was talking, he'd also kept one eye on the monitor and noticed Peter Holland's interview being paused and DCs Virgil and Kolesnyk leaving the room. He found them chatting in the corridor outside.

'You saw?' Virgil asked.

Bliss nodded. 'He played us. Took the first swing and then settled for landing a single blow. Nothing you could have done to avoid it.'

'Did you believe him? About Walsh killing Mrs Musgrove?'

'I did as it goes. His self-defence story is weak, though. The number and locations of stab wounds, in addition to having no defence injuries himself, don't tally with him having been attacked first. I'm all for taking it to the CPS and charging him.'

'And if they err on the side of caution and want us to consider manslaughter?'

'Push for voluntary. Fight them on it and only accept involuntary if they insist it's that or nothing. I want him on remand whatever.'

DC Virgil nodded. 'Sounds good. No way are we buying self-defence. We can be reasonably certain that he intended to kill Walsh, but I agree that voluntary manslaughter ought to be the minimum charge.'

Bliss was determined and firm. 'Go back in. Give him one last chance to explain himself in greater detail. Catch him out in as many lies or half-truths as you can. If he stays schtum, then close the interview, have him taken back to a holding cell, then draw up a charging package for the CPS. I'll make a note in the policy book, and I'll authorise the charge. If the CPS lawyer even tries to sit on the fence, let me know and I'll intervene.'

'Will do, Jimmy. I think what we have is enough.'

'It has to be,' Bliss said. 'Anything to keep him off the streets. Proving our case in court is another matter, but we take it one step at a time as usual.'

Bliss reflected on his conversation with Chandler concerning his role in the grander scheme of things. It was this final piece of the puzzle, in which the team steadily built the right case to earn a just sentence, that he was missing out on. But not this time. Not if he could help it.

FORTY

BLISS REMOVED HIS READING glasses and tossed them onto a pile of folders and printed paper stacked high on his desk. He'd taken refuge in the UCT office long after Foley and Corry had left for the day. Beth Greenhill had remained in the hope that she might persuade him to go for a drink afterwards. He'd agreed but had insisted on writing up his SIO policy book and cold case notes before quitting. He'd required almost sixty minutes longer than the thirty he'd promised her, but she had waited patiently while working on their own case files and reports.

He checked the time on his laptop. 6.11pm. He stretched and yawned, which provoked a short bout of coughing. Glancing across at Greenhill, Bliss noticed her frown of concern. He offered up a smile. 'I'm all right,' he said. 'It's been a long old day, that's all.'

'You sure?' she asked him. 'No spins?'

'A few minor disturbances in the Force, but that's about it.'

'Whatever that means.'

Now it was his turn to frown. 'You not a Star Wars fan, Beth?'

'Not so's you'd notice. Science fiction is not my cup of Darjeeling, if you know what I mean.'

'And Darjeeling is not really my cup of tea. No offence.'

'None taken. Are you done?'

'Just about. I'm…' his voice trailed off as he became distracted by the sound of footsteps and voices approaching along the corridor. Moments later, the office door burst open and in came Chandler, quickly followed by Bishop, Warburton, Edwards and Fletcher. A DS, DI (Acting), DCI, DSI, and DCS; almost the entire force alphabetti spaghetti inside this one tiny room. Bliss thought it sounded like the beginning of a joke.

Bishop, a six-pack of beer tucked under one arm, cried, 'Stop whatever you are doing, Jimmy Bliss! The gang is all here. We thought if the mountain wouldn't come to Mohammed…' This time it was his turn to trail off, having caught sight of Beth Greenhill on the far side of the office.

'Sorry,' he blurted, staggering to a halt. 'Have we interrupted anything?'

Bliss looked at Greenhill. Greenhill looked at him. They both shook their heads. 'Not at all,' Bliss said. 'Just catching up on some paperwork. What's this all about?' He gestured towards the others.

'The CPS are interested,' Detective Chief Superintendent Fletcher told him, offering a wide grin. 'And while that's not exactly the most emphatic endorsement, for the CPS it's the next best thing. They want some dotting and crossing finalised, but essentially, they tell us they'll look favourably on charging Peter Holland for murder.'

Bliss sighed and hung his head in relief. His mind had only half been on his policy book and case notes, the other fifty percent fretting about keeping Holland in custody. Only now did he realise how much anxiety he'd been suppressing.

'No need for me to rattle my sabre, then,' he said eventually, looking back up at the eager, delighted faces surrounding him. 'What a pleasant change that makes.'

'We brought beer to kick off the celebrations,' Bishop said, hoisting the pack. 'Sorry, Beth, we had no idea you'd be here. You can have mine if you like.'

Before Greenhill could respond, DCS Fletcher jumped in. 'Not at all. I wasn't going to have one anyway, so there's a spare. Sorry, I wanted to offer my congratulations but have to forego the drink as I still have a late meeting to attend. Please, go ahead and enjoy. And the first drink down the pub is on me.' With that, she pulled a couple of twenties from her purse and handed them to DCI Warburton.

While Bishop opened up the bottles and passed them out, Bliss and his colleagues exchanged handshakes, smiles, and congratulations. Dories and Walsh were dead. Danek had only ever been a loose end. There was still much to be done before Holland could be remanded, but the Crown Prosecution Service normally played their cards close to the chest, so for them to imply agreeing to the suggested charges must mean they simply wanted the paperwork cleaning up in respect of legalese. It was a result, and one worthy of celebration.

Amidst the backslapping and animated chatter, Chandler found time to slink over to whisper in his ear. 'Are you sure we weren't interrupting anything? I can always shepherd them all out and leave you alone with Beth, if you prefer.'

Bliss shook his head. 'No, thank you. As I explained the other night it's nothing like that. We were going to have an after-work drink is all.'

'So have it. We'll bugger off and celebrate elsewhere.'

'There's no need. Besides, it's an MCU Op, so I'm in if you lot are moving on to a pub.'

'I don't think that's what Beth had in mind when she stayed behind, do you, Jimmy?'

He didn't reply at first. In his opinion, Chandler was making more out of his relationship with Greenhill than it warranted. He and Beth were no more than colleagues and friends. Occasionally, they got together for a drink and the odd meal, just as he always had with Chandler. But that was the extent of it. He eventually told her she was fussing over nothing, that whatever he and Greenhill had was collegial and purely platonic.

'Is that so?' she said, a familiar twinkle in her eyes. 'Tell me, then, Jimmy, if that really is the case, how many times have you done the same with Ben and Guy?'

Bliss shook his head. 'No, no. It's not the same thing at all. They both have family waiting for them at home. It's the same as you and me. I never went for drinks or meals with Bish, because other than team get-togethers he also had a home to go to.'

'Oh, nice. So now you're saying I have no life.'

'Well, let's face it, Pen, it's not much of one when so often the best you can do for companionship is me.'

Rolling her eyes, Chandler said, 'True, that is a fate worse than death. But first, it's my decision. A bad one that doesn't say much about the choices I've made in life, but ultimately still my decision. And second, don't call me Pen.'

Ignoring her last comment, Bliss said, 'Yeah, and it's Beth's decision as well. She has nobody to rush home to. Neither do I. It's about company, so don't read anything else into it. And don't interfere by trying to make it something more, either.'

Chandler placed a hand on her chest. 'Me? As if I would.'

They were interrupted by DCS Fletcher, who had wandered across. 'I'm off,' she said, 'but the others are moving it on to the Woodman, if you're interested. And well done on this case. Both of you. I'm hearing good things about your performance as DI, Penny. I have to say I'm pleased for you. This step up is long overdue and I'm glad to see you making a good fist of it.'

Beaming with pleasure, Chandler said, 'Thank you, ma'am. That means a lot to me.'

'Please. We're off the clock, so it's Marion.'

'Of course. But the thing is, somehow it was easier to use your first name when you were the DSI. You becoming chief has strangely made it harder to say over these past eight months or so.'

'Then don't let it. Formal only in formal situations, remember. As for you, Jimmy,' Fletcher said, turning to Bliss. 'Your efforts haven't gone unnoticed, especially given the cold case you also have on your hands.'

'Thank you,' he said. 'A team effort, as always. But when we have our debriefing there's something I want to run by you. I know you have to be getting off, so it can wait until then.'

'Are you sure? I can spare a few minutes.'

'Thanks, but no thanks. This might need longer, and I think both Diane and Alicia will want to be in the room when we talk.'

Fletcher frowned. 'Sounds serious.'

'Not really. But it's not unimportant, either.'

Their leader left with a promise to schedule extra time for the debrief meeting. When she was gone, Chandler turned to him. 'So, you're actually going ahead with it, then? You're going to request that additional case involvement.'

Bliss shrugged. 'Beginning to end. That's what I'm going to ask for. What do I have to lose? Either they go for it, and we see how it pans out, or they deny it and I see if I can accept their answer.'

Chandler cocked her head. 'What is it with you, Jimmy? You're never bloody satisfied.'

'Truth?' he said.

'Always.'

'I still miss being a copper. The sharper edge, anyway. My twin roles are fulfilling in so many ways, but handing them over to you or others for those final hard yards doesn't sit well with me. I can just about cope with it when it comes to the cold cases, probably because they're still a relatively new thing. But in respect of the active investigations, it's like my manager substituting me when I'm on a hat-trick with the opposition reduced to ten men and the ball sitting on their penalty spot.'

'But you're always complaining about that part of the job. We all do. It's the aftermath of an adrenaline rush, the shitty end of the investigation stick. You get to walk away from all that, which in my book makes you the lucky one.'

'Bollocks,' he replied, unmoved by her attempt to apply a sheen of gloss to his undercoat. 'Of course, we all complain about it because the heat and intensity of the chase is over and all we have left is the grunt work needed to make sure somebody gets put behind bars. But we also know that's the cherry on top of the icing on top of the cake. I miss the cherry.'

'But you don't like cherries,' Chandler said innocently.

'Oh, fuck off! You know what I mean.'

When she'd finished mocking him, she nodded and said, 'Okay. Of course I know what you mean. It's the worst part of the job, but in some ways it's also the most meaningful. It's the final forty percent that makes the previous sixty mean something worthwhile.'

'There you go, then. You know. You understand. It's not about the absence of a warrant card anymore, Pen. I've come to terms with that. It's not about slapping cuffs on chummy's wrists. It hasn't been about that for me in a long time. I just need to see these cases through.'

Chandler might have said more, but their colleagues were drawing closer. Excited and still full of themselves, they were keen to get to the pub. Bishop called out to Beth Greenhill who remained on the other side of the room, demanding she come with them to continue their celebrations. She looked over at

Bliss, who shrugged, smiled, and nodded. Adding a wink at the end, she did the same.

Bliss didn't go directly to the pub. He headed instead to the Holiday Inn, where there were two more people waiting for some good news. Paul and Iris Musgrove had lost their mother, but now at least they could have some closure before they said their final goodbyes. It wasn't exactly hollow justice, but neither was it a complete victory, either. The man who had taken Mrs Musgrove's life was himself now deceased, and without the possibility of conviction there was no point in charging Patrick Walsh with murder. Matt Dories was also dead, which meant he would serve no time for his own role in the tragic incident. As for Peter Holland, once the team had his murder charges wrapped up, they would do whatever was necessary to also charge him as an accomplice in the murder of Mrs Musgrove under the joint enterprise rule.

It wasn't quite enough, but it was the best he and his colleagues could do for the grieving siblings. And Bliss was determined they at least got that much.

FORTY-ONE

The Greek etymology suggested base, groundwork, and foundation. Somewhere around the 1650s, it generally came to mean a proposition, assumed and taken for granted, used as a premise. Either way, the preferred word in police parlance was *hypothesis*. Not a supposition, not a theory, and never, ever an assumption. That much Bliss had learned early on after making Detective Constable. It was, as he stated clearly the following morning in the Unsolved Cases Team office, something they needed to agree upon there and then in reference to the Daisy Vincent murder.

'We've discussed it and talked all around it,' he said, regarding his three coworkers. 'Now is the time to nail our colours to the mast. I brought this case to you, so I'll begin. Following our previous briefings and from everything we have learned so far, my hypothesis is this: at some point shortly after his disagreement with Daisy Vincent, Stephen Wrigley reversed his car and drove back to where she got out. Believing she'd taken the path alongside the abbey, he pulled up and walked that route, probably from the spot where she would have emerged from the park as opposed to where she entered. After spotting her having sex with Jack Maguire, he took his anger and jealousy out on her and ended up strangling the poor girl. Then, the day after his daughter's body was discovered, Dougie Vincent was told by a police source that they were about to arrest Wrigley. Vincent, either alone or with the help of his two sons, got to Wrigley first. They murdered him in an act of revenge. Do any of you have a different slant on how this went?'

'I think it sounds about right,' Guy Foley said, cementing his support. 'The only known fact included in that entire premise is Maguire and our girl having sex. Even that we know only because he says so. But the pieces are all there for me.'

Ben Corry nodded. 'Me, too. We could be wrong about absolutely everything, but this makes sense. Enough to want to prove it, anyway.'

That left Beth Greenhill. She had joined Bliss's Major Crime colleagues the previous night and had enjoyed herself so much that she'd had to get a cab home and a lift to work from a friend who was driving into Peterborough that morning. Bliss knew she'd be nursing a hangover, so gave her some time to either commit or object. Finally, she went along with it.

'I'm not the happiest I've ever been putting my support behind a hypothesis,' she said. 'But I think this is the closest we've come to one so far. It occurred to us pretty early on and nothing has come along since to shake it off. Whether that's because it's sensible and logical or simply that we have bugger-all else, I'm not sure, but yes, I say we go with it.'

Bliss nodded, pleased he had complete agreement. 'Good. Then all that remains of this briefing is to decide what our next move ought to be. Given the lack of witnesses, forensics, and digital intel, and also in the absence of Stephen Wrigley himself to question, I'm in favour of working backwards. The last act of our hypothesis is the murder of Daisy's boyfriend, or ex-boyfriend, as he might have been. If we begin there and succeed, we might just open a door to additional information. To that end I'm proposing we run a bluff on Dougie Vincent. The Vincent family, in fact.'

'Beth mentioned it. This is where you intend to suggest to them that we have a lead on Stephen Wrigley's final resting place, yes?' Foley said, seeking clarification.

'Yes. In the hope that, first, they buried him somewhere after killing him, and second, that we can draw them out to that burial site.'

'I'm thinking this sounds more like an act of desperation.'

'It is,' Bliss agreed. 'Because we are. Desperate, that is. Look, other than wasting some time I'm not seeing a downside. I'm proposing that Beth and I visit them again, only this time we tell them about Jack Maguire. I realise that's a risk, because instead of doing what I want them to do they might decide to act against him. But we'll limit that possibility by ensuring they understand he played no part in Daisy's murder. I'm sure they'll be relieved to discover she wasn't raped, which will help to soften the blow. At that point, I'll casually mention Wrigley. No details, just that we believe we're close to discovering his whereabouts.'

'Jimmy and I already discussed this approach,' Greenhill interjected. 'It needs to come over as a throwaway remark as we're on our way out the door, but we'll drive it home at the same time by suggesting there's a good chance of finding DNA and forensics. We'll put it to them that this is a good thing, whereas our hope is it will spur Dougie Vincent on to revisit the burial site.'

'At which stage a surveillance team will play their part, I presume,' Corry said confidently.

'You presume wrong,' Bliss told him. 'When Beth and I leave, we'll withdraw and swap over to her car. Meanwhile, I'm hoping you two will move in and sit on them. And yes, that does mean I'm asking you to work additional hours if necessary. If I'm right and Dougie or he and his lads buried Wrigley, he or they will probably wait for the cover of darkness before they act.'

'And if you're wrong and they go after Maguire instead?' Foley asked.

'Then we intercept. Show them the error of their ways. Beth and I will take care of that aspect, so we won't needlessly expose you to them.'

'One thing does occur to me,' Corry said. 'Have you forgotten how cold it is out there? Jimmy, the ground is frozen solid. Has been for weeks. They're not digging anything up at this time of year.'

Bliss had forgotten. Neither had he considered the weather conditions while forming his plan. Even so, he wasn't put off his stride. 'It's a valid point, Ben. But if they take the bait and genuinely believe we're getting close, then I think they'll do whatever it takes. Even if they have to use a mechanical digger.'

'And if instead of burying him back in 2014 they chopped him up and fed him to pigs?'

'Then I'm going to look like a total prick, and we're going to have to think again. From scratch.'

The four were quiet for several seconds. Bliss eventually looked around at each member of the team and gave a sympathetic nod. 'This is it,' he said. 'This is all we have. As always, I'm open to suggestions, but I'm guessing you'd have already presented an alternative if you had one.'

Nobody spoke. Nobody needed to.

'Are you all in?' Bliss asked.

Once again nobody spoke. Once again nobody needed to.

'Our friends across the pond call this a Hail Mary,' Bliss said. 'But I think we can stick with shit or bust.'

*

As they made their way back to the car from the Vincent home later that evening, Bliss imagined his exterior countenance was every bit as confused as his brain. He glanced at Greenhill and said, 'Tell me what you got from that encounter, Beth. Because I suddenly feel out of my depth.'

The early exchanges had gone pretty much as expected. The reaction to Bliss telling the remaining members of the Vincent family that Daisy had been involved with Jack Maguire was entirely predictable: an explosion of animated fury, followed by both veiled and overt threats against the man's person. The temperature in the room initially climbed, but then just as quickly plummeted as the family members took umbrage against the two investigators for concealing this fact until that moment. When Bliss pointed out that this revelation meant Daisy hadn't been raped and should therefore be regarded as a positive, he met only with derision and further outbursts of barely controlled rage. But it was at this moment that he chose to slip into the conversation his bluff concerning Stephen Wrigley's remains.

'You mean their reaction to what you told them?' Greenhill asked, having briefly considered his question.

Bliss nodded. 'Who were you focussed on at the time?'

'I admit I was drawn to Mrs Vincent. As a mother myself, I couldn't help but concentrate on her.'

Bliss understood. He nodded. 'Okay, I get that. Me, I never took my eyes off Dougie. My intention was to keep it casual, and hopefully I pulled it off. But in hindsight, I probably looked at him for too long. The thing is, I don't know what the hell to make of what I saw.'

'How do you mean?' Greenhill regarded him with narrowed eyes.

'I mean it made no sense to me. Whether he killed Wrigley or not, he ought to have had some kind of reaction to what I told them. But there was nothing. It reminded me a bit of Peter Holland. No internal acknowledgement whatsoever. Not that I could tell, and I'm usually pretty good at that bit.'

'To be fair, if he did it, he's had a decade to prepare for that disclosure. If he killed Wrigley, the possibility of his actions being exposed at some point will have played on his mind on a regular basis. Probably every time he thought of his daughter over these past ten years.'

'Okay. That makes sense I suppose. And to be honest, it's just about the only thing that does because if he didn't do it then he surely would have had a very different response. Any response.'

Greenhill nodded. 'So, then he did it.'

Bliss sighed and said, 'Yes. I think he must have.'

'Now all we have to do is wait for him to act on the news we just broke to them. Admittedly, none of them were in the right frame of mind by then to say much, but you could feel the animosity towards Wrigley in that room.'

Greenhill was right about that. Bliss had felt it, too. And as he played it back through his memory, it occurred to him for the first time that one or more of the five family members who heard what he said might now be immensely relieved to know for certain that the man they believed had killed Daisy hadn't escaped abroad to live a free life. Just as one or more had almost certainly known all along that Wrigley never left the village alive.

FORTY-TWO

They didn't have to wait until nightfall. Dusk had started to wrap around them like a grainy mist when Bliss took the call he and Greenhill had been waiting for.

'Is he on the move?' he asked, excitement prompting his heartbeat to quicken. Corry and Foley had positioned themselves in a side street facing the Vincent property, providing them with an excellent view of the front door and the vehicles parked outside. It was Foley who had phoned.

'He is. As are his sons. But… there's bad news, too. Dougie climbed into his truck. Eddie and Tommy got into a white transit van. Dougie turned right and is headed your way, but his lads went left. We're following them.'

Bliss was not overly dismayed. It split his team, but it also separated the Vincents. 'We'll pick up on Dougie. He won't have seen Beth's wheels before, and there's plenty of traffic around. How about going your way?'

'Yeah, enough for us to lose ourselves in. Especially with lights now on.'

Bliss was disappointed at not having been able to get a lump on Dougie Vincent's truck earlier that evening. But what he had managed to do during a single covert visit was punch a hole in the coloured plastic covering the rear offside lights on all four vehicles parked outside the Vincent home. It made following them a great deal easier, because instead of having a mass of red lights bunched together ahead of them, one of the vehicles projected a piercing white dot to home in on.

'You still on the Wisbech Road?' Bliss asked just as the truck they had been waiting for passed by. Greenhill allowed two more vehicles to go through before indicating and pulling out smoothly to fall in behind.

'SatNav says we are,' Foley told him. 'We've just gone by the only turning along this stretch of road, so the A47 is coming up next.'

Bliss gave that some thought, running through the permutations. 'I can't see why they would turn left because that bypass will only take them right back to the tip of Thorney. If they'd wanted to go in that direction, they'd've just followed their old man. But if they turn right towards Thorney Toll that takes them to Ring's End in the Isle of Ely.'

'The SatNav is also showing us a road straight over the roundabout, Jimmy.'

'You'd better hope they don't take that. Narrow lanes across this flat countryside are a surveillance nightmare. You'll have to drop back as far as you can while still keeping them in sight.'

'This is not our first time out in the field,' Foley said, only half-jokingly.

'Of course. Sorry about that. We are now headed north, so like you we also have the A47 ahead. Let's take a breath to see what both vehicles do.'

Bliss mentally projected himself ahead, considering potential destinations. The rugby club was a distinct possibility. Dusk was deepening to a deep purple almost by the minute, but he'd seen floodlights alongside the pitches so there might be a training session running. Peterborough and Newborough were the next most likely alternatives, though for all Bliss knew Vincent might be visiting a pub or meeting up with friends. Only then did Jack Maguire's name pop into his head.

'Beth,' he said urgently. 'Can you remember Maguire's home address?'

Nodding, she said, 'Yes. Actually, by the look of it, it's just up ahead. Station Road, on the left somewhere. Oh, shit! You don't think…'

They both held their breath, letting go only when Vincent's truck rolled by the Maguire property. 'I'm slipping,' Bliss muttered, his heart fluttering. 'I should have anticipated that much earlier.'

'He wasn't going there, so what's the problem?' Greenhill said casually.

'My lack of awareness. He didn't go there, but he could have done. And I didn't see it coming, even though we discussed the possibility during our briefing.'

'We did. And what you said was we'd intercept them if that happened. Which we would have done. So forget it and concentrate on where he might be going instead. Hold on, here's the roundabout now.'

Just then, Bliss heard a voice on the phone. 'Damnit!' Ben Corry said. 'They've gone north at the roundabout, Jimmy. I can already see what you mean about the road. It's long, straight, narrow, and dark. No way they won't spot our headlights in their mirrors.'

'Just do your best,' Bliss said. 'Let's hope they reach their destination sooner rather than later. Listen, Ben, ask Guy if he thinks he can lose the lights but still get closer to the brothers.'

Corry, perhaps wisely, muted the following conversation. When he came back, he sounded sceptical but gave a verbal thumbs-up. 'We'll give it a whirl, Jimmy. But it's much darker out here than it was back on the other side of the roundabout. Guy says he'll use the SatNav as much as he can to guide us while I keep my eyes on the van.'

'Okay. Keep me informed. We've just gone over the main road as well, so I'm confident we're heading to the rugby club. And now that I think about it, this might make for a decent burial site. I noticed when we came here the other day that the pitches are bordered by some thick hedgerow. Stick a body in a hole in the ground back there and nobody's going to stumble across it by accident.'

A moment later Corry told them they'd gone dark. Less than ninety seconds after that he came back on. 'Jimmy, we've turned right. Archers Drove by the look of it. Long and straight again, fields on either side. No turns. It's… hold on, what's that? Up ahead, I can see a bunch of wind turbines.'

'I think I have an idea where you are,' Bliss told him. 'And Dougie has just pulled into the rugby club car park.'

'You think this is it, Jimmy? You think he's going for the body?'

With a sudden dull ache in his gut, Bliss hissed between his teeth and said, 'That's a big fat no, Ben. The floodlights are on and there are players already out on one of the pitches. No way is he digging up remains here and now.'

'That doesn't mean he won't stay on after they've all gone,' Greenhill pointed out.

His partner was right. Only that didn't help them out, because there was nowhere for them to park without being conspicuous. Bliss thought quickly and spoke into his phone. 'Ben, tell me where you are. Dougie is doing nothing here for the time being, so we can turn around and be with you in minutes.'

'Got you. We've just turned right onto Scolding Drove. Hold on… oh, shit! We've lost him.'

'Don't panic. He must have turned off somewhere so focus.'

But panicked was precisely how Corry sounded. 'Not according to the SatNav he couldn't, because there are no other roads. Hold on, hold on. Okay, we've just driven past a property. It looks like… yes, it's a farm. The farmhouse itself and the buildings are all in darkness. But I just caught sight of the van slipping behind a barn. I don't know what's going on here, but it doesn't look right.'

'Okay. Park up as soon as you can and head back on foot. Let's get eyeball on them. It could be anything, so prepare for all eventualities. We're on our way to you now. We'll follow the route you took, so we'll hunt down your motor and join you. Keep your phones on but turn your volumes down to zero. Text only from this point on, because voices will carry a long way across those fields.'

'Understood. We're stopped. Sounds going off.'

Greenhill put her foot down until they reached the roundabout. Even on the B roads across country she didn't slow a great deal. When they reached Scolding Drove she killed the lights, allowing the surrounding darkness to swallow them whole. Despite being prepared for it, Bliss felt momentarily disorientated by the abrupt change in vision. But Greenhill kept her cool and they soon came upon Guy Foley's Kia pulled off the road and parked on the grassy verge.

Once out of the car they scuttled back towards the farm. As they emerged from between a knot of elderly trees, Bliss checked his phone for messages. He'd received two in quick succession.

Walk behind silo and take path through trees.
We have eyeball.

It took less than a minute for them to make their way around the back of the farm and as the treeline thinned once more they came upon their colleagues, both of whom were squatting beside a long row of dense undergrowth. Foley stuck out an arm to his left. Bliss followed its direction and caught sight of a van illuminated only by the pale moon.

In a hushed voice, Ben Corry said, 'At first we thought they were interested in that barn with the curved metal roof, but there's something in the ground about a dozen paces east of it. It might be some kind of underground storage container, but we can't quite make it out. I don't know what this pair are up to but it's not good, that's for sure.'

Bliss was silent, lost in thought. But it was Beth Greenhill who spoke next. 'No, I don't think that's a container. Not the kind you're thinking of, anyway. My uncle is a farmer in Suffolk, and he has something similar at the back of his property. I think what we're looking at here is a cesspit of some kind. A septic tank.'

'What would this pair want with a septic…' Corry began and then stopped. 'Oh, Jesus! You don't think…?'

In the gathering darkness, Bliss nodded even though nobody could see the gesture. 'It looks to me as if they didn't bury Stephen Wrigley after all,' he said in a sombre tone. 'Not in a grave, at least, shallow or otherwise.'

FORTY-THREE

'Those tanks usually need to be emptied on a regular basis,' Greenhill said in a steady whisper. 'But there's no sign of life around here, which makes me suspect the farm is inactive. If that's the case, the tank could have remained unemptied for years.'

'But we're looking at more than a decade,' Ben Corry said. 'How likely is that?'

'More than you'd think. Some of these family farms are eventually inherited by youngsters who don't want to farm. But many opt to keep the land and rent it out. If the main properties are no longer being used by either humans or animals, then in theory the septic tanks are just left as they were at the time.'

'Hold on a sec. I can see the brothers now,' Foley said. 'They're doing something there at the top of that mound, but I can't tell what it is from this distance.'

'My guess is they're about to drain it,' Greenhill said. 'The slurry is supposed to be pumped out, but that takes time. There are usually emergency release valves for when a tank is pulled back out of the ground. They're not for use in normal circumstances because it's illegal to discharge that kind of sludge direct into the ground. But these two aren't going to care about the mess or the stench.'

'Maybe not when they're gone, but they do right now. I was wondering why they both put on breathing apparatus.'

Bliss looked over at Greenhill. 'You're up on this kind of thing, Beth. What sort of access are we looking at with these tanks?'

'Usually an inspection pipe, more likely two. Plus a manhole with cover. The main release pipe will lead to a buried trench of some kind, for drainage and filtering.'

'So essentially their intention is to pull the plug to empty the tank. Then what? Surely they wouldn't dream of climbing down into it hoping to find the remains?'

'I wouldn't rule it out. But my guess is they'll probably just set it alight. After ten years down there, Stephen Wrigley won't amount to much more than mush, bones, hair, and teeth. But with the methane and numerous other gases trapped inside, it'll burn well and destroy any remaining evidence.'

Bliss looked back towards the tank and could just about make out the two figures huddled together close by. They appeared to be deep in conversation. He nodded to himself. 'If I'm them, that's what I'm going to do. Drain it, set a fuse of some kind, wait nearby to ensure it goes up, and then scarper. Our evidence along with it.'

'There might be one problem with that scenario,' Greenhill said urgently. 'If it doesn't go up with a whump, it might go up with an enormous bang. Because if they get it wrong, if they misjudge the spread and depth of fumes created by the gases, or create an unexpected spark, the whole thing could explode.'

'Shit!' Bliss said.

'Shit indeed.'

'What do we do now?' Corry asked.

'Change of plan,' Bliss said. 'We were hoping for a body, the remains of one at least. Something we could catch them handling having removed it from the ground. Now we have to stop them lighting that tank up and hope we're right about what's inside.'

By now both Corry and Foley were standing upright, the four gathered closely together watching the activity in the distance. The air froze on their skin, and across the closest field Bliss could see a low-lying mist creeping closer as if stalking its prey. It would descend upon them within minutes, making their job harder still.

'Okay, listen up,' he said. 'Beth and I will go back the way we came and creep around the other side of the barn. While we're doing that, you two move in as close as you can without giving away your position. If you keep inside the treeline, you can get pretty adjacent. I'll send a "Go" text when we're ready to take them down.'

'You did hear Beth when she mentioned a potential explosion, right?' Corry said, clearly alarmed by the possibility. 'Now you want us to move even closer?'

'Can you think of another way to protect those remains, Ben?' Bliss asked. 'They're all we have if we're going to make a case against the Vincents.'

'We don't know if Wrigley is even down there,' Corry argued.

'He's down there,' Bliss insisted. 'And we're about to lose that evidence.'

'Isn't that better than losing our lives? If that was a person down there, Jimmy, I wouldn't hesitate.'

'But it is a person, Ben. Not a living, breathing one, of course. But a person all the same. He was murdered, and it's our job to prove that and lock up the bastards who did it.'

'Ah, Jimmy,' Foley said falteringly. 'Do I need to remind you that we no longer have powers of arrest?'

'Not necessary, Guy. We have enough reasonable belief and justification to make a citizen's arrest. We restrain and detain. The moment we have them down on the ground and out of action, I'll call for backup.'

'Are you sure you want to do that?'

'Yes. Absolutely. Look, I admit this didn't go the way I hoped it might. For a start, I imagined it would be Dougie doing the grunt work. My plan was to call for uniform once we'd seen him shifting the remains. We don't have time to call and wait for backup to arrive, because this pair could be setting that fuse any minute now. Let's just do this and feel our way through what follows.'

'I don't want to sound picky,' Corry said, 'but I'm going to remind you one last time that if the tank does go up, we'll be that much closer to the blast zone.'

'Not if we get there first,' Bliss said. 'But listen to me now. None of you have to come with me if you don't want to. It's not your job, frankly, so you have every right to refuse. I'm going, but if any of you decide to stay here or return to your motor, then I have no problem with that.'

Bliss took their silence for agreement.

'Wait for my text unless you see them setting up a fuse,' Bliss said. 'But whatever you do, don't let them light it.'

With that, he was gone, back into the thicket. Beth Greenhill followed in his wake. The pair moved with haste but took care not to make the slightest sound. Around the side of the silo, turning right to walk the length of the solid barn. At the end he paused to peer around the corner of the structure. The two brothers had their backs to him and Greenhill. He looked to his right but saw no sign of Corry and Foley yet felt confident they were both in place where he needed them to be.

This was as close as they were going to get without stepping out into the open. At this angle, it was perhaps fifteen steps. Bliss swallowed; it had to be enough. His thoughts drifted to the possibility of an explosion, but he dismissed them just as quickly as they had come. This was not the time to second guess himself. He entered the two letters into his text app and pushed the icon to send. Waited five seconds for it to reach its destination and for their colleagues to react. Then he turned to Greenhill and said, 'Shit or bust.'

In his sixty years on the planet, Bliss had watched an awful lot more rugby than he had played. But as he approached the closest Vincent brother, he imagined making the perfect tackle; dropping just before climbing into his opponent; taking shorter, choppier strides as he lined up his prey; bringing his shoulder down to hip height and then driving into the thigh as if his real target was a foot further on; wrapping both arms around the legs while pumping his own to maintain enough momentum and power to slam his man to the ground; and most of all, tucking his head to the side to avoid taking a concussive blow.

It was never entirely down to sheer brute force, as it often seemed, though height and weight could be a decent advantage. The Vincent brothers were tall, rangy, solidly built, and because they played the game they knew how to take a hit, though not necessarily a sneak attack from behind. For Bliss the tackle didn't entirely go to plan, but he got enough of the right components in the right order to smash his man forwards, up, and then down again with a groan of pain, a bone-jarring crunch, and an 'Ooofff' of breath smashed out of the man's lungs as his ribs slammed into the turf.

The next rule of tackling was to get back up and prepare to go again, only on this occasion Bliss was too focussed on keeping his weight pressed down on the lad's back, Greenhill doing the same with both legs. Whichever Vincent son they had driven to the ground, he took a good ten seconds to gather his breath and his wits, but by then his two attackers had gained ideal grips and positions to keep their man restrained.

Ben Corry was younger, taller, heavier, and fitter than his colleagues, so it was no surprise when his somewhat more practiced tackle had the other brother under control, minus the wriggling and squirming. The Vincent brothers shouted and swore and made threats of retribution, but they were contained and had nothing more to offer.

'Guy,' Bliss called out. 'Get backup here now. We've got our hands full.'

The Vincent brothers continued to curse and struggle but were easily restrained by the four investigators who simply remained on top of the two men and kept the pressure on their backs. It seemed to take no time at all for the night sky to pulse blue, the colour deepening as numerous vehicles closed in at high speed, sirens screeching and wailing as their wheels swallowed up the frozen roads beneath them.

By the time the cavalry arrived, Bliss had leaned into what he believed was Tommy Vincent's face. 'What happened?' he asked with a snarl. 'Your old man too much of a coward to come back to the place where he murdered Stephen Wrigley?'

Dougie's older son said nothing, but to Bliss's astonishment he did cough up a chuckle amidst the vitriol. His face was still buried in the turf, so the sound emerged muffled and indistinct. Grabbing hold of the man's hair, Bliss yanked his head backwards and leaned closer. 'What's so funny, fuckwit? It might have escaped your attention, but we have you and your brother attempting to dispose of the evidence. And inside that container, we're going to find everything we need to bury your old man as deep as he buried Daisy's boyfriend.'

'Think again, you thick fuck,' Tommy Vincent grunted, spitting grass as he turned his head.

'Oh, what, you think none of that is true?'

'I know it's not, dickhead. The old man doesn't know this place even exists. He's never been here. So I don't know what traces or DNA you might find in that literal shithole, but I can tell you now, none of it will be his.'

FORTY-FOUR

Penny Chandler sat at her kitchen table flicking through files on her laptop while chewing her favourite snack. That Jimmy-bloody-Bliss, she thought. It was he who had introduced her to the sumptuous delights of cheese spread and peanut butter in a sandwich. As an act of rebellion, she had turned his creation into her own by using a toasted bagel in place of bread, but she had to admit he'd worked his way inside her head with his culinary triumph.

It was his fault she was still up after midnight, but given the circumstances she forgave him. Earlier on that afternoon it had been too cold to open her balcony doors, so they'd stood together gazing out through the glass. The river had looked beautiful, with its gently flowing surface shredded by jagged shards of pale sunlight that dominated a cloudless sky. Bliss always enjoyed the view from her flat, but claimed it was even lovelier at night, beneath a bright moon that added its own glimmering dance to the Nene's water as it made its way south.

They'd talked for over an hour and when he left, he'd barely touched the hot drink she'd made him. He'd been too consumed with Dougie Vincent, whose sons had sworn their father had no idea they had interrupted Stephen Wrigley a decade ago as he was about to make a run for it. Nor was he aware that the pair of them had beaten and tortured the man before ending his life in the same way he had ended their sister's.

Bliss had ignored their protestations and ordered DS Bishop and DC Virgil to bring Dougie Vincent in for questioning. He couldn't be sure that a polite request would suffice, and needed their authority should an arrest be necessary. On being informed about the earlier apprehension of his two sons, Vincent had come willingly, albeit he was an angry man on a short fuse. Even so, something about the patriarch's ability to rise above everything Bliss put to him left a sour taste in the mouth. For a man whose only living children were well on their way to losing their liberty, he was too cool, too calculated, and far too detached.

'He's not quite adding up for me,' Bliss had said to Chandler, unable to find the words to better describe what he meant. 'He's upset about his sons, that much is certain. No faking that. But I still have the overwhelming feeling that he was involved. I don't know when, I don't know how, but something about that man screams guilt at me, Pen. I can't unhear that or ignore it.'

'I get you,' she'd told him. 'I do, Jimmy. But according to everything you've told me, both sons relate exactly the same story. They acted alone, their sole impetus to kill being a deep and urgent desire to avenge their sister. They insist their father knew nothing about what they did. You were there. You watched their interviews. Did you get the impression they were covering for him?'

'No,' he admitted. 'But perhaps they're both chips off the old block when it comes to their ability to lie. All three are stoical and so difficult to read.'

'Which is why you can't pinpoint what it is about Dougie Vincent that bothers you so much.'

He nodded, shoulders slumping. She could tell how exhausted he was. Looking his age having been on the go for two full days with no sleep. Perhaps burdened further by the sheer toll of accumulated experiences. In his weary features, she recognised why he had come to her.

'What do you want me to do, Jimmy?' she asked him.

With great reluctance, he'd asked if she would consider going through the original cold case crime files as a favour to him, but only after first watching the appeal item on a digital recording of the *Golden Hour* television documentary. Not wishing to steer her towards anything specific or share his own misgivings, he hadn't pointed her in any particular direction, simply asking for an opinion initially on the appeal and then on any potential connection to that appeal elsewhere in the files. The particular aim, he told her, was to work out why Jack Maguire had lost his shit in prison to the point where he revealed his secret to a fellow inmate. That moment, Bliss insisted, was crucial and he had to know why.

After he'd gone, Chandler sat down to watch the recording. The section of the documentary featuring the Vincent family was relatively short. She had watched it three times and saw nothing that might explain the prisoner's subsequent erratic behaviour. She thought Bliss had to be right; that Maguire's reaction had been sparked by something he'd seen or heard during that appeal that either did or did not tally with what he believed to be true. The chances of that information being hidden away in the files were remote, but it wasn't often that Jimmy Bliss found himself so completely baffled and she badly wanted to find the connection he had missed – if it even existed. Not to rub his face in her eventual success, which she obviously would do at the appropriate time, but more to prove herself worthy of his respect and trust.

Personally, Chandler wasn't entirely convinced of Jack Maguire's innocence. True, she hadn't interviewed him and knew of the man only through what she'd read and heard from Bliss, but while his version of events was feasible, it also bothered her. Daisy Vincent had started off that fateful evening with her boyfriend and had subsequently spent time having sex with Maguire. He was now asking everyone to believe that the girl had then been misfortunate enough to encounter a third man later that same night. A man who, seemingly for no reason, had strangled her to death.

Yet if you ignored the possibility of Maguire being a suspect, and also ruled out the notion of a third man, that left you with an irate Stephen Wrigley. Now that idea she did like, so much that she could picture it. The boyfriends' initial anger at Daisy's betrayal had spilled over during their drive home. Close to the rectory one or maybe even both of them decided enough was enough. Either Daisy demanded he stop to let her out, or Wrigley stood on the brakes and forced her to leave. Maguire's story could then have gone precisely as described, including the moment of his departure, while Daisy was presumably still glowing from their sexual encounter. It didn't take much for Chandler to imagine Wrigley hurtling back to Thorney, scoping out the path she'd most likely taken. He could easily have arrived in time to witness their lovemaking only to see Maguire walk away, leaving Daisy lying on her back staring up at the sky. At which point, a now enraged Wrigley pounced, kneeling on the poor girl's arms and shoulders, before his hands slipped purposefully to her neck where they fastened around her throat and squeezed the life out of her.

After her snack break, Chandler returned to the appeal recording to give it another shot. This time, she viewed it with a different purpose. It had occurred three days after the murder, two days after Wrigley had supposedly fled. Focussing intently on the faces only, neither brother looked either fierce or determined enough to wish harm on the man who had taken their sister's life. Their eyes were blank, dulled. Possibly by grief. More likely in the knowledge that they had already exacted their revenge and were merely playing their part. Mrs Vincent sobbed incoherently throughout, mourning in full view of the cameras. It was left to Dougie to do all the talking, which he did hollow-eyed and seemingly grief stricken. Which he was, of course. But could he have pulled that off knowing he had already taken or helped to take Wrigley's life? His reaction was in stark contrast to that of his sons, possibly for good reason.

Bliss was looking for a sign that would prove Dougie's involvement, yet this footage did his cause no favours that she could see. Rather, it suggested everything Tommy and Eddie had said was true. About to turn her attention once more to the files, Chandler reacted to her phone, which had started to shuffle across the table. It was a text from Bliss.

Pen. Just been reading some intel from SB. Apparently Daisy Vincent's mobile automatically uploaded photos to the cloud. There's a page in the crime logs containing links, one of which should be to her storage area online. Suggest you download and take a look, just in case you spot something of interest. I'll do the same and we can compare notes.

He must have assumed she'd be asleep, which is why he had texted. His relationship with Sandra Bannister at the *PT* no longer bothered Chandler in the way it once had; she knew of few people with more integrity than Jimmy Bliss, and she had faith in his ability to draw the lines in all the right places. She thought about this link and wondered why nobody from the original investigation had downloaded photos from the account to include in the case files. Or perhaps they had, but they'd been discarded as non-essential to the case.

Having found the link, Chandler clicked on it and used the password that had been provided alongside the URL. The contents were in reverse chronological order, and when she opened the most recent folder, she felt an instant chill on the back of her neck upon seeing images of Daisy Vincent taken on the night somebody took her life. There were a couple of dozen selfies from the young woman's evening out, one of which captured Stephen Wrigley standing in the background. Daisy looked happy and vibrant, everything she ought to have been for many more years to come.

One photo in particular caught her attention. She clicked on it and zoomed in on one particular section. Something about what she saw niggled at her. It bothered her because she instinctively knew it was incongruous, only she just couldn't think why.

What's here that shouldn't be? Chandler asked herself. Or, thinking about it another way, what's here that also features somewhere else when it shouldn't. She clicked on the 'plus' icon to increase the size one more time. Frustratingly, the image blurred. On a roll now and not wanting the momentum to dissipate, she picked up her phone and texted Gul Ansari.

If you're awake, please call me.

She didn't even have time to place the device back down on the table before it rang. 'Please tell me you have something for me to do,' Ansari pleaded with her.

'Woah, hold your horses,' Chandler said. 'First things first: how are you doing?'

'I'm great, Penny. Seriously. No symptoms other than a headache. The worst part is going crazy with boredom.'

Chandler smiled. It was good to hear her friend sounding so enthusiastic. 'Okay. Well, then, officially, this is a health check call. Unofficially, if I ping you over a file can you work your magic and improve the image for me?'

'I can certainly try. You want it brought closer or just sharpened.'

'Both, if possible.'

'I hear you. Zoomed in, but not so much that we lose the clarity of pixelation. Let me have it.'

'You sure? I know it's late.'

'Just send the bloody file!'

Chandler sent the bloody file. Ten minutes later she heard a tone telling her a message had dropped into her inbox, and at the same time her phone rang again.

'If only the task could have lasted longer,' Ansari said. 'But it did feel good to be useful again. Anyway, unfortunately I wasn't able to go too far before I ran up against the blur factor. I have improved it, but probably not as much as you would have liked.'

'That's fine, Gul. Really. Thank you so much.'

'You want to tell me more?'

Chandler paused to consider the request but realised she wasn't really sure what she thought about it herself. 'If I get anything, I'll call you in the morning,' she said.

Ansari had been less than thrilled, but the pair said their goodbyes. Chandler opened the file and maximised the window until the image filled her laptop screen. Despite her protestations, Gul had improved the clarity enormously. Chandler pulled the device closer and squinted hard, eyes flitting from left to right, right to left. And again. And one more time.

That was when the item that had been stuck in her subconscious appeared to leap out of the screen at her. That was when she remembered where she had previously seen it. That was when she knew with a sickening certainty what had happened that night.

That was when she knew everything.

FORTY-FIVE

Dougie Vincent was not a man to drop his guard. Although he'd been made fully aware of just how much trouble his sons were in, he kept his feelings facing inward. That Bliss had elected to interview Vincent himself this time owed much to the aloofness and apparent disregard the man had displayed over his boys taking a life.

And, as it transpired, the life of someone entirely innocent.

'You can come after me all you like,' Vincent began, immediately disregarding his own solicitor's advice. 'But I never knew what my lads did until last night, when your lot turned up on my doorstep. Believe it or don't, you'll never touch me for it. As for Tommy and Eddie, if they did what you say they did, then it was only what any brothers would do for their sister.'

'And what was that, Dougie?' Bliss asked deliberately.

'Murder Stephen Wrigley. Or so you say.'

'They did. After beating and torturing him, they took it in turns to throttle the life out of him. We know this because both of them independently saw sense in buying themselves a few years off their sentence by formally confessing to it. Now, you say you didn't know what your boys did to Wrigley, but when my partner and I first spoke with you and your wife at the rugby club you gave each other a look that told me you were guilty. If I was wrong about that, then what it really said was that you knew he was dead and who was responsible for killing him.'

'That's just not the case at all,' Vincent said, shaking his head defiantly. 'Not in the sense you mean, at any rate. Yeah, I was pretty sure that dickhead boyfriend of Daisy's wasn't about to show up anytime soon. Or ever, in fact. I was as confident as I could be that he was dead. That didn't mean I did it, or that I had any idea my lads did.'

Bliss remembered the moment well. The exchanged look that passed between the couple. At the time, it convinced him of the man's guilt. And upon reflection, perhaps the look in Mrs Vincent's eyes was more one of bemusement. He might well have got that wrong. But perhaps not all of it.

'We'll see about that,' he said. 'But let me take you back to something you just said. In your opinion, they only did what any brothers would do. They took the life of the man who had taken the life of their sister. On a human, purely gut level, I understand that point of view. And while I can't condone it, I even understand why they went ahead and did it. But the problem in this case is that your boys got it wrong, didn't they, Dougie? They went and killed the wrong man.'

Vincent shook his granite head. You could almost hear it scraping against his neck as it moved from side to side. 'That's complete and utter bollocks, and you know it. They... or whoever topped Wrigley, put the bastard who murdered my daughter in the ground. He did it. He murdered my Daisy. And I don't know why you're sitting there trying to pretend otherwise.'

'Funny,' Bliss said. 'Because I could say much the same thing.' He took two printed images from DI Chandler and laid them face upwards on the table. 'Take a look at these,' he said.

Leaning forward to run his eyes over them, Vincent frowned. Bliss could only imagine the thoughts that passed across the man's mind at that point. 'What the fuck is this about?' Vincent asked, indicating the photos.

Bliss also leaned forward, his gaze never shifting. 'My colleague here pieced this whole thing together, Dougie. She spotted what I'd missed. The image on your left is a close-up shot of your daughter's bracelet. Daisy took the photo herself, one of many selfies she took in her lifetime. Only, the thing about this one is it was taken the night she was murdered.'

'What of it?'

'Do you recognise it?'

'Should I?'

'It was Daisy's favourite. The photos we've found in her cloud storage area prove she wore it all the time. Perhaps because you had it made for her, Dougie.'

'Okay, so what of it? Why are you showing me these?'

Bliss ignored him. 'Tell me about the little characters attached to the bracelet. The four characters right at the front.'

'They're Japanese symbols. They spell out my daughter's name.'

'Yes, they do. I looked them up, in fact. In Japanese culture, daisies symbolise beauty, peace, hope, and innocence. All the things you imagined your daughter to be, I suspect.'

Vincent's hands formed into fists. His breathing became laboured. 'What the fuck is this all about? Why are you doing this to me?'

Bliss sensed a shift in the man's emotions. 'Well, now here's the thing, Dougie. That bracelet was not listed among your daughter's personal effects. She was wearing it when she went out, as the selfie image proves. But it was missing when she was found dead just a short while later.'

'And? All that proves is somebody stole it. Wrigley, most likely. Or maybe even that prick Maguire.'

'Except you know it was neither of them, don't you?'

'Me? How would I know?'

Bliss persisted, the interview going precisely the way he had hoped it would. 'See that same bracelet in the second photo, Dougie?'

A quick glance, no more. 'Yes.'

'You admit it's the same one, then?'

'Of course it is. I had it made for her, as you pointed out?'

'So I did. It's unique, wouldn't you say?'

'A complete one-off. And not just because of the Japanese characters with Daisy's name. It's platinum, you see, not silver or white gold.'

Bliss wanted to smile, but kept it from his lips. He'd got Vincent to open up, having first weakened his defences. The man was proud of this gift he'd had made for his little girl, and he wanted them to know that.

'Nice,' he said. 'Sounds expensive.'

'Cost don't come into it when it's your loved ones.'

'I agree. But the reason I'm showing you two separate images of the same bracelet, Dougie, is that while the one on the left was taken with the bracelet on Daisy's wrist, in the second image it's not being worn at all. You can see it's not on the wrist but instead being twisted between fingers. A bit like worry beads, which is what I first thought they were.'

Vincent's eyes sprang wide open. He knew then what Bliss had known going into the room.

Bliss released the smile this time. 'I can tell you're seeing the full picture now, right? I knew you would. Because you know who those hands belong to.'

Vincent said nothing.

'They're your hands, Dougie. Your hands clutching your own daughter's bracelet. The bracelet she wore the night she died. A bracelet you couldn't possibly have unless you took it from her cold, dead wrist.'

'You don't have to respond,' Vincent's solicitor said, his voice urgent and concerned.

Only Dougie Vincent wasn't listening.

'These photos have been doctored,' he said with a sneer. 'You might look at me and see a country bumpkin, but I've heard of AI and Photoshop. You lot did this. You tried making a case against me in the murder of Stephen Wrigley, and when that failed, you had this fucking rubbish doctored up. It's not enough that you have my boys. You want me as well.'

'You won't be able to prove that, Dougie. Because while these images have been enhanced and enlarged, they have not been physically altered in any other way. The second image is actually a still taken from a television documentary in which you and your family made an appeal for your daughter's killer to come forward. Your boys sat through the whole thing knowing that could never happen. But you knew otherwise.'

'These,' Vincent said, slapping the photos away, 'prove nothing. I don't even know what you're trying to say with all this nonsense.'

Bliss let it sit and stir for a moment or two. Then he said, 'You should know that my colleagues have today carried out a search of your home, Dougie. You hid it well, but not well enough. They discovered the hidden compartment at the back of your hallway cupboard. They also got it open, so you'll know what they found.'

'DI... sorry, Mr Bliss,' the solicitor said. 'Where is this going? You're not asking questions, which tells me this is a fishing trip. Please, stick to questions and stop this laboured nonsense.'

'Fair enough.' Bliss was happy to oblige. 'Mr Vincent, how is it you come to have your daughter's bracelet? The same bracelet you were playing with during your recorded appeal. The same bracelet Daisy was wearing the night she was murdered.'

'No comment,' he replied.

The solicitor folded his arms. 'There you have it. My client has nothing further to say. You dragged my client in here today to discuss the alleged murder of Stephen Wrigley. What does this bracelet business have to do with that?'

'Nothing,' Bliss admitted. 'And you're right, that is why we initially wanted to talk to your client. But circumstances have changed. Your client is now facing a charge of murder.'

'But we've just discussed this. My client's sons have, according to you, admitted to the murder of Mr Wrigley, while at the same time exonerating their father. On what basis are you looking to charge him for that crime?'

'Oh, I'm not. Of course, I can't charge him with anything. But my colleague, DI Chandler, will go over the essentials with you when I'm done. No, you see, we are charging your client with murder. Just not of Stephen Wrigley.'

'Then who?'

'He'll be charged with the murder of Daisy Vincent.'

'What? That's preposterous.'

'Is it? Take a long, hard look at your client's face, Mr Hudley. Think about it: Daisy wore the bracelet when she went out that night. She never reached home. The bracelet was not among her personal effects. Therefore, how could your client be in possession of that same bracelet?'

Realisation dawned on the solicitor's face. 'I need to pause this interview immediately. I want to speak with my client alone.'

'I'm sure you do. Just as I'm sure you'll create what you regard as a perfectly reasonable explanation. But I can assure you, whatever you do come up with has no chance of working.'

Bliss was about to say more, but when he looked across at Vincent, he saw the man's head lowered, his chest and shoulders heaving as he sobbed, emitting a low and terrible wail of loss and misery. This continued for several minutes; a broken man physically purging himself of all the pain and sorrow he'd stored away for more than a decade. When he was finished, he looked up, cuffed tears from his cheeks and mucus from his nose, philtrum, and chin.

'I always knew my bastard fucking temper would get the better of me one day,' he said, his voice low and harsh. He blinked his harrowed, moist eyes a couple of times. 'I just never imagined it would be my own daughter who would suffer for it.'

Hudley advised him not to say another word, but Bliss could tell Vincent wasn't done.

'Daisy told me she was breaking up with Wrigley that night. So, when she still hadn't arrived home long after her usual time, I became worried. Whenever she fell out with any of us, she'd go for a walk around the park to wind down, so I thought she might be there after telling him it was all over. I went to the park to look for her. But instead of finding her miserable and alone, I saw her... saw her with...'

'You discovered her making love with the son of your bitter enemy,' Bliss finished for him.

Vincent's eyes narrowed as he clamped his teeth together. He gave a mute nod.

'For the recording, please.'

'Yes. Well, they were finished by the time I almost stumbled on them, but it was obvious what had been going on.'

'You felt betrayed, yes?'

'You're fucking right I did!' Vincent said, far more animated this time. 'Sleeping with the enemy. Isn't that what they call it?'

'I've heard the expression. So, what happened next, Mr Vincent?'

'You don't have to say another word,' Hudley said, leaning in to stress the significance of the moment.

'Yeah, but the thing is I really do. I need to get this weight off my chest.'

'Do go on,' Bliss insisted.

'The tragic, awful truth is at first I walked away. I could feel the rage building inside me, and I knew that could only end badly. I thought if I took myself out of there I might calm down before Daisy got home.'

'But it didn't work out like that.'

'No. I tried. I really tried. But I couldn't let it go. I wanted to rip that fucker apart.'

'You mean Jack Maguire.'

Vincent nodded, his cheeks flushed and his breathing ragged. 'I was going to follow him. Wait for my chance and jump him when he was alone. But when I got back he'd already left, and Daisy was sitting there on her own.'

'But you still had all that anger raging inside you,' Bliss said, probing away. 'And it had to go somewhere.'

For a few seconds they sat in silence. Then Dougie Vincent slowly shook his head and said, 'In those days I could never control my temper. Once I got riled up, I had to do something about it. It wasn't like this red mist you hear about. For me, it was as if everything went black, and then just as suddenly became bright again. Only in between any amount of time might have passed, and only then would I find out how much damage I'd done.'

'And that was how it went with Daisy.'

'I didn't want it that way. I didn't even know what I was doing. You have to believe me. One moment I was walking towards her, the next I was squatting over her, my hands wrapped around her neck.'

'You were choking her.'

'No. That's just it. I'd already choked her. Choked the life right out of her.'

Vincent allowed his head to slump forwards again, and he began to weep once more. Bliss took a breath and finished on his behalf.

'You removed her bracelet as a keepsake, possibly in a moment of realisation and horror at what you'd done. Obviously, you were never going to admit to your family what had happened. I can understand that. I even understand your anger, though as I said earlier, I'm condoning neither.'

'Yes, I took it back. I wanted to... hold on to something of hers. Something that had brought us close.'

Overwhelmed by the unexpected confession, Bliss was about to wind things down when a thought occurred. He knew he could leave it; should leave it. But doing so didn't feel right. He'd been asked to consider letting it go, but he couldn't. Not when he had a chance to complete the job.

'I'm sure it meant a lot to her, Mr Vincent,' he said. 'But now that you've admitted to the worst of it, please tell me about Stephen Wrigley.'

After a moment, the still weeping man looked up. 'What about him?'

'I'd like to know how you came to hear he was our prime suspect.'

Silence.

'Was it through one of my colleagues? Is that it? Did you have a police officer in your pocket?'

'Who didn't?' Vincent growled.

Bliss chose his words carefully. 'It was a long time ago. The officer on your payroll at the time might well have left the job since, so he's of no use to you now. No reason you shouldn't provide us with his name.'

'You think you know who it was?'

'Me? Oh, no. I don't have a clue.'

'Would you be surprised to learn it was your current PCC's son?'

'I'd be shocked. Are you saying it was Jeremy Benning?' Bliss could hardly keep the tremor from his voice.

'That's the one. Slimy little prick he was, too.'

Got him, Bliss thought. Nailed a bent cop without having to reveal what I already knew. It was enough, and what's more it was now on record.

'So Benning told you Wrigley was in the frame. And of course, having murdered Daisy, you couldn't very well punish him for a crime you'd committed. But tell me, what did you make of him vanishing off the face of the earth?'

'I didn't think anything of it.'

'You never wondered if your boys had stepped up?'

'I didn't think anything of it,' Vincent repeated.

Bliss decided he'd taken matters as far as he could for the time being. He nodded and met Vincent's hollowed out gaze. 'Dougie, I can only imagine how you must have felt when you saw your daughter with Jack Maguire that night. The sense of treachery, your anger at the dishonour, the lack of respect. All human emotions, resulting in a shocking and heartbreaking conclusion. In all honesty, I very much doubt that you intended to kill Daisy. But we both know that was the end result of your actions, the consequence of your loss of temper on that one awful occasion. Your family may never forgive you for what you did, but I think you owed it to your daughter to do the right thing here today. You're still here. Your wife and sons are still here, and time heals most wounds. But Daisy is gone. Because of you. You can't bring her back. But you can let her go. Perhaps your confession will take you one step closer to that.'

Bliss wasn't sure if that was true, only that he meant every word he said.

FORTY-SIX

'Who the fuck are you?' Nick Nevin demanded to know. He glared at Bliss, looking him up and down. Then his eyes narrowed as he sought some glimmer of recognition. 'I was told to expect somebody I know. I don't know you. What is this? What's going on?'

Staff at the prison had warned Bliss to expect this reaction because Nevin's condition was worsening daily. Subsequent to DCS Fletcher's recommendation, the prison service was looking at moving Nevin to HMP Grendon, a little more than twenty minutes away. However, the doctor monitoring the prisoner's illness was of the opinion he wouldn't survive long enough. He'd also voiced his concern that transferring the patient away from the familiar might have an adverse effect. The man's deterioration in such a short time was marked, but Bliss had been advised that moments of lucidity were still commonplace.

'You do know me,' he said. 'Just think about it. Look at me. Look closely at my face. I'm Bliss, remember? Jimmy Bliss. DI Bliss as was.'

Liquid eyes stared back, uncomprehending and fearful. 'What's that you say? What about bliss?'

'No, no. That's my name. Jimmy Bliss. I know you know me, Nevin. It's in there somewhere. You just have to reach inside and pull it out.'

'I do?' The confused man's frown deepened as he struggled to recollect. 'Jimmy, you say. How do we know each other?'

A dark part of Bliss wanted to tell him. To tell him everything. To shout and roar his hatred and contempt for this killer. But his mind instead flashed to a memory of his first superintendent in Peterborough, a man by the name of Sykes with whom he'd had many verbal battles. The two had despised each other. But then many years later he had encountered Sykes when the ex-cop was residing in a hospice, his body weakened, his mind long gone. All Bliss had felt then was pity.

Of course, there could be no such feelings for the man who had so brutally and callously murdered his wife. Hazel would have wanted him to. Not to forgive or forget, but to retain enough humanity to feel sympathy towards another human being suffering and waiting to die. It would have been a bone of contention between them. Looking at Nevin now, half the man he used to be, his mind turned to mush, Bliss couldn't put a name to what he did feel. Or even if he felt anything at all.

'It doesn't matter,' he finally said. 'I'd anticipated you sitting there having a laugh at my expense, what with you leading me into a potential bent cop hazard. In the end, I suppose it takes one to know one, but I was confident there was more to your story than you were letting on.'

Bliss paused, searching once more for any sign of awareness, a glint of triumph in those rheumy eyes. All he saw was bemusement. He nodded to himself and pulled out a chair. 'That's okay, Nevin. I came here to talk, not to listen,' he said. 'So if it's all right by you, I'll sit for a while and tell you everything that's happened since we last met. You might take some of it in, you might not. Either way, I need to bring an end to this.'

*

Before leaving Peterborough that day, Bliss had paid a visit to county HQ. He'd needed a word with DCS Fletcher, and she had half an hour to spare. The first thing she did was congratulate him on the successful conclusion of both investigations.

'I work with two great teams,' he told her. 'And actually, "conclusions" is precisely why I wanted to speak with you.'

'Oh, how so?' They sat not at her desk but in the less informal meeting area close by, with soft furnishings and a coffee table arranged neatly by the room's shelving units.

'Well, the truth is we both know I've concluded nothing. Unlike my warranted turns as SIO I'm taking the case to the point where we decide on charges but then stepping back to allow the MCU to complete the task of bringing everything to the stage where we're ready for court.'

'That's what we agreed, was it not?'

'Yes. It is. But the fact is I'm not satisfied. I don't see any good reason why I shouldn't stick with it all the way. The lack of a warrant card doesn't preclude me from doing so. The fact is, I feel frustrated at leaving it here. I want to know we have our case in great shape for the CPS, and while the team is perfectly capable of getting it there without my help, it feels as if I'm missing out.'

Fletcher smiled, shook her head, and said, 'You are one cantankerous bugger, Jimmy Bliss. Most of us would opt out of that stage if we could, but you're unhappy at *not* being involved.'

Bliss allowed himself a sheepish grin. 'What can I say, Marion? Leopard, spots, all that. The point is there's no reason for me not to stick it out. Agreed?'

'Legally, procedurally, none that I can immediately think of, no. But practically speaking, would your time not be better spent working cold cases?'

'I will be. This is merely an extension of my SIO role.'

'True. But it's also the longest part. Many months of work. Come on, Jimmy, you know as well as I do how much of a hard slog it can be between getting someone like Peter Holland put away on remand and having that turn into a sentence following a guilty verdict.'

'Of course. But I'm not asking to do it all, am I? I just want to lead the team through that difficult period. Look, hear me out. How about we give it a try? Let me stick with this one and we'll see how it goes.'

Fletcher nodded. 'We could do that, yes. And what happens if a few weeks in we get another murder, and I want you to be SIO on it? How will you split your time, then?'

'I divide my time between it and whichever cold case we're working and help prepare the court case as and when I am able. I'm not suggesting I devote every hour of every day, just asking not to be cast aside at such an early stage.'

He waited while Fletcher gave herself time to mull it over. Eventually, she nodded. 'Okay. I'll give you this one case, Jimmy. When it's over, I'll decide on how we carry on from there. And it will be my decision, you hear me?'

He had, and he'd accepted with gratitude.

Bliss was on his way out of the door when DCS Fletcher forestalled him simply by stating his name. He turned and raised his eyebrows. 'I heard and saw what you did in that interview room,' she told him. 'Getting Vincent to give up Jeremy Benning.'

He shrugged. 'That's precisely what happened. He gave up Benning. I didn't.'

'I know.' She smiled. 'I wasn't going to bollock you for it. I wanted to thank you. Since it arose during a recorded interview we cannot ignore it. The allegation will have to be investigated. You did well, Jimmy. Saved me from having to make an awkward decision.'

'It wasn't really a decision, though, was it?' Bliss said. 'You would have sent it upstairs. You would have paid the price. Now you don't have to.'

*

'How did it go?' Chandler asked when he got back to the car following his meeting with Nick Nevin. She had wanted to be there to offer emotional support should he need it.

Bliss buckled up but did not switch on the engine. Instead, he sat upright, staring out of the windscreen at the grey concrete car park wall. 'He's gone,' he said.

'You mean…?'

He shook his head abruptly, his left index finger tapping against his temple. 'No, I mean he's gone up here. He had no idea who I was. There's nothing left of the Nick Nevin I once knew.'

'He should be in a home.'

Bliss sighed softly. 'I don't know about that. The kind of home you mean is really just a place where you go when your body has outlived your mind.'

'Isn't that what's happened to him?' she pointed out.

'Yes. But if there are rare sparks of awareness, no matter how brief, do you really want to know that's what you've become?'

'Perhaps not. I'm not sure what the answer is.'

'Me neither. But it's odd. With him in this condition, it's like I don't know how to feel about him anymore. I have nowhere else for all that pent-up anger to be. I've carried it around with me all these years, and now… now it has nowhere left to go.'

'So pull the plug on it and let it drain away.'

Bliss nodded. 'I know that's what I should do. And I know how ridiculous this might seem, how stupid I must sound, but I feel as if I'd be doing Hazel a disservice if I let go of it so easily.'

Chandler stroked his arm. 'You're right,' she said.

He looked at her. 'I am?'

'Yes. It does seem ridiculous. You do sound stupid.'

He closed his eyes, a smile thinning his lips. They were quiet for a minute or so before Bliss got them moving and back on the road. 'Back to the ranch?' he said.

Chandler shook her head. 'Could we take a detour to Thorney?'

'For what reason?'

'I was thinking about Fearn Vincent while you were gone. That poor woman. When this is all done and dusted, she will have lost both her sons and her husband to the prison system. Worse still, she'll know her boys killed the wrong man and that her husband murdered their only daughter. Can you imagine having to live with that knowledge? I've never even met the woman, but somehow I feel the need to tell her and to be a shoulder for her to cry on.'

Bliss nodded. He thought about how tough the conversation would have been with Wrigley's mother were she still alive. How tragic that she had died not knowing the truth about her only son. It was only natural for his mind to drift in that direction, but Chandler wasn't even part of the cold case investigation yet had nonetheless taken it upon herself to comfort Mrs Vincent. Yes, the Major Crime Unit was going to be just fine in this woman's hands. And so was he. 'There was another reason why I was pleased you came along today,' he said. 'I wanted to talk about the future.'

'You're not going to ask me to marry you, are you?' Chandler asked.

'Fuck no.'

She turned to look at him. 'Well, thank you and fuck you, too. Need I remind you that of the two of us, I am the catch?'

Bliss laughed. 'Shut your cakehole for a minute will you? I'm being serious. It's about, well, it's about what happens to me if I go doolally and also when I croak.'

'*If* you go doolally? Oh, Jimmy, I know you don't realise this in your sorry state, but that ship has sailed.'

'Yeah, yeah. I could have a single brain cell left and still have twice your IQ, so don't get me started. Anyway, listen to me. The thing is, I've started the process of legally drawing up plans for the future. I haven't told Molly yet, but I'm leaving everything to her. Except for my dry cereal and my Porcupine Tree albums – they're all yours.'

'Oh, goody. Just what I always wanted. Thank you so much, Jimmy.'

'You're very welcome. But what I need to discuss with you right now is my Power of Attorney. If I lose the ability to make decisions about my health or become unable to manage my finances, I want to name you as my primary replacement attorney. It's just legal jargon, but in essence I want you to make decisions for me and act on my behalf when or if the time comes.'

'Jimmy, I'm honoured that you would choose me,' Chandler said, a sad smile on her face. 'But why wouldn't you want Molly to do that for you as well?'

'Too much pressure on young shoulders,' he replied with a shake of the head. 'You'll do it for me, though, won't you?'

'Of course. I'll happily do that for you. In fact, is there any chance I can pull your plug now and get it over and done with?'

'Do you ever miss a chance to take the piss?' he asked, shooting her a look of affected disapproval.

'I hope not. You'd only be disappointed in me if I did.'

Bliss nodded. 'The sad thing is, Pen, not only are you my first choice, you're also my only bloody choice. How fucking sad is that?'

'It's a shame, but not sad.'

'It's not? It's the same thing as you being my best friend by virtue of the fact you're my only friend.'

'Which is patently untrue,' she scoffed. 'What about Lenny Kaplan? Or Gary Griffin? Then there's Bish. And don't you count Diane as a friend? How about Phil and Alan? Gul? Just because they're not dumb enough like me to be at the end of a phone for you in the dead of night whenever you have a bright idea doesn't mean they're not friends. And what about outside the job? Sandra Bannister… what is she if not a friend? And didn't you and Emily part company on good terms?'

'All right, all right,' he said as he navigated yet another roundabout. 'I have friends. But you're the only one I'd ask to do this. And thank you for agreeing. It means a lot to me.'

'So, do I get to decide which home to put you in? I already have a lovely one picked out.'

This time, the look he gave her was firm. 'You put me in one of those places and when I pop my clogs I'm coming back to haunt you. That's a promise.'

'I thought you didn't believe in all that claptrap.'

'For you, I'll make an exception.'

In the silence that followed, Bliss had an idea what Chandler was thinking. 'Don't worry,' he said. 'You won't end up like me. You'll meet the right bloke. And even if you don't, you have Anna. She's flesh and blood, Pen. Family. You know how much I think of you, and I couldn't love Molly more if she was my own kid. But real family is everything. I don't think we ever truly appreciate that while they're around, but when they're gone you can't fill that void in your life. Not with all the friends in the world.'

'Not even a friend like me?'

Bliss took a breath and smiled. 'There are no friends like you, Pen. There's just you.'

Chandler nudged his arm and grinned back at him. 'Then that's good enough for both of us,' she said. 'But Jimmy...'

'I know, I know. Don't call you Pen.'

'No, that's not what I was going to say.'

'What were you going to say, then?' Bliss asked.

Chandler cocked her head and said, 'I was going to say, Jimmy, from now on you can call me Pen any time you like.'

Bliss chuckled. 'Really?'

'Really.'

He shook his head. 'No, I don't think so. Thanks, but no thanks.'

'How come?' she asked, looking bewildered.

'Because where would be the fun in that?' Bliss said. 'Penny.'

ACKNOWLEDGEMENTS

This time around I really must begin with a group of unselfish, dedicated people who give freely of their time to review my books and blog about me. Alyson Read, Amanda Oughton, Jill Burkinshaw, Karen Cole, Lynda Checkley, Nicki Murphy, Sarah Hardy, Donna Morfett, Sharon Rimmelzwaan, and Yvonne Bastion, my sincere gratitude to you all for your longevity, your steadfast support, and for being so kind to me along the way. I'd also like to thank anybody who has taken time over the years to review or post an article about me – please know that I greatly appreciate it.

When doling out the thanks I cannot possibly overlook the support of my beta and ARC reviewers, most of whom are also in my Facebook group, whose support I continue to enjoy and cherish. And to fellow authors Maggie James and Liz Mistry for their friendship, words of wisdom, and wonderful reviews.

I'm also extremely grateful to my cover designer, formatter, and editor, along with my wife who gets a hard copy to read and make notes on, for helping me prepare the final package. I've said it before, but it takes a village. And if not a village in this case, then perhaps a tiny hamlet, or at the very least an isolated dwelling, maybe the shed at the bottom of my garden... where was I? Oh, yes, well you get my drift. It takes more than just me is what I'm saying.

Finally, a whopping great 'thank you' to you, dear reader, for purchasing this book. I sincerely hope you enjoyed it, and that perhaps you'll stick around for Bliss #14, *The Stonemason's Song*, which will hopefully be available later this year.

Best wishes to you all from deepest, darkest West Sussex in 2025.

Tony

Printed in Dunstable, United Kingdom